ESAU AND JACOB

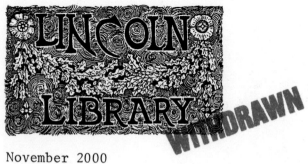

OXFORD

ESAU AND JACOB

A Novel by
JOAQUIM MARIA MACHADO DE ASSIS

Translated from the Portuguese by
ELIZABETH LOWE

EDITED WITH A FOREWORD
BY DAIN BORGES
AND AN AFTERWORD BY CARLOS FELIPE MOISÉS

OXFORD
UNIVERSITY PRESS

2000

OXFORD
UNIVERSITY PRESS

Oxford New York
Athens Auckland Bangkok Bogotá
Buenos Aires Calcutta Cape Town Chennai Dar es Salaam
Delhi Florence Hong Kong Istanbul Karachi
Kuala Lumpur Madrid Melbourne
Mexico City Mumbai Nairobi Paris São Paolo Shanghai
Singapore Taipei Tokyo Toronto Warsaw

and associated companies in
Berlin Ibadan

Copyright © 2000 by Oxford University Press, Inc.

Published by Oxford University Press, Inc.
198 Madison Avenue, New York, New York 10016

Oxford is a registered trademark of Oxford University Press, Inc.

Library of Congress Cataloging-in-Publication Data
Machado de Assis, 1839–1908.
[Esaú e Jacob. English]
Esau and Jacob : a novel by / Joaquim Maria Machado de Assis;
translated from the Portuguese by Elizabeth Lowe;
edited with a foreword by Dain Borges;
and an afterword by Carlos Felipe Moisés.
p. cm. — (Library of Latin America)
ISBN 0-19-510810-8 (cloth) — ISBN 0-19-510811-6 (pbk.)
1. Lowe, Elizabeth, 1947–.
II. Borges, Dain Edward.
III. Title.   IV. Series.
PQ9697.M18 E713   2000
869.3'3—dc21   00-036330

1 3 5 7 9 8 6 4 2

Printed in the United States of America
on acid-free paper

Contents

Series Editors'
General Introduction

The Library of Latin America series makes available in translation major nineteenth-century authors whose work has been neglected in the English-speaking world. The titles for the translations from the Spanish and Portuguese were suggested by an editorial committee that included Jean Franco (general editor responsible for works in Spanish), Richard Graham (series editor responsible for works in Portuguese), Tulio Halperín Donghi (at the University of California, Berkeley), Iván Jaksić (at the University of Notre Dame), Naomi Lindstrom (at the University of Texas at Austin), Francine Masiello (at the University of California, Berkeley), and Eduardo Lozano of the Library at the University of Pittsburgh. The late Antonio Cornejo Polar of the University of California, Berkeley, was also one of the founding members of the committee. The translations have been funded thanks to the generosity of the Lampadia Foundation and the Andrew W. Mellon Foundation.

During the period of national formation between 1810 and into the early years of the twentieth century, the new nations of Latin America fashioned their identities, drew up constitutions, engaged in bitter struggles over territory, and debated questions of education, government, ethnicity, and culture. This was a unique period unlike the process of nation formation in Europe and one which should be more familiar than it is to students of comparative politics, history, and literature.

The image of the nation was envisioned by the lettered classes—a minority in countries in which indigenous, mestizo, black, or mulatto peasants and slaves predominated—although there were also alternative nationalisms at the grassroots level. The cultural elite were well educated in European thought and letters, but as statesmen, journalists, poets, and academics, they confronted the problem of the racial and linguistic heterogeneity of the continent and the difficulties of integrating the population into a modern nation-state. Some of the writers whose works will be translated in the Library of Latin America series played leading roles in politics. Fray Servando Teresa de Mier, a friar who translated Rousseau's *The Social Contract* and was one of the most colorful characters of the independence period, was faced with imprisonment and expulsion from Mexico for his heterodox beliefs; on his return, after independence, he was elected to the congress. Domingo Faustino Sarmiento, exiled from his native Argentina under the presidency of Rosas, wrote *Facundo: Civilización y barbarie*, a stinging denunciation of that government. He returned after Rosas' overthrow and was elected president in 1868. Andrés Bello was born in Venezuela, lived in London where he published poetry during the independence period, settled in Chile where he founded the University, wrote his grammar of the Spanish language, and drew up the country's legal code.

These post-independence intelligentsia were not simply dreaming castles in the air, but vitally contributed to the founding of nations and the shaping of culture. The advantage of hindsight may make us aware of problems they themselves did not foresee, but this should not affect our assessment of their truly astonishing energies and achievements. It is still surprising that the writing of Andrés Bello, who contributed fundamental works to so many different fields, has never been translated into English. Although there is a recent translation of Sarmiento's celebrated *Facundo*, there is no translation of his memoirs, *Recuerdos de provincia (Provincial Recollections)*. The predominance of memoirs in the Library of Latin America series is no accident—many of these offer entertaining insights into a vast and complex continent.

Nor have we neglected the novel. The series includes new translations of the outstanding Brazilian writer Joaquim Maria Machado de Assis' work, including *Dom Casmurro* and *The Posthumous Memoirs of Brás Cubas*. There is no reason why other novels and writers who are not so well known outside Latin America—the Peruvian novelist Clorinda Matto de Turner's *Aves sin nido*, Nataniel Aguirre's *Juan de la Rosa*, José de

Alencar's *Iracema,* Juana Manuela Gorriti's short stories — should not be read with as much interest as the political novels of Anthony Trollope.

A series on nineteenth-century Latin America cannot, however, be limited to literary genres such as the novel, the poem, and the short story. The literature of independent Latin America was eclectic and strongly influenced by the periodical press newly liberated from scrutiny by colonial authorities and the Inquisition. Newspapers were miscellanies of fiction, essays, poems, and translations from all manners of European writing. The novels written on the eve of Mexican Independence by José Joaquín Fernández de Lizardi included disquisitions on secular education and law, and denunciations of the evils of gaming and idleness. Other works, such as a well-known poem by Andrés Bello, "Ode to Tropical Agriculture," and novels such as *Amalia* by José Mármol and the Bolivian Nataniel Aguirre's *Juan de la Rosa,* were openly partisan. By the end of the century, sophisticated scholars were beginning to address the history of their countries, as did João Capistrano de Abreu in his *Capítulos de história colonial.*

It is often in memoirs such as those by Fray Servando Teresa de Mier or Sarmiento that we find the descriptions of everyday life that in Europe were incorporated into the realist novel. Latin American literature at this time was seen largely as a pedagogical tool, a "light" alternative to speeches, sermons, and philosophical tracts—though, in fact, especially in the early part of the century, even the readership for novels was quite small because of the high rate of illiteracy. Nevertheless, the vigorous orally transmitted culture of the gaucho and the urban underclasses became the linguistic repertoire of some of the most interesting nineteenth-century writers—most notably José Hernández, author of the "gauchesque" poem "Martín Fierro," which enjoyed an unparalleled popularity. But for many writers the task was not to appropriate popular language but to civilize, and their literary works were strongly influenced by the high style of political oratory.

The editorial committee has not attempted to limit its selection to the better-known writers such as Machado de Assis; it has also selected many works that have never appeared in translation or writers whose work has not been translated recently. The series now makes these works available to the English-speaking public.

Because of the preferences of funding organizations, the series initially focuses on writing from Brazil, the Southern Cone, the Andean region, and Mexico. Each of our editions will have an introduction that places the work in its appropriate context and includes explanatory notes.

We owe special thanks to Robert Glynn of the Lampadia Foundation, whose initiative gave the project a jump start, and to Richard Ekman of the Andrew W. Mellon Foundation, which also generously supported the project. We also thank the Rockefeller Foundation for funding the 1996 symposium "Culture and Nation in Iberoamerica," organized by the editorial board of the Library of Latin America. We received substantial institutional support and personal encouragement from the Institute of Latin American Studies of the University of Texas at Austin. The support of Edward Barry of Oxford University Press has been crucial, as has the advice and help of Ellen Chodosh of Oxford University Press. The first volumes of the series were published after the untimely death, on July 3, 1997, of Maria C. Bulle, who, as an associate of the Lampadia Foundation, supported the idea from its beginning.

—*Jean Franco*
—*Richard Graham*

Foreword

Dain Borges

Take heed how you go in, and whom you trust;
Let not the gate deceive you by its width!
—*Inferno*, Canto V

When he composed *Esau and Jacob* (1904), Joaquim Maria Machado de Assis stood at the peak of his career. Over the previous two decades, he had published three brilliant novels, *The Posthumous Memoirs of Brás Cubas* (1880), *Quincas Borba* (1891), and *Dom Casmurro* (1899), which established him as Brazil's leading writer. He had also lived a self-imposed intellectual isolation in the midst of this acclaim. Neither his closest friends nor the sharpest critics, who were schooled to read naturalist realism, caught the ambiguities in his writing. No Brazilian reader of his latest novel had yet deciphered the clues suggesting that the narrator, Dom Casmurro, may have deluded himself into imagining his wife's adultery. Although Machado never found a Henry James to read him, and he must have felt the temptation to set his audience straight, he refrained from revealing his tricks to the public.

Instead, in *Esau and Jacob*, he adopted a wistful voice even more disingenuous than the openly insolent and unreliable narrators he had used before. This narrator, who sometimes is (and sometimes is not) the diplomat Counselor Aires, offers to entertain hasty readers with a romantic love story, a transparent political allegory, and facetious anecdotes of society life. At the same time, he promises careful readers that, if they ruminate with "four stomachs in their brain" and reread the text through certain "spectacles" he provides, they can solve his puzzles and recognize his enigmas. In *Esau and Jacob*, more than any of his five mature novels, Machado invented deliberately artificial "chess piece" characters who come to life just when they elude the narrator's minute analysis of their moves.

If Machado felt trapped in Rio de Janeiro's philistine society, he was trapped near the top. When he was born, in 1839, Rio was the sleepy capital of a backward, agrarian empire, a tropical Russia. Its racial hierarchy worked loosely enough to afford free men of color haphazard chances in life. A few poor, self-educated mulatto boys like Machado, with talent and lucky connections, entered Rio's middle class. Starting as a typesetter's apprentice, he broke into journalism and theater criticism in the 1860s, got a steady government clerkship from political friends in 1867, and slowly rose toward the highest civil service rank in the Ministry of Agriculture and Public Works. By 1869 he was settled enough to marry Carolina Novais, the sister of a Portuguese poet he had befriended, stranded in Rio after nursing her dying brother. As a young man, Machado could entertain actresses, retell a joke for weeks on end with fresh enthusiasm, and charm Rio's French expatriates into letting him practice his French on them. For a full year he edited a Liberal party newspaper single-handedly, while translating French plays and writing for other journals under pen names. Without committing himself recklessly to the Liberal party or to any other position, he made friends of ministers of the empire, radical abolitionists, republicans, and monarchists alike. He made only a handful of literary enemies in an age when self-promotion through polemics was the rule. However, he went out of his way to attack the two strongest naturalists of his generation, the Brazilian Sílvio Romero and the Portuguese Eça de Queirós. In 1888, Emperor Pedro II named him an Officer of the Order of the Rose (just below the rank of honorary baron that Santos obtains in chapter XX). In 1897, Machado founded the Brazilian Academy of Letters, on the French model, hoping it would dignify literary careers. He was its president until his death in 1908. Like Aires, who has learned to disagree while appearing to agree, Machado knew how to move within Brazil's ruling circle while denouncing it in a style that its members found acid but agreeably philosophical.

Machado achieved that style only in the middle of his life, after securing his career. The Paraguayan War of 1865–70, a pointless Bismarckian war of aggression, alienated him from Emperor Pedro II and the regime. But he abstained from expressing his political opinions directly. He never joined the abolitionist movement, although he detested slavery and wrote pseudonymous columns dissecting slave owners' "generosity" in granting freedom to their slaves. Instead, during the 1870s, he continued to write facile, witty columns in the newspapers. He saved his stronger themes for short stories, where he sketched morbidly egotistical characters and explored metaphysical paradoxes. In 1879, after illness gave him a retreat of several months, he finally combined his frivolous and meditative registers into the first voice of his mature novels: the arrogant, exhibitionist, flippant, world-weary Brás Cubas, writing from beyond the grave in his *Posthumous Memoirs*. Machado's later novels explored storytelling through different combinations of an assertive narrator and short, digressive chapters. Each of them examined intersections between the private lives of the upper class and the public life of Rio de Janeiro. *Esau and Jacob* extends farthest beyond the Rio de Janeiro of barefoot slaves and mule carts, court of the empire (1822–89), into the Rio of electric streetcars and Copacabana beach, the federal capital of the First Republic (1889–1930). *Esau and Jacob* also has the most explicit political allegory, one that almost obscures its moral concerns.

The political commentary of *Esau and Jacob* was meant to seem comfortably familiar to Machado's Brazilian readers, and the characters themselves speak of it. The Santos and Batista families live for their political ambitions and see their lives synchronized with national events. Natividade gives birth to the twins Pedro and Paulo in 1870, at the end of the Paraguayan War, a time when the Brazilian political elite split between conservatives and reformers. Conservatives ousted the Liberal party during the war; the Republican party was founded in 1870; everyone sensed a new beginning. Dona Cláudia recalls giving birth to Flora during the Conservative party's 1871 Rio Branco Ministry, which passed the Law of the Free Womb declaring children born to slave mothers free at adulthood. The vote on this first emancipation measure followed sectional lines and cut across Conservative and Liberal party lines. In itself that was not unusual during the empire. Parties meant little in ideological terms, particularly on a burning issue such as slavery. Even the Republican party refused to take a position on abolition, for fear of dividing its meager bases of support. Thus, Batista's jump from the Conservative to the Liberal party pains him as a shift of loyalties more than of ideas; he finds politics "less an opinion than an itch." The empire fancied itself as an English constitutional monarchy, but its politics centered on exchanges of favors between Rio and backwoods strongmen. Batista is representative of many career politicians appointed in rotation to administer the provinces, rigging elections in connivance with landlords, electoral court judges, and police chiefs, mediating their relations with Rio de Janeiro. And thus, Pedro and Paulo's monarchism and republicanism are platonic fetishism of heroes' portraits and slogans, "neckties of different colors," until the abolitionist campaigns of the 1880s.

During the 1880s, the imperial political system disintegrated over the question of emancipation and other reforms, taking with it many careers like Batista's. Although slavery had declined in most of Brazil since the end of the slave trade, and free Brazilians of color outnumbered slaves at least three to one in 1870, slavery had intensified on the expanding coffee plantations in Rio de Janeiro and São Paulo. Politicians committed to the planters conceded that slavery should end—someday. They defended it through cynical delaying tactics in parliament. Abolitionists turned to direct action around 1885. The government, fearing that the mass escapes, plantation strikes, and civil disobedience in 1887 had reached the point of civil war, declared abolition on May 13, 1888. This conflict is mentioned only in passing in *Esau and Jacob*. Discussion of abolition was inhibited after 1888, so perhaps Machado found it hard to treat abolition and the republic in a single novel. In his last novel, *Counselor Aires's Memorial* (1908), he used "Aires's notebooks" again, selecting diary entries for 1888 and 1889 that trace the connections between a young widow's remarriage and Brazil's process of abolition without land distribution. In *Esau and Jacob*, he focused instead on the unexpected political outcome of abolition, the collapse of the empire and rise of the republic. Both Pedro and Paulo support abolition; Paulo sees it as the dawn of national liberation. Yet perversely the republican movement grew as a reactionary backlash against abolition. Within eighteen months, resentful planters joined the Republican party and disgruntled army officers to overthrow Emperor Pedro II. The regime's politicians did little to stop the conspiracy. In chapter XLVIII, Flora, her family, and many of the characters in the novel attend the emperor's ball for Chilean naval officers in Rio's harbor. This ball, on the eve of the coup of November 15, 1889, became famous as the emblem of the monarchy's smug misjudgment of its true circumstances.

To Aires, with his memories of diplomatic service in Caracas, the 1889 republican revolution opens with comic-opera overtones of a South American palace coup. Many commentators at the time shared this view. The first administration set off a speculative stock market and banking bubble, the *Encilhamento* (1890–91), whose arbitrary redistribution of fortunes seemed both silly and sinister. In the novel it elevates the sordid speculator Nóbrega overnight to the level of the banker Santos, and above the Batista family. But republican politics soon turned entirely grim. The military dictatorships of Deodoro da Fonseca (1889–91) and Floriano Peixoto (1891–94), assassinations, a bloody civil war in southern states (1892–95), and battles between the army and navy in the harbor of Rio de Janeiro (1893–94) became more reminiscent of the French Revolution than a Caracas *golpe*. The state of siege mentioned during the funeral in chapter CVII is one decreed by Floriano Peixoto, perhaps that of April 10, 1892. During such periods of censorship and repression under Floriano's dictatorship, Machado himself had remained unharmed, but close literary friends such as Joaquim Nabuco and Rui Barbosa had fled into exile. Batista's interview with Floriano in chapter LXXVI, in which the dictator discerns his lukewarm loyalty to the republican principles and leaves him with an ominous handshake, resembles many anecdotes that circulated about the impassive "Iron Marshal." In 1894, foreign pressure (largely from U.S. President Grover Cleveland) and near-bankruptcy during the civil war drove Floriano to hand over the presidency to a civilian from the state of São Paulo. Rather than establish democracy, however, the São Paulo politicians crafted an interstate compromise to perpetuate the incumbent political machines in each state. All of Machado's readers would have read between the lines to the irony that the "brilliant careers" of Paulo and Pedro in Congress after 1894 fulfill the *cabocla*'s prediction of greatness only superficially. Underneath such statesmanship in Congress lay a stillborn democracy of back room deals between country bosses and courthouse machines.

Machado made contemporary politics the most accessible key to an allegorical interpretation of the plot. If the twins are the empire and the republic, then Natividade is the old Brazil who gave them life and Flora is the new nation. But what exactly is she? The future nation who cannot choose between them, or who cannot tell them apart, or who wishes she could fuse them, or whom neither will take? In fact, the allegory is ambiguous. Machado also contrived some puzzles that can be worked out with knowledge of political events. Just as Flora will not choose between the twins, and just as Batista wavers between the Liberal and Conservative parties, so also the neighborhood baker Custódio evades commitment. On the day after the republican coup, Custódio consults Aires on how to keep street mobs from misinterpreting the old signboard of his teashop, "*Confeitaria do Império* [of the Empire]," and breaking his windows. He must change it. But if he changes it to "*Confeitaria da República*," one day restorationist mobs might break his windows. After discarding several alternatives, such as adding a line to the sign to make it "Teashop of the Empire—of the Law," Custódio appears to accept Aires's diplomatic solution: that he name it after himself, "Teashop of Custódio." Custódio's signboard symbolizes the political indifference of Rio's common folk to the change of regime and counterpoints the equally timorous and opportunistic responses of the banker Santos and the politician Batista. Yet with historical hindsight, the ruminative reader of 1904 could deduce Machado's wry joke: that Custódio's neutral choice of his own name would lead to an unforeseen disaster. In 1893, Admiral Custódio José de Melo led the naval uprising in Rio's harbor, and the name "Custódio" became anathema to republican mobs. Those who will not make political or moral choices in *Esau and Jacob* have special punishments in store for them. Their agonies are

Batista's despair that he didn't speak his mind at the right time, Paulo's restlessness when he can't fraternize with the republican troops, Aires's regret that the twins are not his sons, Flora's insomnia over deciding between the twins. They are different from Dostoevsky's heroes, tormented by the whirlwind of ideologies in Russian politics. Machado's unheroic characters suffer precisely because Rio de Janeiro's placid and inarticulate politics nourishes ambitions rather than purposes.

The moral concerns of *Esau and Jacob* emerge in light of its literary allusions. Carlos Felipe Moisés's "Afterword" to this volume discusses the curious relations of the biblical Esau and Jacob to this story. Other allusions suggest additional interpretations of the plot. The narrator first describes Nóbrega in chapter III, when Natividade and Perpétua leave him alms for the souls. Nóbrega is neither poor nor rich: "Ni cet excès d'honneur, ni cette indignité; neither such an excess of honor, nor such an indignity." This unexplained and unattributed quotation encapsulates another key to the relationships in *Esau and Jacob*. It is the line with which Junia rejects the seduction of Nero in Racine's tragedy *Brittanicus*. And *Brittanicus* chronicles the day in which the young emperor Nero first unleashes his monstrous nature: misled by his mother Agrippina and the evil tutor Narcissus, he poisons his half brother Brittanicus in order to steal Junia. Junia flees him to become a vestal virgin. Certainly this could mean that Flora's rejection of Nóbrega's marriage proposal echoes Junia's rejection of Nero, and that Nóbrega is to blame for Flora's fate, that millionaires are Brazil's new Neros. Or it could mean that Paulo and Pedro fighting over Flora should remind us of the usurper Nero and his half brother Brittanicus (just as they are dim reflections of Esau and Jacob, Peter and Paul, and Castor and Pollux). Or it could also mean that the ambitious Natividade is an unnatural mother like Agrippina and that Counselor Aires, who agrees to act as "a sort of nanny or tutor" to her sons, is partly responsible for their acts. More clues and conundrums appear if we reconsider the action of *Esau and Jacob* in light of other texts Machado cited: Goethe's *Faust*, Shakespeare's *Macbeth*, Voltaire's *Candide*, and Dante's *Divine Comedy*.

The narrator warns us early on that we must consider Dante, that the epigraph, "Dico, che quando l'anima mal nata," "serves as a pair of spectacles with which the reader can penetrate what is less clear or totally obscure." We should listen to the narrator here, because every one of Machado's novels engaged *The Divine Comedy*. Who, then, is the "ill-born soul" of this line? In Aires's diary (chapter VII), it is the guests at a dinner party, born hopelessly insipid. In Canto V of *Inferno*, it is each damned soul who appears before the judge Minos in the outer circle of hell, "confesses all," and is assigned to its destined place in the pit. In the epigraph to *Esau and Jacob*, whose alternate title is *Ab Ovo*, "ill-born soul" points to the newborn twins whose destiny is to be divined by the cabocla. Are they alone born damned? The novel is full of souls, spirits, alms-collectors for the souls in purgatory, and quack spirit mediums. Every character is in some way a sinning soul judged by Aires, and everyone intentionally or unintentionally confesses their secrets to Aires—or to any judging eye. All of us, after all, are motivated by "that irresistible desire to know another's business"; secrets themselves want to be known, as "there is a force that drags out everything that people try to hide."

Aires is a special sort of judge, loving solitude but also loving other people, "to hear them, smell them, taste them, touch them, and apply all his senses to a world that could kill time, immortal time." The narrator uses Aires's point of view because only he has the detective insight needed to reconstruct the episode of Natividade and Perpétua's visit to the cabocla, twenty years later, from "old and obscure stories that he remembered, iinked, and deciphered," or to imagine what the twins dream at night. The reader may use him, too, but should beware. If *Esau and Jacob* is a novel with moral mysteries (for example: who killed Brazil's future?), and Aires is their detective, then he does not give us all the solutions, and he himself must always be a suspect. After all, Aires's talent lies in his combination of reasoning and imagination with memory. Reasoning can deceive us; Nóbrega misinterprets every person he encounters. Imagination lures Aires into reading a dialogue on freedom and bondage in the patient eyes of a donkey; "the eye of man serves as photograph of the invisible." Memories, triggered by an inkwell, a book, a shout, or a place, often overwhelm him, and he cultivates those reveries partly in despairing hope that he may "kill the dragon of Time." Machado, who was in his sixties and facing his wife's death when he wrote the novel, must have been very conscious of resorting to such stratagems against aging himself. With regard to the enigmas of life and death Machado addressed through this novel, Aires is far from a disinterested observer.

Aires's great enigma is Flora. Things and people move in and out of focus in this novel, and at times she seems a flat, allegorical figure in a cartoon of "the Nation." At other times she seems nothing but a conventional nineteenth-century stereotype of feminine mystery. But she is lovingly rounded out in a series of incomplete investigations. Aires reasons a hypothesis to explain her, and she outflanks it; he deepens his analysis again and never reaches bottom. All souls have "abysses," but Flora is "inexplicable." Her origins can hardly be explained by the naturalistic hereditary theories that satisfy us that the twins are the foredoomed product of Natividade's ambition wedded to Santos's greed, or that Nóbrega is a born thief. Dona Cláudia and Batista shouldn't have been able to produce an ethereal daughter. Flora's actions show Aires hope, when through music she transcends the pettiness, egotism, and masquerading that condemn all social relations and all politics. But she transcends them as a real girl who hides her drawings, makes immature demands, and is just learning about adults. Her fate satisfies other characters as a sign of reconciliation that Aires, to his credit, cannot accept. Like Joseph Conrad with Marlowe and Kurtz in *Heart of Darkness*, or like Natsume Soseki with student and Sensei in *Kokoro*, Machado de Assis used the incomplete, half-comprehended character to resist the dehumanization of persons implicit in the omniscience of twentieth-century psychologies and literary naturalism. Aires reveals Flora as a sketch that the reader must patiently complete with imagination, reason, and love.

ESAU AND JACOB

Contents

A Note to the Reader

When Counselor Aires died, seven notebooks in manuscript were found in his desk, firmly bound in cardboard. Each one of the first six was numbered in order, with roman numerals I, II, III, IV, V, VI penned in red ink. The seventh bore this title: "Last."

The reason for this special designation was not known then nor is it known now. Indeed, this was the last of the seven notebooks, with the distinction that it was the thickest, but it was not part of the *Memoirs*, the diary of remembrances that the counselor had been writing for many years and which constituted the subject of the previous six. It did not bear the same order of dates, indicating both the hour and the minute, in the previous ones. It was a single narrative; and although the very figure of Aires played a prominent role in it, with his name and title of counselor, and by allusion, some of his adventures, it did not thus belong to the previous six. Why, indeed, "Last"?

The hypothesis that the desire of the deceased was to publish this notebook after the others, is not a natural one, unless he wanted to force the reader to read the previous six, in which he wrote about himself, before they acquainted themselves with this other story, written from the perspective of a unique interior monologue, throughout its diverse pages. In this case, it was the vanity of the man who thus spoke, but vanity was not one of his failings. And if that was his intention, would it be worthwhile to honor it? He did not play an important role in this world; he pursued a diplomatic career and retired. In his leisure time he wrote the *Memoirs*, which if you separate out from them the dead or dark pages, would only do (or still might suffice) to kill time on the launch to Petrópolis.

That was the reason for publishing only this narrative. As for the title, several were suggested that would summarize the topic. *Ab ovo*, for example, in spite of the Latin; what prevailed, however, was the idea of giving it the two names that Aires himself once quoted:

ESAU AND JACOB.

Dico, che quando l'anima mal nata ...
—Dante

I

Things of the Future!

It was the first time that the two had gone to Morro do Castelo hill. They began the ascent from the Rua do Carmo. There are many people of the city of Rio de Janeiro who have never been there, indeed many will die and many more will be born and die who will never set foot there. Not everyone can claim to know an entire city. An old Englishman, who in fact roamed the world, confided to me many years ago in London, that of London he only knew his club well, and that was enough for him of both the metropolis and the world.

Natividade and Perpétua were familiar with other parts of the city, besides Botafogo, but Morro do Castelo, for all they had heard about it and the *cabocla*, a half-breed Indian fortune-teller, who reigned there in 1871, was as strange and remote to them as the Englishman's club. The steep incline, the uneven and poorly paved path up the hill, mortified the feet of the poor ladies. Nevertheless, they continued to climb, as if it were a penance, slowly, faces downcast, veils lowered. The morning brought with it a certain bustle. Women, men, children who walked up and down the hill, washwomen and soldiers, one or another clerk, shopkeeper,

3

priest, all looked at them with some surprise; while they were simply dressed, their bearing revealed a certain breeding that can't be hidden, which stood out in those heights. The very slowness of their gait, compared to the swiftness of the others, betrayed the fact that this was the first time they had ventured there. One black woman remarked to a sergeant: "You'll see they're on their way to see the cabocla." And both stood watch, taken by that irresistible desire to know another's business, which sometimes is the sum of all human need.

In fact, the two ladies searched discreetly for the number of the fortune-teller's house, until they found it. The dwelling was like the others, perched on the hillside. One reached it by a little stairway, narrow, dark, appropriate to the adventure. They wanted to enter quickly, but they bumped into two fellows who emerged from the doorway and who lingered there. One asked in a familiar way if they were going to consult the cabocla.

"You're wasting your time," one concluded furiously, "you'll hear a lot of nonsense."

"He lies," laughed the other, "the cabocla knows what she's doing."

The women hesitated a little; but quickly they realized that the words of the first one were a certain sign of the prescience and frankness of the fortune-teller. Not all would have the same happy fortune. The future of Natividade's sons could be miserable, and then . . . While they considered these things a mailman went by, which prompted them to hurry in, to escape yet more eyes. They had faith, but they were also embarrassed about what others might think, like a devout who crosses himself in secret.

An old half-breed Indian gentleman, father of the fortune-teller, led the ladies to the parlor. It was a simple room, with bare walls, nothing to suggest mystery or incite fear, no fetishes, stuffed beasts, skeletons, or horrid scrawls. At worst, an image of the Virgin pasted to the wall suggested a mystery, worn and tattered as it was, but it did not inspire fear. On a chair, a guitar.

"My daughter will be right in," said the old man. "What are your names, ladies?"

Natividade gave only her Christian name, Maria, as if it were a veil darker than the one she wore over her face, and she was given a card, because there was to be only one consultation, with the number 1,012. Don't be dismayed by the numeral. The clientele was numerous, and it represented many months of consultations. Not to mention an old, most ancient custom. Reread Aeschylus, my friend: reread *The Eumenides,* and there you will see Pythia calling those who came to consult her: "If there are any Hellenes here, let them draw lots, so enter, as the custom is. My prophecy is only as the god may guide." By lot then, numbering now, all is done so that truth adjusts to priority and no one loses their turn for a consultation. Natividade kept the card, and both ladies went to the window.

To tell the truth, each one harbored her own little fears, Perpétua less than Natividade. The adventure seemed daring, and some danger was possible. I won't describe their gestures here. Imagine that they were nervous and a little confused. They did not speak. Natividade confessed afterward that she had a lump in her throat. Fortunately the cabocla did not take long; after three or four minutes, her father brought her by the hand, lifting the curtain at the back of the room.

"Come in, Barbara."

Barbara entered, while her father picked up the guitar and went out the door on the left to the stone stair landing. Barbara was a light, slight creature, embroidered skirts, little slippers on her feet. One couldn't deny her a graceful figure. Her hair, swept up to the crown of her head and bound by a piece of soiled ribbon, made her a natural cap, with a tassel of a sprig of bitter rue. There was something of the priestess in her bearing. The mystery was in her eyes. They were opaque, but not so much that they were not also bright and sharp, and in this last regard also large, so large and so sharp they pierced you, skewered your heart, and retreated, only to penetrate and pierce again. I don't lie saying that the two were somewhat fascinated. Barbara interrogated them. Natividade stated her mission and showed her the pictures of her sons and locks of their hair, which she had been advised would suffice.

"That's enough," confirmed Barbara. "Are the boys your sons?"

"They are."

"The one is the spitting image of the other."

"They're twins. They were born a little over a year ago."

"Ladies, please sit down."

Natividade whispered to her companion that "the cabocla is very nice," so softly that the fortune-teller could not hear her; but it could be that, fearful of her prediction, the mother wished for exactly that, to assure a good destiny for her sons. The cabocla went over to the round table at the center of the room and sat down, facing the two of them. She put the photographs and the locks of hair in front of her. She looked alternately at the pictures and at the mother, asked a few questions of her client, then stared at the portraits and the locks of hair, her mouth slightly open and her eyelids dropped. I hesitate to tell you that she lit up a cigarette, but I do so, because it's true, and the weed fits the occupation. Outside the father strummed the guitar, softly singing a song of the Northeast backlands:

Girl in the white skirts
Skipping from rock to rock in the stream

As the cigarette smoke curled upward, the face of the fortune-teller changed expression, radiant or somber, now quizzical, now authoritative. Barbara leaned over the portraits, clutched a lock of hair in each hand, and stroked them, smelled them, listened to them, without the affectation that you might believe these lines convey! Such gestures would be difficult to recount casually. Natividade did not take her eyes off the seer, as if she wanted to read what was inside her. And it was not without some shock that she heard her ask whether the boys had fought before their birth.

"Fight?"

"Yes, my lady, fight."

"Before they were born?"

"Yes, madam, I ask if they had not fought in their mother's womb. Can't you remember?"

Natividade, whose pregnancy had not been easy, replied that in fact she had felt unusual repeated movements, pains, insomnia. . . . But, then, what was it? Why had they fought? The cabocla did not reply. She rose shortly thereafter and walked around the table, slowly, like a somnambulist, her eyes open and staring; then she once again shifted her gaze between mother and sons. Now she became more agitated, breathing heavily. Her whole being, face and arms, shoulders and legs, all was little to wrench a pronouncement from Destiny. Finally, she stopped, sat down, exhausted, until she sprang up and approached the two, so radiant, her eyes so bright and warm, that the mother hung on their expression, and could not hold herself back from grasping the woman's hands and asking anxiously, "Well then, tell me, I can hear everything."

Barbara, full of spirit and laughter, gave a satisfied sigh. The first word seemed to rise to her mouth, but it retreated back to her heart, virgin of her lips and others' ears. Natividade insisted on a reply, that she tell her everything, without fail . . .

"Things of the future!" the cabocla finally murmured.

"But are they bad things?"

"Oh, no, no! Good things, things of the future!"

"But that's not enough; tell me the rest. This woman is my sister and can be trusted with secrets, but if she needs to leave, she will; I'll stay and you can tell me alone . . . will they be happy?"

"Yes."

"Will they be great?"

"They will be great, oh very great! God will give them many blessings. And they will rise, rise, rise. . . . They fought in their mother's womb, so what? People fight out here too. Your sons will be glorious. And that's all I will tell you. As for the quality of the glory, things of the future!"

From within, the voice of the old man once again continued the song of the backlands:

Climb up that coconut palm
Throw my coconuts down

And the daughter, not having any more to say, or not knowing what to explain, moved her hips to the melody, which the old man repeated from behind the door:

Girl in the white skirts
Skipping from rock to rock in the stream,

7

Climb up that coconut palm,
Throw my coconuts down.
Coconut break, missy,
In the coconut grove,
If it falls on your head,
Breaks open for sure.
I'll laugh out loud
I'll love that coconut milk
Coco, lala, nana.

II

Better Going Down than Going Up

All oracles speak with a forked tongue, but they can be understood. Natividade finally understood the cabocla, even though she heard nothing more from her. It was enough to know that things of the future would be good, and her sons great and glorious, for her to feel happy and to pull a 50,000 *réis* note from her purse. It was five times the customary price, and it was worth as much or more than the rich gifts of Croesus to Pythia. She carefully placed the portraits and the locks of hair back in her bag, and the pair left, while the cabocla retreated to the back rooms of her dwelling, to wait for the next clients. There were already some customers at the door, with their numbers, and the women retreated hastily down the stairs, their faces veiled.

Perpétua shared the joy of her sister, and so did the stones underfoot, the wall facing the sea, the shirts hanging from window sills, the banana peels in the path. The very shoes of an alms collector about to turn the corner from the Rua da Misericórdia to the Rua São José seemed to squeak with glee, when they really were groaning with exhaustion. Natividade was so elated that, on hearing his call "For the all souls' Mass!" she pulled out of her purse a 2,000 réis bill, brand new, and laid it in the alms bowl. Her sister pointed out the mistake to her, but it was not a mistake—it was for the souls in purgatory.

And light-footed they moved quickly to their waiting carriage, which stood in the space between the church of São José and the Chamber of Deputies. They had not wanted their coach to take them to the foot of the hill, so that the coachman and the lackey would not suspect their mission. Everyone in the city was talking about the cabocla on the Morro do Castelo. It was the talk of the town. They attributed infinite powers to her, a series of miracles, sudden fortunes, lost things found, marriages. If they were found out they were lost, although many good people went there. Seeing them give alms to the alms collector, the lackey jumped up onto the carriage step and the coachman tugged at his reins to set his horses in motion; the carriage came to fetch them and headed back to Botafogo.

The Alms of Happiness

" **M** ay God multiply your blessings, my devout lady!" exclaimed the alms collector as he saw the banknote fall on top of two 5 *tostão* pieces and some old *vintém* coins.

"May God give you all the happiness of heaven and earth, and the souls of purgatory ask the Holy Virgin Mother to recommend you to her divine son!"

When fortune smiles, all of nature smiles too, and the heart rejoices with all around it. That was the explanation that, in less poetic language, the alms collector gave about the 2,000 note. The suspicion that it might be counterfeit did not take root in his brain. That was just a rapid hallucination. He understood that the women were happy, and being accustomed to thinking out loud, he said, winking an eye, while they climbed into their carriage: "Those two have seen the bluebird of happiness, for certain."

He arrived directly at the conclusion that the two ladies were returning from an amorous adventure, and he deduced this from three facts, which I am obliged to display here so as not to leave this man suspect of gratuitous slander. The first was their happiness, the second the value of the donation, and the third the carriage that awaited them in an alley, as if they wished to hide from the coachman the location of the lovers' tryst. Now, do not conclude yourself that he had once been a coachman, driving young ladies to and fro before entering his vocation of serving souls. Also do not believe that he had once been rich and adulterous, openhanded in saying farewell to his lady friends. "Neither such an excess of honor, nor such an indignity." He was just a poor devil with no other occupation than that of being a devout. Besides, he would not have had sufficient time. He was only 27 years old.

He waved to the ladies when their carriage passed. Afterward he stared at the banknote, so crisp, so valuable, a note that the souls would never see pass from his hands. He kept walking up the Rua de São José. He no longer had the energy to beg. The banknote was turning into gold and the idea of it being counterfeit was returning to his head, now more frequently, until for a few minutes he was consumed with it. If it were false . . . "For the Mass of the dead!" he moaned at the door of a grocery shop and they gave him a vintém, a coin so dirty and sad, lying at the foot of the note so new it seemed just off the printing press. Next was the entry to a townhouse. He entered, climbed the stairs, begged, and they gave him two vinténs, the double of the other coin in value and corrosion.

And the banknote still clean, a 2,000 note that seemed like 20,000. No, it wasn't false. In the hallway he picked it up, looked at it closely. It was real. Suddenly he heard a doorway open and rapid footsteps. He, more quickly still, folded the note and stuck it in his trouser pocket. There only remained the sad, corroded coins, the widow's mite. He left the building, and went on to the next workshop, the next store, the next hallway, begging loudly and mournfully: "For the Mass of the dead!"

In the church, after he removed his cloak and after delivering the alms bowl to the sacristan, he heard a weak voice like that of a lost soul asking him of the 2,000 note. The 2,000 réis, said another less weak voice, which was naturally his, who in the first place also had a soul and in the second place had never received such a large offering. Whoever wants to give that much comes into church or buys a candle, they don't put a banknote like that in an alms bowl.

If I am lying, it is not intentional. In fact, the words did not come out quite that well articulated and clearly, neither the weak ones nor the less weak. They all buzzed in the ears of his conscience. I translated them into spoken language so that they will be understood by those who read me. I don't know how one would transcribe to paper a deaf roar and one less deaf, one after the other and all of them jumbled together, until the second remained alone: "he didn't take the note from anyone . . . the lady put it in the bowl with her own hand . . . he too was a soul." At the door of the sacristy which led to the street, once he closed the heavy blue curtain bordered in gold, he heard nothing more. He saw a beggar holding out his tattered, greasy hat. He carefully put his hand in his waistcoat pocket, also torn, and ventured forth two copper coins, which he dropped into the beggar's hat, quickly, in secret, as the Gospel preaches. They were two vintém pieces. He had 1,960 left. And the beggar, as he left quickly, sent after him these words of thanks, similar to his own: "God multiply your blessings, my dear sir, and give you . . ."

I V

The Carriage Mass

Natividade kept thinking about the cabocla on Castelo hill, about the prediction of greatness and the notice of the fight. She began to remember that, in fact, her pregnancy had not been easy. But what remained in her awareness was the good fortune of glory and greatness. The fight faded from her awareness, as if it hadn't happened at all. The future, yes, that was the most important thing, everything in fact. She said nothing as they rode by Santa Luzia beach. At the Largo da Lapa she questioned her sister about what she thought of the fortune-teller. Perpétua answered that she had a good impression, that she believed her, and both agreed that she seemed to speak of her own sons, such was her enthusiasm. Perpétua did, however, scold her sister about the 50,000 réis given in payment; 20,000 would have been enough.

"It's all right. Things of the future!"
"What things will these be?"
"I don't know, future things."

They sank once again into silence. When the carriage entered Catete, Natividade recalled the morning she had passed that very place in this same carriage, and she confided to her husband that she was expecting. They were returning from a memorial Mass at the Igreja São Domingos . . .

"Today at the Igreja São Domingos there will be a Mass for the soul of João de Melo, deceased in Maricá." So went the announcement that one can read even today in some of the newspapers of 1869. The day escapes me, but the month was August. The announcement is correct, it was precisely that, no additional information, not even the name of the person or persons who ordered the Mass, no time or invitation was given. It did not even say that the deceased was a court clerk, an office he gave up only at his death. In fact, it seems they even took a name away from him. He was, if I am correctly informed, João de Melo e Barros.

Not knowing who had ordered the Mass, nobody went. The church that was chosen gave even less importance to the act. It was not grand or sought out, but somewhat shabby, without pomp or populace, tucked away in the corner of a small square, appropriate for an obscure, anonymous Mass.

At eight o'clock a carriage stopped at the church door. The lackey jumped down, opened the coupé door, removed his cap, and stood at attention. Out came a gentleman, who gave his hand to a lady; the lady emerged and took the gentleman's arm, they crossed the little square, and entered the church. In the sacristy all was in a state of alarm. The soul who to such a place would attract a luxurious carriage, thoroughbred horses, and two elegant people would not be like the other souls tended here. The Mass was heard without condolences or tears. When it was over, the gentleman went to the sacristy to give his offering. The sacristan, folding in his cassock the note of 10,000 réis that he was given, thought this proved the sublimity of the deceased. But what kind of a dead man was this? The same would occur to the alms box, if it could think, when the gloved hand of the lady let fall inside a silver piece of 500 réis. Already gathered in the church were half a dozen raggedy children, and now people were at the doors and in the square, waiting. The gentleman, arriving at the door, surveyed the scene slowly and saw that he and his wife were objects of curiosity. The lady kept her eyes lowered. And the two entered the carriage; with the same gesture, the lackey shut the door and they left.

The local folk spoke of nothing else on that and the following days. The sacristan and the neighbors recalled the carriage with pride. It was the Mass of the carriage. Other Masses came and went, all on foot, some with tattered shoes, not infrequently barefoot, old capes, torn linen, Masses in calico on Sundays, clog Masses. Everything returned to normal, but the carriage Mass lived in their memory for many months. Finally they spoke no more of it—it was forgotten like a fancy ball.

Well, the carriage was this very same one. The Mass was ordered by that gentleman, whose name is Santos, and the deceased was his relative, even if a poor one. He too had been poor. He had also been born in Maricá. Arriving in Rio de Janeiro, on the occasion of the stock market fever (1855), they say he revealed extraordinary ability to earn money quickly. He earned a lot quickly, and he made others lose it. He married this Natividade in 1859, who was then 20 and had no money, but she was beautiful and she loved him passionately. Fortune blessed them with riches. Years later they had a fancy home, carriages, horses, and new, important social relations. Of Natividade's two poor relatives, her father died in 1866. She had only a sister left. Santos had some family in Maricá, to whom he never sent money, whether out of stinginess or cleverness. Stinginess, I think not. He spent lavishly and gave many alms. Let it be cleverness. It took away their taste for asking for more.

That didn't work with João de Melo, who one day appeared to ask him for a job. He wanted to be, like Santos, a bank director. Santos quickly arranged for him a place as court clerk in Maricá and sent him off with the best advice in the world.

João de Melo left with his clerkship and, they say, with a great passion as well. Natividade was the most beautiful woman of the time. Even at the end, with her sexagenarian gray hair, she lived up to her reputation. João de Melo became infatuated when he saw her. She recognized this and behaved properly. She did not present an angry countenance, it is true, and she was more beautiful this way than angry. Also she did not close her eyes to him, which were black and warm. She just closed her heart, a heart

14

that must love as no other, was the conclusion that João de Melo reached when he saw her bare-shouldered at a ball. He had the impulse to possess her, sink with her, to fly, to be swept away. . . .

And instead, a clerkship in Maricá. It was an abyss. He fell into it and three days later he left Rio de Janeiro, never to return. At first he wrote many letters to his relative, hoping she would read them and understand that some of the words were for her. But Santos did not answer him, and time and absence turned João de Melo into an excellent clerk. He died of pneumonia.

That the motive of Natividade's little silver piece thrown into the alms box was to repay the adoration of the deceased, I will say neither yea nor nay. I lack details. But it could be so, because this lady was not less grateful than chaste. As for the largess of her husband, don't forget the relative was dead, and a dead man meant one less relative.

V

There are Contradictions that Can Be Explained

D on't ask me to explain the cause of such modesty in the advertisement and the Mass and so much publicity with the carriage, lackey, and livery. There are contradictions that can be explained. A good author, who made up his story or placed importance on the apparent logic of events, would transport the Santos couple by foot or by public carriage or rented coach; but I, my friend, I know how things happened, and I relate them exactly as they were. At most, I explain them, with the condition that such a custom will not become a habit. Explanations eat up time and paper, they hold up the action and end up in boredom. It's best to read with attention.

As to the contradiction we are discussing here, it is obvious that in such a remote and modest little square, no one they knew would run into them, while they would enjoy local admiration. Such were the reflections of Santos, if one can give such a name to an interior process that leads one to do one thing rather than another. There remains the Mass. The Mass itself only needed to be known in heaven and in Maricá. The couple was dressed up for an audience in heaven. The luxury of the couple tempered the poverty of the prayers; it was a type of homage to the deceased. If the soul of João de Melo had seen them from above, he would have been pleased at the elegance in which they went to pray for a poor clerk. It is not I who state this. Santos is the one who thought it.

V I

Maternity

At first they rode in silence. Natividade only spoke to complain of the dirty church, which had soiled her dress.

"I'm full of fleas," she continued. "Why didn't we go to St. Francis de Paula or Glória, which are closer and cleaner?"

Santos changed the topic and talked about the poorly paved streets, which made the carriage jolt. Certainly, it would break the springs.

Natividade did not reply, she sank into silence, as in that other chapter, twenty months later, when she returned from Morro do Castelo with her sister. Her eyes did not shine with wonder as they would that day. They were fixed and somber, as in the morning and the night before. Santos, who had noticed this, asked her what was the matter. I don't know if she answered him in words. If she said anything, it was so brief and muffled that it was lost entirely. Perhaps it was nothing more than a glance, a sigh, or something like that. Whatever it was, when the carriage had reached mid-Catete, the two were holding hands and the expression on their faces was beatific. They took no further notice of people on the streets, perhaps not even of themselves.

Reader, you will certainly have guessed the cause of that expression and those intertwined fingers. It was already mentioned before, when it would have been better to let you guess, but probably you would not have guessed it, not because you are short of intelligence or foresight, but because each man is different from the next, and you perhaps might have worn the same expression, simply knowing you would go dancing on Saturday. Santos did not dance. He preferred the game of whist as a distraction. The cause was virtuous, as you know. Natividade was with child, and she had just told her husband.

At 30 years of age it was not too early or too late, it was unexpected. Santos felt more than she the pleasure of new life. Here at last was the fulfillment of a dream he had held for ten years, a creature taken from Abraham's thigh, as the good Jews said, whom we burned later and who now generously lend their money to firms and to nations. They take interest for the loans, but the Hebrew sayings are given for free. That is one of them. Santos, who only understood the part about the loans, identified unconsciously with the saying and delighted in it. Emotion tied his tongue. His eyes, which caressed his wife and held her, were those of the patriarch. His smile rained light on his loved one, blessed and beautiful among the beautiful.

Natividade didn't feel exactly this way in the beginning. Little by little she was conquered, and already she wore an expression of hope and of maternity. In the first days, the symptoms disconcerted our friend. It is hard to say so, but it's true. There went balls and parties, there went liberty and leisure. Natividade mingled in the highest circles of the time. She had just become a part of society, with such art that she seemed to have been born there. She exchanged letters with great ladies, she was familiar with many, and with some used the intimate *tu*. She not only had the house in Botafogo, but also another in Petrópolis, not just one car, but also a box in the Lyric Theater, not counting the balls at the Fluminense Casino, those of her friends and her own, all the repertory, in sum, of the elegant life. She was written about in the newspapers, she belonged to that dozen planetary names who shine amid the plebeian stars. Her husband was a capitalist and director of a bank.

In the midst of all this, why should a child come who would deform her for months, force her to retire from society, rob her of sleep, with teething problems and the rest? Such was the first sensation of the mother, and the first impulse was to crush the seed. She became angry at her husband. The second sensation was better. Maternity, arriving at midday, was like a new and fresh dawn. Natividade saw the figure of her son or daughter playing in the grass of their country home or in the lap of their nanny, 3 years old, and this scene would come when she was 34, giving her the appearance of a mere twenty-some years . . .

That is what reconciled her with her husband. I don't exaggerate. I don't dislike the lady. Some would be frightened, most would feel love. The conclusion is that, through one or another door, love or vanity, what the embryo wants is to enter life. Caesar or João Fernandes, all is to preserve life, to assure the dynasty and leave the world as late as possible.

The couple was silent. Arriving at Botafogo beach, the view of the bay brought the customary pleasure. The house appeared in the distance, magnificent. Santos delighted in the sight of it, saw himself in it, he grew with it and ascended within it. The statue of

Narcissus in the middle of the garden smiled as they entered, the sand became a lawn, two swallows swooped overhead, their fluttering wings expressing the happiness of the pair. The same ceremony was repeated as they descended. Santos still paused for a few moments to see the carriage turn, leave, and head for the carriage house. Then he followed his wife into the foyer.

V I I

Gestation

U pstairs, Perpétua was waiting for them, that sister of Natividade's who accompanied her to the Morro do Castelo and stayed in the carriage, where I left them to narrate the origins of the boys.

"Well, were many people there?"

"No, nobody. Fleas."

Perpétua also had not understood the choice of church. As for who would attend the service, it seemed to her there would be few people or none at all. But her brother-in-law was entering the room, so she said nothing more. She was a circumspect person, who would not allow herself a careless word or gesture. Nevertheless, it was impossible to silence her amazement, when she saw her brother-in-law come in and give his wife a long, tender embrace, sealed with a kiss.

"What is this?" she exclaimed, astonished.

Without taking notice of his wife's embarrassment, Santos embraced his sister-in-law, and he was about to kiss her too, if she had not recoiled forcefully and immediately.

"But what is this, have you won the Spanish lottery?"

"No, something better—new folks coming."

Santos kept some mannerisms and ways of speech from his early years, that the reader will perhaps not call exactly familiar. But you don't need to call them anything at all. Perpétua, who was used to them, smiled and congratulated the couple. Then Natividade left them to change her clothes. Santos, a little discomfited by his expansiveness, became serious and talked about the Mass and the church. He agreed that it was decrepit and in a bad location, but he alleged spiritual reasons. That prayer is always prayer, no matter where the soul communicates with God. That the Mass, strictly speaking, does not even need an altar. The rite and the priest are enough for the sacrifice. Perhaps this reasoning was not entirely his own, but heard from someone, memorized effortlessly, and repeated with conviction. The sister-in-law nodded her head in agreement. Then they spoke about the deceased relative and agreed piously that he was an ass. They didn't use that word, but the totality of their estimation could be summed up that way, adding honest, honest to a fault.

"He was a pearl," concluded Santos.

It was the last obituary; peace to the dead. From there on the new reign of the approaching child began. Their habits did not change at first, and the visits and balls continued as before, until little by little Natividade retreated entirely into the house. Her lady friends came to see her. Gentlemen friends came to visit them or play whist with her husband.

Natividade wanted a son, Santos a daughter, and each one built a case for their choice with such good reasons that they ended up switching positions. Then she kept the daughter, and dressed her in the best lace and cambric, while he dressed the young lawyer in a robe and gave him a seat in parliament, another in a Ministry. He also taught him how to get rich quickly and would help him, beginning with an account at the Savings and Loan, from the day he was born until he was 21. Sometimes at night, if they were alone, Santos took a pencil and drew the figure of his son, with a mustache, or he would sketch a vaporous young girl.

"Stop, Agostinho," his wife told him one evening. "You'll always be a child."

And not too much later, she herself began to draw in words the figure of her son or daughter, and both of them chose the color of eyes, hair, the forehead, stature. You see, she was still a child as well. Maternity has these inconsistencies and joys, and finally hope, which is the childhood of mankind.

Perfection would be for both a boy and a girl to be born. Thus the desires of both mother and father would be met. Santos thought about doing a spiritist séance over this matter. He was starting to be initiated into this religion, and he had the unwavering faith of the novice. But his wife was opposed to this. If they were to consult anyone, first it should be the famous cabocla of Morro do Castelo, who found what was lost and predicted the future. Nevertheless, he refused that too, as unnecessary. Why consult about something that in a few months would be revealed? Santos thought—in relation to the cabocla—that this would be to imitate the credulity of ignorant people. But his sister-in-law objected, and cited a recent case of a distinguished person, a municipal judge, whose appointment had been announced by the cabocla.

"Maybe the minister of justice likes the cabocla," explained Santos.

The two laughed at the thought, and thus was closed the chapter of the fortune-teller, to be opened later. For now let us allow the fetus to develop, the child to turn and twist, impatient to be born. In fact, the mother suffered considerably during the pregnancy, especially in the last weeks. She thought she must be carrying a general beginning his campaign in life, if not a couple falling out of love before their lives started.

VIII

Neither Boy and Girl, nor a General

Neither boy and girl, nor a general. On April 7, 1870, twin boys came into being, so identical that each seemed to be the shadow of the other, if it was not simply the optical illusion of the eye seeing double.

They were ready for anything else but the twins, and not for the great astonishment was their love any less. This is understandable without my needing to insist, just as one understands that the mother would give her two sons that full and divided loaf of the poet. I add that the father did the same thing. He spent the first days contemplating the boys, comparing them, measuring them, weighing them. They were the same weight and they grew in equal measure. The changes occurred apace in both. The long face, dark brown hair, long thin fingers such that, when those of the right hand of one were crossed with the fingers of the left hand of the other, it was impossible to tell they were two separate individuals. They would come to have different temperaments, but for now they were the same cautious little creatures. They started to smile on the same day. The same day saw them baptized.

Before the delivery, they had agreed to give the name of the father or of the mother, depending on the sex of the child. Since it was a pair of boys and there was no masculine form of the mother's name, and the father did not want to use only his own name, they began to scrounge around for others. The mother proposed French or English names, depending on which novels she was reading. Some Russian novels in fashion suggested Slavic names. The father accepted some, but consulted third parties, and did not get definitive opinions. Generally those who were consulted brought up yet another name, which was not accepted at home. They also tried the ancient Lusitanian onomasticon, without better luck. One day, when Perpétua was at Mass, she recited the Creed and her attention was caught by the words, "the holy apostles St. Peter and St. Paul," and she could hardly finish the prayer. She had found the names; they were simple and paired. The parents agreed with her, and the dispute was over.

Perpétua's joy was almost as great as that of the father and the mother, if not greater. Greater it was not, but it was great even if short-lived. The naming of the boys was almost as important as producing them. A widow, without children, she did not judge herself incapable of having them, and it was something to name them. She was about five or six years older than her sister. She had married an artillery lieutenant who had died a captain in the Paraguayan War. She was on the short side and she was fat, contrary to Natividade who, without being thin, did not carry the same amount of flesh, was tall, and stood erect. Both brimmed with health.

"Pedro and Paulo," said Perpétua to her sister and brother-in-law. "When I pronounced those two names in the prayer, I felt something in my heart."

"You will be the godmother of one," said her sister.

The little ones, who were differentiated by a colored ribbon, received gold medals, one with the image of St. Peter and the other of St. Paul. The confusion did not clear right away, but later, slowly and not completely, such a resemblance remaining that even those who knew them would make mistakes most of the time or all of the time. The mother did not need great external signs to tell who were those two pieces of herself. The wet nurses, despite telling them apart, became rivals because of the similarity of their charges. Each one insisted that hers was the more handsome. Natividade agreed with both.

Pedro would be a doctor, Paulo the lawyer. That was the first choice of professions. But soon afterward they would change careers. They also thought of placing one of them in engineering. The navy beckoned to the mother, because of the particular distinction of its school. The only inconvenience was the first distant voyage, but Natividade thought she might have a word with the minister of the navy. Santos talked about making one or both of them a banker. Thus passed the leisure hours. Intimates of the household entered into the calculations. Some would have them become ministers, justices, bishops, cardinals . . .

"I don't ask for that much," said the father.

Natividade said nothing in front of outsiders, she just smiled, as if it were a game at the feast of St. John, a throw of dice and reading in the book of fortunes the square corresponding to the numeral. It does not matter. Inside herself she craved a brilliant destiny for her sons. She believed, she waited, she prayed, she asked heaven to make them great men.

One of the wet nurses, it seems it was Pedro's, knowing about these yearnings and conversations, asked Natividade why she did not consult the cabocla of Morro do Castelo. She claimed that the woman was able to predict everything, what was and what would be. She knew the numbers of the big lottery, only she did not say what they were nor did she buy lottery tickets so as not to steal from the chosen of Our Lord. It seems she was sent by God.

The other wet nurse confirmed this rumor and added others. She knew people who had lost and found both jewels and slaves. The very police, when they could not find a criminal, went to the hill to talk to the cabocla and they would return with the information they needed. For this reason she was not expelled, as the envious would have it. Many did not travel without first making a pilgrimage up the hill. The cabocla explained dreams and thoughts, cured spells . . .

At dinner, Natividade repeated to her husband the suggestion of the wet nurses. Santos shrugged his shoulders. Then he laughed at the alleged prescience of the cabocla—especially the lottery was unbelievable because if she knew the number, then why did she not buy a ticket? Natividade thought this was the most difficult to explain, but it could be an invention of the people. *On ne prête qu'aux riches,*" she added, laughing. Her husband, who the evening before had dined with a judge, repeated his words that "until the police took control of the situation . . ." The judge had not finished his sentence. Santos concluded with a vague gesture.

"But you are a spiritist," commented his wife.

"Excuse me, let us not confuse the two things," he replied gravely.

Yes, he might consent to a consultation with a spiritist. He had already thought of it. Some spiritist might tell him the truth instead of a fake fortune-teller. Natividade defended the cabocla. People in society spoke of her in total seriousness. She did not want to admit yet that she had faith in the woman, but in fact she did. If she had declined to seek her out before, it was of course the lack of motive that had restrained her. What did it matter to know the sex of her child? To know the destiny of the two was much more urgent and useful. Old notions that had been instilled in her as a child now rose from her brain and descended to her heart. She imagined going with the little ones to the Morro do Castelo, under the pretext of an outing. What for? To confirm in her the hope she held that they would be great men. That there might be a contrary prediction did not occur to her. Perhaps if the reader were in the same situation, she might just await destiny. But the reader, besides not believing (not all do believe), might not be more than 20 or 22 years of age, and would have the patience to wait. Natividade, for her part, admitted her 31 years, and feared not seeing the greatness of her children. She might see it, because one can die old, and sometimes of old age, but would it have the same flavor?

After supper, the subject of conversation was the cabocla of the hill, initiated by Santos, who repeated the opinions of the evening before and of dinner. Some of the visitors told what they had heard about her. Natividade did not fall asleep that night before she obtained permission from her husband to visit the cabocla with her sister. There was nothing to lose. It would be enough to take the portraits of the boys and locks of their hair. The wet nurses would know nothing of the adventure.

On the appointed day the two got themselves into the carriage, between seven and eight o'clock, under the pretext of an outing, and away they went to the Rua da Misericórdia. You already know that there they descended, between the Church of St. John and the Chamber of Deputies, and they walked from there to the Rua do Carmo, where it abuts the walkway up the Castelo hill. About to ascend, they hesitated, but a mother is a mother, and now there was just a little way to go to hear destiny speak. You saw them ascend, and descend, give the 2,000 note to the almsman, enter the carriage, and return to Botafogo.

I X

View of the Palace

In Catete, their carriage and a victoria crossed and stopped for a while. A man jumped out of the victoria and walked over to the carriage. It was Natividade's husband, who was now going to the office, a little later than usual, because he had been waiting for his wife's return. He had been thinking of her and business, about the boys and the Rio Branco law then being discussed in the Chamber of Deputies. His bank had loaned money to the planters. Then he also thought about the Morro do Castelo and what the cabocla might have said to his wife . . .

Passing by the Nova Friburgo palace, he fixed his gaze on it with the customary covetousness, a longing to possess it, without foreseeing the high destiny that the palace would come to have in the history of the republic. But who then would have foreseen anything? Who can foretell anything at all? For Santos the question was just to possess it, to host large, unique parties there, which would be celebrated in the press, discussed in the city between friends and enemies alike, full of admiration, anger, or envy. He did not think about the fond memories that matrons of the future would pass on to their granddaughters, less still about the books of chronicles, written and printed in this next century. Santos did not have the imagination to contemplate posterity. He saw only the present and its wonders.

Already it was not enough to be what he was. The house in Botafogo, while beautiful, was not a palace, and then, it was not as visible as here in Catete, a thoroughfare that all had to travel. Everyone would look at the great windows, the great doors, the huge eagles decorating the corners of the palace, their great wings spread. Whoever saw it from the seashore would see the back of the palace, its gardens and ponds . . . Oh, infinite pleasure! Santos imagined the bronzes, marbles, lights, flowers, dances, carriages, music, dinners . . . All this he thought rapidly, because the victoria, although it was not speeding (the horses had been restrained to slow their pace), still did not move slowly enough for Santos to finish his daydream. Thus it was that before arriving at the Glória beach, the victoria sighted the family coupé, and the two carriages stopped at a short distance from each other, as previously mentioned.

X

The Vow

I t was also said that the husband got out of the victoria and walked over to the coupé, where the wife and sister-in-law waited, and anticipating his questions, they smiled.

"Don't tell him anything," advised Perpétua.

Santos's head appeared, with his short sideburns, the close-cropped hair, and trimmed mustache. He was an attractive man. When he kept still, he wasn't bad at all. The agitation with which he approached, leaned into the coupé, and spoke, took away the gravity of his demeanor in the victoria, his hands placed on the gold handle of his walking stick and the walking stick propped between his knees.

"Well? Well?" he asked.

"I'll tell you later."

"But what happened?"

"Later."

"Good or bad? Just tell me if it was good."

"Good. Things of the future."

"Is she a serious person?"

"Serious she is. I'll see you later," repeated Natividade, extending her fingers.

But the husband could not tear himself away from the coupé. He wanted to know everything on the spot, the questions and answers, the people who were waiting, if it was the same destiny for both, or if each had his own. Nothing of this was as I write it here, slowly, so that the bad handwriting of the author does not affect his prose. No sir, Santos's words tumbled out in a rush, falling over each other, jumbled together, without a beginning and an end. The lovely wife already had her ears so tuned to her husband's speech, especially in times of emotion or curiosity, that she understood everything, and kept saying no. Her head and her finger emphasized the negative. Santos had no choice, and said good-bye.

On the way, he realized that, if he didn't believe in the cabocla, it was pointless to insist on knowing her prophecy. It was more: it was to acknowledge that his wife had been correct. He vowed not to ask any more when he returned. He did not promise to forget, and thus the persistence with which he often thought of the oracle. And finally, they would tell him everything without his asking anything, and that certainty brought him peace for the day.

Do not conclude from this that the bank customers suffered any loss of service from his distraction. All went well, as if he did not have a wife or sons, or as if there was no Castelo or a cabocla. It was not just his hands that did their work, signing papers. His mouth kept talking, giving orders, calling and laughing, if necessary. Nevertheless, the anxiety persisted and the figures paraded back and forth in his mind's eye. In an interval between two drafts, Santos decided one way or the other, if not both at the same time. Entering the carriage in the afternoon, he gave himself entirely to the oracle. He rested his hands on his walking stick, the walking stick rested between his knees, as in the morning, but he thought about his boys' destiny.

When he arrived home, he saw Natividade contemplating the boys, both in their cribs, their wet nurses at their feet, a little astonished by the insistence with which their mother had sought them out that day since early morning. She didn't just look at them, or gaze off into space and time. She would kiss them and press them to her heart. I forgot to say that in the morning, Perpétua changed her clothes before her sister did and found her standing at the foot of the cribs, dressed as she had returned from the hill.

"I see you came to see the great men," she said.

"I did, but I don't know in what way they will be great."

"However it is, let's have lunch."

At lunch and throughout the day, they spoke often of the cabocla and her prediction. Now, in seeing her husband come in, Natividade read the feigned indifference in his eyes. She wanted to remain quiet and wait, but she was so anxious to tell him everything, and it was so good, that she changed her mind. Except she had no time to do so. Even before she began, he had already asked what had happened. Natividade recounted the ascent, the consultation, the reply, and the rest; she described the cabocla and her father.

"And so, great destinies?"

"Things of the future," she repeated.

"Certainly of the future. It's just the matter of the fight that I don't understand. Why fight? And how did they fight? And did they really fight?"

Natividade recalled her sufferings during pregnancy, confessing she did not complain so as not to worry him. Naturally that is what the fortune-teller interpreted as fighting.

"But why would they fight?"

"That I don't know, nor do I believe it was anything serious."

"I'm going to consult . . ."

"Consult whom?"

"A person."

"I know, your friend Plácido."

"If he were just a friend, I would not consult him, but he is my spiritual adviser and my mentor, he has a clear and broad vision of things, a gift from heaven . . . I'll consult him as if it were a hypothetical case. I won't give our names."

"No, no, no!"

"Just as a hypothetical case."

"No, Agostinho, don't tell him. Do not ask anyone on my behalf, do you hear? Go now, promise you will not speak of this to

29

anyone, neither spiritists nor friends. The best is to keep it to ourselves. It's enough to know they will have good fortune. Great men, things of the future . . . Swear, Agostinho."

"But didn't you go in person to see the cabocla?"

"She does not know me, not even by name; she saw me only once, she will never see me again. Please swear to me!'

"You are a strange one. Well, now, I promise. And what does it matter if I do speak about it, by the way?"

"I simply don't want you to. Swear you won't!"

"Is this something worth a vow?"

"If you don't, I cannot trust you," she said, smiling.

"I swear."

"Swear by God our Lord."

"I swear by God our Lord."

X I

A Unique Case!

Santos believed in the sanctity of vows. For this reason, he resisted, but finally he gave his promise. Nevertheless, the thought of the intrauterine battle of the two boys never left him. He wanted to forget it. He played whist that night, as usual. The next night he went to the theater. On the next he paid a visit. Then went back to his usual card game of whist, while the fight stayed with him. It was a mystery. Perhaps it was a unique case. . . .

Unique! A unique case! The singularity of it made him cling even more tenaciously to the idea, or the idea to him. I cannot explain any better this intimate phenomenon, occurring where no man's eye can penetrate, and where neither reflection nor conjecture suffices. Even so, it didn't take very long. On the first Sunday, Santos took himself off to the house of "Doctor" Plácido, Rua do Senador Vergueiro, a low-standing house, with three windows and a large lot facing the sea. I don't believe it exists any longer: it dates from the time that the street was called the Caminho Velho, to differentiate it from the Caminho Novo.

Forgive these minutiae. The action could go on without them, but I want you to know which house it was, and on which street, and what is more, I will tell you that it was a kind of club, temple, or spiritist place of worship. Plácido was both priest and president. He was an old man with a thick beard, blue, piercing eyes, cloaked in a large silk robe. Put a wand in his hand, and he would be a magician, but truthfully, the beard and the robe were not worn to produce that effect. Unlike Santos, who would have altered his face ten times were it not for the opposition of his wife, Plácido had a full beard since early manhood and the robe for a good ten years.

"Come, come," he said, "come help me convert our good friend Aires. For the last half hour I have tried to inculcate in him the eternal truths, but he resists."

"No, no, no, I am not resisting," chimed in a man of about 40, extending his hand to the new arrival.

XII

That Man Aires

The man Aires who just appeared still retains some of the virtues of the times, and almost none of the vices. Do not attribute such qualities to any motive. Nor should you believe that homage is intended to that person's modesty. No sir, it is the pure truth and a natural attribute. In spite of his 40 years, or 42, and perhaps because of this, he was a fine specimen of a man. A career diplomat, he had arrived just a few days before from the Pacific, on a six-month leave.

I will not take too long to describe him. Just imagine that he wore the marks of his profession, the approving smile, the soft, cautious speech, the well-timed gesture, the appropriate turn of phrase, all so well distributed that it was a pleasure to hear and see him. Perhaps the skin of his clean-shaven face was just about to betray the first signs of age. Even so, his mustache, which was youthful in color and in the energy with which it twirled into fine, stiff points, would give an air of freshness to his face, when the half century of his life arrived. His hair would do the same thing, just vaguely graying, parted in the middle. On the top of his head was the beginning of a bald spot. In his buttonhole an eternal flower.

There was a time, it was on occasion of his previous leave, when he was just a second secretary, there was a time when he too was fond of Natividade. It was not exactly passion. He was not a man for that type of thing. He liked her, the way he appreciated jewels and rare objects, but as soon as he saw it was not reciprocated, he changed the subject. It was not weakness or coldness on his part. He liked women enough and even more so if they were beautiful. The issue was that he did not want them by force nor did he want to have to persuade them. He was not a general for frontal attacks, or to undertake lengthy sieges. He was content with simple military exercises, long or brief, depending on if the weather was clear or cloudy. In sum, extremely sensible.

An interesting coincidence: it was around this time that Santos thought of marrying him to his sister-in-law, recently widowed.

She seemed to be interested. Natividade was opposed; no one ever knew why. It was not jealousy, I don't think it was envy. The simple desire not to have him enter the family through the side door is just one conjecture which is as good as the first two rejected hypotheses. The displeasure of ceding him to another, or having them happy at her feet, it could not be, although the heart is the abyss of abysses. Let us suppose that it was to punish him for loving her.

It may be, in any case, that the greatest obstacle would come from himself. Although Aires was a widower, he had never been exactly married. He did not care for marriage. He married because his profession expected it. He understood that it was better to be a married diplomat than a single one, and he asked the first young woman who seemed fit to join him in his destiny. He was mistaken. The difference of temperament and spirit was so great that, even though he lived with the woman, it was as if he lived alone. He did not suffer with the loss. He had the vocation for bachelorhood.

He was sensible, I repeat, although this word does not express exactly what I wish to say. His heart was ready to accept everything, not because it was inclined to harmony, but because of an aversion to controversy. To appreciate this aversion, it would have been sufficient to see him enter the Santos household on a visit. The guests and the family were talking about the cabocla of the hill.

"You are just in time, counselor," said Perpétua. "What do you think about the cabocla of the Castelo?"

Aires thought nothing, but he realized that the others did, and he made an ambivalent gesture. Since everyone insisted, he chose neither of the two opinions, but he found another, a compromise, which satisfied both sides, a rare thing for compromise. You know that the fate of compromise is disdain. But that Aires, José da Costa Marcondes Aires, had it that in controversies a skeptical or compromising opinion can be a healing agent, like a pill, and he fashioned his so that the patient, if not cured, at least did not die, which is the most that pills do. Don't think badly of him because of this. The bitter medicine is swallowed with sugar. Aires opined slowly, delicately, with circumlocutions, wiping his monocle with a silk handkerchief, dripping his grave and obscure words, rolling his eyes up as one who searches for a recollection, and finds it, and thus rounded out his opinion. One of the listeners accepted it right away, another diverged a little and ended up in agreement, thus the third, and fourth, and then the whole room.

Do not think he was not sincere; he was. When he did not manage to have the same opinion, and it was worthwhile to write his down, he wrote it. He was also in the habit of keeping notes on his discoveries, observations, reflections, criticisms, and anecdotes, keeping for this purpose a collection of notebooks which he gave the name *Memoirs*. That evening he wrote these lines:

"An evening at the Santos home, without a game of whist. The conversation was about the cabocla of the Morro do Castelo. I suspect Natividade or her sister wants to consult her. It would not be on my account.

"Natividade and a Padre Guedes, a fat old gentleman, were the only two interesting people there. The rest were insipid, but insipid from necessity, not being capable of being anything but insipid. When the Padre and Natividade left me in the hands of the other insipid ones, I tried to escape into my memories, recalling sensations, reliving scenes, travels, people. That is how I thought about Capponi, whom I caught a glimpse of from behind today on the Rua da Quitanda. I met her here at the old Hotel Dom Pedro, years ago. Poor Capponi! She was walking, her left foot slipped out of her shoe, and showing through the heel of her stocking was a little hole of longing.

"I finally went back to the eternal insipidness of the others. I cannot understand how this lady, who is in fact so fine, can organize evenings like this one. It's not that the others did not try to be interesting, and if intentions were enough, no book would be enough for them. But they were not, as hard as they tried. Well, there they go, let's hope that other nights bring better company with no effort. What the cradle gives, only the grave takes away, says an old adage. I can, truncating a verse of my poet Dante, write of these insipid ones: *Dico, che quando l'anima mal nata. . . .*"

XIII

The Epigraph

Well, that is precisely the epigraph of the book, if I wanted to write one for it and none other occurred to me. It is not only a way of completing the characters in the narrative with the ideas they evoked, but it also serves as a pair of spectacles with which the reader can penetrate what is less clear or totally obscure.

On the other hand, there is an advantage in having my characters collaborate in the story, helping the author, through an act of solidarity, a kind of exchange of services, between the chess player and his pieces.

If you accept the comparison, you will distinguish the king and the queen, the bishop and the knight, knowing that the knight cannot substitute for the rook nor can the rook become the pawn. There is also the difference of color, white and black, but that does not restrict the movements of any piece, and finally one or the other can win the game, which is how the world works. Perhaps it would be a good idea, from time to time, to insert a diagram of beautiful or difficult positions, just as they do in chess literature. Not having a chessboard, this means of following the moves is a great help, but it could be that you have enough vision to reproduce by memory the different moves. I think so. Away with diagrams! Everything will happen as if you really were watching a game between two players, or more clearly, between God and the Devil.

XIV

The Lesson of the Pupil

"Stay, please stay, counselor," said Santos, gripping the
diplomat's hand. "Learn the eternal truths."

"Eternal truths demand eternal hours," mused the latter,
checking his watch.

That fellow Aires was not easy to convince. Plácido spoke to
him about scientific laws to avoid any taint of sectarianism, and
Santos followed suit. All the spiritist terminology came out, and
also the cases, phenomena, mysteries, testimonies, written and
verbal affidavits. Santos offered an example: two spirits might return together to this world. And, if they fought before they were
born?

"Children don't fight before they are born," replied Aires, tempering his affirmation with a questioning intonation.

"So you deny that two spirits . . . ? That one is mine, counselor!
What then prevents two spirits . . . ?"

Aires saw the abyss of a controversy and protected himself
from vertigo with a concession, saying: "Esau and Jacob fought in
their mother's womb, that is true. And the cause of the conflict is
known. As for others, if they also fight, all lies in knowing the
cause of the conflict and not knowing it, because Providence
hides it from human awareness. If it were a spiritual cause, for example . . ."

"For example?"

"For example, if the two children wanted to kneel at the same
time to worship the Creator. There is a case of conflict, but of
spiritual conflict, whose processes elude human sagacity. There
could also be a temporal motive. Let us suppose the need to el-
bow one another to adjust their position in the womb. It is a hypothesis that science would allow. That is, I don't know. There is
still the case of each one competing to be primogenitor."

"What for?" asked Plácido.

"While that privilege today is limited to royal families, the
House of Lords and I don't know what all, it still has a sym-

36

bolic value. The simple pleasure of being born first, without any other social or political advantage, could be instinctive, particularly if the children are destined to climb the heights of this world."

Santos cocked his ear to this point, remembering "things of the future." Aires said a few more pretty words, and added a few more ugly ones, allowing that the fight could be a premonition of grave conflicts on earth. But he quickly tempered this notion with another: "It doesn't matter; let us not forget the words of one ancient, that 'war is the mother of all things.' In my opinion, Empedocles, referring to war, did not do so only in the technical sense. Love, which is the first art of peace, can be viewed as a duel, not of death but of life," concluded Aires, smiling wanly as he spoke softly, and he excused himself.

X V

"Teste David Cum Sybilla"

"And so," said Santos. "Now hasn't the counselor, instead of learning, taught us a thing or two? I think he gave some good arguments."

"At the very least, they were plausible," added Master Plácido.

"It's a shame he had to leave," continued Santos, "but fortunately my business is with you, sir. I have come to consult you, and your insights are the truest in the world."

Plácido thanked him, smiling. The praise was not new, to the contrary. But he was so accustomed to hearing it that the smile had become a habit. He could not keep himself from paying his disciples in this coin.

"It is about . . ."

"It is about this. That hypothesis that I came up with is a real case. It happened to my sons . . ."

"What?"

"That's what it seems to me, and just what I came here to explain. I never mentioned it to you for fear that you would think it absurd, but I have thought about it, and I suspect that such a fight happened, and that it is an extraordinary case."

Santos then laid out his case, gravely, with a particular way that he had of popping out his eyes to stress its unique details. He did not forget or hide anything; he recounted the visit of his wife to Morro do Castelo, with disdain, it's true, but moment by moment. Plácido listened attentively, asking questions, repeating, and then he meditated for a few moments. Finally he declared that the phenomenon, had it occurred, was rare, if not unique, but possible. Just the fact that their names were Pedro and Paulo indicated some rivalry, because these two apostles had also fought over their differences.

"Pardon me, but the christening . . ."

"It was afterward, I know, but the names could have been predestined, even more so because the choice of names came, as you told me, through an inspiration of the boys' aunt."

"Exactly."

"Dona Perpétua is very devout."

"Very."

"I believe that the very souls of St. Peter and St. Paul would have chosen that lady to inspire her with the names that are in the Creed. Acknowledging that she says the prayer frequently, but it was on that occasion that the names came to her."

"Exactly, exactly!"

The doctor went to the bookshelf and picked up a leather-bound Bible with large metal clasps. He opened it to the Epistle of St. Paul to the Galatians, and read the passage in Chapter II, verse 11, in which the apostle recounts that, going to Antioch, where St. Peter was, "he opposed him to his face."

Santos read the passage and then had an idea. Ideas wish to be celebrated, when they are beautiful, and examined, when new. His was both new and beautiful. Dazzled, he raised his hand and slapped the page, braying: "Without adding that this numeral II of the verse, composed of two identical numerals, one and one, is a twin number, isn't it?"

"Of course. And more: it is the second chapter, that is, *two*, which is the number of the twins."

Mysteries engender mysteries. There was more than one intimate link, substantial and hidden, that connected everything. A fight, Peter and Paul, twin brothers, twin numerals, all these were the mysterious waters in which they thrashed, swimming and flailing forcefully. Santos went deeper. Would the two boys not be the very spirits of St. Peter and St. Paul, that were now reborn, and he, father of two apostles? Faith transfigures; Santos had an almost divine look about him, he ascended into himself, and his eyes, usually expressionless, seemed to hold the flame of life. Father of apostles! Plácido was almost about to believe it too. He found himself in a turbid dark sea, where the voices of the infinite became lost, but soon it occurred to him that the spirits of St. Peter and St. Paul had reached perfection. They would not return here. No matter, they must be others, great and noble ones. Their destinies could be brilliant; the cabocla was right, even though she didn't know what she was talking about.

"Leave the ladies to their childish beliefs," he concluded. "If they have faith in that woman on the hill, and they think she is a vehicle of truth, don't discourage them for now. Tell them that I agree with their oracle. *'Teste David cum Sybilla.'*"

"I'll tell them, I'll tell them! Do write the verse."

Plácido went to the desk, wrote the verse, and gave him the paper, but then Santos realized that showing it to his wife would be to confess the spiritist consultation, and naturally his perjury. He told his friend about Natividade's scruples and asked that they keep this confidential.

"When you see her, don't tell her what has passed between us."

He left immediately thereafter, regretting his indiscretion, but dazzled at the revelation. He went full of scriptural numerals, of Peter and Paul, of Esau and Jacob. The street air did not dispel the dust of mystery; to the contrary, the blue sky, the calm sea, the green mountains encircled him and covered him with a veil that was even more transparent and infinite. The boys' squabble, a rare or unique fact, was a divine distinction. Contrary to his wife, who was concerned only with the future distinction of her sons, Santos thought about the past conflict.

He entered his house, ran to the little ones, and caressed them with such a strange expression that the mother suspected something and wanted to know what it was.

"It's nothing," he answered, laughing.

"It is something, come on, tell me."

"What could it be?"

"Whatever it is, Agostinho, tell me."

Santos begged her not to be angry and told her everything, the fate, the fight, the Scripture, the apostles, the symbol, all so jumbled that she could barely understand, but she finally understood and answered with clenched teeth: "Oh, you, you!"

"Pardon me, little friend; I was so anxious to know the truth. . . . And please notice that I believe in the cabocla and the doctor does too. He even wrote this verse for me in Latin," he concluded, taking out and reading the slip of note paper: "Teste David cum Sybilla."

XVI

Paternalism

After a little while, Santos took his wife's hand, who let him hold it, limply, without returning his grasp. Both gazed at the boys, forgetting their anger to be just parents.

This was no longer spiritism, or any other new religion. It was the oldest of all, founded by Adam and Eve, which you might call, if you wish, paternalism. They prayed wordlessly, they crossed themselves without using their fingers, a kind of gentle, mute ceremony, which embraced the past and the future. Which was the priest and which the sacristan, I don't know, nor is it necessary to define. The Mass was the same and the Gospel began as in St. John (emended): "In the beginning there was love, and love became flesh." But let us go to our twins.

XVII

Everything that I Leave Out

The twins, having nothing else to do, nursed. This job they performed without rivalry, except when the wet nurses were on good terms with each other, and they nursed side by side. Each one would then seem to want to prove to the other that he nursed more and better, running his fingers over the friendly breast and sucking with all his heart and soul. The nurses, for their part, reveled in the glory of their breasts and compared them. The little ones, sated, finally let go of the nipples and laughed at them.

If it were not for the need to get these boys on their feet, and turn them into grown men, I would stretch out this chapter. Really the spectacle, while common, was lovely. The little rascals nourished themselves differently than their parents, without the arts of the chef, nor with the sight of foods and drinks placed in crystal and porcelain to alter or color the crude need to eat. They did not even see their food. The mouth connected to the breast did not even allow the milk to appear. Nature showed itself satisfied through their laughter and their sleep. When it was sleep, each nurse carried her boy to a cradle and then left to take care of other things. That comparison could fill three or four solid pages.

One page would suffice for the rattles that entertained the little ones, as if they were the very music of heaven. They smiled, stretched out their hands, sometimes became angry when they were out of reach, and then they quieted down when the objects were handed to them, not even needing to play with them. With respect to rattles, one would say that these instruments do not leave memories of themselves. Whoever sees one in a child's hands, if they think it reminds them of their own, is deluded and soon realizes that the memory has to be more recent, some experience last year, or last night's cow bell.

The operation of weaning could be told in half a line, but the regrets of the wet nurses, the farewells, the little gold earrings that the mother gave to each of them as a final present, all this demands a page or more. A few lines suffice for the dry nurses, therefore we will not dwell on whether they were tall or squat, ugly or pretty. They were gentle, zealous in their work, friends to the little ones and to each other. Hobby horses, little flags, puppet theaters, tin soldiers and drums, all the claptrap of childhood could occupy much more space than their names.

All of this I leave out, so as not to bore the gentle reader who is curious to see my boys become adult men. We'll see them soon, darling. In a little while they will be grown up and strong. Then I will leave them to their own devices. Let them open their own ways to life and to the world, whether it be with weapons or words, or simple elbowing.

XVIII

How They Grew Up

And here they are, growing up. The similarity between them was still great, although the tendency to confuse one with the other was now less frequent. The same pale, alert eyes, the same pleasing smile, the fine hands and high color in their cheeks which made it seem as if they were painted with blood. They were healthy. Except for their teething crises, they had no other ailments, because I will not tell about the occasional indigestion from candy which their parents gave them or they sneaked. They both had a sweet tooth, Pedro more than Paulo and Paulo more than anyone.

At age 7 they were two masterpieces, or rather one in two volumes, as you prefer. In truth, on that whole stretch of beach front, and in Flamengo, Glória, Caju, and other neighborhoods, there was not one, not to mention two, children as precious. Note that they were also robust. Pedro would knock down Paulo with one blow. In compensation, Paulo would kick Pedro to the ground. They raced each other frequently in the yard. Sometimes they wanted to climb trees, but their mother forbade it. It wasn't proper. They contented themselves with peering up at the fruit from below.

Paulo was more aggressive, Pedro more wily, and since both ended up eating the fruit from the trees, it was a little black boy who would climb to get them, either because of a sock in the head from one or a bribe from the other. The bribe was never delivered. The blow, because it was paid in advance, was always delivered, and sometimes repeated after the job was done. I don't mean to imply that either of the twins did not also know how to be aggressive or deceitful. The difference is that each one had his own preferred method, which is so obvious it is tedious to write about it.

They obeyed their parents without too much effort, even though they were stubborn. They did not lie more or less than any other boys in the city. After all, a lie is sometimes half a virtue. Thus it is that when they said they had not seen anyone steal their mother's watch, an engagement present from their father, they lied consciously, because the maid that took it was caught by them in the act of the theft. But she was so friendly to them! And with tears she begged them not to tell anyone, so that the twins absolutely denied having seen anything. They were 7 years old. At 9, when the girl had already been long gone, they disclosed the old story, I don't know why. Their mother wanted to know why they had been silent then. They did not know how to explain themselves, but it is clear that the silence of 1878 was an act of care and pity and thus half virtuous, because it is something to repay love with love. As for the revelation of 1880, that can only be explained by the distance of time. The good Miquelina was no longer present. Perhaps she was already dead. And, it came out so easily. . . .

"But why didn't you tell me until now?" insisted their mother.

Not knowing what to say, one of them, I think Pedro, decided to accuse his brother.

"It was his fault, Mommy!"

"Me?" retaliated Paulo. "It was him, Mommy, he's the one who wouldn't say anything."

"It was your fault!"

"Yours!"

"It was you, don't lie!"

"He's the liar!"

They confronted each other. Natividade intervened quickly, but not before they had exchanged the first blows. She grasped their arms in time to avoid others, and instead of punishing or threatening them, she kissed them so tenderly that they did not find a better moment to ask her for a candy. They got candies. They also got an excursion that afternoon, in their father's carriage.

On the way back, they were friends or reconciled. They told their mother about the excursion, the people on the street, the other children who looked at them enviously, one who put his finger in his mouth, another who put it in his nose, and the girls at the windows, some who thought they were cute. On that last point they disagreed, because each one took all the credit for the admiration, but their mother intervened: "It was for both of you. You are so alike, that it could only have been for both. And do you know why the young ladies admired you? It was because they saw how friendly you were with each other, how you sat next to each other nicely. Handsome boys don't fight, much less brothers. I want to see you both be nice friends, playing together without tussles. Do you understand?"

Pedro answered yes; Paulo waited for his mother to repeat the question and then gave the same answer. Finally, because she insisted, they embraced, but it was an embrace without sincerity, without strength, almost armless. They leaned up against each other, touched their hands to each other's backs, and then let them fall.

That evening, in their bedroom, each one concluded privately that he owed the treats of the afternoon, the candies, the kisses, and the carriage, to the fight they had, and that another fight might yield as much or more. Wordlessly, like a fantasia for the piano, they resolved to go for each other at the first opportunity. What should have been a tie bound by their mother's tenderness brought to the heart of each a particular sensation, that was not just consolation and vengeance for the blow received that afternoon, but also the satisfaction of an intimate desire, profound and necessary. Without hate, they said a few words to each other from bed to bed, they laughed at one or the other remembrance of the street, until sleep entered with its wool feet and closed beak, and took over the room.

XIX

Just Two — Forty Years — Third Reason

O ne of my intentions in this book is not to bring you to tears. However, I cannot be silent about the two tears that welled out of Natividade's eyes, after a squabble between the little ones. Just two, and they died at the corners of her mouth. As quickly as they came out she swallowed them, unwillingly repeating in mute speech the end of those children's stories: "came in one door, went out the other, the king commands you, to tell us another." And the second child told the second story, the third told a third, the fourth a fourth, until they got bored or sleepy. People who date from the time when such stories were told affirm that children did not put into that formula any monarchical intent, whether absolute or constitutional. It was a way of linking their *De-cameron*, inherited from the old Portuguese kingdom, when kings commanded whatever they wanted and the nation said so be it.

The two tears swallowed, Natividade laughed at her own weakness. She did not call herself stupid, because these insults are rarely used, even in private. But in her heart of hearts, deep down, where no man's eye penetrates, I believe she felt something like this. Not having any clear proof, I limit myself to defending our lady.

Truthfully, any other mother would live in trembling for the fate of her sons, since the former, interior fight had taken place. Now the fights were more frequent, and the hands ever more ready, and all made the mother fear that they would end up butchering each other. But then the idea of greatness and prosperity surfaced— things of the future!—and that hope was like a handkerchief that dried the eyes of the lovely lady. The Sybils told not only of evil, nor did the Prophets, but also of good and mostly the latter.

With this green handkerchief she dried her eyes, and there would be other hankies if that one got torn or wrinkled. One, for example, not green as hope but blue, like her soul. I haven't told you yet that Natividade's soul was blue. There I'll leave it. A sky blue, bright and transparent, that sometimes clouded, rarely stormed, and never darkened by night.

No, reader, I have not forgotten the age of our friend. I remember as if it were today. Thus she reached her 40th birthday. It makes no difference. The sky is older and has not changed color. As long as you do not attribute any romantic significance to the blue of her soul, it's all right. At most, on the day she reached that age, our lady felt a chill. What was happening? Nothing, one day more than the day before, just a few hours. All a question of numbers, less than numbers, the name of the number, that word *forty*, that's the only evil. Thus the melancholy with which she said to her husband, thanking him for the birthday remembrance: "I'm old, Agostinho!" Santos playfully tried to strangle her.

Well, he would do wrong if he did strangle her. Natividade still had the figure of the time before her pregnancy, the same flexibility, the same tiny, lively grace. She kept the bearing of a 30-year-old woman. The seamstress accentuated all the remaining attributes of her figure and even lent her a few more from her sewing kit. Her waist refused to thicken and her hips and thighs were upholstered as firmly as before.

There are regions of the world where summer mingles with autumn, as in our land, where the two seasons differ only in temperature. Not even in temperature. May had the heat of January. She, at 40, was the same green lady, with the very same blue soul.

That color came from her father and grandfather, but her father had died young, before her grandfather, who lived to 84. At that age he believed sincerely that all the delights of this world, from morning coffee to peaceful slumber, had been invented just for him. The best cook in the land had been born in China, with the sole purpose of leaving family, country, language, religion, everything, to come braise his cutlets and make his tea. The stars gave *his* nights splendor, the moonlight too, and the rain, if it rained, was for him to rest from the sun. There he is now in the cemetery of St. Francis Xavier. If anyone could hear the voice of the dead, in the grave, they would hear his, calling out that it is time to close the cemetery gate and not let anyone else in, since he is there to rest for eternity. He died blue. If he had lived to be 100, he would not have changed color.

Well, if nature wished to spare this lady, wealth gave a hand to nature, and from one and the other was produced the most beautiful color that a soul can have. All converged thus to dry her tears quickly, as we saw before. If she drank those two solitary tears, she could have drunk others because of the years yet to come, and that is yet more proof of that spiritual shade. Thus she will show that she has few, and swallows them to save them.

But there is still a third reason why this lady had a blue soul, a reason so special that it deserves its own chapter, but it won't for the sake of economy. It was her immunity, it was having crossed through life intact and pure. The Cape of Storms turned into the Cape of Good Hope, and she conquered her first and second age of youth, without the winds capsizing her ship or the waves swallowing it. One would not deny that a stiff gust might carry off her foresail, as in the case of João de Melo or worse, like Aires, but they were yawns of Adamastor. She quickly mended the sail, and the giant was left behind with Thetis, while she continued on course to India. Now she remembered the safe voyage. She was honored by the futile, lost winds. Memory brought her the taste of dangers past. And thus the uncharted lands, her two sons, born, raised, and beloved of fortune.

X X

The Jewel

Her 41st birthday did not give her a chill. She was already used to being in her 40s. She did experience a great shock.

She woke up and did not see the accustomed present, her husband's "surprise" at the foot of the bed. It wasn't on the dressing table. She opened drawers and looked around, but nothing. She concluded that her husband had forgotten the day and was sad. It was the first time! She came down the stairs looking around her. Nothing. Her husband was in the study, quiet, self-absorbed, reading newspapers, and barely greeted her. The boys, even though it was Sunday, were studying in a corner. They came to give her the usual kiss and returned to their books. The mother kept searching the corners of the room with her eyes, to see if she could find some little remembrance, a picture, a dress, it was all in vain. Under one of the newspapers on the chair in front of her husband, could it be . . . Nothing. Then she sat down, and opening the newspaper, said to herself: "Is it possible that he doesn't remember what day today is? Is it possible?" She started to scan the newspaper distractedly, her eyes jumping back and forth on the page.

Facing her, husband observed wife, paying no attention to what he pretended to be reading. Thus passed a few minutes. Suddenly Santos saw a new expression on Natividade's face. Her eyes seemed to grow larger, her mouth opened slightly, her head shot up and his too, both left their chairs, took two steps, and fell into each other's arms, like two desperate lovers. One, two, three, many kisses. Pedro and Paulo, astonished, stood up in their corner. The father, when he could speak, said to them: "Come kiss the hand of the Baroness Santos."

They did not understand right away. Natividade did not know what to do. She gave her hand to her sons, her husband, and then returned to the newspaper to read and reread that in the imperial dispatch of the evening before, Mr. Agostinho José dos Santos was graced with the title Baron de Santos. She understood everything. That was her present. This time the goldsmith was the emperor.

"Go, go, now you can go play," said the father to his sons.

And the boys ran out to spread the news around the house. The servants were happy at the change in their masters. The very slaves seemed to receive a morsel of freedom and decorated themselves with it. "Missy Baroness!" they exclaimed, jumping with glee. And João pulled Maria to him, snapping his fingers. "People, who is this black girl?" "I'm the slave of Missy Baroness!"

But the emperor was not the only goldsmith. Santos took out of his pocket a little box, with a brooch on which the new crown sparkled in diamonds. Natividade thanked him for the jewel and consented to put it on, so her husband could see it. Santos felt himself the designer of the jewel, inventor of shape and stones. But he let her take it right off and put it away, and he picked up the newspapers so he could show her that all of them carried the story, some with the adjective "respected," in others, "distinguished," etc.

When Perpétua entered the study she found them walking back and forth, arm in arm, talking quietly, looking at their feet. She also gave and received embraces.

The whole house was happy. In the garden the trees seemed greener than before, the budding flowers justified the leaves, and the sun covered the earth with an infinite clarity. The sky, to collaborate with the others, stayed blue all day long. Soon arrived cards and letters of congratulations. Later on, visitors. Men of the courts, men of business, men of society, many ladies, some with titles as well, came or sent greetings. Debtors of Santos showed up promptly, others preferred to remain forgotten. There were names that they could only recognize with some inquiry and heavy use of the directory.

XXI

An Obscure Point

I know there is an obscure point in the previous chapter. I write this one to clarify it.

When his wife inquired about the antecedents and circumstances of the dispatch, Santos gave the requested explanations. Not all of them would be strictly true; time is a gnawing rat that diminishes or alters things by giving them another appearance. What's more, the subject lent itself so well to rejoicing that it would easily confuse the memory. There are, in the gravest events, many details that are lost, others that imagination invents to supplant the losses, and not for this does history die.

Suffice it to say (this is the obscure point) it is difficult to explain how Santos could be silent for many days about such an important event for himself and his wife. Truthfully, more than once he was about to tell her in word or in gesture, if he could find one, that rare secret. But a force greater than himself always silenced him. It seems that the anticipation of a new and unexpected happiness was what gave him patience. In that study scene, all had been composed beforehand, the silence, the indifference, the sons whom he had placed there, all for the effect of that phrase: "Come kiss the hand of the Baroness Santos!"

XXII

Now a Leap

That the twins shared in the aristocratic honeymoon of their parents is not something I need to write about. Their love of them is enough to explain it, but I would add that, because the title had produced two opposing sentiments in other boys, esteem and envy, Pedro and Paulo concluded that they had received a very special honor. When later Paulo adopted the republican opinion, he never included that family distinction in his criticism of institutions. The states of mind born of this are sufficient material for a special chapter, if I did not prefer at this point to leap to the year 1886. It's a big leap, but time is an invisible fabric upon which one can embroider everything: a flower, a bird, a lady, a castle, a tomb. One can also embroider nothing. Nothing, on top of the invisible; that is the most subtle work of this world, and for that matter, of the other.

XXIII

When You Have a Beard

That year, on an August evening, there were guests at the Botafogo house, and it happened that one of them, I don't know whether it was a man or a woman, asked the brothers how old they were.

Paulo answered: "I was born on the day that Pedro I fell from the throne."

Pedro replied: "I was born on the day that His Majesty ascended to the throne."

The replies were simultaneous, not successive, so much so that the person asked them to speak one at a time. Their mother explained: "They were born on April 7, 1870."

Pedro repeated slowly: "I was born on the day His Majesty ascended to the throne."

And Paulo followed: "I was born the day that Pedro I fell from the throne."

Natividade scolded Paulo for his subversive reply. Paulo defended himself, Pedro disputed the explanation and gave another, and the room would have turned into a debate club, if their mother had not accommodated them in this way: "This must come from groups at school. You are not old enough to talk about politics. When you have a beard."

The beards did not want to come, much as they tugged at their chins with their fingers, but political and other opinions formed and flourished. They were not exactly opinions, as they did not have large or small roots. They were (a bad comparison) like neckties of a particular color, that they wore until they got tired of the color and another one came along. Naturally each one had his own. One could also believe that the color each one wore suited his personality. Since they got the same good grades on examinations, they lacked reasons for envy. And if ambition would divide them one day, for now it was not an eagle or a condor, or even a chick, at most, an egg. At the Dom Pedro II School, all liked them well enough. The beards did not want to come. What is one to do, when one's beard does not want to grow? Wait until it shows up on its own, grows, turns white, which is the custom, except for those that never turn white, or just partly and temporarily. All this is common knowledge, but it provides occasion to talk about two beards of the latter sort, famous at the time and now totally forgotten. Not having any other place to talk about them, I use this chapter, and the reader may turn the page, if he prefers to go on with the story. I will stay for a few more lines, recalling the two deceased beards, without understanding them now, any better than we understood them then, the most inexplicable beards in the world.

The first beard belonged to a friend of Pedro's, a Capuchin monk, an Italian, Friar ***. I could write his name, nobody would recognize him, but I prefer this triple sign, a mystery number, expressed in stars, which are the eyes of heaven. He was a monk. Pedro didn't know his beard when it was black, but when it was already gray, long and full, adorning a manly and handsome head. His mouth was smiling, the eyes sparkling. He laughed with his mouth and eyes, so sweetly that he brought people into his heart. He had a broad chest and strong shoulders. His bare feet, in sandals, showed they carried the body of a Hercules. All of this was gentle and spiritual, like a page of the Scriptures. His faith was living, his affection secure, his patience infinite.

One day Friar *** said farewell to Pedro. He was going to the interior, to the states of Minas Gerais, Rio de Janeiro, and São Paulo, I believe also to Paraná. A spiritual voyage, like that undertaken by other brothers in his order, and there he stayed half a year or more. When he returned he brought everyone great happiness and even greater astonishment. The beard was black, I don't know if as much or more than before, but very black and very shiny. He did not explain the change, nor did anyone ask him about it. It could be a miracle or a caprice of nature. It could also be a man-made improvement, since the latter was more difficult to believe than the former. This color lasted for nine months. When he traveled again for thirty days, the beard appeared, white as silver or snow, whichever seems whiter to you.

As for the second of these beards, it was even more shocking. It did not belong to a friar, but to a vagabond, a fellow who lived off his debts and who, in his youth, amended an old saying of our language this way: "Pay what you owe, and see what you *don't* have left." He reached the age of 50 penniless, jobless, and friendless. His clothes were just as old, his shoes no younger. His beard, however, never reached 50. He dyed it black and badly, probably because it was not good dye and he did not own a mirror. He was always alone, he walked up and down the same street. One day he turned the corner of Life and fell into the court of Death, his beard piebald because there was no one to dye it in the charity hospital.

Ora, bene, as my friar would say, why did he and the vagabond go from gray to black? My reader should guess, if she can: I'll give you twenty chapters to figure it out. Perhaps I, by that time, can work up an explanation, but for now I do not know and I will not venture anything. Let malicious tongues attribute some worldly passion to the friar. Even so, one does not understand why he would reveal it in that fashion. As for the beggar, what ladies would he wish to attract, to the point of exchanging bread for dye? That one or the other would want to give in to the desire to hold on to their fleeting youth is plausible. The friar, learned in the Scriptures, knowing that Israel wept for the onions of Egypt, might have also cried, and his tears fallen black on his cheeks.

It could be, I repeat. That desire to capture time is a need of the soul and of the chin. But God gives time a habeas corpus.

X X I V

Robespierre and Louis XVI

The opinions of Pedro and Paulo grew so strong that one day they attached themselves to something. They were walking down the Rua da Carioca. A glazier's shop was located there, with mirrors of varying sizes and, more than mirrors, it also had old portraits and cheap engravings, with and without frames. They stopped for a few seconds, just browsing. Then Pedro saw a portrait of Louis XVI, entered, and bought it for 800 réis. It was a simple engraving hanging from the counter wall by a string. Paulo wanted to have equal good fortune, appropriate to his opinions, and he discovered a Robespierre. Since the shopkeeper asked 1,200 for this one, Pedro got a little upset.

"So then, sir, you sell a king more cheaply, and a martyr king at that?"

"You'll have to forgive me, but this other engraving cost me more," countered the old shopkeeper. "We sell according to the price we get. See, it's newer."

"That's not it," added Paulo. "They are from the same period, but this one is worth more than the other one."

"I heard that he was also a king . . ."

"No king!" the two answered.

"Or he wanted to be one, I don't know exactly. Who am I to talk about history, I just know about the Moors, whose history I learned in my own land from my grandmother, some stories in verse." And he added, "There are still some lovely Moorish ladies, for example, this one. In spite of her name, I think she was a Moor, or still is, if she's alive . . . May she taste bad to her husband!"

He went to a corner and brought out a portrait of Madame de Staël, with the famous turban on her head. The power of beauty! The boys forgot their political opinions for a moment and stared at the figure of Corinne. The shopkeeper, despite his 60 years, had moist eyes as he looked at the portrait. He was careful to emphasize the shapes, the head, the slightly fleshy but expressive mouth, and he said that the portrait was not expensive. Since neither one wanted to buy it, perhaps because there was only one, he told them he had another, but this one was "a bit naughty," a phrase that the gods would forgive him, when they found out that all he wanted to do was whet the appetite of his customers. And he went to a closet, removed, and brought over a Diana, as naked as she had lived here on earth, in the forests. Not even with this did he make a sale. He had to be satisfied with the political portraits.

He still wanted to see if he could make some more money, selling them a framed portrait of Pedro I, which hung from the wall. But Pedro refused because he did not have any more money, and Paulo said he wouldn't give a vintém for that "face of a traitor." Better if he had said nothing! The shopkeeper, as soon as he heard the answer, dropped his obsequious manners, put on an indignant expression, and roared that yes, sir, the young man was right!

"You are very right. He was a traitor, a bad son, a bad brother, a bad everything. He did all the evil that he could to this world. And in hell, where he is, if religion does not lie, he must still be doing evil to the Devil. This young man spoke a while ago of a martyr king," he continued, showing them a portrait of Dom Miguel de Bragança, in profile, waistcoat, and hand on his chest. "This one was truly martyred by that one, who stole the throne, which was not his, to give it to someone it didn't belong to. And my poor king and master went to die a pauper, they say in Germany, I don't know where. Ah, those constitutional bandits! Ah, spawn of the Devil! You young gentlemen cannot imagine what that rabble of liberals was like. Liberals! Liberal with other people's property!"

"They are all flour ground from the same mill," reflected Paulo.

"I don't know if they were made of flour, I do know they took a beating. They won, but they really took a beating. My poor king!"

Pedro wanted to counter his brother's malicious remark, and he set out to buy the portrait of Pedro I. When the shopkeeper came back to his senses, he began to negotiate the sale, but they could not agree on a price. Pedro offered him the same 800 réis as the other one, the shopkeeper asked 2,000. He pointed out that the picture was framed, and Louis XVI was not. Besides, it was newer. And he brought the portrait over to the door, for better light, drawing his attention to the face, principally the eyes, what beautiful expression they had! And the imperial robe . . .

"What difference does it make for you to pay 2,000?"

"I'll give you a thousand, will that do?"

"No, it will not, the portrait cost me more than that."

"Well then . . ."

"Look, isn't this worth at least 3,000? The paper is not faded, the engraving is fine."

"One thousand, I already told you."

"No sir, for a thousand take this one of Dom Miguel; the paper is well preserved, and for a little more money, I'll put a frame on it. Here you go, a thousand."

"If I'm not already regretting this . . . a thousand for the emperor."

"Oh, not that! It cost me 1,700 three weeks ago; I make just 300 réis, almost nothing. I can make even less with Lord Dom Miguel, but I also agree he is in less demand. This one of Pedro I, if you come by tomorrow, you probably won't find it here. So, what about it?"

"I'll come by later."

Paulo was already walking off and looking at the Robespierre. Pedro caught up with him.

"Look, take the Dom Miguel for seven tostões."

Pedro shook his head.

"Will six tostões do?"

Pedro, next to his brother, unrolled his engraving. The old shopkeeper still wanted to shout out, "five tostões!" but they were far away, and it would not look good to bargain that way.

X X V

Dom Miguel

"Be that as it may," thought the old man. "I won't sell this if I roll it up and put it away. I'll have it framed. A few old sticks here . . ."

Dom Miguel turned to him his dark, sad eyes of reproach. Thus it seemed to the glazier, but it could have been an illusion. In any case, it also seemed to him that the eyes returned to their place, staring ahead, far off . . . Where? Toward where there is eternal justice, the shopkeeper thought naturally. Since he was contemplating the portrait with such concentration at the door of the shop, a man stopped, entered, and looked at the portrait with interest. The shopkeeper noticed his expression. He could be a loyalist to Dom Miguel, or just a collector.

"How much are you asking for this?"

"This? You must forgive me. You want to know how much I ask for my dear lord Dom Miguel? Not much, it's a little faded, but you can still make out his features. How regal he is! It is not expensive. I'll give it to you at cost. If it were framed it would be worth 4,000 réis. Take it for 3,000."

The customer calmly took the money out of his pocket, while the old man rolled up the picture. And, after exchanging one for the other, they said farewell, courteously and satisfied. The shopkeeper, after going to the door, returned to his customary chair. Perhaps he was thinking of the misfortune he had barely escaped of selling the picture for a thousand. In any case, he stared ahead, far off, where there is eternal justice . . . 3,000 réis!

XXVI

The Battle of the Portraits

There is almost no need to talk about the fate of the portraits of the king and the commissioner. Each boy hung his at the head of his bed. This situation did not last long, because both of them started to deface the poor engravings, which were not guilty of anything. There appeared donkey's ears, ugly words, animal drawings, until one day Paulo tore up Pedro's and Pedro tore up Paulo's. Naturally, they avenged themselves with blows. Their mother heard the noise and ran upstairs. She restrained her sons, but they were already scratched up, and she went to bed sadly. Would that cursed rivalry never end? She silently asked herself that question, lying on her bed, with her face in the pillow, which this time stayed dry but her soul was weeping.

Natividade placed her trust in upbringing, but upbringing, as much as she refined it, only altered the exterior traits of the boys' behavior. Their essential characters remained unchanged. Their embryonic passions struggled to live on, to grow and to break out, just as she had felt the two in her own womb during gestation. And she recalled that distant crisis and ended up cursing the half-breed of the Castelo. Really, the fortune-teller should have remained silent. The evil that is not spoken does not change, but is not known. Now, it could be that her not remaining silent confirms the opinion that the cabocla was sent by God to tell men the truth. And after all, what did she say to Natividade? She did nothing more than ask a mysterious question. The prophecy was luminous and clear. And once again the words of the Castelo rang in the mother's ears, and her imagination did the rest. Things of the future! There they are, great and sublime. A few childish squabbles, what do they matter? Natividade smiled, got up, went to the door, and found her son Pedro, who came to explain.

"Mama, Paulo is bad. If you just could hear the horrors that come out of his mouth, Mama would die of fear. I can hardly control myself from going for his face. It's lucky I haven't put out his eye."

"Son, do not speak that way, he is your brother."

"Then he should not bother me, annoy me. What foul language he comes out with! While I prayed for the soul of Louis XVI, he, to hurt me, prayed to Robespierre. He made up a little hymn calling Robespierre a saint and he sang it very softly under his breath so you and Father would not hear him. I gave him a few cuffs . . ."

"There you go!"

"But he hit me first because I drew donkey's ears on Robespierre. So should I take it lying down?"

"Not lying down and not standing up to him."

"Then how? Am I just supposed to take it?"

"No, sir. I forbid fighting. The best is that you both forget everything and care for each other. Don't you see how much your parents love each other? The fights are over for good. I do not want to hear complaints or quarrels. After all, what do you fellows have to do with a bad character who died years ago?"

"That's what I say, but he won't change his ways."

"He will. Good breeding amends childish ways. When you are a doctor you will have to fight sickness and death. It is much better than beating up your brother. What is that? I don't want threats, Pedro. Calm yourself and listen to me."

"Mama is always against me!"

"I am not against anyone, I am for both of you, both are my sons. And twins besides. Come here, Pedro. Do not think I disagree with your political opinions. I like them. They are mine, they are ours. Paulo will come to have them, too. At his age one accepts foolishness, but time will correct that. Look, Pedro, my hope is that you will be great men, but on the condition that you will be great friends."

"I am ready to be a great man," conceded Pedro innocently, almost with resignation.

"And a great friend, too."

"If he will, I will."

"Great men!" exclaimed Natividade, giving him two hugs, one for him and one for his brother when he came in.

But Paulo came right in, and received the whole, genuine embrace. He also came to complain, and grumbled something, but his mother did not wish to hear him and again spoke the language of greatness. Paulo also consented to be great.

"You will be a doctor," said Natividade to Pedro, "and you a lawyer. I want to see who does the best cures and wins the hardest cases."

"I will," said both in unison.

"Sillies! Each of you will have his own special career, his own special science. Is your nose better? There, no more bleeding. Now the first to hurt his brother will be demoted."

It was a wise idea to separate them. One would stay in Rio, studying medicine. The other would go to São Paulo, to study law. Time would do the rest, not least when each one married and made his own future with his wife. That would be perpetual peace. Then perpetual friendship.

XXVII

About an Inopportune Thought

And here comes a thought from the reader. "But if two old engravings can push them to blows and bloodshed, will they be happy with their wives? Won't they want the very same and only woman?"

What you want, dear madam, is to arrive right away at the chapter about love or loves, which is your particular interest in novels. Thus the importance of the question, as if you said,

"Look, you have not yet shown us the lady or ladies that will be loved or courted by these two young enemies. I'm already tired of hearing that the boys do not get along or get along poorly. It is the second or third time that I listen to the mother's coddlings or to your quarrelsome friends. Let's move on quickly to love, to the two young ladies, if it is not just one person."

Frankly, I don't like it when people go about guessing and composing a book that is being written methodically. Your insistence in talking about one single woman is bordering on impertinent. Suppose that they really do like one single person. Will it not seem that I am telling you what you asked me for, when in truth I only write down what happened and what can be confirmed by dozens of witnesses? No, my lady, I did not take pen in hand to satisfy the whims of those who give me suggestions. If you want to write the book, I offer you the pen, paper, and an admiring reader. But if you wish only to read, be still, go line by line. I will allow you a yawn between chapters, but wait for the rest, have faith in the narrator of these adventures.

XXVIII

The Rest Is True

Yes, there was a person, younger than they by one or two years, who made them lock horns whether by force of habit or of temperament, if not because of both. Before her, there may have been others, even older than they were, but the notes used for this book do not refer to them. If they fought over these other ones, there was no memory of it, but it is possible, since they had identical tastes. If it were otherwise, they would have too, like the medieval knights who defended their ladies.

All of this is conjecture. It was natural that, handsome and elegant as they both were, given to life and to excursions, conversation and dances, not least of all heirs, it was natural that more than one girl would favor them. Those who saw them pass by on horseback, on the beach, or on the avenue would fall in love with the perfect harmony of their posture and movements. Even the horses were just alike, almost twins, and beat their hooves with the same rhythm, the same strength, and the same grace. Don't think that the swishing of the tails and manes of the two animals was simultaneous. It's not true and could make you doubt the rest. Because the rest is true.

XXIX

The Younger Person

The younger person does not already enter the scene in this chapter for a valid reason, which is that it is proper to introduce her parents first. It is not that one cannot see her well without them. One can, the three are different, even opposite, and as special as you might find her, it is not necessary for the parents to be present. Children do not always reproduce their parents. Camões affirmed that from a certain father one could only expect such a son, and science confirms this poetic rule. For my part I believe in science and in poetry, but there are exceptions, my friend. It happens sometimes that nature does something different, but not for this do plants stop growing or stars stop shining. What one must believe without faltering is that God is God. And if a young Muslim girl is reading me, substitute the name of God with that of Allah. All languages lead to heaven.

X X X

The Batista Family

The Batista family met the Santos family at I don't know what plantation in the province of Rio. It was not in Maricá, although the father of the twins had been born there. It would have been some other municipality. Whatever it was, that is where the two families met, and since they lived near each other in Botafogo, repetition and sympathy helped the fortunate association along.

Batista, the father of the young woman, was a man of 40-some years. He was an attorney in private practice, former governor of a province, and member of the Conservative party. The trip to the plantation had been precisely for a political meeting having to do with elections, but the meeting was so unproductive that he returned from there without a shred of hope. Despite having friends in government, he had gotten nothing, not the post of deputy or of governor. He had interrupted his career since he had been relieved of that post "by special request," said the decree, but the complaints from the one relieved of duty would have us believe something else. In fact, he had been responsible for the loss of the elections and he attributed the loss of his post to this political disaster.

"I don't know what else he wanted me to do," said Batista, talking about the minister. "I surrounded churches, no friend asked for police protection that I did not deliver, I tried about twenty people, and others went to jail without trial. Did I have to hang people for him? Even so there were two deaths at the Ribeirão das Moças."

The latter claim was an exaggeration, because the deaths were not his work. At most, he ordered a halt to the investigation, that is, if you can call a simple conversation about the ferocity of the two deceased an investigation. In sum, the elections were bloodless.

Batista said that because of the elections he had lost the governorship but another version was going around, a water deal, a concession made to a Spaniard at the request of the brother of the governor's wife. The request was authentic, the insinuations about a payoff were false. No matter. It was enough for the opposition press to say that there had been a good "family arrangement" in the deal, adding that since it was about water, it must have been a clean deal. The administration newspaper retorted that if there was water, there wasn't enough to wash off the soot of the coal dust left by the liberal administration of the governor's predecessor—a deal to supply the statehouse. That was not true; the opposition paper dredged up records of the old trial and showed that the defense had been convincing. It could have stopped there, but it continued that "since we were now in Spanish territory," the governor edited the Spanish poet, who had written the epitaph:

"Brothers-in-law and friends,
Must be they've reached their end."

and he changed it so as not to be obliged to kill off someone, but rather he gave life to himself and his, saying in our language:

"The family that survives
Takes wits to stay alive!"

Batista immediately responded to the slanderous charges, declaring the concession canceled, but this just gave the opposition ammunition for more volleys: "We have the confession of the accused!" was the headline of the first article that the opposition newspaper devoted to the gubernatorial act. The correspondents had already sent articles to Rio de Janeiro reporting the concession, and the government ended up removing its representative from office. In truth, nobody but the politicians paid any attention to the business. Dona Cláudia just mentioned the press campaign, which was very violent.

"It wasn't worth it to leave here," said Natividade.

"Oh no, baroness!"

And Dona Cláudia affirmed that it had been worth it. One suffered, oh well. It was so good to arrive at the provinces! Everything officially announced, the visits on board, the landing, assuming office, the greetings. . . . It was nice to see the magistrates, the employees, the officers, very bald, a lot of white hair, the country's finest, in fact, with their long, drawn-out courtesies, all at curves and angles, and the printed praise. The very insults of the opposition were agreeable. To hear them call her husband a tyrant, when she knew he had the heart of a dove, did her soul good. The thirst for blood they attributed to him, he who did not even drink wine, the iron glove of a man who was like kid glove, the immorality, the unscrupulousness, the lack of brio, all the unjust, crude names they called him that she liked to read as if they were eternal truths, where were they now? The opposition paper was the first that Dona Cláudia would read when they were in the governor's mansion. She also felt pilloried and this made her feel voluptuous, as if it were lashes or a whip on her own skin; it gave her a better appetite at lunch. Where were the whiplashes of those days? Now she could barely find his name in print at the bottom of some legal document or on the list of people who went to visit the emperor.

"Not always," explained Dona Cláudia. "Batista is very modest. Occasionally he visits the palace in São Cristóvão so that it doesn't look as if he is trying to be remembered, as if that were a crime. On the contrary, never to go there would seem like a slight. Note that the emperor never ceased to receive him benevolently, and me, too. He never forgot my name. I had not been there for two years, and when I went, he asked me right away: 'How are you, Dona Cláudia?'"

Besides this nostalgia for power, Dona Cláudia was a happy creature. The liveliness of her words and manners, her eyes that seemed not to see anything because they never stopped darting about, the benevolent smile, and constant admiration, all these attributes were at work in her to cure the melancholy of others. When she kissed her friends or looked at them, it was as if she wanted to eat them alive, eat them for love not hate, put them inside herself, in the deepest part of herself.

Batista was not that expansive. He was tall, and his calm manner gave him the appearance of someone suited for government. All he lacked was action, but his wife could inspire him. He never failed to consult her during the crises of the governorship. Even now, if he had listened to her, he would have already asked something from the government. But on that point he was firm, a firmness that was born of weakness. "They will call me, don't worry," he would say to Dona Cláudia when there was a vacancy in provincial government. It is certain that he felt the need to return to an active life. For him, politics was less an opinion than a rash. He had to scratch himself frequently and forcefully.

Flora

T hat was the political couple. A child, if they had a son, could be the fusion of their opposing qualities, and perhaps a statesman. But heaven denied them that dynastic consolation.

They had an only daughter who was completely their opposite. Neither the passion of Dona Cláudia nor the governmental bearing of Batista distinguished the soul or the figure of young Flora. Whoever met her in those days could have compared her to a brittle vase, or to a flower that would bloom only for a day, and would have had material for a sweet elegy. Already she had big clear eyes, less knowing, but gifted with a particular look that was not the darting of her mother or the dullness of her father, but rather tender and pensive, so full of grace that it would soften the face of a miser. Add an aquiline nose, sketch out a half-smiling mouth, forming a long face, smooth her red hair, and there you have the girl Flora.

She was born in August 1871. Her mother, who dated things by Ministries, never denied the age of her daughter.

"Flora was born during the Rio Branco administration, and she learned so fast that already in Sinimbu's administration she could read and write proficiently."

She was retiring and modest, averse to public festivities, and reluctantly agreed to learn to dance. She liked music and preferred the piano to singing. At the piano, left to her own devices, she was capable of forgetting to eat for a whole day. There is a little exaggeration there, but hyperbole is the way of this world, and people's ears are so clogged that only by force of a lot of rhetoric can one fill them with a breath of truth.

To this point, there is nothing that extraordinarily distinguishes this young woman from others, her contemporaries, since modesty goes with grace and at a certain age daydreaming is as natural as mischief. Flora, at 15, was inclined to keep to herself. Aires, who met her around this time at Natividade's house, believed that the girl would become an inexplicable creature.

"What did you say?" asked the mother.

"Really, I say nothing," Aires corrected himself. "But if you permit me to say something, I will say that this young lady sums up the rare gifts of her mother."

"But I am not inexplicable," replied Dona Cláudia, smiling.

"On the contrary, my lady. All, however, is in the definition we give to the word. Perhaps there is none that is exact. Let us suppose a creature for whom perfection does not exist on earth, and who judges that the most beautiful soul is nothing more than a point of view. If everything changes with one's point of view, perfection . . ."

"Perfection is trumps," injected Santos.

That was an invitation to play cards. Aires did not feel like accepting, with Flora staring at him with her restless, questioning eyes, curious to know why she was or would become inexplicable. Besides, he preferred conversation with women. This is a sentence from his *Memoirs:* "In a woman, the sex corrects banality, and in a man, it aggravates it."

It was not necessary to accept or refuse Santos's invitation. Two habitués of the game of whist arrived. With them was Batista, who was in the next room. Santos retired to his nightly diversion. One of the players was old Plácido, "doctor" of spiritism. The second was a commercial broker named Lopes who loved cards for the sake of cards and suffered less with losing money than losing the game. There they went to play whist, while Aires stayed in the drawing room to listen to the ladies sing. All the while Flora's eyes stayed fixed on him.

The Retiree

B y this time, this ex-diplomat was retired. He returned to Rio de Janeiro after a last look at the many things he had seen, to live here for the rest of his days. He could have done it in any city, he was a man for all seasons, but he had a particular love for his country, and possibly was also tired of other places. He did not admit to the many calamities attributed to his country. Yellow fever, for example, because he had denied it so often to the outside world, he had lost his belief in it; and when the cases were reported, he was already infected by the belief that all diseases were first a list of names. Perhaps it was because he was a healthy man.

He had not changed completely. He was the same, or almost. He had gotten balder, it is true. He carried a little less weight, a few wrinkles. In sum, a fit old age of 60. His mustache still twirled up into two elegant points. His step was firm, his gestures grave with that touch of gallantry which he never lost. In his buttonhole was the same eternal flower.

The city did not seem to have changed a lot either. He noticed more traffic, a few less operas, white hair, dead friends, but the old city was the same. His own house in Catete was well preserved. Aires dismissed his tenant with the same polish with which he would pay his respects to the minister of foreign affairs, and he installed himself there with a servant, in spite of his sister wanting him to take him to Andaraí.

"No, sister Rita, let me stay in my little corner."

"But I am your only relative," she said.

"Tied by blood and our heartstrings, of course," he agreed. He could add that she was the kindest relative of all and the most pious. "What happened to your hair? You don't need to lower your eyes. You cut your hair to put it in the coffin of your departed husband. Those that are left have turned white. But those that stayed with him are black, and more than one widow would have kept all of them for her second nuptials."

Rita enjoyed hearing that reference to the past. Back then, she would not have. Shortly after she became a widow, she was embarrassed by her sincere act. She thought herself almost ridiculous. What good did it do to cut her hair because she had lost the best of husbands? But as time went by, she began to see that she had done well, to feel satisfied when people told her so, and privately to remember it. Now the reference allowed her to reply: "Well, if I am that, why do you prefer to live with strangers?"

"What strangers? I will not live with anybody. I will live with Catete, the Largo do Machado, Botafogo beach, and Flamengo. I speak not of the people who live there but of the streets, the houses, the fountains, and the shops. There are some funny things in those neighborhoods, but who knows whether what I would find on Andaraí would be as topsy-turvy as my own? Let us be content with what we know. There in my old neighborhood my feet walk by themselves. There are things that are frozen in stone and immortal people, like that Custódio of the Imperial teashop, remember?"

"I remember, the Confeitaria do Império."

"It was established forty years ago. That was back in the time when carriages had to pay a transit tax. Well, the devil is old but he is not finished. He will still bury me. He seems like a young man, he shows up there every week."

"You too look like just a boy."

"Don't kid me, sister, I am finished. I am an old dandy, it could be, but that is not to please the young ladies, it's because that is how I turned out. And by the way, why don't you come and live with me?"

"Ah! well, I'll have you know I also enjoy my own company. I'll visit you once in a while, but I'm not leaving here until it's time to go to the cemetery."

They agreed to visit each other. Aires would dine with her on Thursdays. Dona Rita asked what he would do if he got sick, to which Aires replied that he never got sick, but if he did he would come to Andaraí. Her heart was a better cure than any hospital. Perhaps in all these refusals was also the need to avoid disagreements, because his sister knew how to invent occasions for discord. That same day (it was at lunch) he thought the coffee was delicious, but his sister said it was vile, forcing him with much effort to reverse his opinion and declare it disgusting.

At first, Aires kept to his solitude, separated himself from society, and stayed at home. He did not visit anyone, or rarely and at infrequent intervals. Truthfully he was tired of men and women, of parties and late nights. He organized his life. Because he was fond of classical literature, he found a translation by Father Bernardes of that psalm: "I would flee to a far-off place and make my lodging in the wilderness." That was his motto. Santos, if he had one, would have had it engraved in stone at the entrance to his drawing room, for the amusement of his numerous friends. Aires kept his counsel. At times he liked to recite it silently, in part because of the meaning and in part for the beauty of the old language: "I would flee to a far-off place and make my lodging in the wilderness."

Thus it was in the beginning. On Thursdays he would dine with his sister. In the evenings he would stroll on the beach or along the streets of his neighborhood. Most of the time was spent in reading and rereading, composing the *Memoirs* or revising the manuscript, to relive past events. These were many and of diverse character, from joy to melancholy, burials and diplomatic receptions, an armful of dried leaves which seemed green to him now. Sometimes people were designated by an X or ***, and he could not remember immediately who it was, but it was amusing to look for them, find them, and complete them.

He ordered a glass-encased cabinet to be made, where he put all the relics of his life, old photos, gifts from government officials and private citizens, a fan, a glove, a ribbon and other feminine mementos, medals and medallions, cameos, pieces of Greek and Roman ruins, an infinity of things I will not list so as not to waste paper. The letters were not there, they lived inside a suitcase, catalogued alphabetically, by city, by language, and by sex. Fifteen or twenty would provide material for as many chapters and would be read with interest and curiosity. A note, for example, smudged and without a date, young as an old note, signed with initials, an M. and a P., which he translated with longing. It's not worth telling the name.

Solitude Is Also Tedious

B ut everything becomes tedious, even solitude. Aires began to feel a twinge of boredom. He yawned, napped, he began to develop a thirst for living people, strangers, it did not matter who, happy or sad. He began to frequent eccentric neighborhoods, he climbed the hillsides, he went to the old churches, to the new streets, to Copacabana and Tijuca. The sea there, here the forest and the view, awoke in him an infinity of echoes which seemed to him to be the very voices of the ancients. All this he wrote, at night, to fortify his resolve to continue his solitary life. But there is no resolve against need.

Strangers had the advantage of taking away his solitude without engaging him in conversation. The formal visits he made were few, brief, and almost without conversation. And all of this was just the first steps. Little by little he started to notice the taste for his old habits, nostalgia for the salons, the longing for laughter, and it was not long before the retired diplomat was reinstated to the occupation of recreation. Solitude, as much in the biblical text as in the priest's translation, was archaic. Aires changed a word and the meaning: "I would flee to a far-off place and make my lodging in society."

Thus went the plan for a new life. He wanted to see other people, to hear them, smell them, taste them, touch them, and apply all his senses to a world that could kill time, immortal time.

Inexplicable

T hat is how we left him, just two chapters ago, in a corner of the Santos drawing room, in conversation with the ladies. You will remember that Flora did not take her eyes off him, anxious to know why he thought her inexplicable. The word tore at her brain, wounding her without an incision. What was inexplicable? She knew it meant something that cannot be explained. But why?

She wanted to ask the diplomat this, but she did not find the opportunity and he left early. The first time, however, that Aires went to São Clemente, Flora asked him familiarly the favor of a more detailed explanation. Aires smiled and took the young lady's hand. There was only time to invent this answer to the young woman standing in front of him: "Inexplicable is the word we use to describe artists who paint without finishing their painting. They put on paint and more paint, another kind of paint, a lot of paint, a little paint, new paint and it never seems to them that the tree is a tree or the cabin a cabin. And if the painting has people in it, good-bye. As much as the eyes of the figures speak, these painters always think they say nothing. And they touch it up with so much patience that some die in between eyes, and others kill themselves from despair."

Flora thought the explanation obscure. And you, my lady reader, if you are by chance older and more polished than she, it could be that you don't find it any clearer. He did not add anything, so as not to be included in that category of artist. He patted Flora's palm paternally and asked about her studies. The studies were going well, why would they not? And sitting at his feet, the young lady confessed that she had in fact been thinking about learning drawing and painting, but if she were going to be putting too much or too little paint on the picture, better not to paint and to stick with music. She did well with music, and French too, and English.

"Well then, just music, English, and French," agreed Aires.

"But will you promise me that you will no longer think me inexplicable?" she asked sweetly.

Before he could answer, the twins entered the room. Flora forgot this subject for another, and the boys took her attention away from the old man. Aires did not stay longer than to see her laughing with them and to feel something like remorse. Remorse at getting old, I think.

X X X V

About the Young Lady

At that time the twins were both at the university, one at the School of Law in São Paulo and the other at the School of Medicine in Rio. It would not be long before they were graduated and ready, one to defend people's rights and wrongs and the other to help them live and die. All contrasts reside within man.

It was not politics that made them forget Flora, nor was it Flora who made them forget politics. And neither one was enough to do harm to their studies or to their pastimes. They were at the age in which all combines without disturbing the essence of each thing. That they had both come to love the girl with equal force is what could be acknowledged right away, without her having to attract them willfully. On the contrary, Flora laughed with both of them, without especially rejecting or accepting either one of them. It could be that she did not even notice anything. Paulo was absent longer. When he came back for vacations he found her livelier. That was when Pedro multiplied his attentions so as not to be outdone by his brother, who came well supplied with them. And Flora received all of this with the same friendly face.

Please note, and this point should be brought to light of day, that the twins continued to look alike, and they grew ever more slender. Perhaps they lost by being together, because the similarity diminished the individual features in each of them. What is more, Flora pretended sometimes to confuse them in order to laugh at them. And she would say to Pedro: "Dr. Paulo!"

And to Paulo: "Dr. Pedro!"

In vain they switched from left to right and from right to left. Flora changed their names, too, and the three would laugh together. Familiarity excused the act and grew with it. Paulo liked conversation more than the piano. So Flora conversed. Pedro favored the piano over conversation. So Flora played. Or she would do both things, and talk as she played, loosening the reins from her fingers and her tongue.

These arts, at the service of such graces, really served to inflame the twins, and that is what happened little by little. Her mother, I believe, noticed something, but at first she did not give it much thought. She, too, had been a girl and a young lady, and she, too, divided herself while giving herself to no one. It could even be that, in her opinion, it was an exercise necessary for the eyes of the spirit as well as of the face. The point is not to let them be corrupted, nor chase after songs, as the popular saying goes, which thus expresses the charms of Orpheus. On the contrary, Flora was Orpheus and she was the song. In time, she would choose one of them, thought the mother.

Their intimacy had long intermissions, besides the obligatory absences of Paulo. In spite of not leaving, Pedro did not always seek her out, nor did she go often to the house on the beach. They would not see each other for days and days. That they might have thought of each other, it is possible. But I have no documentation of this. The truth is that Pedro had his school friends, his street flirtations, his adventures, his theater parties, his excursions to Tijuca, and other local attractions. As for the rest, the brothers were still at the stage of referring to her in their letters, praising her, describing her, saying a thousand sweet things, without jealousy.

Discord Is Not as Ugly as Is Said

D iscord is not as ugly as they say, my friend. It is neither ugly, nor sterile. Count only how many books it has produced, from Homer to the present day, not excluding . . . not excluding what? I was going to say this one, but Modesty waves to me from afar that I should stop here. I stop here, and long live Modesty, which hardly can stand the capital letter I give her, the letter and the hurrahs, but she will have to go with it and with them. Hurrah for Modesty, and let us exclude this book. Leave only the great epics and tragedies that Discord gave life to, and tell me if such effects do not prove the grandeur of the cause. No, discord is not as ugly as it is painted.

I insist on this so that sensitive souls do not begin to tremble for the young lady or the young lads. There is no need to tremble, even more so because the discord of the two began with a simple accord, that night. They walked shoulder to shoulder along the beach, silently, each with his own thoughts until both, as if they were talking to themselves, emitted this single sentence: "She is getting very pretty."

And turning to each other: "Who?"

They both smiled, amused at the simultaneity of the reflection and the question. I know that this phenomenon is exactly like the one in chapter XXV, when they told their age, but do not blame me. They were twins and they might speak like twins. The main thing is that they did not become surly. It was not yet love that they felt. Each one expressed his opinion about the charms of the girl, her gestures, voice, eyes, and hands, all in such good spirits that it excluded the notion of rivalry. At most, they differed in their choice of the nicest feature, which for Pedro were the eyes and for Paulo the figure. But since they ended up in agreement on the harmony of the whole, it was evident that they would not fight on account of this. Neither one attributed to the other the vague thing or whatever it was that they were beginning to feel, and they seemed more like aesthetes than young men in love. In fact, even politics left them in peace that night. They fought over nothing. Maybe they even felt something opposite, with the view of the sea and the sky, which was beautiful. A full moon, calm water, a few scattered voices, one or another carriage at a slow walk or a trot, depending on whether it was empty or carried passengers. An occasional fresh breeze.

Imagination carried them to the future, a brilliant future, such as it is at that age. Botafogo would have a historical role, an imperial port for Pedro, a republican Venice for Paulo, without doge, or council of ten, or then a doge with another title, a simple president, who would marry in the name of the people with this little Adriatic. Perhaps he himself would be the doge. That possibility, in spite of his green years, swelled the soul of the young man. Paulo saw himself at the head of a republic, in which the ancient and the modern, the future and the past, would mix together, a new Rome, a National Convention, a French Republic, and the United States of America.

Pedro, for his part, constructed in midstroll a palace for the national parliament, another for the emperor, and he saw himself both minister and president of the council. He spoke, he commanded the crowd and public opinion, he wrested a vote from the Chamber of Deputies or then expedited a decree dissolving parliament. It's a minor detail but deserves to be inserted here: Pedro, dreaming of the government, thought especially about the decrees of dissolution. He saw himself at home, with the signed act, approved by Congress, copied, sent to the newspapers and the chambers, read by secretaries, filed in Ministries, and the deputies leaving with their heads down, some grumbling, others irate. Only he was tranquil, in his office, receiving friends who paid their respects and asked for messages for their provinces.

Such were the broad strokes of imagination of the two. The stars received in the heavens all the boys' thoughts, the moon remained still, and the surf stretched on the beach with its customary laziness. They returned to the present in front of their home. One or another impulse wanted to lead them to discuss the weather and the evening, the temperature and the bay. A vague murmur may have made them move their lips and begin to break the silence, but the silence was so august that they agreed to respect it. And soon they each found privately that the moon was splendid, the bay beautiful, and the temperature divine.

XXXVII

Discord in Accord

D o not forget to mention that, in 1888, a grave and most serious issue also made them agree, although for different reasons. The date explains the fact: it was the emancipation of the slaves. They were at the time living at a great distance from each other, but opinion united them.

The only difference between them was about the meaning of the reform, which for Pedro was an act of justice and for Paulo was the beginning of the revolution. He himself said it, concluding a speech in São Paulo on the twentieth of May: "Abolition is the dawn of freedom. Let us await the sun. Now that the blacks are emancipated, what remains to be done is to emancipate the whites."

Natividade was speechless when she read this. She picked up her pen and wrote a long and maternal letter. Paulo responded with thirty thousand expressions of tenderness, declaring at the end that he could sacrifice everything for her, including his life and his honor, but not his opinions. "No, Mother, not my opinions."

"Not my opinions," repeated Natividade when she finished reading the letter.

Natividade did not understand the feelings of her son, she who had sacrificed her opinions to her principles, as in the case of Aires, and continued to live without a stain on her character. So how then not to sacrifice? She did not find an explanation. She reread the sentence in the letter and of the speech. She feared he would lose his political career, if it was politics that would make him a great man. "Once the blacks are emancipated, what remains is to emancipate the whites." That was a threat to the emperor and the empire.

She did not grasp the meaning of this; mothers do not always grasp things. She did not grasp that the phrase of the speech did not exactly belong to her son. It did not belong to anybody. Someone had pronounced it one day in a speech or a conversation, in a gazette or on a voyage by land or by sea. Someone else had repeated it until many people made it their own. It was new, energetic, it was expressive, and it became common property.

There are other felicitous phrases. They are born modestly, like poor people. When one least expects it, they are governing the world, just like ideas. Ideas themselves do not always keep the name of their father. Many appear as orphans, born of nothing and of no one. Each one takes them from the next, makes of them what they can, and carries them to the marketplace, where all take them for their own.

X X X V I I I

A Timely Arrival

W hen, at two o'clock in the afternoon on the next day, Natividade boarded the trolley to go on I don't know what shopping errands at the Rua do Ouvidor, she carried the phrase with her. The view of the bay did not distract her, nor the people passing by, nor the bumps of the street, nothing. The phrase went before her and inside her, with its threatening tone and character. In Catete, someone jumped aboard without stopping the vehicle. You may guess that it was the counselor. Guess, too, that with his foot on the running board and seeing our friend in front of him, he made his way over to her quickly and accepted the corner of the bench that she offered him. After the first greetings, he remarked: "It appears to me that you look frightened."

"Naturally, I did not imagine that you were capable of that feat of acrobatics."

"A matter of custom. My legs jump by themselves. One day they will let me fall and the wheels will run me over."

"However it was, you arrived just in time."

"I always arrive in time. I have already heard this from you, once, many years ago, or was it your sister . . . Now, wait, I have not forgotten the motive. I think you were speaking about the cabocla of Castelo. Don't you remember that half-breed who lived on the Castelo hill and guessed people's futures? I was here on leave, and I heard all sorts of old wives' tales. Since I always had faith in Sibyls, I believed in the cabocla. Whatever became of her?"

Natividade looked at him, as if fearing that he had discovered her consultation with the fortune-teller. It seemed, though, that he had not; she smiled and called him an unbeliever. Aires denied he was an unbeliever. On the contrary, being tolerant, he professed virtually all the beliefs of this world. And he concluded: "But after all, why did I arrive just in time?"

Either the past or his person, with his discreet manners and serene spirit, or all this together, gave this man in the eyes of this lady a trustworthiness that she did not find any more in anyone else, or would find in few. She spoke to him about a confidential matter, a document that she would not show her husband.

"I want advice, counselor. And more, why should I trouble my husband? At most I will tell this to sister Perpétua. I think it better not to say anything to Agostinho."

Aires agreed that it was not worth troubling him, if that were the case, and waited. Natividade, without mentioning the cabocla, first related the rivalry of her sons already manifest in politics, and, referring especially to Paulo, repeated the phrase of the letter and asked what she should do. Aires interpreted this as the ardor of youth. Not to insist, for if she insisted he would change his words, but not his feelings.

"So you think Paulo will always be like this?"

"I won't say forever. Nor do I say the contrary. Baroness, you demand definitive answers, but tell me what is definitive in this world, except for your husband's game of whist? Even that fails.

How many days has it been that I have not drawn a card? It's true that I have not paid you a visit recently. And truly, the pleasure of conversation well repays the game of cards. I wager that the married men who go there are of another opinion?"

"Perhaps."

"Only bachelors can value women's ideas. A widower without children, like myself, is as good as a bachelor. I lie, at 60 as I am, I'm worth two or three. As far as young Paulo is concerned, do not give his speech another thought. I, too, gave speeches when I was a young man."

"I am trying to marry them."

"Marriage is good," Aires assented.

"I don't mean that they should marry now, but in two or three years. Perhaps first I will take a trip with them. What do you think? Come now, don't answer me by repeating what I say. I want your own thoughts. Do you think a trip? . . ."

"I think a trip . . ."

"Finish."

"Voyages do a lot of good, especially at their age. They will graduate at the end of this year, correct? Well then! Before they start any career, married or not, it is useful to see other countries. But why do you need to go with them?"

"Mothers . . ."

"But I, too—excuse me for interrupting you—but I too am your son. Don't you think that the habit of your company, your good face, your grace, your affection, and all the gray curls that adorn your face make up a kind of maternity? I confess that I would become an orphan."

"Well then, come with us."

"Ah! Baroness, for me there is nothing in the world worth a steamship ticket. I have seen everything, in various languages. Now the world starts here on the docks of Glória or the Rua do Ouvidor and ends at the Cemetery of São João Batista. I hear there are fearsome seas beyond the Ponta do Caju, but I am an unbelieving old man, as you said before, and I do not accept that news without absolute visual proof, and to seek it, I lack energy in my legs."

"Always the joker! Did I not see you leap on them just now? Your sister told me the other day that you have the agility of a 30-year-old."

"Rita exaggerates. But returning to the voyage, have you bought the tickets?"

"No."

"Have you even reserved them?"

"Also not."

"Then let us think of something else. Every day brings its cares, all the more weeks and months. Let us think of something else, and let Paulo call for his republic."

Natividade thought to herself that perhaps he was right. Afterward she thought of something else, and that was the idea she had at the beginning. She had not mentioned it right away, she had preferred to converse for a few minutes. It was not difficult to talk with this fellow. One of his qualities was the ability to talk with women, without falling into banalities or soaring to the clouds. He had a particular way about him, she was not sure whether it was his ideas, or his gestures, or his words. It is not that he spoke ill of anyone; in fact, that would be a distraction. I rather suppose that he did not speak ill out of indifference or caution. Provisionally, let us call it charity.

"But my lady still has not told me what you want from me besides advice. Or do you not need anything else?"

"It is hard for me to ask."

"You may always ask."

"You know that my twins do not agree on anything, or just a little, as much as I have tried to bring them around to a certain harmony. Agostinho does not help me. He has other worries. I do not have the strength anymore, and so I thought that a friend, a moderate man, a man of society, able, fine, cautious, intelligent, educated . . ."

"I, in sum . . .?"

"You guessed."

"I did not guess. You painted my very portrait. But what do you think I can do?"

"You could correct their manners, make them unite even when they disagree, and let them disagree seldom or never. You cannot imagine. They seem to do it on purpose. They do not disagree on the color of the moon, for example, but when he was 11 Pedro discovered that the shadows on the moon were clouds, and Paulo said they were flaws in our vision, and they clashed. I had to separate them. Imagine in politics!"

"Imagine in love, I say. But that is not exactly this case . . ."

"Oh, no!"

"In the others it is equally useless, but I was born to serve even if uselessly. Baroness, your request is equivalent to appointing me nanny or tutor. Do not make gestures, I am not diminished by this. Providing you pay me a salary. And do not be frightened. I ask little. Pay me in words, your words are like gold. I have already told you that any action of mine is useless."

"Why?"

"It's useless."

"A person of authority, such as yourself, can do a lot, providing you love them, because they are good, believe me. Do you know them well?"

"Hardly."

"Get to know them more and you will see."

Aires agreed, laughing. For Natividade this was worth a new try. She trusted in the action of the counselor and to say it all . . . I don't know if I should . . . I will. Natividade counted on the old inclination of the aging diplomat. White hairs would not take away his desire to serve her. I do not know who reads me on this occasion. If it is a man, perhaps he will not understand right away, but if it is a woman, I think she will understand. If no one understands, oh well. It is enough to know that he promised what she wanted and also promised not to say a word about it. That was the other condition she imposed. All of this was polished, sincere, and unbelieving.

XXXIX

A Thief

They arrived at the Largo da Carioca, got off the trolley, and said good-bye. She went to the Rua Gonçalves Dias, and he headed for the Rua da Carioca. Midway down that street, Aires encountered a knot of people standing, then moving toward the square. Aires wanted to reverse his direction, not from fear but from horror. He had a horror of the crowd. He saw that there were not that many people, fifty or sixty, and he heard them crying out against the arrest of a man. He entered an alley, waiting for the throng to pass. Two policemen held the prisoner by the arms. From time to time he resisted, and then it was necessary to drag or force him another way. It was, apparently, about the theft of a wallet.

"I didn't steal anything!" shouted the prisoner, slowing his steps. "I am falsely accused. Let me go! I am a free citizen! I protest, I protest!"

"You're going to the station!"

"I won't go!"

"Don't go!" cried the anonymous crowd. "Don't go! Don't go!"

One of the policemen tried to convince the crowd that it was true, that the fellow had stolen a wallet, and the unrest seemed to diminish a little. But as the guard walked along with his partner and the prisoner, each one holding one of his arms, the crowd resumed its protest against the violence. The prisoner was encouraged, and now lamenting, now aggressive, incited the defense. It was then that the other guard drew his sword to open way. The people fled, not gracefully like a swallow or dove searching for its nest or for food, but stampeding, jumping here and there, pushing out to all sides. The sword returned to its sheath and the prisoner went along with the guards. But soon the hearts of the populace took over their legs, and an insistent, long, affronted clamor filled the street and the soul of the prisoner. The multitude once again formed a compact mass and walked toward the police station. Aires continued on his way.

The voices subsided somewhat, and Aires entered the offices of the Ministry of the Empire. He did not find the minister, it seems, or the meeting was short. It is certain that, going out into the square, he encountered small clusters of the crowd that were returning from the station, commenting on the arrest and the thief. They did not say thief, but crook, thinking it less offensive, and as much as they had shouted their protest at the police, they now laughed about the prisoner's misfortune.

"That poor slob!"

But then? . . . you ask. Aires asked nothing. After all, there was a kernel of justice in that dual and contradictory manifestation. Those were his thoughts. Then he imagined that the shouts of the protesting crowd were spawned from an old instinct of resistance to authority. He was reminded that man, once created, immediately disobeyed his Creator, who in fact had given him a paradise in which to live. But there is no paradise worth as much as the relish of opposition. That man should become accustomed to laws, indeed; that he bend his back to force and at the whims of others, also; that is what happens with a plant when the wind blows. But for man to bless force and obey the laws always, always, and always is to violate the primitive instinct for freedom, the freedom of old Adam. That is what Counselor Aires was thinking as he walked along.

Do not attribute all these ideas to him. He thought this way, as if he were speaking out loud, at table or in someone's salon. It was a gentle and delicate process of social criticism, so full of conviction on the surface, that a listener, someone searching for ideas, just might catch one or two.

He was going to head toward the Rua Sete de Setembro, when the memory of the crowd's roar brought him another, larger and more remote.

Memories

T hat other larger and more remote din would not have a place here, if it were not for the need to explain the sudden gesture with which Aires stopped on the sidewalk. He stopped, came back to himself, and continued to walk with his eyes on the ground and his soul in Caracas. It was in Caracas, where he had served as attaché to the diplomatic mission. He was at home, entertaining a fashionable actress, an amusing and lively person. Suddenly they heard a loud clamor, excited voices, vibrant, growing louder . . .

"What noise is that, Carmen?" he asked, between caresses.

"Don't be frightened, my friend. It's the government falling."

"But I hear cheers . . ."

"Then it is the government rising. Don't be frightened. Tomorrow is time enough to pay your respects."

Aires let himself float down the river of that old memory, which now rose from the noise of fifty or sixty people. That type of memory had more effect on him than others. He reconstructed the hour, place, and person of the *sevillana*. Carmen was from Sevilla. The ex-young man still recalled the popular song that she trilled in farewell, after clasping shut her garters, arranging her skirts, and placing her comb in her hair, at the moment she threw her mantilla around her shoulders, swaying her body gracefully:

"The girls of Sevilla
On their mantilla
Have a sign that says
Viva Sevilla!"

I cannot give you the melody, but Aires still knew it by heart and repeated it to himself softly as he walked. At times he thought about his lack of a diplomatic vocation. The rise of a government, of whatever regime, with its new ideas, its fresh men, laws, and proclamations, was worth less to him than the smile of the young comedienne. Where would she be now? The shadow of the young lady swept everything else away, the street, the people, the crook, to stand alone in front of old Aires, swaying her hips and trilling the Andalusian melody:

"The girls of Sevilla,
On their mantilla . . ."

XLI

The Incident of the Donkey

If Aires followed his inclinations, and I his, neither he would continue to walk, nor I would start this chapter. We would remain in the previous one, without ever finishing it. But there is nothing in memory that lasts, if some more forceful event claims our attention, and a simple donkey made Carmen and her song disappear.

In this case a cart was stuck, blocking the entrance to the Travessa de São Francisco, not allowing any other vehicles to pass. The cart driver was beating his donkey on the head. While common, this spectacle made our Aires stop, not less concerned for the ass than the man. The force expended by the latter was great, because the ass ruminated over whether it should leave its place or not. But in spite of demonstrating this superiority, he took a devil of a beating. Already a few people had stopped to watch.

This situation went on for five or six minutes. Finally the donkey preferred to move than to be beaten, pulled the cart out of the way, and went on.

In the round eyes of the animal, Aires saw an expression of profound irony and patience. It seemed to him the plain face of invincible spirit. Then he read in them this monologue: "Come, boss, you load up this cart with cargo to earn the hay that you feed me. You walk on the ground to buy the shoes for my hooves. Not because of this can you stop me from calling you a dirty name, but I call you nothing. You are always my dear master. While you break your back to earn a living, I think that your dominion over me is not worth much, since you cannot take away my freedom to be stubborn."

"Well, you can almost hear the animal thinking aloud," Aires noted to himself.

Then he laughed to himself and went on his way. He had made up so many things in the diplomatic service that perhaps he had made up the donkey's monologue. Thus it was: he had read nothing in the animal's eyes, except irony and patience, but he could not keep himself from giving form to the expression in words, with their rules of syntax. The very irony might have been in his own retina. The eye of man serves as a photograph of the invisible, just as the ear serves as the echo to silence. All it requires is that its owner have a flash of imagination to help his memory forget Caracas and Carmen, her kisses and her political experience.

XLII

An Hypothesis

V isions and reminiscences thus ate up the counselor's time
and space, to the point that they made him forget Natividade's request. But he did not forget it entirely, and the words exchanged with her jumped out at him from the cobblestones on
the street. He considered that he had nothing to lose in studying
the two boys. He even was able to grab hold of an hypothesis, a
kind of swallow that flies between the trees, swooping down and
then up again, landing here, landing there, taking off again, and
dissipating in a flurry of motion. The vague and colorful hypothesis was this: that if the twins had been born from him they would
hardly have diverged at all, thanks to the equilibrium of his spirit.
The soul of the old man began to sprout shoots of I know not
what retrospective desires, and to review that hypothesis, another
Caracas, another Carmen, he the father, these boys his, the whole
swallow which took flight in a silent rustling of movement.

XLIII

The Speech

N atividade had no distractions of any kind. Her entire sense
of self resided in her sons and now especially in the letter
and the speech. She began by not answering Paulo's political effu-

sions. That was on the advice of the counselor. When her son returned from vacation he had forgotten the letter he had written.

He did not forget the speech, but who forgets the speeches he makes? If they are good, memory engraves them in bronze. If bad, they leave a bitter taste that lasts a long time. The best of remedies, in the latter case, is to suppose they are excellent, and if reason does not accept this imagining, to consult people who do accept it and believe them. Opinion is an old incorruptible oil.

Paulo had talent. The speech of that day may have sinned in this or that emphasis and one or another vulgar, tired idea. Paulo indeed had talent. In sum, the speech was good. Santos thought it was excellent, read it to his friends, and resolved to reprint it in the newspapers. Natividade did not oppose him but thought that some words should be cut.

"Cut, why?" asked Santos, waiting for a reply.

"Well, don't you see, Agostinho? These words have a republican message," she explained, rereading the phrase that had troubled her.

Santos heard her read, read them to himself, and found her to be right. However, not for this reason should they be omitted.

"Well then, the speech should not be printed."

"Oh, no! The speech is magnificent, and it should not die in São Paulo. The Court must read it, and the provinces too, and I might even have it translated into French. In French it might sound even better."

"But Agostinho, this could do harm to the boy's career. The emperor might not like it."

Pedro, who had been listening to the debate for a few minutes, intervened sweetly to say that his mother's fears were baseless. It was good to leave the sentence as it was, and strictly speaking, it did not differ much from what the liberals had said in 1848.

"A liberal monarchist could well have signed this part," he concluded after rereading his brother's words.

"Precisely!" agreed the father.

Natividade, who saw her sons' rivalry in everything, suspected that Pedro's intent was precisely to compromise Paulo. She looked at him to see if she could discern this twisted motive, but her son's face was bright with enthusiasm. Pedro read passages of the speech, repeating the newer phrases, praising the rounder ones, turning them around in his mouth, all in such good spirits that his mother forgot her suspicions and the reprinting of the speech was resolved. They also had a pamphlet edition printed, and the father had six copies richly bound in leather, which he took to the ministers, and one even more luxurious was presented to the princess regent.

"Tell her," counseled Natividade, "that our Paulo is an ardent liberal."

"An 1848 liberal," completed Santos, remembering Pedro's words.

Santos complied to the letter. The delivery was made naturally and in Princess Isabel's palace, the definition of "1848 liberal" was pronounced with more spirit than the other words, either to diminish the revolutionary smell of the phrase condemned by his wife or because it had historical value. When he returned home, the first thing he told her was that the regent had asked after her, but in spite of being flattered by the consideration, Natividade wanted to know what impression the speech had made, if she had already read it.

"It seems it was good. She told me she had already read the speech. But I did not fail to say that Paulo's sentiments were good. That if we noticed a certain ardor in his words, we understood that they were those of an 1848 liberal . . ."

"Did you say that, Father?" asked Pedro.

"Why not, if it's true? Paulo is what can be called an 1848 liberal," repeated Santos, wanting to convince his son.

XLIV

The Salmon

W hen he was home for vacation, Paulo found out about the interpretation that his father had given to the princess regent about that part of the speech. He protested against it, at home. He wanted also to make it public, but Natividade intervened in time. Aires put water on the flames, saying to the future lawyer: "It is not worth it, young man. What matters is that everyone has his ideas and fights for them until they triumph. Now, if others interpret your words incorrectly, it should not trouble the author."

"Trouble, yes sir. It may seem that that is the case . . . I will write an article about something else, and I won't leave any doubts."

"Why?" asked Aires.

"I do not want them to suppose . . ."

"But who doubts your sentiments?"

"They may doubt them."

"Come now! In any case have lunch with me one of these days. Look, come on Sunday, and your brother Pedro too. We will be three at table, a bachelors' lunch. We will drink a certain wine given to me by the German ambassador."

On Sunday, the two went to Catete, less for the lunch than for the host. Aires was beloved of both of them. They liked to listen to him, to question him, to ask him to tell political anecdotes from another time, descriptions of dances, society news.

"Hurrah for my two young men," said the counselor, "hurrah for my two young men who have not forgotten their old friend. How is your father? Your mother?"

"They are well," said Pedro.

Paulo added that both sent their regards.

"And Aunt Perpétua?"

"She is also well," said Paulo.

"Still practicing homeopathy and telling her stories about Paraguay," added Pedro.

Pedro was in high spirits and Paulo preoccupied. After the first greetings and exchange of news, Aires noticed that difference and thought it was good, because it took away the monotony of their resemblance. But then, he did not want sullen faces, and he asked the law student what was wrong.

"Nothing."

"That cannot be. You seem to be down in the dumps. Well, I woke up in the mood to laugh and I want you both to laugh with me."

Paulo growled a word that neither one of them understood and pulled a sheaf of papers out of his pocket. It was an article.

"An article?"

"An article in which I remove all doubts with regard to my opinions, and I ask you to listen to it, it is short. I wrote it last night."

Aires proposed that he listen to it after lunch, but the young man asked him to do it right away, and Pedro agreed with this proposal, alleging that on top of lunch, it could spoil their digestion like the bitter pill that it must naturally be. Aires gave in to their insistence and consented to listen to the article.

"It is short, seven pages."

"Tiny writing?"

"No sir, medium."

Paulo read the article. Its epigraph was from Amos: "Hear this word, you fat cows of Bashan, who are in the mountain of Samaria . . ." The fat cows were the members of the regime, explained Paulo. He was not attacking the emperor, out of respect for his mother, but he was violent and sharp with the principle of monarchy and the rest of the court. Aires saw in him what at the time was called the "taste for combativity." When Paulo was finished, Pedro said in a bored voice: "I've heard all of that before, they are *Paulista* ideas."

"Your ideas are colonial," replied Paulo.

Worse words could have grown from that challenge, but fortunately a servant came to the door announcing that lunch was served. Aires rose and said that he would give his opinion at the table.

"First lunch, because we have a salmon, something special. Let's enjoy it."

Aires wanted to keep his promise to Natividade. Who knows if the idea of being the boys' spiritual father, the father of mere desire, the father that he was not, that he could have been, did not give him a special affection and a higher calling than that of simple friend? Nor it is out of the question that he was merely looking for new material for the blank pages of his *Memoirs*.

At lunch they still talked about the article: Paulo with love and Pedro with disdain, Aires without one or the other sentiment. The lunch did its work. Aires studied the two boys and their opinions. Perhaps these were nothing more than a rash on the skin of youth. And he smiled, made them eat and drink, and talked about young women, but here the boys, vexed and respectful, did not accompany the ex-minister. Talk of politics began to dwindle. Truthfully, Paulo still declared himself capable of overthrowing the monarchy with ten men, and Pedro of routing out the republican germ with a decree. But the ex-minister, without more of a decree than a casserole nor any more army than his cook, engaged the two regimes in the same delicious salmon.

X L V

Muse, Sing . . .

When lunch was finished, Aires gave them a quote from Homer, in fact two, one for each one, telling them that the old poet had sung about them separately, Paulo at the beginning of the *Iliad:*

> "Muse, sing the wrath of Achilles, Peleus's son, ill-boding wrath for the Greeks, that sent to Pluto's house many strong souls of heroes and gave their bodies to be a prey to birds and dogs."

Pedro was at the beginning of the *Odyssey:*

> "Muse, sing that astute hero who wandered so many years after the destruction of sacred Ilium."

It was one way to define each one's character and neither took the illustration badly. To the contrary, the poetic quotation served as a private diploma. The fact is that both smiled with faith, acceptance, thanks, without finding one word or syllable with which to contradict the aptness of the verses. That he, the counselor, after citing them in our prose, repeated them in the original Greek, and that the twins felt themselves more epic still, is as true as that translations are not as good as the original. What they did was to give a depressing twist to what had been said about their brother.

"You are right, counselor," said Paulo. "Pedro is a sneak."

"And you're a raging lunatic."

"In Greek, boys, in Greek and in verse, which is better than our own language and the prose of our time."

XLVI

Between Acts

Those lunches were repeated, the months passed, holidays
came, holidays went, and Aires had penetrated the twins
well. He wrote them into the *Memoirs*, where one reads about the
consultation with old Plácido and what he said about the pair and
also the visit to the cabocla of the Castelo hill and the fight before
they were born, old and obscure stories he remembered, linked,
and deciphered.

As the months pass, pretend you are in the theater, between
acts, talking. Inside they move the scenery and the actors change
their costumes. You don't go backstage. You let the leading lady,
in her dressing room, laugh with her friends about what she wept
over on stage. As for the garden they are constructing, don't try to
look at it from behind. It is just old, unpainted canvas, because
only the part visible to the spectator has leaves and flowers. Allow
yourself to remain out here, in the box of this lady. Examine her
eyes. They are still filled with the tears that the leading lady drew
from her. Talk with her about the play and the actors. That it is
obscure. That they don't know their lines well. Or that everything
is sublime. Afterward survey the boxes with your opera glasses,
distribute justice, call the beautiful ones beautiful and the ugly
ones ugly, and don't forget to tell of anecdotes which disfigure the
pretty ones and of virtues which make the ugly ones prettier. The
virtues must be great and the anecdotes amusing. There are also
banalities, but the same banality in the mouth of a good narrator
becomes rare and precious. And you will see how tears dry
quickly and reality substitutes for fiction. I speak in images. You
know that everything here is pure truth and tearless.

Matthew 4:1-10

If there is much laughter when one party rises to power, there are also many tears in the other that loses, and it is with laughter and tears that the first day of the new incumbency is made, as in Genesis. Let us turn to the evangelist who serves as title for this chapter. The liberals were called to power, which the conservatives had to relinquish. It is not redundant to say that the disappointment of Batista was great.

"Just now, when I had such hopes," he said to his wife.

"For what?"

"Well, for what! For a governorship. I said nothing because it could have failed, but it is almost certain that it would not. I had two interviews, not with ministers but with an influential person who knew, and it was just a question of waiting one or two months more . . ."

"A good governorship?"

"A good one."

"If you had worked hard . . ."

"If I had worked hard, I could already be holding the position, but we'd be coming home now with our tails between our legs."

"That is true," agreed Dona Cláudia, looking to the future.

Batista paced, hands behind his back, face down, sighing, without being able to foresee the time when the conservatives would come back to power. The liberals were strong and resolute. The same ideas danced in Dona Cláudia's head. This couple was not only of the same will, their ideas were sometimes so similar that if they were to take on a physical form out here, no one could tell which were his or which were hers, they seemed to come from a single brain. At that moment neither one found immediate or remote hope. Just a vague idea. And it was here that Dona Cláudia's will put its feet on the ground and grew tall. I don't speak just figuratively. Dona Cláudia rose quickly from her chair and shot off this question to her husband: "But Batista, what more can you expect from the conservatives?"

Batista stopped and with a dignified look answered simply: "I hope they come back."

"Come back? Wait eight or ten years, until the end of the century? And then do you know if they will appoint you? Who will remember you?"

"I can start a newspaper."

"Forget newspapers. And if you die?"

"I'll die in a position of honor."

Dona Cláudia stared at him. Her little eyes bored down into his like two patient drills. Suddenly, she lifted her arms and opened her hands: "Batista, you were never a conservative!"

Her husband grew pale and stepped back, as if he had heard the very ingratitude of his party. Had never been a conservative? But what was he then, what was left for him in this world? What had earned him the esteem of his superiors? That was the last straw. Dona Cláudia did not heed his protests, she repeated the words and added: "You were with them, like someone who attends a ball, where it is not necessary to share the same ideas in order to dance the same quadrille."

Batista smiled lightly and quickly. He liked witty images and this one seemed to him to be very witty indeed, so that he agreed right away. But his star inspired him to a quick rebuttal.

"Yes, but people don't dance with ideas, they dance with their legs."

"However they dance, the truth is that all your ideas were in the liberal camp. Remember the dissidents in the province accused you of supporting the liberals . . ."

"That was false, the government asked me to be moderate. I can show you the letters."

"What moderation! You're a liberal."

"Me, a liberal?"

"Quite a liberal. You were never anything else."

"Think of what you are saying, Cláudia. If anyone hears you they might believe it and spread it around . . ."

"And what if they do? They will be spreading the truth, spreading justice, because your real friends will not leave you in the street, now that everything is being organized. You have personal friends in the Ministry. Why don't you seek them out?"

Batista recoiled in horror. The business of climbing the stairs of power and telling them that he was at their service was hardly conceivable. Dona Cláudia admitted it was not, but a friend could do it for him, an intimate friend of the government who would say to the viscount of Ouro Preto: "Viscount, why don't you invite Batista? He was always liberal in his ideas. Give him a little governorship."

Batista shrugged his shoulders and raised his hand in a gesture of silence. His wife did not stop talking. She kept saying the same things, now more serious because of the insistence and the tone. In her husband's soul the catastrophe was tremendous. Considering it, he would not refuse to cross the Rubicon. He just lacked the necessary strength. He wanted to desire it. He wanted not to see anything, not the past, not the present, not the future, not to know about men or things, and to obey the dice of fate, but he could not.

And let us do justice to the man. When he thought only of the faithfulness to his friends, he felt better. The same faith existed, the same habits, the same hope. The evil came when he looked across to the other side. And it was Dona Cláudia who pointed with her finger at his career, his happiness, their life, the steady long march to the governorship, the Ministry . . . He rolled his eyes and stayed put.

Alone with himself, Batista thought a lot about his personal and political situation. He palpated himself morally. Cláudia could be right. What was there in him that was properly conservative, except that instinct for survival common to every creature that helps it to get along in this world? He found himself a conservative in politics because his father had been, his uncle, family friends, the parish priest, and he began in school to vilify the liberals. And then he was not exactly a conservative, but a *Saquarema,* just as the liberals were called *Luzias.* Batista clung now to these obsolete and depressing designations that changed the style of the parties. So that today there was not the great abyss between them that had separated them from 1842 to 1848. And he remembered the viscount of Albuquerque or another senator who had said in a speech that there was nothing more like a conservative than a liberal and vice-versa. And he evoked examples, the Progressive party, Olinda, Nabuco, and Zacarias; who were they but conservatives who understood the new times and removed from the liberal ideas that revolutionary blood, to cover them in a lively yet serene color? Nor did the world belong to the hardheaded. That caused a chill to run down his spine. Just at that moment, Flora appeared. Her father embraced her tenderly and asked if she wanted to go to the provinces, if he were to be named governor.

"But haven't the conservatives fallen?"

"Yes, they have fallen, but suppose that . . ."

"Oh, no, Father!"

"No, why?"

"I don't want to leave Rio de Janeiro."

Perhaps Rio de Janeiro was for her Botafogo and precisely Natividade's house. Her father did not inquire further into the reasons for her refusal. He supposed them to be political, and he summoned up new strength to resist the temptations of Dona Cláudia. "Begone, Satan! For it is written, you shall worship the Lord your God and Him only shall you serve." And it followed as in the Scriptures: "Then the Devil left him, and behold, angels came and ministered to him." The angels were just one, who was worth many. And her father said, kissing her lovingly: "Very well, very well, Daughter."

"Isn't it so, Father?"

No, it was not the daughter who stayed the desertion of her father. On the contrary. Batista, if he were to give in, would give in to his wife or to the Devil, synonymous in this chapter. He did not give in, out of weakness. He did not have the strength to betray his friends, much as they seemed to have abandoned him. There are virtues made of reticence and timidity, and not for this are they less lucrative, morally speaking. Not only stoics and martyrs have worth. Maiden virtues are also virtues. It is true that his language, regarding the liberals, was no longer made of hate or impatience. It approached tolerance and brushed on justice. He agreed that the alternation of parties was a principle of public necessity. What he did was to encourage his friends. They would soon return to power. But Dona Cláudia had the opposite opinion. For her, the liberals would last to the end of the century. At most, she admitted that at the first moment in power they would not welcome a last-minute convert. It was necessary to wait a year or two, a vacancy in the Chamber, a commission, a lieutenant-governorship in Rio . . .

X L V I I I

Terpsichore

None of these things bothered Natividade. She was more concerned with the ball on the Ilha Fiscal which took place in November to honor the Chilean naval officers. Not that she herself still danced, but she enjoyed watching others dance and now had the opinion that dance is a pleasure of the eyes. This opinion is one of the effects of that bad habit of growing old. Do not fall into that habit, reader. There are others, also bad, none worse, this is the worst. Let the philosophers say that old age is a useful state because of the experience and other advantages. Do not grow old, my friend, as much as the years invite you to leave Spring behind. At best, accept Summer. Summer is good, warm, the nights are brief, it is true, but the dawns do not always bring fog, and the sky is born blue. Thus you will dance forever.

I know there are people for whom the dance is above all a plea-sure of the eyes, nor the dancers anything more than professional women. I, too, if it is licit to refer to oneself, I also think that dance is a pleasure of the eyes more than of the feet, and the rea-son is not only my long gray years but also another I will not mention because it is not worth it. After all, I am not telling about my life, or my opinions, or anything else that does not have to do with the characters who enter the book. These I do have to put down here in their totality, with their virtues and imperfections, if they have them. This should be understood, without having to note it down, but nothing is lost in repeating it.

For example, Dona Cláudia. She also thought about the ball on the Ilha Fiscal, without the least inclination to dance or the aesthetic reason of the other lady. For her, the ball on the island was a political fact, it was the ball of the Ministry, a liberal party, which could open the doors to a governorship for her husband. She already saw herself with the imperial family. She heard the princess: "How are you, Dona Cláudia?"

"Perfectly well, Most Serene Highness."

And Batista would converse with the emperor, in a corner, in front of the envious eyes of those who would try to overhear the dialogue, forced to view them from afar. Her husband, however . . . I don't know what I should say about her husband relative to the ball on the island. He planned to go, but he thought he would not be at ease. It could be that they would translate this act as a half-conversion. It is not that only liberals went to the ball, conservatives would go too, and here fit Dona Cláudia's aphorism that it is not necessary to have the same ideas to dance in the same quadrille.

It was Santos who did not need ideas to dance. He would not even attempt to dance. When he was young he danced a lot, quadrilles, polkas, waltzes, the sliding waltz, and the jumping waltz, as they said then, without my being able to better define the difference. I presume that in the former the feet do not leave the ground, and in the latter they do not come down from the air. All this until he was 25. Then business got hold of him and put him in that other contradance, in which one does not always return to the same place, or never leaves it. Santos left, and we now know where he is. Lately he was entertaining the fantasy of becoming a deputy. Natividade shook her head, no matter how he explained that he did not want to be an orator or a minister, but just make the Chamber of Deputies a stepping stone to the senate, where he had friends, persons of merit, and which was eternal.

"Eternal?" she interrupted with a thin, pale smile.

"Lifelong, I mean to say."

Natividade insisted no, that his position was commercial and financial. She added that politics was one thing and industry another. Santos replied, citing the baron of Mauá, who merged both. Then his wife declared dryly and harshly that at 60 nobody begins a political career as deputy.

"But that is just temporary. Senators are old."

"No, Agostinho," concluded the baroness with a definitive gesture.

I do not mention Aires, who would probably dance, in spite of his years. Nor do I speak of Dona Perpétua, who would not even attend. Pedro would go and it is natural that he would dance, and a lot, notwithstanding his perseverance and passion for his studies. He was bewitched by Medicine. In his room, in addition to the bust of Hippocrates, he had the portraits of some of Europe's medical luminaries, many engravings of skeletons, many illustrations of diseases, chests cut open vertically to expose the cavities, dissected brains, a cancer of the tongue, some pictures of deformities, all things that his mother, were it up to her, would have thrown out, but it was the chosen science of her son, and that was enough. She resolved not to look at the pictures.

As for Flora, too green for the wiles of Terpsichore, she was shy or skittish, according to her mother. And that was the least of it. She would get bored quickly, and if she could not go home right away, she would feel ill the rest of the evening. Note that, being on an island, the sea would be all around; but if she consoled herself with the hope of looking out at it, she would find that the dark night would steal her consolation. What a multitude of factors in life, reader! Some things are born from others, bump into each other, repel each other, are confused with one another, and lose each other, and time marches on without losing itself.

But where would Flora's tedium come from, if it came? With Pedro at the ball, it would not. He was, as you know, one of the two who cared for her. Except if she principally cared for the one who was in São Paulo. A dubious conclusion, since it is not certain that she preferred one more than the other. If we have already seen her talk to both with the same sympathy, which she did for Pedro now in Paulo's absence, and which she would do for

Paulo in Pedro's absence, there will undoubtedly be a reader who will presume a third possibility. A third one would explain everything, a third who did not go to the ball, some poor student, friendless and coatless with only his green, warm heart. Well, not even this, curious reader, not a third, not a fourth, not a fifth, no one else. A strange girl, as her mother called her.

No matter, the strange girl went to the ball on the Ilha Fiscal with her mother and father. So did Natividade, her husband, and Pedro, so did Aires, and all the other people invited to the great party. It was a beautiful idea of the government, reader. Inside and out, from the sea to the land, it was a Venetian dream. All of that society lived a few sumptuous hours, new for some, bringing back tender memories for others, and the future to all. Or at least, for our friend Natividade and for the conservative Batista.

She was considering the destiny of her sons—things of the future! Pedro, as minister, could inaugurate the twentieth century and the third reign. Natividade imagined another, greater ball on that same island. She arranged the decorations, saw the people and the dances, a magnificent ball that would go down in history. She would also be there, seated in a corner, her years resting lightly on her, once she saw the greatness and prosperity of her sons. That is how she would focus her eyes ahead through time, spending in the present her future happiness, in case she should die before the prophecies came true. It was the same sensation given her now by that basket of lights in the middle of the dark, tranquil sea.

Batista's imagination did not go as far as Natividade's. I mean to say that it did not go all the way to the end of the century, God knows if it even went to the end of the year. To the sound of the music, surrounded by elegance, he heard some local Rio de Janeiro witches, who resembled the Scottish ones, at least, in the words that were analogous to those that greeted Macbeth: "Hail, Batista, ex-governor of the province!" "Hail, Batista, next governor of the province!" "Hail, Batista, one day you will be minister!" The language of these prophecies was liberal, without a shadow of solecism. It is true that he felt guilty listening to them and struggled to translate them back into the old conservative idiom, but he lacked dictionaries. The first word still carried the old accent: "Hail, Batista, ex-governor of the province!" But the second and last were both in that other liberal language, which always had seemed to him to be some language of the blacks. Finally, his wife, like Lady Macbeth, said in her eyes what the latter said with her mouth, that is, that she already felt within her those future events. The same message was repeated to him the next morning, at home. Batista, trying to suppress a smile, disbelieved the witches, but his memory stored the words from the island: "Hail, Batista, next governor to be!" To which he answered with a sigh, "No, no, daughters of the Devil!"

To the contrary of what was said before, Flora did not get bored on the island. I supposed wrongly, and correct myself in time. She could have gotten bored for the reasons already stated and others that I spared the hurried reader; but truthfully, she spent the night well. The novelty of the party, the surrounding sea, the ships lost in the shadows, the city on the horizon with its gas lanterns, high and low, on the beaches and mountains, these were new sights that enchanted her during those fleeting hours.

She did not lack partners, or conversation, or enjoyment, her own and that of others. All of her shared the happiness of those around her. She saw, she heard, she smiled, she forgot the rest to enjoy herself alone. She also envied the imperial princess, who would become the empress one day, with the absolute power to dismiss ministers and ladies, visitors and petitioners, and then to remain alone, in the innermost rooms of the palace, luxuriating in contemplation and music. That was how Flora defined the task of governing. These ideas came and went. Once someone said to her, as if to spur her on: "Every free soul is an empress!"

It was not another of those voices like the witches of her father or those that spoke inwardly to Natividade about her sons. No, that would be putting in too many mysterious voices, something that, besides the tedium of repetition, would belie the reality of the facts. The voice that spoke to Flora came out of the mouth of old Aires, who sat down at her feet and asked: "What are you thinking about?"

"Nothing," answered Flora.

Well, the counselor had seen something in the expression on the girl's face and he insisted on knowing what it was. Flora related as best she could the envy that the sight of the princess had given her, not to shine one day, but to flee from bright lights and the duties of office, any time she wished to become her own subject. That was when he murmured to her, as I said above, "Every free soul is an empress."

The phrase was good, sonorous, and seemed to contain the greatest sum of truth that there is on earth and in the solar system. It was worth a page of Plutarch. If a politician had heard it, he could keep it for his days of opposition to the government, when the third reign came. This is what he wrote in his *Memoirs*. With this note: "The darling creature thanked me for these six words."

X L I X

The Old Sign

E veryone returned from the island with the ball in their head, many dreamt of it, some slept badly or not at all. Aires was one of those who woke up late. It was eleven o'clock. At midday he had lunch. Then he wrote in his *Memoirs* the impressions of the evening, he noted various bare shoulders, made political observations, and ended with the words which conclude the previous chapter. He smoked, read, until he resolved to go to the Rua do Ouvidor. As he looked out of one of his front windows, he saw at the door of the teashop an unexpected figure, old Custódio, in a melancholy posture. The spectacle was so new that there he stood for a few moments. That was when the shopkeeper, raising his eyes, noticed him between the curtains, and as Aires turned to go inside, Custódio crossed the street and came into the house.

"Send him upstairs," said the counselor to the servant.

Custódio was received with the usual benevolence and a little more interest. Aires wanted to know what was making him sad.

"I came to tell your excellency about the sign."

"What sign?"

"Please come see with your own eyes," said the shop owner, asking him to come over to the window.

"I don't see anything."

"Well, that's it. I received so much advice to change the sign that I finally consented and had two servants take it down. The neighbors came to watch the work and they seemed to laugh at me. I had already spoken to a painter on the Rua da Assembléia. I did not agree on the price because he wanted to see the work first. Yesterday afternoon my clerk went to look at it, and do you know what the painter had him tell me? That the wood is old and needs to be replaced. The old wood will not take any more paint. I went running to the painter. I could not convince him to paint on the same wood. He showed me that it was splintered and riddled with termites. Well, you didn't notice that from down here. I insisted that he paint on it anyway, and he answered that he was an artist and would not do work that was going to be ruined from the start."

"Well, make a new one. New paint on old wood is worth nothing. Now you will see that it will last the rest of our lives."

"The other would have lasted too. All he had to do was brighten up the letters."

It was too late, the order was made, the wood purchased, sawed, and nailed, and the background painted so that the sign could be painted over it. Custódio did not say that the artist had asked him about the color of the letters, whether they should be red, or yellow, or green on white or vice-versa, and that he, cautiously, had inquired about the price of each color in order to choose the cheapest. It does not matter which they were.

Whatever the colors, it was new paint, new boards, a renovation that he, more out of economy than out of affection, did not want to do. But affection was worth a lot. Now that he was going to exchange the sign, he felt he had lost a part of his body, something that others in the same or another line of business would not understand, such is the pleasure that they find in face-lifting and thus making their clientele grow. Different natures. Aires was thinking about writing a Philosophy of Signs, in which he would put this and other observations, but he never began the work.

"Your Excellency must forgive me the inconvenience I have given you, coming to tell you this, but you have always been so good to me, spoken to me with such friendship, that I dared. Please forgive me?"

"Of course, my good man."

"While Your Excellency approves the renovation of the sign, you will feel with me the loss of the other, my old friend, who never left me, and that I, on the nights of festivals such as St. Sebastian, would illuminate so all could see. Your Excellency, when you retired, found it in the same place you left it when you received your appointment. And I had the strength to separate myself from it!"

"All right, go on. Now get the new one, and you will see how soon you will become friends."

Custódio left bowing, as was his custom, and he hobbled down the stairs. In front of the teashop he paused for a moment to look at the place where the old sign had been. He really did miss it.

Evaristo's Inkwell

"This case proves that one can love anything well, even a piece of old wood. Believe me, it was not just the expense that he naturally felt, it was also that he longed for the old sign. Nobody lets go of such an intimate object, which becomes an integral part of your house and your skin, because the sign was never taken down even for one day. Custódio never had a chance to notice it was rotten. It lived there, like the doors and the wall."

It was dinner time, in Botafogo. Just four people, the two sisters, Santos, and Aires. Pedro had gone to dine in São Clemente, with the Batista family.

Dona Perpétua approved the sentiments of the teashop owner. She cited, apropos, the case of Evaristo da Veiga's inkwell. The sister smiled at her husband and he at her, as if they were saying: "here it comes!" It was an inkwell that had served the famous journalist of the first reign and the regency, a simple artifact, made of clay, just like the inkwells that plain folks bought in the stationery stores of that and this day. Dona Perpétua's father-in-law, who had given it to her as a remembrance, had one just like it in age, size, and shape.

"It went from hand to hand and ended up in mine. It is not like the inkwells of brother Agostinho or Natividade, which are luxurious, but it has great value to me."

"Without doubt," said Aires, "historical and political value."

"My father-in-law said that out of it had come the great political articles in the *Aurora*. To tell you the truth, I had never read those articles, but my father-in-law was a man of truth. He knew Evaristo's life from having heard it from others, and he praised him to the skies."

Natividade tried to divert the conversation to the ball of the evening before. They had already talked about it, but she did not find another distraction. Meanwhile, the inkwell stayed around a while longer. It was not just one of Dona Perpétua's knicknacks, a family relic, it was also one of her ideas. She promised to show it to the counselor. He promised to look at it with pleasure. He confessed that he revered the objects used by great men. Finally, dinner was over, and they went into the parlor. Aires, talking about the bay: "Now here is a work of art that is older than Evaristo's inkwell and Custódio's sign and nevertheless seems younger, isn't that true, Dona Perpétua? The night is clear and warm; it could be dark and cold, the effect would be the same. The bay does not change. Perhaps men one day will fill it in with earth and stones to build houses on it, a new neighborhood, with a great track for horse races. Everything is possible under the sun and the moon. Our happiness, Baron, is to die first."

"Don't speak of death, counselor."

"Death is an hypothesis," countered Aires, "perhaps a legend. Nobody dies of good digestion, and your cigars are delicious."

"These are new. Are they good?"

"Delicious."

Santos appreciated the praise. He perceived it as intended directly for his person, his merits, his name, his position in society, his house, his country cottage, his bank, and his vests. That is perhaps an exaggeration. It would be an emphatic way of explaining the strength of his attachment to his cigars. To him they were worth the sign and the inkwell, with the difference that these only signified affection and veneration, and the cigars, superior because of their aroma and price, were also a miracle, because they were reproduced every day.

Such were the suspicions floating in Aires's brain, while he looked benignly at his host. Aires could not deny to himself the aversion the man produced in him. He did not harbor any ill feelings toward him, certainly; he could even wish him well, if there were a wall between them. It was the person, the sensations, the pronouncements, the gestures, the laugh, the entire soul that made him ill.

L I

Here Present

A round nine o'clock or just afterward, Pedro arrived with the Batistas and Flora.

"We came to bring your boy home," said Batista to Natividade.

"Thank you, sir," said Santos, "but he is no longer of the age to lose himself in the streets and if he does, we know where to find him," he added, smiling.

Natividade did not like the joke, since it was about her son and right in front of her. It was perhaps an excess of modesty. There is much excess of that sort, and the proper thing is to forgive it. There are also opposite excesses, facile condescensions, people who enter with pleasure into the exchange of libertine allusions. They should also be forgiven. In sum, all pardon goes to heaven. Forgive each other, that is the law of the Gospel.

He, the young man, heard nothing. He interrupted the conversation he was having with Flora, and once a few words were exchanged, the two went off to a corner to pick up the thread of their conversation. Aires noticed their attitude. Nobody else paid attention to them. After all, their conversation was in murmurs; nobody could hear them. She listened, he spoke; then it was the opposite, she spoke and he listened, so absorbed that they appeared not to notice anybody, but they did. They had the sixth sense of conspirators and lovers. It is possible they spoke of love; but it is certain they were conspiring. As far as what they were conspiring, you will know it soon, in the next chapter. Even Aires discovered nothing, as much as he wanted to feast his eyes on that dialogue of mysteries. He persuaded himself that it was not serious, because they smiled frequently. But it could be intimate, hidden, personal, and perhaps strange. Suppose it was a string of anecdotes or a long story, something to do with others? Even so, it could have to do with them alone, because there are states of the soul in which the subject of the narration is insignificant, and the pleasure of doing it and hearing it is everything. It could also be that.

See, however, how nature guides the smallest and biggest things, especially if fortune assists her. The conversation which appeared to be so sweet began with an upset. The cause was a letter from Paulo, written to his brother, and which he decided to show to Flora, saying that he had also shown it to his mother, and his mother had gotten very angry.

"At you?"

"At Paulo."

"But what did the letter say?"

Pedro read her the principal point, which took up practically the entire letter. It was about the military affair. The "military affair" had started, a conflict between generals and ministers, and Paulo's language was against the ministers.

"But why did you go and show the letter to your mother?"

"Mother wanted to know what he had written me."

"And your mother got angry, there it is. She may reprimand him."

"All the better. Paulo needs to be reprimanded. But tell me, why do you always defend my brother?"

"So that I also have the right to defend you."

"So he has spoken badly of me?"

Flora wanted to say yes, then no, and finally she remained silent. She changed the subject, asking why they did not get along. Pedro denied that they got along badly. On the contrary, they went well. They might not have the same opinions, and they might have the same likes . . . From that to saying that both loved her was a comma; Pedro placed the period on the sentence. That sly one was also timid. Later he understood that by remaining silent he had done better, and he applauded himself for the choice. But that was false, he had chosen nothing. I do not say this to discredit him. Yes, because fear often makes the right choices, and it is appropriate to leave this reflection here.

Anger flared up. Flora did not reply further, and were it up to her she would not have had dinner, such was her pity for the other. Fortunately, the other was the one present, the same present eyes, the same present hands, the same present words. It was not long before the anger fled from grace, tenderness, and adoration. Blessed are those who are present, for they shall be rewarded.

LII

A Secret

Here, now, is what the conspiracy was about. It was on the walk from São Clemente that Pedro, having spent most of the evening on the letter and the dinner, could reveal a secret to the young lady.

"Aunty said at home that Dona Cláudia had told her in confidence—don't say anything—that your father is going to be appointed governor of a province."

"I don't know anything about this, but I don't believe it, because Daddy is a conservative."

"Dona Cláudia told Aunty that he is a liberal, almost a radical. It seems that the governorship is a sure thing. She asked for secrecy, and Aunty, when she told us, also asked us to keep it a secret. I also ask you not to say anything, but it's true."

"True, how? Daddy does not associate with liberals. You don't know how conservative my father is. If he defends the liberals, it's because he is tolerant."

"If it were the province of Rio de Janeiro, I would like it, because it would not be necessary to live in Praia Grande but if it was, the trip would only be a half hour, and I could go there every day."

"Would you?"

"Let's bet on it."

Flora, after a moment: "Why, if there is no governorship?"

"Suppose there is."

"That is supposing a lot, that there is a governorship and that it is Rio de Janeiro. No, no, there is nothing."

"Then suppose the half of it. There is a governorship and it is Mato Grosso."

Flora felt a chill. Without admitting the possibility of an appointment, she trembled at hearing the name of the province. Pedro also named Amazonas, Pará, Piaui . . . It was infinite, especially if her father were a good administrator, he would not return so soon. Already the young lady resisted the idea less, thought it possible and abominable, but she said this to herself, in her heart. Suddenly, Pedro said, almost halting his steps: "If he goes, I'll ask the government for the post of secretary and I will go too."

The intermittent light of the shops, reflecting on the face of the young lady while they walked under them, helped the street lamps and showed the emotion of that promise. Flora's heart must have been beating fast. Shortly, however, she began to think of something else. Natividade would never consent. And that a student . . . It could not be. She imagined a scandal. That he would run away, book passage, go after her . . .

All of this was seen or thought in silence. Flora did not question herself about thinking so much and so daringly. It was like the weight of her body, which she did not feel. She walked, she thought, just as she breathed. She did not calculate even the time she spent in imagining and undoing ideas. That this gave her more pleasure than displeasure, is certain. Next to her, Pedro walked with care, with his eyes on his feet and his feet in the clouds. He did not know what to say in the middle of such a long silence. Nevertheless, he could see only one solution. He no longer thought about the governorship of Rio. He wanted to be with her in the most remote part of the empire, without his brother. The hope of exiling themselves thus from Paulo started to sprout in Pedro's soul. Yes, Paulo would not go. His mother would not allow herself to remain alone. To lose one son would be enough; not both.

To whomever this monologue might seem egotistical, I ask on behalf of the souls of his parents and friends, who are in heaven, and ask that you consider the causes well. Consider the state of mind of the young man, the closeness of the young woman, the roots and flowers of passion, Pedro's age, the evils of the earth, the good of the same earth. Consider, too, the will of heaven, which watches over all creatures who love each other, except if just one loves the other, because then heaven is an abyss of iniquities, and this image is meaningless. Consider it all, friend. Let me go on telling badly just what happened in that short transit between the two houses. When they arrived, they were again conversing aloud.

Above, as you saw, they continued to talk, until the subject of the governorship arose again. Flora noticed then the cautious insistence with which Aires looked at them, as if he were trying to guess the subject of the conversation. She was sorry that he was not there too, listening and talking with them, and finally promising to do something for her. Aires could, yes—he was her friend and everyone held him in high esteem. He could intervene and destroy the project of the governorship.

Without knowing or wanting to know, she may have said just this with her eyes to the old diplomat. She averted her gaze, but of their own accord they repeated the monologue and perhaps asked something that Aires could not understand and which must be interesting. It could be that they reflected the anguish or whatever hurt her inside. It could be. The truth is that Aires remained curious, and as soon as Pedro left his place to answer his mother's call, he left Natividade to speak to the young woman.

Flora, already on her feet, hardly had time to exchange two words, those that cannot be interrupted without pain or at the least an itch. Aires asked if he had ever told her that he had the ability to divine.

"No, sir."

"Well, I do. And I guessed just now that you had a secret to tell me."

Flora was astonished. Not wanting to deny or confess, she answered that he had only guessed half the truth.

"The other half is?"

"The other is to ask you a favor of friendship."

"Ask."

"No, not now. We're on our way. Mother and Father are saying good-bye. Unless you can walk back to São Clemente with us?"

"With great pleasure."

L I I I

Confidences

O ne understands that was not exactly the case. It was not with greater or lesser pleasure. It was a rule of society, since Flora had asked him to, I am not sure whether discreetly. That politeness might have also been linked to some desire to learn a secret, I will not be the one to deny, nor you, not even he himself. After a few minutes, Aires felt how this little one revived in him some dead voices, barren or unborn, voices of a father. The twins had only given him that same sensation once because they were Natividade's sons. Here it was not the mother, it was Flora herself, her gestures, her speech, and perchance her fate.

"But it seems to me that this time she is hooked. She has finally made her choice," thought Aires.

Flora spoke to him of the governorship but did not ask him to keep it a secret, as others had. She confessed she did not want to leave this place, to go anywhere, and ended by declaring that all was in his hands. Only he could dissuade her father from accepting the governorship. Aires thought this request so absurd that he almost laughed, but he contained himself. Flora's words were grave and sad. Aires answered softly that he could do nothing.

"You can do a lot. Everyone listens to your advice."

"But I do not give advice to anyone," said Aires. "The title of counselor is one that the emperor conferred on me, because he thought I deserved it, but it does not oblige me to give counsel. Even to him, I would give advice only if he asked for it. Imagine now if I were to go to a man's house, or call him to mine, to tell him not to become the governor of a province? What reasons would I give him?"

The young lady had no reasons, she had needs. She appealed to the talents of the ex-diplomat, that he should find a good reason. He did not even need reasons, his talk was enough, the gift God had given him to please everyone, to influence, to get what he wanted by bringing people around to his way of thinking. Aires saw she exaggerated to attract him, and that did not seem bad to him. Nevertheless, he rebutted those merits and virtues. God had given him no gift, he said, but the young woman insisted such that Aires suspended his protests and made a promise.

"I'll think about it. Tomorrow or afterward, if I find a way, I will try." That was a palliative. It was also a way of stopping the conversation, since their house was nearby. He did not count on the girl's father, who insisted on showing him, at that hour, a novelty, or rather an antiquity, a document of diplomatic value. "Come, please come in, just five minutes, counselor."

Aires sighed to himself, and bowed his head to fate. One does not fight against it, you will say. The best is to let Destiny grab you by the hair and drag you wherever it wants to lift one up or drop one down. Batista gave him no time to reflect, he was all apologies.

"Five minutes and you will be free of me, but you will see that I will repay your sacrifice."

The office was small. A few good books, formal furniture, and a portrait of Batista in the uniform of governor, an almanac on the table, a map on the wall, a few souvenirs from his term as governor of the province. While Aires looked around, Batista went in search of the document. He opened a drawer, took out a folder, opened it, and took out the document which was not alone, but with others. It was immediately recognizable because it was on old, yellow paper, parts of it torn. It was a letter from the count of Oeiras, written to the minister of Portugal in Holland.

"Today is the day for antiquities," thought Aires. "The sign, the inkwell, this autograph . . ."

"The letter is important, but long," said Batista. "We cannot read it now. Do you want to take it with you?"

Batista did not give Aires time to answer. He picked up a large envelope and placed the manuscript inside it, with this note: "To my most excellent friend, Counselor Aires." While he did this, Aires scanned the spines of some of the books. Among these were two *Reports* from Batista's governorship, richly bound.

"Don't attribute that luxury to me," volunteered the ex-governor. "That was a courtesy of the secretariat of the government who had never done such a thing for anyone. They were a very distinguished staff."

He went to the bookshelf and removed one of the reports so that it could be examined more easily. Opening it, he pointed out the print job and the text. It demonstrated both the style and the prosperity of the administration. Batista limited himself to the totals. Expenditure: 1,294 *contos,* 790,000 réis. Receipts: 1,544 contos, 209,000 réis. Balance: 249 contos, 419,000 réis. Verbally, he explained the balance, which he achieved by reducing some services and a small increase in taxes. He reduced the provincial debt, which he inherited at 384 contos and left at 350. He initiated public works and important repairs. He built a bridge . . .

"The binding is worthy of the contents," said Aires, to conclude the visit.

Batista closed the book and countered that he could not go before giving him some advice.

"Everything backward," he concluded. "In the morning I take care of problems and now at night I am the one who asks for help."

That was the introit, but from the introit to the Creed is always a long step, and the main part of the Mass for him was in the Creed. Not finding the text of the missal, he showed him a seal, a golden feather pen, and a copy of the Criminal Code. The code, while old, was worth thirty new ones, not that it had a handsomer face, but it had the handwritten notes of a great jurist, so-and-so. Having spent a great part of his life overseas, the counselor hardly recognized the author of the notes, but since he heard him called great, he assumed the appropriate expression. He picked up the code carefully and read a few of the notes with veneration.

Meanwhile, Batista got his second wind. He composed a phrase with which to initiate the consultation and only waited for Aires to close the book to release it. But his guest lingered in his examination of the code. It could have been a bit of malice, but it was not. Aires had eyes with a particular characteristic, less unusual than it seems because others may possess it in a less obvious way. His eyes may not have left the page, but in truth he was able to see beyond it. Time, people, life, things past sprang from the pages of the book, and Aires could see them as they had lived and a Rio de Janeiro that was not this one, or just barely resembled it. And don't think they were just judges and convicts, but outings, streets, parties, old and dead revelers, fresh young men now rusted like himself. Batista coughed. Aires returned to himself and read some of the notes that the other must have known by heart, but they were so profound! Finally he examined the binding, found the book well-preserved, closed it, and returned it to the library shelf.

Batista did not lose a second; he went right to the subject, afraid of seeing him pick out another book.

"I confess that I have a conservative temperament."

"I also hold on to old presents."

"It isn't that. I refer to my political temperament. Really there are opinions and temperaments. A man can very well have a temperament opposed to his ideas. My ideas, if we compare them with political programs around the world, are above all liberal, and some ultraliberal. Universal suffrage, for example, for me is the cornerstone of a good representative regime. On the contrary, the liberals demanded and introduced the restricted vote. Today, I am more progressive than they. I accept what exists, for now, but before the end of the century it will be necessary to revise two or three articles of the Constitution."

Aires hid his astonishment. Invited thus at such a late hour . . . A profession of political faith . . . Batista kept on with the distinction between temperament and ideas. A few old friends, who knew of this moral and mental duality, were insisting that he accept a governorship, and he did not want to. Frankly, what did the counselor think?

"Frankly, I think you are mistaken."

"I am mistaken about what?"

"You are mistaken to refuse."

"Well, in fact I have refused nothing. There is a great effort under way, and my desire," he added with more clarity, "is that my old wise friends tell me if such a thing is correct. It does not seem so to me."

"I think it is."

"Such that, if it were you . . ."

"It couldn't be me. You know that I no longer belong to this world, and politically I never made a show. Diplomacy has the effect of separating the official from parties and leaves him so distant from them that it is impossible to give one's opinion truthfully, much less with certainty."

"But did you not say you think . . ."

"I do."

"That I can accept a governorship if they offer me one?"

"You can. One should accept a governorship."

"Well then, know all. You are the only person in society with whom I can open myself so frankly. The governorship was offered to me."

"Accept, accept."

"It is accepted."

"Already?"

"The decree will be signed on Saturday."

"Then accept my congratulations."

"Strictly speaking, the initiative did not come from the Ministry. On the contrary, the Ministry did not make up its mind until it determined whether I had actually turned an election against the liberals years ago. But as soon as they found out that I was dismissed for not persecuting them, they accepted the nomination of the political leaders, and I received this note shortly after."

The note was in his pocket, inside his wallet. Any other person, excited by the forthcoming nomination, would take time to find the note amid his papers. But Batista had the feel for texts. He took his wallet and with his fingers calmly retrieved the minister's note inviting him for a conference. In the conversation, all was agreed.

L I V

Alone at Last!

A lone at last! When Aires finally found himself on the street, alone, free, unfettered, back to his own devices, loosened from the chains of duty and consideration, he breathed deeply. He talked to himself in a monologue, which he then soon interrupted, remembering Flora. All she had not wished had happened. There went her father to a governorship, and she with him, and the recent inclination toward young Pedro would be stopped in midpath. However, he did not regret what he had said and even less what he had not said. The dice were cast. Now he could take care of other business.

L V

"Woman Is the Undoing of Man"

W hen he said good-bye, Aires had a thought which I transcribe here in case some reader might have had the same idea. The thought was the work of astonishment, and that astonishment arose from seeing how a man who had such difficulty ceding to his wife's insistence (Begone, Satan, etc.; see chapter XLVII) simply threw caution to the winds. He didn't find an explanation, nor would he have, if he hadn't learned what they told him later, that the first steps of the man's conversion had been taken by his wife. "Woman is the undoing of man," said I don't know which socialist philosopher, I think Proudhon. It was she, the widow of the governorship, who by various and secret means, arranged her second marriage. When he found out about the courtship, the banns had already been posted, and he had no choice but to consent and get married too.

Even so, he paid dearly for it. The clamor of those close to him already rang in his ears, his soul blundered ahead blindly, dizzily, but his wife was his guide and support, and in a few hours Batista saw the way clearly and stood firm.

"We are at the threshold of the third reign," reflected Dona Cláudia, "and certainly the Liberal party will not relinquish power that soon. Their men are able, the tendency of the times is to liberalism, and you . . ."

"Yes, I . . . ," sighed Batista.

Dona Cláudia did not sigh, she sang victory. Her husband's pause was the first step to acquiescence. She did not say so point blank. Nor did she reveal unbridled happiness. She spoke always the language of cold reason and righteous will. Batista, feeling himself supported, walked to the abyss and jumped into the darkness. He did so neither without grace nor with it. Since his will was borrowed, he did not lack a desire given life and soul by his wife's will. Thus the responsibility he invested himself with and ended up confessing.

Thus was Aires's conclusion, as one reads it in the *Memoirs*. It will be the reader's conclusion, too, if he cares to make conclusions. Note that here I spared him Aires's work. I did not oblige him to find out for himself what other times he had to discover. The attentive reader, truly ruminant, has four stomachs in his brain, and through them he passes the facts and deeds back and forth, until he deduces the truth, which was or seemed to be hidden.

The Blow

The next day brought the young girl Flora the big news. Saturday the decree would be signed; the governorship was in the north. Dona Cláudia did not notice her pallor or feel her cold hands, continuing to talk about the assignment and the future until Flora, wanting to sit down, almost fell. Her mother reached out to help her.

"What is it, what's the matter?"

"Nothing, Mother, it's nothing."

Her mother made her sit down.

"I got dizzy, it's all right now."

Dona Cláudia gave her a little vinegar to sniff and rubbed her wrists. Flora smiled.

"This Saturday?" she asked.

"The decree? Yes, this Saturday. But don't tell anyone for now. They are secrets of government. It is a sure thing. Finally, someone did us justice, probably the emperor. Tomorrow you will go shopping with me. Make a list of what you need."

Flora needed not to go and could only think about that. Since the decree was ready to be signed, there was no way to undo the nomination. All she could do was stay. But how? All sorts of dreams fit into a child's sleep. It wasn't easy, but it wouldn't be impossible. Flora imagined everything, and began to construct a plan. She could not take her mind off Aires, and now Natividade entered into her thoughts as well. The two of them could do it, or rather the three, if you counted the baron, and if you counted his sister-in-law, then four. Join the four to the five stars of the Southern Cross and the nine muses, the angels and archangels, virgins and martyrs . . . Join them all, and they all could accomplish that simple task of impeding Flora's departure for the provinces. Such were her vague hopes, rapid thoughts that ran through her to substitute for the sadness visible on her face, while her mother, attributing this to the effect of the vinegar, twisted the cap back on the bottle and put the bottle back into the cabinet.

"Make a list of what you need," she repeated to her daughter.
"No, Mother, I don't need anything."
"Yes, you do, I know what you need."

L V I I

The Shopping Trip

I would not write this chapter if it were really about the shopping trip, but it is not. Everything is an instrument in the hands of Life. The two left the house, one with a light step, the other melancholy, and they went to choose a quantity of items for travel and personal use. Dona Cláudia thought of the dresses for the first reception and the official visits. She also thought about what to wear on disembarking from the ship. She had an order from her husband for a few ties. The hats, however, were the principal article on the list. In Dona Cláudia's opinion it was the hat that gave the true indication of a woman's taste, of the manners and culture of a society. It was not worth accepting a governorship to wear boring hats, she said without conviction, because in her heart she thought that a governorship made everything lively.

They were in fact in the millinery, on the Rua do Ouvidor, seated, their eyes focused on objects near and far, when the true subject of this chapter appeared. It was the twin, Paulo, who had arrived by overnight train and knowing they were shopping, had gone out to find them.

"Sir!" they exclaimed.

"I arrived this morning."

Flora had risen from her seat with the excitement that the un-expected sight of Paulo had given her. He ran to them, clasped their hands, asked after their health, and acknowledged that they radiated health and joy. The impression was true. Flora now demonstrated an agitation that contrasted with her depression that sad morning and a laugh that made her gay.

"I kept up with news of you ladies which Mother gave me, and Pedro, sometimes. From you, madam, I received two letters," he said, addressing Dona Cláudia. "How is your husband?"

"Well."

"So, finally I'm here!"

And Paulo divided his eyes between the two, but the best part naturally went to the daughter. Then shortly all his attention was for her. Dona Cláudia returned her attention to the hats, and Flora, who until now had nodded her opinion, abandoned that gesture. Paulo sat in the chair that a clerk brought him and looked at the young woman. They talked about trivial things, their own or concerning others, all that was needed to retain them discreetly in contemplation of each other. Paulo had returned the same as before, the same as Pedro, except with a personal charac-teristic that she could not put her finger on, much less define. It was a mystery. Pedro had his own special way as well.

Dona Cláudia interrupted them now and then about the choice. But everything comes to an end, even choosing hats. They went on to the dresses, and Paulo, not knowing about the gover-norship, took advantage of their mission to accompany them from store to store. He told anecdotes about São Paulo without great interest to Flora. The news that she gave him about her girlfriends was more or less dispensable. Anything served the purpose of the two interlocutors. The street aided that reciprocal absorption. Peo-ple who came and went, ladies and gentlemen who stopped or did not, served as the point of departure for a digression. The digres-sions gave way to silence, and the two continued with their eyes looking into the distance and their heads held high, he more than she, because a little touch of melancholy began to rob from the face of the girl the happiness of a short while ago.

On Rua Gonçalves Dias, on the way to the Largo da Carioca, Paulo sighted two or three republican politicians from São Paulo, apparently plantation owners. Having just seen them there, he was surprised to see them here, without remembering that the last time he had seen them had been some time ago.

"Do you know them?" he asked the two.

No, they did not know them. Paulo told them the names. The mother might have asked a political question, but she noticed that something on her list was missing, and proposed they go back to buy it. That was accepted with docility by both, in spite of the veil of sadness closing over the face of the young woman. Those errands on the list already had the feel of boat tickets, the ship was on its way, they would rush to pack their bags, make arrangements, say their good-byes, check into their cabins, get seasick, and then go on to that other sea and land sickness which would kill her, for certain, Flora thought. Thus the growing silence, which Paulo could hardly overcome from time to time. And yet, she was comfortable with him and liked to listen to him tell stories, some old, some new, recollections from the time prior to his departure from here to São Paulo.

Thus they let themselves be guided by Dona Cláudia, who had almost forgotten them. In the middle of that truncated conversation, more sustained by him than by her, Paulo felt the impulse to ask her, whispering into her ear on the street, if she had thought of him, or at least dreamt of him some nights. Hearing that she had not, he would unleash his rage, and hurl insults at her. If she ran, he would run after her, until he grabbed her by the ribbons of her hat or the sleeve of her dress, and instead of strangling her, he would sweep her up into a Strauss waltz or a polka. Then he laughed at these wild thoughts, because despite the girl's melancholy, the eyes she lifted to him were those of someone who had dreamed and thought a lot about someone, and were now trying to discover if that someone were the person they were looking at. Thus it seemed to the law student. So when he turned his face, it was to repeat the experiment and to see again the eyes enlivened by the same critical and inquiring spirit. As for the time the three spent in this agitation of purchases and choices, visions and comparisons, there is no memory of it, nor need to remember. Time is properly the work of a watch, and none of them consulted the watch they wore.

L V I I I

The Reunion

Well, you have now seen how Flora received Pedro's brother; just as she would have received Paulo's brother. Both were apostles. Paulo thought her prettier than a few months before and told her so that same afternoon in São Clemente, with this familiar and cordial phrase: "Madam, you are lovelier than ever."

Flora thought the same thing, regarding the law student. She kept silent about her impression. Either her sadness or some other private sensation made her reluctant at first. She did not take long, however, to find again the twin in the twin, and for them to begin to make up for the time apart.

How you make up for the sad longing absence engenders is something that one cannot explain clearly. Longing is not something one can kill with steel or fire, rope or poison, and still it expires, sometimes to resurrect before the third day. There are those who believe that, even dead, longing is sweet, more than sweet. This point, in our case, cannot be aired, nor do I wish to develop it as I should.

Longing subsided, not entirely and not right away, but in part and so slowly that Paulo accepted the invitation to dinner. It was the day he arrived. Natividade wanted him with her at the table next to Pedro, to cement the peacemaking begun by distance. Paulo did not even bother to send word home. He let himself remain with the lovely creature, between her mother and father who had their minds on another thing, close in time and remote in space. Knowing what it was, Flora passed from pleasure to tedium, and Paulo did not understand this shift of sentiments. From time to time, seeing the mother agitated and preoccupied, but with another expression, Paulo questioned the daughter. Instead of giving an explanation, Flora put her hands over her eyes and for a few moments did not remove them. The action of the law student should have been to pull her hands away, look her in the eyes, closely, closer, and repeat the question in such a way that the eloquence of the gesture would make speech unnecessary. If he had such an idea, it did not come out into the open. Nor did she offer more than the question took to ask: "What's the matter?"

"Nothing."

"Something is the matter," he insisted, wanting to take her hand.

He did not complete the gesture, which he did not even begin. He just opened and closed his fingers, while Flora smiled to shake off her sadness and let herself return to the reunion.

L I X

The Night of the 14th

Everything was explained that evening at the Santos family home. The ex-governor of the province confessed his hopes for a new appointment. His wife affirmed the importance of the act. Thus the public announcement of the news which a little before Dona Cláudia had only spoken of in secret. Now there were no more secrets to hide.

Paulo learned everything then, and Pedro, who had been aware of some preliminaries, found out the rest. Both naturally felt the coming separation. Pain made them friends for a few moments. That is one of the advantages of that great and noble feeling. I don't remember any more who affirmed, to the contrary, that it is a shared hate that most connects two people. I think so, but I do not deny my proposition, for the reason that one thing does not contradict the other, and both can be true.

Besides, pain was still not despair. There was even a consolation for the twins. The young woman would be far away from both of them. Neither one would have the exclusive pleasure at their doorstep. There is no evil that does not bring a little good, and for this reason what is bad is useful, often indispensable, sometimes delicious. The two wanted to speak to their little friend, in private, to sound out her feelings about the separation, now certain, but neither one was able to fulfill their wish. They watched each other, that is certain. When they spoke to her, it was always together and about familiar and ordinary things. Flora's appearance did not reveal her state of mind. That could have been light, melancholy, or indifferent, it did not show on the outside. In fact, she spoke little. Her eyes did not say much, either. More than once, Pedro caught her looking at Paulo, and he sighed at the preference. But he also was the preferred one later and found consolation in this. Then Paulo was the one to gnash his teeth, figuratively. Natividade, completely absorbed in her reception, which was the last of the year, did not follow the moral agitation of the trio very closely. When she noticed them, she felt it too.

Little by little the guests left. Just a few were left, and an intimate note prevailed. When most were gone, just the family intimates were left, three or four men in a corner of the room talking and laughing at jokes and anecdotes. They were not speaking of politics, when in fact subject matter would not have been lacking. The young ladies, for the second or third time, exchanged impressions of the recent grand ball. They also spoke about music and theater, the forthcoming holidays in Petrópolis, the people who would go this year, and those who would go only in January. Natividade divided herself among all of them until, able to spend a few minutes with Aires, she confessed to him her misgivings about the love of the two boys and, at the same time, the pleasure that the prospect of a long separation from Flora gave her. The counselor did not discourage her from her fear or her hope.

"It's a blessing that Batista was nominated and will take his daughter away from here," she said.

"Certainly, but . . ."

"But what?"

"Certainly he will take her, but you may not know the girl well."

"I think she is good."

"I think so, too. Goodness, however, has nothing to do with the rest of the person. Flora is, as I said a long time ago, inexplicable. Now it is late to explain the basis for my feelings. I will tell you later. Note that I like her very much. I find a special flavor in that contrast of her opposing characteristics: at the same time so human and so removed from this world, so ethereal and so ambitious at the same time, with a hidden ambition. Please forgive these badly packaged words, and until tomorrow," he concluded, extending his hand. "Tomorrow I'll come to explain them."

"Explain them now, while the others seem to be laughing at some funny joke."

In fact, the men were laughing at some joke or riddle. Aires wanted to speak but he held his tongue and excused himself. The explanation was long and difficult and it was not urgent, he said.

"I don't know if I even understand myself, baroness, or if I am close to the truth; it may be. In any case, my good friend, until tomorrow or until Petrópolis. When do you think you will go to the mountains?"

"Toward the end of the year."

"So then we will still see each other a few times."

"Yes, and if you don't see me, I want you to see my boys and to receive them with esteem. They hold you in high regard. They do you justice. Pedro thinks you have the finest spirit, and Paulo thinks you are the backbone of our land."

"See how you raise them, teaching them to think wrongly," said Aires, smiling and making a gesture of thanks. "I, a back-bone?"

"The strongest and finest."

The last habitués of the house came to bid the hostess good-night. Ten minutes afterward, Aires said good-bye to the Santos couple.

The night was clear and calm. Aires reconstructed a part of the evening to include in his *Memoirs*. A few lines, but interesting ones, in which Flora was the principal figure.

"May the Devil decipher her, if he can. I, who am not his match, will never understand her. Yesterday she seemed to like one of them, today she liked the other. A little before the good-byes, she liked both of them. I have run into alternating and si-multaneous sentiments like this before. I myself have been one and the other thing, and I always understood myself. But that girl, that young lady . . . The fact that she is dealing with twins explains the double inclination. It could also be that some quality is lacking in one that the other has, and vice-versa, and she, be-cause she likes both, cannot choose definitively. It is fantastical, I know. Less fantastical if they, destined to be enemies, found in this creature a narrow field for hatred, but that would explain them, not her. Whatever happens, our political system is useful. The governorship of the province, by taking Flora away from here for a time, will remove the girl from the situation in which she finds herself, like Buridan's ass. When she returns the water will be drunk and the hay eaten. A decree will assist nature."

That done, Aires got into bed, mumbled an ode of his Horace and closed his eyes. This did not help him sleep. He tried then a page of his Cervantes, another from Erasmus, closed his eyes again, until he slept. He slept little. At five forty he was up again. In November, you know when daylight has arrived.

L X

The Morning of the 15th

When things like this occurred, it was Aires's custom to leave the house early for a stroll. He did not always get it right. This time he went to the Passeio Público. He arrived at seven thirty in the morning, walked through the entrance up to the terrace, and looked out at the sea. The ocean was choppy. Aires began to walk back and forth along the terrace, listening to the waves and looking over the rail from time to time to see them crash against the seawall and retreat. He liked it when the sea was like this. He thought of the waves as having a strong soul that moved them to intimidate the earth. The water, curling over itself, gave him a sensation, more than of life, of a person, who did not lack nerves and muscles and who possessed a voice with which to shout out his anger.

Finally he tired and retraced his steps, in the direction of the lake, through the tree-lined streets, and he wandered at random, reliving men and things, until he sat on a bench. He noticed that the few people there were not seated, as usual, casually looking around, reading newspapers, or yawning from a sleepless night. People were standing around, talking among themselves, and those who came by caught pieces of the conversation without knowing who the speakers were. That's how it seemed to him, at least. He heard a few loose words, Deodoro, battalions, field, Ministry, etc. Some, spoken in a loud voice, by chance reached his ears, as if trying to arouse his curiosity, as if trying to attract one more listener to the news. I do not swear it was thus, because it was long ago and the people were strangers. Aires himself, if he suspected such a thing, did not tell anyone. Nor did he try to capture the rest. On the contrary, remembering something private, he wrote a note to himself in pencil in his notebook. That was enough to make the curious disperse, not without some epithet of praise, some for the government and others for the army: he might be a friend of one or the other.

When Aires left the park he suspected something and went on to the Largo da Carioca. There was little conversation, hushed clusters of pedestrians with frightened faces, figures rushing to open way in the street, but no clear or complete news. On the Rua do Ouvidor, he discovered that the military had led a coup, heard descriptions of the assault and of the protagonists, and contradictory accounts. He returned to the Largo da Carioca, where three carriages competed for his business. He hailed one that was closest and ordered the driver to take him to Catete. He asked nothing of the driver. The driver, however, filled him in on everything and all the rest. He spoke of a revolution, of two dead ministers, one a fugitive, the rest prisoners. The emperor, apprehended in Petrópolis, was returning to the city.

Aires looked at the coachman, whose words dripped with the delicious news. This fellow was not unknown to him. He had seen his type before, without the coach, on the street or in a salon, at Mass or on board, not always a man, sometimes a woman, dressed in silks or calico. Aires wanted to know more, showed himself to be curious and interested, and ended up asking if what had been narrated had really happened. The driver said he had heard everything from a man he had brought from the Rua dos Inválidos and taken to the Largo da Glória, and who was indeed distressed, he could hardly speak, asking that the driver hurry and he would pay double. And he did.

"Maybe he was someone involved in the confusion," suggested Aires.

"It could have been, because his hat was askew, and at first I thought that he had blood on his fingers, but I looked closer and I saw it was mud. Certainly he had climbed over some wall. But thinking about it, I think it was blood. Mud is not that color. The truth is he paid double fare and rightly so, because the city is not safe and people run a great risk driving folks back and forth."

They had just arrived at Aires's door. He asked the driver to stop, paid the usual fare, and alighted. Walking up the stairs to his house, he was naturally thinking about possible events. At the top of the stairs he found his servant, who knew everything and asked if it was true.

"What is there that is not true, José? It is more than true."

"That they killed three ministers?"

"No, there is just one wounded."

"I heard there were even more, they spoke of ten dead."

"Death is a phenomenon just like life. Perhaps the dead lived. In any case, don't pray for their souls, because you are not a good Catholic, José."

L X I

Reading Xenophon

How can it be that having heard of the death of two and three ministers, Aires acknowledged only that one had been wounded, correcting the news from the servant? It can only be explained in two ways—either as a noble sentiment of pity or as the opinion that all public news grows by two-thirds, at least. Whatever the cause, the version of the wounding was the only true one. A little afterward, the stretcher bearing the wounded minister was carried down the Rua do Catete. Learning that the others were alive and well and that the emperor was expected from Petrópolis, Aires did not believe in the change of regime that he had heard about from the coach driver and from the servant José. He reduced everything to a disturbance that would end with a simple change of personnel.

"We have a new cabinet," he said to himself.

He lunched calmly, reading Xenophon. "I considered one day how many republics have been toppled by citizens who desire another kind of government, and how many monarchies and oligarchies are destroyed by the uprising of the people, and of those who climb to power, some are toppled quickly and others, if they last, are admired for being able and happy." You know the conclusion of the author, in favor of the thesis that man is difficult to govern. But soon after, the figure of Cyrus demolishes that conclusion, showing a single man who reigned over millions of others, subjects who not only feared him but even fought to do his bidding. All of this in Greek, and with such pause, that he concluded his lunch without finishing the first chapter.

"Stop on 'D'"

"**B**ut His Excellency is having lunch," said the servant on the stair landing, to someone who asked to speak to the counselor.

That was not true; Aires had just finished lunch. But the servant knew that his master liked to enjoy a cigar after lunch without interruption. Now he was on the sofa, and he heard the dialogue on the landing. The person insisted on having a word.

"That is impossible."

"I'll wait. As soon as His Excellency is finished . . ."

"It would be better to come back later. Don't you live across the street? Well come back in an hour or two."

The person was Custódio and he went home, but the old diplomat, hearing who it was, did not wait to finish his cigar. He sent for him to come over. Custódio ran back, climbed the stairs, and came in with a worried look on his face.

"What's going on, Mr. Custódio?" asked Aires. "Are you leading revolutions?"

"I, sir? Oh, sir! If Your Excellency only knew!"

"If I knew what?"

Custódio explained himself. Well, let us summarize the explanation.

The evening before, having to go downtown, Custódio went to the Rua da Assembléia, where his sign was being painted. It was already late. The painter had stopped work. Only a few letters had been painted, the word *Confeitaria*—and the letter "d." The remaining letters of the name of the teashop were traced in chalk. The letter "o" and the word *Império* were only outlined in chalk. He liked the paint and the color, he reconciled himself to the shape of the sign, and he barely forgave himself the expense. He urged haste. He wanted the sign inaugurated on Sunday.

Upon waking the next morning, he was not aware of what had happened in the city, but little by little the news reached him. He saw a few battalions march by, and he believed those who claimed a revolution had occurred and the vague references to a republic. At first, in his shock, he forgot the sign. When he remembered it, he saw it would be necessary to put a hold on the painting. He dashed off a note, and sent a clerk over to the painter. The note only said: "Stop at the 'd.'" Indeed, it was not necessary to paint the rest, which would be wasted, nor to lose the beginning, which could be used. There was always some word that could take the place of the remaining letters. "Stop at the 'd.'"

When the messenger returned, he brought back the news that the sign was ready.

"Did you see that it was finished?"

"I saw it, boss."

"Did it have the old name on it?"

"Yes, sir, it did: "Confeitaria do Império," "Teashop of the Empire."

Custódio pulled on an alpaca jacket and flew to the Rua da Assembléia. There was the sign, in fact, covered with a piece of calico. A few boys who had seen it in passing by on the street had wanted to smash it. The painter, after defending it with good words, thought it better to cover it. Lifting the cloth, Custódio read: "Confeitaria do Império." It was the old name, the very one, the famous one, but now it meant ruin. He could not keep the sign another day, even if in a dark alley, much less on the Rua do Catete.

"You are going to have to redo this sign," he said.

"I don't understand. That is, first pay me what you owe me. Then I will paint something else."

"But what do you lose by changing the last word for another? The first one can stay, and even the 'd.' Didn't you read my note?"

"It came too late."

"And why did you paint it, after such serious events?"

"You were in a hurry, and I got up at five thirty this morning to serve you. When they gave me the news, the sign was done. Didn't you tell me you wanted to hang it on Sunday? I had to put a lot of drying agent in the paint, I spent time and effort."

Custódio wanted to reject the work, but the painter threatened to put the number of the teashop and the name of the owner on the sign and expose him that way, so the revolutionaries would break his windows on Catete. There was no solution except to capitulate. Let it wait; he would think about the replacement. In any case, he asked for a discount on the price. He got the promise of a discount and returned home. On the way, he thought of what he was losing by changing the name. Such a famous house, known for years and years! May the Devil take the revolution! What name could he use now? That is when he thought of his neighbor Aires and ran to seek his counsel.

L X I I I

A New Sign

Having recounted what had just transpired, Custódio confessed everything he was losing with the name and the expense, the damage that keeping the name of the house would do, the impossibility of finding another, an abyss, in sum. He did not know what he was looking for. He lacked resourcefulness and peace of mind. If he could, he would sell the teashop. And after all, what did he have to do with politics? He was a simple merchant and baker, esteemed, sought out by his clientele, respected and principally respectful of public order . . .

"But what is the matter?" asked Aires.

"The republic has been proclaimed."

"Is there a government?"

"I think so, but please tell me, Your Excellency, have you ever heard anyone accuse me of attacking the government? Nobody. Nevertheless . . . a fate! Come to my aid, Excellency. Help me out of this predicament. The sign is ready, the name all painted, 'Confeitaria do Império,' the paint is bright and beautiful. The painter insists I pay him for his work, before he will make another. If the job had not been already finished, I would change the name, whatever it cost, but do I have to lose the money I have already spent? Your Excellency, do you believe if I keep the name 'Império' they will break my windows?"

"That I don't know."

"Really, there is no reason. It is the name of the house, the name it has had for thirty years, nobody knows it by any other name . . ."

"But you can call it 'Confeitaria da República.'"

"That occurred to me along the way, but I also remembered that if in one or two months there is a counter-revolution, I'd be back where I am now, and I would lose money again."

"You are right. Sit down."

"I'm all right."

"Sit down and smoke a cigar."

Custódio refused the cigar, he did not smoke. He accepted the chair. They were in the study, in which a few objects would have interested him, were it not for his troubled spirits. He continued to implore the help of his neighbor. His Excellency, with the great intelligence that God had given him, could save him. Aires proposed a compromise, a title that would fit both scenarios, "Confeitaria do Governo," "Teashop of the Government."

"It will serve equally well for one regime as for the other."

"I don't say no, and were it not for the lost expense. . . . There is, however, a reason against it. Your Excellency knows that no government lacks an opposition. And the oppositions, when they come down the street, could give me a hard time, imagine that I am challenging them, and break up my sign. Meanwhile, what I want is the respect of all."

Aires understood very well that terror went hand in hand with avarice. Certainly, his neighbor did not want disturbances at his door, or gratuitous harassment, or hatred from anyone, no matter who they were. But he was no less distressed by the expense that he would have from time to time if he did not find a definitive name, popular and impartial. Losing the one he had, he had already lost his fame, aside from losing the paint job and having to pay more money. Nobody would buy a condemned sign. It was already bad enough to have his shop listed in *Laemmert's Almanac*, where some busybody could read it and go with others to punish him for what had been published there since the beginning of the year.

"Not that," interrupted Aires. "You will not recall an edition of the almanac."

And after a few moments: "Look, I'll give you an idea that might be used, and if you don't think it's good, I have another one which might work and it will be the last. But I think either one will work. Leave the sign painted the way it is, and under the title have these words written, which will explain the name: 'Founded in 1860.' Wasn't it in 1860 that you opened the house?"

"It was," replied Custódio.

"Well . . ."

Custódio thought about it. One could not tell if he thought yes or no. Speechless, his mouth half open, he did not look at the diplomat, or at the floor, the walls, or furniture, but out into the air. Since Aires insisted, he woke up and confessed that this was a good idea. Really, he could keep the name and remove what was seditious about it, which was enhanced by the freshness of the paint. Meanwhile, the other idea could be just as good or better, and he wanted to compare the two.

"The other idea does not have the advantage of stating the date the house was founded, it only has that of defining the name, which will be the same, in a manner neutral to the regime. Leave the word, 'Império' and add underneath, in the middle, these two which don't need to be big letters: 'das leis,' 'of the Law.' Look, it would be this way," concluded Aires, sitting at his desk and writing on a piece of paper what he was saying.

Custódio read, reread, and thought the idea was useful. Yes, it didn't seem bad. He only saw one problem. Since the letters underneath were smaller, they could not be read as quickly and clearly as those above, which would be noticed by most who passed by. Thus if a politician or some personal enemy did not quickly grasp the subtitle . . . The first idea had the same problem and this one besides: it would seem that the pastry chef, by emphasizing the date of opening the shop, boasted about being old. Who knows if this was not worse than nothing?

"Everything is worse than nothing."

"We'll see."

Aires found another name, the name of the street, "Confeitaria do Catete," not realizing that, since there was another teashop on the street, it would seem to attribute exclusivity to Custódio for the local designation. When the neighbor pointed this out to him, Aires thought that was fair, and he appreciated the man's delicate sensitivity. But soon afterward, he discovered that what made Custódio uncomfortable was the idea that the name would be shared by the two establishments. Many people would not pay attention to the written name and would buy at the first shop they came to, so that not only would he alone pay for the sign painting, but on top of that he would lose business. Realizing this, Aires did not lose his admiration for a man who, in the midst of such tribulation, could calculate the bad fruits of a mistake. He said to him then that the best would be to pay for the sign he had ordered and not put anything else on it, unless he wanted to use his own name, "Confeitaria do Custódio." Many people certainly did not know the house by any other name. A name, the very name of the owner, did not have any political or historical significance, not hate or love, nothing that would call the attention of either regime and consequently put into peril his Santa Clara tarts, much less the life of the proprietor and of the employees. Why not adopt this solution? He would spend something to exchange one name for another, Custódio instead of Império, but revolutions always bring expense.

"Yes, I'll think about it, Excellency. Perhaps it would be good to wait one or two days, to see how things turn out," said Custódio, thanking him.

He bowed, backed away, and left. Aires went to the window to see him cross the street. He imagined that he would take with him from the house of the retired minister an inner glow that would make him forget for a few moments the crisis of the sign.

Not everything in life is expenses, and the glory of social relations can soften the trials of this world. He did not get it right this time. Custódio crossed the street without stopping or looking back and entered the teashop with all of his despair.

L X I V

Peace!

That, in the midst of such grave events, Aires would have enough leisure and clarity to imagine such a discovery in his neighbor can only be explained by the skepticism with which he took the news. Custódio's distress did not concern him. He had seen many false rumors be born and die. One of his maxims was that man lives to spread the first street story that comes along, and that it is possible to make one hundred people together or separately believe anything. Only at two in the afternoon, when Santos arrived at his house, did he believe in the fall of the empire.

"It's true, counselor, I saw the troops coming down the Rua do Ouvidor, I heard the cries for the republic. The stores are closed and the banks too, and the worst is if they do not open again, and we fall into public disorder. It is a disaster."

Aires wanted to calm him. Nothing would change. It was possible that the regime would, but one also changes clothes without changing skin. Commerce is necessary. The banks are indispensable. On Saturday, or at most on Monday, everything would return to the way it was the day before, except the Constitution.

"I don't know, I am afraid, counselor."

"Don't be afraid. Is the baroness aware of what has happened?"

"When I left home, she did not know, but now it is probable."

"Well, go back and comfort her. She is certainly upset."

Santos was worried about shootings. For example, what if they shot the emperor, and with him people of society? He remembered that the French Terror—Aires took the Terror out of his head. Opportunity makes the revolution, he said, without intending to coin a phrase, but he liked the ring of it. Then he brought up the soft nature of the people. The people would change governments without touching persons. There would be gestures of generosity. To prove what he said, he told of a case that an old friend had told him about, Marshal Beaurepaire Rohan. It was in the time of the regency. The young emperor had gone to the São Pedro de Alcântara Theater. At the end of the show, his friend, then a young man, heard a loud noise next to the São Francisco church, and he ran to see what it was. He spoke to a man who was bellowing with indignation and learned that the emperor's coachman had not taken off his hat at the moment that the emperor had returned to enter the door to his carriage. The man added: "I am a *ré.* . . ." At that time the republicans, for brevity, were called thus. "I am a ré. But I will not consent that they show lack of respect to that boy!"

No change in Santos's expression indicated that he appreciated or understood that anonymous gesture. On the contrary, his entire being seemed to be given over to the present, to the moment, to the suspension of commerce, to the closed banks, to fear of a total paralysis of business for an indeterminate amount of time. He crossed and recrossed his legs. Finally, he arose and sighed.

"So, what do you think?"

"Go home and rest."

Santos accepted the advice, but there is a long way from acceptance to compliance, and his appearance was very different from the state of his heart. His heart was pounding. His mind's eye saw everything crumble in front of him. He wanted to say good-bye, but he made two or three attempts before setting foot outside the study and walking to the stairs. He insisted on certainty. When he had seen and heard the republic, then maybe . . . In any case, peace was necessary and would there be peace? Aires was inclined to think so, and again invited him to take a rest.

"Good-bye," he concluded.

"Why don't you come have dinner with us?"

"I have a dinner engagement with a friend at the Hotel dos Estrangeiros. Later, perhaps, or tomorrow. Go, go on and comfort the baroness and the boys. Will the boys be all right? They will fight, for sure. Well, go keep them in line."

"You could help me with that. Come over tonight."

"Maybe. If I can, I will. Tomorrow certainly."

Santos left. His carriage was waiting, and he entered and went on to Botafogo. He did not bring peace with him, and he could not give it to his wife, or to his sister-in-law, or to his children. He wanted to get home, because he was nervous about the streets, but he also wanted to stay on the street, because he did not know what words or advice to give to his own. The space in the carriage was small and enough for one man; but after all he could not stay there all afternoon. For the rest, the streets were quiet. He saw people gathered at storefronts. At the Largo do Machado he saw someone laughing, another one quiet, there was excitement but not exactly fear.

LXV

Between the Sons

W hen Santos arrived home, Natividade was restless, not having received exact and definitive word of the events. She did not know about the republic. She had not heard from her husband or her sons. Her husband had left before the first rumors started to circulate, and her sons set off to do the same thing, once news started to reach them. Their mother's first gesture was to prevent them from leaving, but she could not, it was too late. Not able to retain them, she latched on to the Virgin Mary, asking her to save them, and she waited. Her sister did the same. It was close to midday. That was when the minutes seemed like centuries.

The anxiety of the mother was naturally higher than that of the aunt. Natividade saw time move with iron shackles on its feet. There was no excitement that would attach wings to those long hours on the house clock or on the watches they wore at their waists, hers and her sister's. Time limped along on both legs. Finally they heard the carriage wheels on the sand in the driveway. It was Santos.

Natividade ran to the front steps. Santos came up and their hands reached out and clasped each other. A long life together ends up turning tenderness into a grave and spiritual act. Nevertheless, it seemed that the husband's gesture was not original but secondary, the child of, or imitation of, his wife's. It could be that the string of sensibility was less vibrant on his lyre than on hers, since many years ago, that other gesture in the carriage when they returned from the Mass at São Domingos, do you remember? About this I wrote some lines that would not be bad if I finished, but I retreat in time and scratch them out. It is not worth while to go scrounging around after crossed-out words. Better to delete them.

Let the four clasped hands suffice for now. Natividade asked about her sons. Santos thought she should not be afraid. There was nothing, everything seemed to be the very way it was the day before, the streets calm, the faces quiet. Blood would not flow, commerce would continue. All of Aires's confidence now flowed in him, with the same freshness and the same style.

The sons arrived late, separately, Pedro earlier than Paulo. The melancholy of one fit the soul of the house, the happiness of the other clashed with it, but both were so deep that, in spite of the expansiveness of the second, there was no reprisal or fight. At dinner, they spoke little. Paulo related events lovingly. He had spoken with some fellow party members and heard what had happened last night and in the morning, the march and the rendezvous of the battalions on the field, the words of Ouro Preto to Field Marshal Floriano, his reply, the proclamation of the republic. The family listened and asked questions, did not argue, and this moderation contrasted with Paulo's enthusiasm. Pedro's silence was like a challenge. Paulo did not know that his own mother had begged his brother with many kisses to remain silent, and that was a motive that went with the tightness in the boy's heart.

Paulo's heart, on the contrary, was free, it let his blood flow like happiness. His republican sentiments, in which his principles were embedded, lived there strong and hot, and they hardly let him see Pedro's discouragement and the subdued mood of the rest of his family. At the end of the dinner he drank to the republic, but quietly, without ostentation, just looking at the ceiling and raising his glass a little more than usual. Nobody replied with another gesture or word.

Certainly young Pedro wanted to pronounce some phrase of compassion for the imperial regime and the Bragança family, but his mother did not take her eyes off him, as if imposing or begging for silence. Besides, he did not believe anything had changed, despite decrees and proclamations. Pedro imagined that all could remain as before, just altering the people in government. It would take little, he said softly to his mother as they left the table, all the emperor has to do is talk to Deodoro.

Paulo left, right after dinner, promising to return early. His mother, fearful that he would get into trouble, did not want him to go out; but another fear made her consent, and that was that the two brothers would finally fight. Thus one fear overcame the other, and people end up giving what they deny. It is no less certain that she reasoned for a few minutes before deciding, the same way that I wrote a page before the one I am about to write now. But both of us, Natividade and I, ended up letting events happen, without opposition from her and without commentary from me.

LXVI

The Club and the Spade

Friends of the household came to visit, bringing news and rumors. They varied little, and generally there was no sure opinion about the result. Nobody knew if the victory of the movement was a good or an evil; they just knew it was a fact. Thus the naiveté with which somebody proposed the usual game of whist, and the good will of others in accepting the proposal. Santos, while he declared that he would not play, ordered the cards and the chips brought out, but others were of the opinion that a player was missing, and without him it would not be the same. He wanted to resist. It would not be fitting that on the very day the monarchy had fallen or would fall, he give himself to recreation. He did not think this aloud or softly, but to himself, and perhaps he read it in his wife's face. He could find a pretext to resist if he looked for one, but his friends and the cards would not let him look for anything. Santos ended up accepting. Probably that was his inner leaning. There are many that need to be enticed out here as a favor or a personal concession. In fact, the ace of clubs and the ace of spades did their job that night, like the butterflies and the rats, the winds and the waves, the brilliance of the stars and the sleep of the citizens.

L X V I I

The Whole Night

L eaving his house, Paulo went to the home of a friend, and the two began to seek others of the same age and same intimacy. They went to the newspaper offices, to the barracks at the Campo, and spent some time in front of Deodoro's house. They enjoyed seeing the soldiers, on foot or on horseback, they asked their permission to pass, spoke to them, and offered them cigarettes. It was the soldiers' only concession. None of them offered to tell what had happened and not all knew anything.

It did not matter, they were full of themselves. Paulo was the most enthusiastic and the most assured. For the others, youth was what mattered, and that is a doctrine, but Santos's son had fresh in his mind all the ideas of the new regime, and he had still others that were not yet accepted. He would fight for them. He even had the desire to find someone on the street who would let out a shout, which would now be seditious, and smash his head with his cane. Note that he had forgotten or lost his cane. He didn't notice. If the opportunity arose, he would use his bare hands.

He proposed singing the *Marseillaise*. The others did not want to go so far, not out of fear but because they were tired. Paulo, who resisted fatigue more than they did, suggested they wait for dawn.

"Let's wait for sunrise on top of a hill or on Flamengo beach. We will have time to sleep tomorrow."

"I can't," said one.

The others repeated the refusal and agreed to return to their homes. It was about two o'clock. Paulo accompanied all of them, and only after seeing the last one home did he return alone to Botafogo.

When he entered, he found his mother waiting for him, restless and regretting having let him go out. Paulo could not find an excuse and scolded his mother for not sleeping and waiting for him. Natividade confessed she could not rest until she knew he was home safe and sound. They spoke in low voices and said little; having kissed each other before, they kissed again and said good-night.

"Look," said Natividade, "if you find Pedro awake, don't tell him or ask him anything. Sleep, and tomorrow we will know everything and more of what has gone on tonight."

Paulo entered his room on tiptoe. It was still that vast room in which the twins had fought over the two old portraits of Robespierre and Louis XIV. Now there was more than the portraits, a revolution just a few hours old and a new government. Obeying his mother's advice, Paulo did not try to see if Pedro was asleep, though he suspected that he was not. In fact, he was not. Pedro saw Paulo's caution and also followed his mother's counsel. He pretended to see nothing. The advice went that far; but a little gloating prompted Paulo to mouth to himself the first verse of the *Marseillaise* that his friends had refused to sing outside.

Allons, enfants de la patrie,
La jour de gloire est arrivé!

Pedro recognized the song and concluded that the intention of the other was to irritate him. It was not, but it could have been. He vacillated between a reply and silence until a fantastic idea

crossed his mind, to intone softly the second part of the verse—
"*Entendez-vous dans vos campagnes*"—which refers to foreign
troops, but to change the verse from its historical meaning to al-
lude to national troops. It was a vague kind of vengeance, the idea
passed quickly. Pedro contented himself with simulating the
supreme indifference of sleep. Paulo did not finish the song. He
quickly got undressed without taking his thoughts off the victory
of his political dreams. He did not get into bed immediately. He
went first to his brother's to see if he was asleep. Pedro breathed
so naturally, as if he had lost nothing. He had an impulse to wake
him, scream at him that he had lost everything, if in fact the defeated institution was anything at all. He recoiled in time and
climbed into the sheets.

Neither one slept. While sleep did not arrive, they thought of
the events of the day, both shocked at how quickly and easily they
went. Then they mulled over what might happen the next day
and the possible repercussions of the events. Don't be surprised
that they did not arrive at the same conclusions.

"How the devil did they do it without anybody catching on?"
reflected Paulo. "It could have been more turbulent. There was
certainly a conspiracy, but a barricade wouldn't have done any
harm. However it was, the battle was won. Now it is important
not to let the iron go cold, to keep on striking it and renewing the
cause. Deodoro is a wonderful figure. They say that the marshal's
entrance to the barracks and his exit, spurring on the troops, was
magnificent. Perhaps too easy; the regime was rotten and fell on
its own."

While Paulo's head turned over these ideas, Pedro's was thinking the opposite. He called the movement a crime.

"A crime and an impertinence, besides ungrateful. The emperor should have taken the ringleaders and had them executed.
Unfortunately, the troops were with them. But not everything is
over. This is a brush fire. In a few days it will burn out, and what
was before will be restored. I will find two hundred good and
ready lads, and we'll put this mess back in order. The appearance
it gives is of solidity, but that's a sham. They will see that the emperor will not leave this place, and even if he doesn't want to, he
must govern. Or his daughter will, and if not her, the grandson.

He himself began to govern as a boy. Tomorrow will be early enough. Right now all it amounts to is flowers. There are still a handful of men . . ."

The suspension points at the end of the monologue indicate that the ideas were becoming fragmented, fuzzy, and repetitive until they dissipated entirely and the boys fell asleep. During their slumber, revolution and counter-revolution stopped, there was no monarchy or republic, Dom Pedro II or Field Marshal Deodoro, nothing that smelled of politics. One and the other dreamed of the beautiful Botafogo bay, a clear sky, a sunny afternoon, and a single person: Flora.

L X V I I I

Morning

Flora opened the eyes of both and vanished so quickly that they could hardly see the hem of her dress and hear a little soft, remote word. They glanced at each other, without apparent rancor. The fear of one and the hope of the other set a truce. They ran to the newspapers. Paulo, a little dizzy, feared a betrayal at dawn. Pedro had a vague idea of restoration and hoped to read in the papers of an imperial amnesty decree. Neither a betrayal nor a decree. Hope and fear fled from this world.

LXIX

At the Piano

While they dreamed of Flora, she did not dream of the republic. She had one of those nights in which imagination sleeps too, without eyes or ears, or at most, one's retinas do not allow one to see clearly, and one's ears confuse the sound of a river with the barking of a faraway dog. I cannot give a better definition, nor is it needed. Each one of us will have had such mute and darkened nights.

She did not even dream about music, and she had, in fact, played some of her favorite pieces that evening. She played them not only because she liked them, but also to escape from her parents' consternation, which was considerable. Neither one could believe that institutions had fallen, others been born, that all was changed. Dona Cláudia even held out hope for the next day and asked her husband if he had really understood what he had seen, and asked him to repeat it. He bit his lips, slapped his hand on his leg, got up, paced, and again narrated the events, the news posted at the doors of the newspaper offices, the imprisonment of ministers, the incumbents, everything was extinct, extinct, extinct . . .

Flora was not averse to pity or to hope, as you know. But she could not identify with her parents' agitation, and she took refuge with her piano and her music. She chose I don't know what sonata. That was enough to remove her from the present. Music had for her the advantage of not being present, past, or future. It was something outside of time and of space, a pure ideal. When she stopped, she heard loose phrases from her father or her mother: "But how was it that . . ." "Everything was done secretly . . ." "Was there bloodshed?" Occasionally one of them would make a gesture, but she did not see the gestures. Her father, his soul limping, talked a lot and incoherently. Her mother brought another kind of vigor to the conversation. She would remain silent for a few minutes, as if she were thinking, unlike her husband who, when he was silent, would scratch his head, wring his hands, or sigh, when he did not shake his fist at the ceiling.

La, la, do, re, sol, re, re, la, sang the piano of their daughter, with these or other notes, but they were notes that rang to flee from humanity and its discord.

One can also find in Flora's sonata a kind of harmony with the present moment. There was no definitive government. The soul of the young woman was in tune with that first light of dawn or last glow of sunset—as you wish—in which nothing is so clear or so dark that it invites one to leave one's bed or light the candles. At most, there would be a provisional government. Flora did not understand forms or names. The sonata brought the feeling of absolute lack of government, the anarchy of primitive innocence in that corner of paradise which man lost because of his disobedience and one day will regain, when perfection brings the eternal and only order. Then there will be no progress or regression, but stability. Abraham's bosom will enfold all things and persons, and life will be a clear sky. That is what the keys told her without words, re, re, la, sol, la, la, do . . .

LXX

A Mistaken Conclusion

Events kept happening, just as the flowers kept blooming. Some flowers bloomed to decorate the last ball of the year. Others died on the eve of the revolution. Poets of one and the other regime drew images from this fact to sing the joy and melancholy of the world. The difference is that the latter muffled their sighs while the former celebrated their bacchanal. The flowers continued to bloom and die, just as regularly as before.

Dona Cláudia gathered the roses of the last ball of the year, the first of the republic, and adorned her daughter with them. Flora obeyed and accepted them. Foremost the head of a family, Batista accompanied his wife and daughter to the ball. Paulo also attended, because of the young woman and the regime. If, in conversation with the ex-governor of the province, he said all the good things that he thought about the provisional government, he did not hear words of agreement or disagreement. He did not delve deeper into the man's convictions, because the young lady attracted him, and he liked her more than he liked her father.

Flora found a resemblance between the ball of the Ilha Fiscal and this one, although it was modest and private. This one was given by a person who had done propaganda for the republicans, and one of the ministers was there, although he stayed just half an hour. Hence the absence of Pedro, although he had been invited. Flora felt Pedro's absence, just as she had felt Paulo's on the island. This was the resemblance between the two parties: both were marked by the absence of a twin.

"Why didn't your brother come?" she asked.

Paulo hesitated and then, after a few seconds: "Pedro is stubborn," he said. "He insisted on refusing the invitation. He believes naturally that the monarchy had a monopoly on the art of dancing. Don't pay any attention to him, he's a lunatic."

"Don't say that."

"Do you also think that dancing went out with the empire?"

"No, the proof is that we are dancing. No, I meant that you should not call him nasty names."

"So you think that Pedro is sensible?"

"Of course, just as you are, sir."

"But . . ."

Paulo was going to ask her which one of them, if she had to swear on one or the other, would deserve her oath. But he stopped in time. Then she complained of the heat, and he agreed it was hot. He would think it was cold if she complained of the cold. Flora, if she succumbed to what was in her sight, was also capable of accepting all of Paulo's opinions, to follow him. Truthfully, Paulo had a brilliant, petulant manner, looking off into the air, certain that what he had written a year ago had been instrumental in ushering in the republic, even though certain ideas he had proposed and defended were incomplete and would be realized one day. This is what he told the young woman, and she listened with pleasure, without opinion. It was just the pleasure of listening to him. When the memory of Pedro popped back into her head, sadness dimmed her joy, but then happiness quickly overcame the other emotion and thus ended the ball. Between the two, happiness and joy, they found shelter in Flora's heart, like the twins that they were.

The ball ended. It's the chapter that won't end without leaving some space for whoever wants to think about that creature. Neither her father nor her mother could understand her, nor could the young men, and probably Santos and Natividade least of all. You, mistress of young love or student of it, you who listen to all sides, conclude that she was . . .

It's difficult to put a name to her profession. Were it not my obligation to tell the story with the exact words, I would prefer not to mention it but you know what it is, and here it will stay. You conclude that Flora was a flirt, and you conclude wrongly.

Reader, it is better to deny this now than wait for time to tell. Flora did not know the sweetness of love, and much less could you call her a habitual flirt. Flirtation is the bud of hopes and sometimes of reality, if vocation requires it and the occasion permits it. It is also necessary to keep in mind that story about a publicist, a son of Minas Gerais and another century, who ended up as a senator, and wrote against his ministerial adversaries: "A *pi-*

tanga tree does not bear mangos." No, Flora was not suited to having lovers.

The proof of this is that in the state in which she lived for some months in 1891, with her father and mother, for the purpose which I will tell you about shortly, nobody achieved the least look or even complacency. More than one young man spent his time courting her. More than one tie, more than one cane, more than one monocle offered her their colors, gestures, and lenses, without obtaining anything but courteous attention and perhaps a word with no meaning.

Flora remembered only the twins. If neither one of them forgot her, she did not release them from her memory. On the contrary, she sent a letter to Natividade with every mail pouch, asking to have herself remembered by both. The letters spoke little of the land and the people, and did not say anything good or bad. She used the word "longing" frequently, which each one of the twins read as meant for himself. They also wrote to her in the letters they sent to Dona Cláudia and to Batista with the same dual and mysterious intention which she understood very well.

So they had been for a long time, she and the two of them. The old quarrel that disunited them in life continued to disunite them in love. They could each have loved their own girl, married her, and had their children, but they preferred to love the same one, and not to see the world through any other eyes, not hear finer words, nor other music, before, during, and after Batista's commission.

The Commission

The words have escaped me. Yes, a commission was given to her father and I know nothing about it, nor did she. Confidential business. Flora called it the commission from hell. Her father, without going that deep, mentally agreed with her. Verbally he denied the characterization.

"Don't say that, Flora, it is a confidential commission for noble political purposes."

I think so, but from there to knowing the specific and real objective was a long stretch. One also does not know how that special trust of the government ended up in Batista's hands. One knows that he did not turn down the honor when an intimate friend ran and called him to the palace of the *generalíssimo*. He saw that he was being recognized for his subtle character and his capacity for work. It is not less true, however, that the commission became distasteful to him, although in the official correspondence he said exactly the opposite. If such documents always revealed the hearts of their authors, then Batista, whose instructions were in fact to achieve concord, seemed to want to achieve concord by iron and fire. But the style is not the man. Batista's heart closed when he wrote, and he let his hand forge the way, with the key to his heart locked. "It's time," sighed the muscle, "it's time to be a governor."

As far as Dona Cláudia was concerned, she did not want to see an end to the commission, which restored her husband to political action. She lacked only one thing: opposition. No newspaper spoke badly of him. That pleasure of reading the insults of his adversaries every morning, to read and reread them with their ugly names like whips with many lashes, which ripped her flesh and excited her at the same time, that pleasure was not given to her by the confidential commission. On the contrary, there was a kind of contest to find the commissioner just, equitable and conciliatory, worthy of admiration, civic-minded, spotless of character. All of this she had experienced before, but to find it tasty it was always necessary that it be mixed with affronts and slander. Without them, it was lukewarm water. The commission also lacked a ceremonial role appropriate to the highest command, but she did not lack for attention, and that was something.

L X X I I

The "Regress"

When Marshal Deodoro dissolved the national Congress on November 3, Batista recalled the era of the liberal manifestos and wanted to write one. He started it in secret, using the beautiful phrases that he knew by heart, Latin citations, two or three digressions. Dona Cláudia held him at the brink of the precipice with clear and sound reasons. More than anything, the coup d'état could be beneficial. Liberty is often served by seeming to suffocate it. Then, the same man who had proclaimed liberty now invited the nation to declare what it wanted, and to amend the Constitution except in its essential parts. The word of the generalíssimo, like his sword, was enough to defend and consummate the work begun. Dona Cláudia did not have her own style, but she did know how to communicate the heat of her convictions to the heart of a man of good will. Batista, after listening and thinking, patted her on the shoulder confidently: "You are right, my dear."

He did not tear up the written page. He wanted to keep it as a simple reminder, and proof is that he was going to write a letter to the president. Dona Cláudia also got that idea out of his head. There was no need to send his endorsement. It was enough to stay in his commission.

"Isn't the government satisfied with you?"

"It is."

"When they notice your faithfulness to the commission, they will conclude that you approve everything, and that is enough."

"Yes, Cláudia," he agreed after a few moments. On the contrary, anything else that he could write against the seditious assembly that the president had just dissolved would seem a lack of pity. Peace to the dead! "You are right, my dear."

He remained silent and followed his instructions. Twenty days later, Marshal Deodoro turned the government over to Marshal Floriano, Congress was reestablished, and all the decrees of November 3 were annulled.

Learning of these facts, Batista thought he would die. He was speechless for a few moments, and Dona Cláudia did not find the smallest words of consolation to give him. Neither one had expected the rapid march of events, one after the other, in such disorder that it seemed like a crowd of people in stampede. Just twenty days, twenty days of strength and peace, hopes and a great future. One day more and everything collapsed like an old house.

It was now that Batista understood the error of having listened to his wife. If he had finished and published the manifesto on the 4th or the 5th, he would have a document of resistance in his hand to claim some place of honor or at least of esteem. He reread the manifesto, and he thought of printing it, even though it was incomplete. He had good ideas, like this one: "The day of oppression is the dawn of freedom." He quoted the beautiful Roland walking to the guillotine, "Oh, Liberty, how many crimes are committed in your name!" Dona Cláudia made him see that it was too late, and he agreed.

"Yes, it is late. On that day it was not too late, it would have come at the right moment, for the right effect."

Batista crumpled the paper distractedly, then he smoothed it and kept it. He immediately examined his conscience, profoundly and sincerely. He should not have given in. Resistance was better; if he had resisted his wife's words, their situation would be different. He probed his conscience himself, thought that yes, that he could well have closed his ears and gone on. He insisted on this point. If he could he would make time turn back, and he would show how it is that the soul chooses on its own the best side. It was not necessary to know what had happened before. His conscience told him that, in a situation identical to the 3rd, he would do otherwise. Oh, certainly! He would do something very different and change his destiny.

A bulletin or telegram arrived to pull Batista off his confidential political commission. The return to Rio de Janeiro was brief and sad, without the epithets that had delighted him for some months, nor the company of friends. Only one person was happy, his daughter, who had prayed every night for the end to that exile.

"It seems you are pleased with your father's misfortune," said her mother on board the ship.

"No, Mother. I am happy that this boredom is over. Daddy can do politics in Rio de Janeiro, where he is appreciated. You'll see. If I were Daddy, as soon as I disembarked I would go to the marshal right away and explain everything, show my instructions and say what I had done. I would furthermore say that the dismissal was very timely, so as not to seem annoyed. Then I would ask him to appoint me right there."

Dona Cláudia, in spite of the bitterness of the moment, was pleased to see that her daughter thought about politics and gave advice. She did not notice, as the reader will have, that the soul of the girl's speech was not to leave the capital, to establish her congress right here, which would soon be a single legislative assembly, as in Rio Grande do Sul. But which of the chambers, that of Pedro or Paulo, would end up with that exclusive political power? That is what not even she herself knew.

Both presented themselves on board as soon as the steamship entered the port of Rio de Janeiro. They did not go in two launches, they traveled in the same one and jumped onto the boarding ladder with such alacrity that they almost fell in the sea. Perhaps that would have been the best ending for this book. Even so, this chapter does not end badly, because the reason for the alacrity with which they jumped off the launch was their ambition to be the first to greet the young girl, a love bet which once again made them equal in her soul. At last they arrived, and I am not sure which one in fact greeted her first. It could have been both of them.

An Eldorado

Three carriages waited for them on the Pharoux Docks, two
coupés and a landau, with three handsome pairs of horses.
The Batistas were flattered by the thoughtfulness of the Santos
family, and they entered the landau. The twins each rode in his
own coupé. The first carriage had its coachman and lackey, in
brown uniforms, tin buttons on which the coat of arms of the
family could be seen. Each of the other carriages had a single
coachman with identical livery. And all three set off, the smaller
carriages behind the bigger one, the animals' hooves beating
firmly and in rhythm as if they had rehearsed that reception for
many days. From time to time they encountered other liveries,
other pairs, other cavalcades, with the same beauty and the same
luxury.

The capital offered the recent arrivals a magnificent spectacle.
It was still living the glow and bustle of that end of century, the
golden age of the city and of the world, because the total impression it gave was that the whole world was like that. Certainly you
have not forgotten it was called the *Encilhamento*, the period of
speculation, the stage of big business and enterprises of all types.
Whoever did not see that, saw nothing. Cascades of ideas, inven-
tions, concessions poured out each day, with the loud, flashy
promise of making contos of réis, hundreds of contos, thousands,
thousands of thousands, millions and millions of contos of réis.
All financial paper, that is, stocks, rolled out fresh and eternal
from the printing presses. There were railroads, banks, factories,
mines, shipyards, shipping, building, exporting, importing, pack-
aging, loans, all the "amalgamateds," the "regionals," all that those
names signify and more that has been forgotten. Everything circulated on the streets and in the market, with by-laws, organizers,
and lists of shareholders. Words in large type filled the public an-
nouncements, bond issues succeeded one another without repeating themselves, they rarely died and the only ones that died were
the weak, but in the beginning nothing was weak. Each share of

stock came with an intense and liberal life, sometimes immortal, which was multiplied by that other life, the one with which the soul embraces new religions. Stocks were born at high prices, and more numerous than the former offspring of slaves, and with infinite dividends.

People of that time, wanting to exaggerate their wealth, said that money grew out of the ground, but that is not true. At most, it fell from the sky. Candide and Cacambo . . . Oh, our poor Cacambo! You know that is the name of that Indian which Basílio da Gama sang of in *O Uruguai*. Voltaire stole him and put him in his book, and the irony of the philosopher won over the sweetness of the poet. Poor José Basílio! You had your narrow subject and your obscure language against you. The great man didn't take your Lindóia, fortunately, but Cacambo is his, more his than yours, compatriot of my soul.

Candide and Cacambo, as I was saying, upon entering Eldorado, according to Voltaire's account, saw children playing on a street paved with gold, emeralds, and rubies. They gathered a few of these cobblestones, and, at the first inn at which they ate, they tried to pay for dinner with two of them. You know that the owner of the inn laughed heartily, because they wanted to pay him with paving stones, and also because nobody paid for what they ate. The government paid for everything. Thus the hilarity of the innkeeper, along with the liberality attributed to the state, which made us believe in similar phenomena among us, but that is all a lie.

What seems to be true is that our carriages grew out of the ground. In the afternoons, when a hundred of them lined up around the Largo de São Francisco de Paula, waiting for people, it was a pleasure to walk up the Rua do Ouvidor, stop, and contemplate them. The pairs of horses made people's eyes pop; they seemed to descend from the rhapsodies of Homer, although they were steeds of peace. The carriages, too. Juno certainly had dressed them with her golden straps, golden bridles, golden reins, all incorruptible gold. But neither she nor Minerva entered the vehicles of gold to wage war against Ilium. Everything there breathed peace. Coachmen and lackeys, bearded and serious, waiting at attention, gave a fine impression of the profession.

None of them waited for their master, lying inside the carriage with their legs hanging out. The impression they gave was of rigid and elegant discipline, learned in the grand school and maintained by the dignity of the individual.

"There are cases," wrote our Aires, "in which the impassivity of the coachman in the driver's seat contrasts with the agitation of the owner inside the carriage, making it seem that it is the owner, who, for a change, climbed into the driver's seat and took the coachman for a ride."

L X X I V

Textual Reference

Before continuing, it is necessary to say that our Aires did not refer vaguely or in a generic way to a few people but to one particular person. His name then was Nóbrega. Before he was not called anything, he was simply that hawker of souls who met Natividade and Perpétua on the Rua de São José, at the corner of Misericórdia. You have not forgotten that the new mother left a note of 2,000 réis in the bowl of the alms collector. The note was new and beautiful. It went from the bowl to his pocket in a hallway, not without some struggle.

A few months later, Nóbrega abandoned the souls to their own devices, and went on to other purgatories, for which he found other robes, other bowls, and other notes, alms of happy piety. I want to say he went on to other careers. In a little while he left the city and perhaps even the country. When he returned, he brought with him a few contos of réis, which fortune doubled, redoubled, and tripled. Then the famous era of speculation began. That was the great begging bowl, the great alms, the great purgatory. Who knew anymore what became of the alms collector? His old crowd was lost in obscurity and death. He was changed, his features were not the same, but ones that time composed and improved.

If the great bowl or any of the others received notes that suffered the same fate as the first is not known, but it is possible. It was around that time that Aires saw him in a carriage, almost falling out of the window, waving a lot, peering at everything. Since the coachman and the lackey (I think they were Scotsmen) saved the personal dignity of the house, Aires made the observation at the end of the other chapter without any general intention.

Although he had not met any old acquaintance, Nóbrega was afraid of returning to the neighborhood where he had begged for the former souls. One day, however, his nostalgia was so great that he thought of facing the danger, and on he went. He had an itch to see the streets and the people, he remembered the houses and the stores, a barber, the townhouses with their latticed wooden gates, where such and such a young lady appeared. When he was about to give in, he once again became afraid and went on to another location. He would only pass through by carriage. Later he wanted to see everything on foot, slowly, stopping if possible to relive the past.

He went there on foot. He walked down the Rua São José, turned on Misericórdia, stopped at the Praia de Santa Luzia, turned on Rua Dom Manuel, and poked into every alley. At first he looked furtively, quickly, his eyes downcast. Here he saw the barber shop and the barber was another person. Ladies still leaned out of the latticed balconies of the townhouses, old women and young girls, and none was the same. Nóbrega gained courage and began to look at things more freely. Perhaps that old lady had been young twenty years ago. That girl had perhaps been a suckling babe then, but now suckled her own. Nóbrega finally stopped and walked slowly.

He returned more times. Only the houses, which were the same, seemed to recognize him and some almost talked to him. That is not poetry. The ex-alms collector seemed to feel the need to be recognized by the stones, to hear them admire him, to tell them about his life, to force them to compare the modest man of yesteryear with the elegant gentleman of today, and to hear their mute words: "Look, sisters, it's him." He passed by them, looked at them, interrogated them, almost laughed, almost touched them to shake them forcefully: "Speak, you devils, speak!"

He would not confide in a man about that past, but to the silent walls, the old grates, the latticed gates, the old-fashioned lamps if they were still there, all that was discreet, to all that he wished to lend eyes, ears, and mouth, a mouth that only he could hear, and which would proclaim the prosperity of the former beggar.

Once he saw the portal to the church of São José open and he walked in. The church was the same. Here are the altars, here is the solitude, here is the silence. He crossed himself, but he did not pray. He just looked from side to side, walking in the direction of the main altar. He was afraid of seeing the sacristan, who could be the same one, and might recognize him. He heard steps, turned quickly, and left.

Walking up the Rua São José, he leaned against the wall to let a cart pass. The cart rolled up on the sidewalk, and he ducked into a passageway. The passageway could have been any one, but it was the very one in which he had carried out the operation of the 2,000 réis note from Natividade. He looked hard, it was the same. At the end were the three or four stairs of the first stairwell that turned left and joined the larger one. He smiled at the coincidence and for an instant revisited that morning, he saw in the air the bill of 2,000 réis. Others had come into his hands with equal ease, but he never forgot that charming piece of paper decorated with so many symbols, numbers, dates, and promises, handed over by an unknown lady, God knows if it was Santa Rita de Cássia herself. That was the saint to which he gave his special devotion. Without a doubt, he had changed the bill and spent it, but the dispersed parts did nothing but invite other bills into the pocket of their owner, and all followed in droves, obediently and silently so that nobody would hear them grow.

As much as he examined his own life, he did not find another gift like that from heaven or hell. Later, if some jewel captured his eyes, it did not catch his hands. He had learned to respect the property of others, or he had earned enough money to buy it. The note of 2,000 réis . . . One day, daring more, he called it a present from Our Lord.

No, reader, you don't catch me in a contradiction. I know that in the beginning the alms collector attributed the note to the pleasure which the lady had from some adventure. I still remember his words, "Those two saw the bluebird of happiness!" But if he now attributed the banknote to the protection of the saint, he did not lie then or now. It was difficult to hit on the truth. The only sure truth were the 2,000 réis. Nor could one say that it was the same at both of those times. Then, a note of 2,000 réis was worth at least 20,000 (remember the man's old shoes). Now it wasn't more than a tip to a coachman.

There is also no contradiction in crediting the saint now and the lover then. The opposite would have been more natural, when his intimacy with the church was closer. But, reader of my sins, there was lots of lovemaking going on in 1871 just as there was in 1861, 1851, and 1841, no less than in 1881, 1891, and 1901. The next century will tell the rest. And also, you must not forget that the opinion of the alms collector about Natividade was formed prior to his act in the alleyway, when he tucked the banknote into his pocket. It is doubtful that, after this act, his opinion was the same.

LXXV

A Mistaken Proverb

A person to whom I read the previous chapter in confidence wrote to me saying that everything was the fault of the cabocla of the Castelo. Without her grandiose predictions, Natividade's donation would have been minimal or nothing and the act in the hallway would not have happened, for lack of the banknote. "Opportunity makes the thief," concludes my correspondent.

He does not conclude wrongly. There is nonetheless some injustice or forgetfulness, because the reasons for the act in the hallway were all pious. Besides this, the proverb could be wrong. Aires, who also liked to study adages, affirmed that that particular one was not correct.

"It is not opportunity that makes the thief," he said to someone. "The proverb is wrong. The correct form should be: 'opportunity makes the theft; the thief is born, not made.'"

LXXVI

Perhaps It Was the Same One!

Nóbrega finally left the hall, but he was obliged to stop because a woman extended her hand to him: "Kind sir, alms for the love of God!"

Nóbrega put his hand in the pocket of his waistcoat and reached for a coin. There were two there, one of one tostão and the other of two. He took the first, but as he was about to hand it to the woman he changed his mind. He did not give her the coin. He told the old woman to wait and retreated farther into the passage. His back to the street, he put his hand into the pocket of his trousers and pulled out a wad of banknotes. He searched and found a note of 2,000 réis, not new, even somewhat old, as old as the beggar who received it with astonishment, but you know that money does not lose value with age.

"Take it," he murmured.

When the beggar woman recovered from her shock, Nóbrega had just returned the wad of banknotes to his pocket, and he was preparing to leave. The beggar then began to address him in a voice laced with tears: "Dear sir! Thank you, dear sir! God repay you! The Holy Virgin . . ."

She kissed the banknote, and she wanted to kiss the hand that had given her the alms, but he hid it, as in the Gospel, murmuring that no, she should go away. In truth, the words of the beggar had an almost mystical sound, a sort of melody from heaven, a choir of angels, and it did him good to countenance the wrinkled face, the trembling hand holding the bill. Nóbrega did not wait for her to leave; he exited, walked down the street, with the blessings of the woman following him. He turned the corner, walking quickly and thinking about I don't know what.

He crossed the square, passed the cathedral and the Igreja do Carmo, and arrived at the Café Carceler, where he gave his boots to an Italian shoeshine. Mentally he looked up and down, left and right—in any case, far away, and he ended up murmuring this phrase, which could have referred either to the note or to the beggar, but it was probably the banknote: "Perhaps it was the same one!"

No gift, as insignificant as it might be, is forgotten by the recipient. There are exceptions. There are also cases when the memory of a gift bites and pesters like a mosquito. But that is not the rule. The rule is to safeguard it in one's memory, like a jewel in its case. A just comparison, because the offering is often a jewel that the recipient forgot to return to its box.

LXXVII

Lodging

The Batista family was lodged at the Santos house. Natividade could not meet them at the boat, and her husband was busy with "starting a new company." They sent a message with their sons that their rooms were ready in the Botafogo house. As soon as the carriage was moving, Batista confessed that he would be uncomfortable staying there.

"It would be better to stay in a pension, until the São Clemente house is handed over to us."

"What did you want me to do? We had no choice but to accept," pondered his wife.

Flora said nothing but had opposite feelings from her mother and father. Think, she did not. She was so overwhelmed at having seen the two lads that her ideas did not line up in logical formation. Her very feeling was not precise. It was a mixture of oppressive and delicious, of murky and clear, a truncated happiness, a consoling affliction, and all the rest that you might find under the heading of contradictions. I don't put anything else down. Not even she would know how to describe how she felt. She had extraordinary hallucinations.

Now it is necessary to say that the idea of lodging was entirely the work of the two young professionals. They were already university graduates, although they had not yet embarked on their careers as lawyer and doctor. They lived on their mother's love and their father's pocketbook, both inexhaustible. Their father shook his head at the suggestion, but the twins insisted on the offering to such a point that their mother, glad to see them agree on something, retreated from her silence and agreed with them. The idea of having the young woman at their feet for a few days, to try to discern which one she favored and whom she really loved, might also have influenced the vote, but I affirm nothing in this regard. I also cannot guarantee that she was enthusiastic about hosting Flora's mother and father. Nevertheless, the meeting was cordial all around. It was embraces, kisses, questions, an exchange of tokens of affection that never ended. All were fatter, had better color, a better complexion. Flora was a delight to Natividade and Perpétua. Neither knew where such a regal, slender young woman would end up.

"Don't say anything more," interrupted the girl, smiling. "I have the same opinion."

Santos received them later that afternoon, with the same cordiality, perhaps less apparent, but everything is forgiven the one engaged in important business dealings.

"A sublime idea," he said to Flora's father. "The one I got off the ground today was one of the best, and the stocks are already good as gold. It's about sheep's wool, and it begins with breeding this animal on the fields of Paraná. In five years we will dress America and Europe. Did you see the prospectus in the newspaper?"

"No, I have not read the papers since I got on the boat."

"Well, you'll see."

The next day, before lunch, he showed the guest the prospectus and its portfolio information. There were sheaves and sheaves of shares, and Santos recited the worth of each one. Batista usually did not do his arithmetic very well; that time he did it worse. But the numbers multiplied before his eyes, they tumbled over each other, filled space from the floor to the windows, and jumped outside with a clinking of gold that deafened him. Batista left there fascinated and went back to repeat everything to his wife.

LXXVIII

A Visit to the Marshal

Dona Cláudia, when he finished, asked him simply: "Are you going to see the marshal today?"

Batista, returning to his senses, said: "Of course."

They had agreed that he would call on the president of the republic to explain to him the commission that he had carried out, which was confidential and nevertheless, impartial. He would talk about the spirit of concord which guided his actions and the esteem he garnered. Then he would talk about the desirability of a government which, through strength and liberty, would be even better than that of the generalíssimo, concluding with a final, well-studied phrase.

"That I will improvise," said Batista.

"No, it's better to have it ready. I thought of this one: 'Believe me, Your Excellency, God is with the strong and the good.'"

"Yes, that's not bad. You can add a gesture that points to the sky."

"No, not that. You know I am not good at gestures, I am not an actor. I can inspire respect without moving a foot."

Dona Cláudia dropped the gesture, it was not essential. She wanted him to write down the sentence, but he had already memorized it. Batista had a good memory.

That same day, Batista went to see Marshal Floriano. He did not say anything to his hosts, he would tell everyone about it when he returned. Dona Cláudia also said nothing. She waited anxiously. She waited two eternal hours and began to imagine that they had put her husband in jail for intrigue. She was not devout, but fear inspires devotion, and she prayed to herself. Finally Batista arrived. She ran to receive him, excited, took his hand, and they retired to their room. Perpétua (see what personal witnesses can contribute to a story!) exclaimed tenderly: "They are like two love birds!"

Batista said the reception was better than he had hoped, and while the marshal said nothing, he had listened with interest. The phrase? The phrase came out well, with just one change. Not being certain whether he preferred good to strong, or strong to good . . .

"It should have been both words," interrupted his wife.

"Yes, but it occurred to me to use a third: 'Your Excellency should believe that God is with the worthy.'"

In fact, the last word could cover the other two, and it had the advantage of giving the phrase a personal touch.

"But what did the marshal say?"

"He didn't say anything. He heard me with courteous attention and even smiled, a light smile, a smile of agreement . . ."

"Or could it be . . . Who knows . . . You did not do well, it seems. He would have said something to me. Did you tell him everything, just as we had agreed?"

"Everything."

"You laid out the reasons for the commission, the performance, our moderation . . .?"

"Everything, Cláudia."

"And did you shake the marshal's hand?"

"He did not offer me his hand, at first. He made a gesture with his head. And I extended my hand saying: 'Always at your service, Your Excellency.'"

"And he?"

"He shook my hand."

"Did he shake it with conviction?"

"You know, it could not be called a friendly handshake, but it was cordial."

"And not a word? A mere 'be well'?"

"No, it wasn't necessary. I bowed and left."

Dona Cláudia remained pensive. The reception had not been bad, but it could have been better. With her there, it would have been much better.

LXXIX

Fusion, Diffusion, Confusion

A while back I spoke of Flora's hallucinations. Really, they were extraordinary.

On the way, after they disembarked, and in spite of seeing the twins separately and alone, each one in his coupé, she thought she heard them talking, the first part of the hallucination. The second part: the two voices became confused, they were so alike, and ended up as one. Finally, her imagination made one person out of the two young men.

I do not believe that this can be a common phenomenon. On the contrary, there will be someone who absolutely does not believe me and assumes this to be a pure invention, when it is actually the purest truth. Well, it should be known that, during her father's commission, Flora more than once heard the two voices that fused into the same voice and the same creature. And now, in the Botafogo house, the phenomenon repeated itself. When she heard the two, without seeing them, her imagination completed the fusion of her ear with that of sight, and a single man said extraordinary words to her.

All of this is no less extraordinary, I agree. If I followed my tastes, neither the two boys would become one young man, nor would the young woman be a single girl. I would correct nature by doubling Flora. That not being possible, I consent to the unification of Pedro and Paulo. And thus, this optical effect repeated itself in front of them, just as in their absence, when she let herself forget the place and loosened the reins upon herself. At the piano, in conversation, taking a ride in the country, at the dinner table, she had these sudden brief visions which made her smile, at first.

If anyone wants to explain this phenomenon by the law of heredity, supposing that it was an affective form of the political variability of Flora's mother, they would not get support from me nor, I believe, from anybody. They are different things. You know the motives of Dona Cláudia. Her daughter would have others, of which she herself was not aware. The only point of resemblance is that in the mother, as in the daughter, the phenomenon was now more frequent, but in the mother it came from the rapid succession of external events. No revolution is made like a simple walk from one room to the next. Even those revolutions called palace revolts bring some agitation that remains for a certain time, until the water returns to its level. Dona Cláudia yielded to the tumult of the times.

Her daughter was responding to another cause which could not be discovered or understood right away. It was a mysterious spectacle, vague, obscure, in which the visible figures became impalpable, and the doubled became single, the single doubled, a fusion, a confusion, a diffusion . . .

L X X X

Transfusion, Finally

A transfusion, this can best define, as repetition and gradation of forms and states, that singular phenomenon; you may use it in the previous chapter and in this one.

Now that the phenomenon has been discussed, it is necessary to say that Flora found it amusing at first. I lied: at first, because she was far away, she did not think anything at all about it. Later, she felt a kind or fear or vertigo, but as soon as she got used to moving from two to one and from one to two, the alternation seemed enjoyable and she even began to evoke it to divert herself. Finally, not even that was necessary, the alternation occurred by itself. Sometimes it was slower than others, other times it was instantaneous. It wasn't often enough to approach delirium. Finally, she became used to it and enjoyed it.

Occasionally in bed, before she fell asleep, the phenomenon repeated itself, after much resistance on her part, because she did not want to lose sleep. But sleep came, and dreams completed the work of wakefulness. Flora strolled then on the arm of the same beloved, Paulo if not Pedro, and the couple went to admire the stars and the mountains, or the sea, which sighed or stormed, and the flowers and the ruins. It was not rare that they remained alone, in front of a patch of sky, in the moonlight, the night sky sometimes studded with stars like a dark blue cloth. It was at the window, suppose; the song of soft breezes came from outside, a large mirror, hanging from the wall, reproduced images of him and her, confirming her imagination. Since it was a dream, imagination brought unknown spectacles, such and so many that it was hard to believe that the space of one night could hold them all. And it did, with time left over. Flora would wake up suddenly, lose the scene and the face, and persuade herself it was an illusion. Rarely did she fall back asleep. It was early, she got up, walked until she was tired, until she slept again and had another dream.

Other times the vision remained without the dream, and in front of her stood just one slender figure, with the same beloved voice, the same imploring gesture. One night, resting her arms on his shoulders with the unconscious desire of lacing her fingers behind his neck, reality, although it was absent, demanded its rights, and the single man doubled into two similar persons.

The difference gave the two wakeful visions such a ghostly aspect that Flora was afraid and thought of the Devil.

LXXXI

Oh, Two Souls . . .

C ome on, Flora, help me, by quoting something, verse or
prose, which expresses your situation. Quote Goethe, my
friend, quote a fitting verse from Faust:

Oh, two souls live in my breast!

The mother of the twins, the lovely Natividade, could have
quoted that same line, before they were born, when she felt them
fighting inside her:

Oh, two souls live in my breast!

In this respect, the two are alike. One conceived them, the
other received them. Now then, how Flora's choice will be made,
not even Mephistopheles himself can explain with clarity and
certainty. The verse is enough:

Oh, two souls live in my breast!

Perhaps that old Plácido, whom we left in the early pages of this
book, would be able to unravel these later ones. A doctor in obscure
and complicated subjects, he knew the value of numbers very well,
the significance of gestures not just visible but invisible, the statistics
of eternity, the divisibility of the infinite. He had been dead for some
years. You will remember that he, consulted by the father of Pedro
and Paulo about the original hostility of the twins, explained it
promptly. He died while exercising his profession. He was explaining to three new disciples the correspondence of the five vowels with
the five human senses, when he fell flat on his face and expired.
Already at that time Plácido's adversaries, who were found in
his very own sect, affirmed that he had diverged from doctrine
and as a natural consequence, had gone crazy. Santos never let
himself be swayed by these troublemakers against the common
cause, who ended up forming another little church in another

neighborhood where they preached that the correct correspondence was not between the vowels and the senses but between the senses and the vowels. This other formula, seeming to be clearer, led many of the early disciples to join the latter sect, and proclaim now, as a final conclusion, that man is an alphabet of sensations.

The new sect won, and very few stayed faithful to the doctrine of old Plácido. He was invoked some time after his death, and once again he proclaimed his formula as the one and only truth, and he excommunicated those who preached the contrary. In fact, the dissidents had already excommunicated him, too, declaring his memory an abomination, with that firm hate that strengthens man against the softness of pity.

Perhaps old Plácido would unravel this problem in five minutes. But for this, we would have to call back his spirit, and his disciple Santos was involved in some last-minute lucrative cash transactions. Man does not live by faith alone, but also by bread and its components and derivatives.

L X X X I I

In São Clemente

After a few weeks, the Batista family departed from the Santos home and returned to the Rua São Clemente. The goodbye was tender, they began to miss each other before the separation, but affection, habit, esteem, the need, in sum, to see each other frequently compensated for their melancholy, and the Batista people took with them the promise that the Santos folks would visit them in a few days.

The twins kept the promise early. One of them, apparently it was Paulo, went that same night with a message from his mother to inquire whether they had arrived well. They told him yes, Batista adding to abbreviate his visit, that they were quite tired. Flora's eyes contradicted that claim, but in a few moments they were no less sad than happy. The happiness came from Paulo's promptness, the sadness from Pedro's absence. She naturally wanted them both, but how it is that the two sensations manifested themselves at the same time, that you will not understand, either well or poorly. Certainly, her eyes darted to the door several times, and once it seemed to the young girl that she heard noises at the door; it was all an illusion. But these gestures, which Paulo did not see, so happy was he at having beat his brother to the visit, were not such that they made her forget the present brother.

Paulo left late, not just to take advantage of Pedro's absence, but also because Flora detained him, trying to see if the other would arrive. Thus, the same duality of sensation filled the girl's eyes, until the farewell, when the sad part was greater than the happy one, since now there were two absences instead of one. Conclude what you will, my dear lady. She went to bed and recognized that one cannot sleep with a sorrow in one's soul, much less with two.

The Long Night

There are many remedies against insomnia. The most common is to count from one to a thousand, two thousand, three thousand, or more, if the insomnia does not retreat right away. It is a remedy that never made anybody fall asleep, it seems, but that does not matter. Until now, all the effective methods against tuberculosis go hand in hand with the notion that tuberculosis is incurable. It is fitting that men affirm what they know nothing about and, as a rule, the contrary of what they know. Thus that other incurable condition is formed: hope.

Flora, also incurable, if you do not prefer the definition of inexplicable that Aires gave her, charming Flora had her insomnia that night. But it was a little bit her fault. Instead of lying down quietly and sleeping with the angels, she thought it better to stay up with one or two of them, and spend part of the night at her window or sitting in her rocking chair, remembering and thinking, examining and completing, dressed in her linen robe, her hair pinned up for the night.

At first she thought about the one who had been there, and evoked all his charms, which were enhanced by the special virtue of having come to see her that night, even though they had just seen each other that morning. She felt grateful. The whole conversation was repeated in the solitude of her bedroom, with its several intonations, varied subjects, and frequent interruptions, either by others or her own. She, in truth, only interrupted to think about the absent one, and thus did no more than convert the dialogue into a monologue, which in turn ended in silence and contemplation.

Now, thinking of Paulo, she wanted to know why she did not choose him for a suitor. He had an extra quality, the adventurous nature of his soul, and that feature did not displease her. Inexplicable or not, she let herself be carried along by the enthusiasm of the young man, who wanted to change the world and the times into others that would be more pure and happy. That head, very masculine, was destined to correct the mistakes in the course of the Sun. The Moon too. The Moon required more frequent contact with mankind, less variation, and never to wane past half moon. Visible every night, without thus effecting the decadence of the stars, it would modestly continue the work of the Sun and give dreams to sleepless eyes or those just tired of sleeping. All of this would be accomplished by Paulo's soul, famished for perfection. He was a good husband, in sum. Flora closed her eyelids, to see him better, and found him at her feet, with his hands in hers, smiling and ecstatic.

"Paulo, my dear Paulo!"

She bent forward to see him closer and did not lose the moment or the intention. Seen thus, he was more handsome than simply conversing about trivial and fleeting subjects. She stared into his eyes and found herself inside the young man's soul. What she saw there she could not express very well: it was all so new and radiant that the poor retinas of the young woman could not grasp anything with confidence or continuity. Ideas sparkled as if fanned out of a bonfire, feelings battled each other, reminiscences rose freshly, so did longings, and principally ambitions, ambitions with large wings, which created winds just by ruffling the air. Upon this mixture and confusion rained tenderness, much tenderness . . .

Flora averted her eyes; Paulo was in the same position. But next to the door, in the shadows, Pedro's figure appeared, not less handsome, but a bit sad. Flora felt touched by that sadness. It seems that, if she loved the first exclusively, the second could cry tears of blood without getting the least sympathy. Because love, according to both ancient and modern nymphs, has no pity. When there is pity for the other, they say, that means that love has not truly been born or it has already died completely, and thus the heart doesn't mind putting on that first petticoat of affection. Pardon the figure of speech, it is not noble or clear but the situation doesn't give me time to go scrounging around for another one.

Pedro approached slowly; he also kneeled and took the hands that Paulo clasped between his. Paulo rose and disappeared through the other door; the room had two. The bed was between them. Perhaps Paulo had left bellowing with rage. She heard nothing, so sweetly vivid was Pedro's gesture, now without melancholy, his eyes as ecstatic as those of his brother. They were not the same eyes that went out in search of adventure. They had the calm of one who did not want any sun or moon but the ones that go around now, who is content with his share of both, and if he finds them divine, does not try to trade them for new ones. Order, if you wish, stability, the harmony between himself and things around him, were not less attractive to the young woman's heart, either because they carried the notion of perpetual bliss or because they gave the impression of a soul able to withstand all.

Not for all of this did Flora's eyes desist from penetrating Pedro's, until they reached his soul. The secret motive of this other excursion could be the scruple of wanting to examine both to judge them, if it was not just the desire not to seem less curious about one than the other. Both reasons are good, but perhaps neither was true. The pleasure of gazing into Pedro's eyes was so natural that it did not require any particular intent, and a look sufficed to slip and fall into that beloved soul. It was the twin soul of the other, and she saw in it not more or less.

It is just, and here is the sticky part of this chapter, that she found there something indefinable that she had not felt in the other. In compensation she felt in the other something that she could not find here. It was indefinable, do not forget. And this part is rough because there is nothing worse than to talk about nameless feelings. Believe me, my gentleman friend and you, my lady, no less my friend, believe me that I would prefer to count the threads on the lace of the girl's robe, the hairs pinned back on her head, the threads of the carpet, the boards in the roof, and at last the sparks of the dying flame of her lamp. That would be tedious but one could understand it.

Yes, the lamp was burning down, but it could still light Paulo's return. When Flora saw him come in and kneel again, at the feet of his brother, and both share between them her hands, calm and level-headed, she remained for a long time in a state of amazement. It was as long as a Credo, as our ancients said, when there was more religion than clocks. Coming back to her senses, she pulled back her hands, then laid them on their heads, as if trying to feel out the difference between them, the *quid*, the indefinable something. The lamp was dying . . . Pedro and Paulo spoke to her in exclamations, in exhortations, in supplications to which she responded badly and obliquely, not that she failed to understand them but so as not to worsen them, or perhaps because she did not know which one would best receive her response. The last hypothesis has an air of being the most probable. In any case, it is the prologue to what happened next, when the lamp burned down to its last sputters.

Everything gets mixed up in half light. That would be the cause of the fusion of the two figures, which from two became just one. Flora, not having seen either one leave, could hardly believe they were now just one person, but she ended up believing it, mostly because this single, solitary person seemed to complete her internally, better than either one had done separately. It was a lot of doing and undoing, changing and transmuting. She thought she was mistaken, but no. They were just one person, made of the two and of herself, a single person in which her own heart was beating. She was so emotionally tired that she tried to rise and leave the room, but she could not. Her legs seemed like lead and they stuck to the floor. She stayed like that until the lamp, in the corner, died completely. Flora was startled and rose from her chair: "What's that?"

The lamp went out. She walked over to light it. She saw then that she was alone, without either one or the other, neither two nor the one fused from both. The entire illusion vanished. The lamp, newly lit, illuminated her entire bedroom, and her imagination had created everything. That was what she supposed, the reader will understand. Flora understood that it was late, and a rooster sang to confirm this opinion. Other roosters did the same thing.

"Oh, my goodness," exclaimed Batista's daughter.

She got into bed, and if she did not fall asleep right away, nor did she take long to do so. Soon she was with the angels. She dreamed of the cock's crow, a cart, a lake, a scene of a sea voyage, a speech, and an article. The article was real. Her mother came to wake her at ten in the morning, calling her a sleepyhead, and there in the bed read her an article from the morning paper that recommended her husband for a position in government. Flora heard it with satisfaction. The long night was over.

The Old Secret

Natividade slept peacefully in Botafogo, but she woke up thinking about her sons and the young woman in São Clemente. She had been taking notice of the three. It had seemed to her before that Flora did not accept either one or the other, then that she accepted them both, and later, one and the other in turns. She concluded that the girl still felt nothing special and decisive. Naturally she would go along for a time, to see which one really deserved her. They seemed to feel equal inclination and equal jealousy. Thus a possible catastrophe. Separation would not curb everything. But aside from the fact that once the families were separated, she would not always be within their sight, visits could be less frequent and even rare. That was how she wanted it.

What is more, it was time to go to Petrópolis. Natividade planned to make the trip to the mountains with her sons. There were always elegant ladies up there, entertainment, fun. It could even be that they would find young lady friends there. It was enough for one of them to find someone. The one without a new interest would be free to marry Flora. A mother's calculations. There came others that would modify them and others that would restore them. Whoever is a mother may cast the first stone.

No other mother threw the first stone at our friend. I want to believe that the reason for this was Natividade's discretion. Suspicions and calculations accumulated in her heart. She kept silent and waited.

In fact, Flora was growing fonder of Natividade. She loved her as a mother, doubly her mother, since she hadn't yet chosen either one of her sons. The reason could be that their two temperaments fit better than Flora's and Dona Cláudia's. At the beginning she felt, I don't know what, friendly envy, or rather desire, when she saw that the figure of the other, although somewhat eroded by time, still conserved its statuesque lines. Little by little, she discovered in herself the introit of a beauty which should be long and fine, and of a life that could be great.

Flora knew about the prediction of the cabocla of the Castelo regarding the twins. The prediction was no longer a secret to anybody. Santos had spoken of it in time, concealing only Natividade's climb to the Castelo. He edited the truth, saying that the cabocla had come to Botafogo. The rest was revealed in confidence, as it had been to the departed Plácido, and then only after some struggle. Three or four times he attempted to do it and then retreated. One day, his tongue gave seven twists in his mouth, and the secret came out in a fearful whisper, but he lost his fear with the pleasure of showing that the boys would be great. Finally, the secret was forgotten. But Perpétua, for this or that reason, told it now to the Batista girl, who heard it skeptically. What could the cabocla know about the future?

"She knew, and the proof is that she predicted other things, which I cannot tell and which were true. You cannot imagine how that devil of a half-breed could see far into the future. And her eyes could pierce your heart."

"I don't believe it, Dona Perpétua. So then our future . . . ? And great how . . . ?"

"She didn't say that, much as Natividade asked her. She only said they would be great and would rise far. Perhaps they will be ministers of state."

Perpétua seemed to have acquired the cabocla's eyes. She bored them into her friend, straight through to her heart, which in fact did not beat hard or quickly, but as regularly as ever. Nevertheless, since it wasn't impossible that the two fellows would rise to the heights of this world, Flora quit objecting and accepted the prediction without another word other than a gesture, you know which, I believe, a gesture with her mouth, whose corners turned downward, raising her shoulders slightly and opening her hands, as if to say: well it could be.

Perpétua added that, since the regime had changed, it was natural that Paulo would be the first to arrive at his greatness, and here her eyes pierced the girl again. It was a way of gauging Flora's sentiments, baiting her with the elevation of Paulo, since it could well be that she would fall in love with the destiny before the person. She found nothing. Flora continued to refuse to let herself be read. Don't attribute this to calculation, it was not. Seriously, she thought of nothing beyond herself.

Three Constitutions

"Do you really think we will become great men?" Pedro had asked Paulo, before the fall of the empire.

"I don't know. You might become at least prime minister."

After the 15th of November, Paulo returned the question and Pedro answered as his brother had, changing the ending: "I don't know. You could become the president of the republic."

Two years had already gone by. Now they thought more about Flora than about greatness. Good morals demand that we put the public good above our personal wants, but young people in this regard are more like old men, and men of another age, who often think more of themselves than of others. There are noble exceptions, and others more noble still. History records many of them, and poets, both epic and tragic, are full of cases and models of abnegation.

Practically, it would be demanding a lot of Pedro and Paulo to pay more attention to the Constitution of February 24, 1891, than to the Batista damsel. They thought of both, it is true, and the former had already provoked a few acerbic exchanges of words. The Constitution, if it were a living person and standing next to them, would hear the most contradictory statements in this world, because Pedro went to the point of finding it a well of iniquity and Paulo described it as Minerva herself rising out of Jove's head. I speak in metaphors so as not to sink below my style. In truth, they used words that were less noble and more emphatic, and they ended up exchanging the first kind. On the street, where political demonstrations were most common, and notices on the doors of newspaper offices were frequent, everything was an occasion for debate.

When, however, the image of Flora appeared in their imaginations, the debate waned, but the insults continued and even grew, without admitting the new motive, which was even greater than the first. Indeed, they were arriving to the point at which they would give up the two Constitutions, the imperial and the republican, for the exclusive love of the young woman, if it were necessary. Each one would make her his constitution, better than any other in this world.

L X X X V I

Lest I Forget

It is necessary to say one thing before I forget. You know that the twins were both handsome and still looked alike. On that score they had no reason to envy each other. On the contrary, each found in himself something that accentuated, if not enhanced, their common charms. It was not true, but it is not truth that prevails, but conviction. Convince yourself of an idea, and you will die for it, wrote Aires around this time in the *Memoirs,* and he added: "The greatness of sacrifice is none other, but if truth coincides with conviction, then the sublime is born, and after it, the useful . . ." He did not finish or explain that sentence.

Between Aires and Flora

That quote from old Aires reminds me of one way in which he and young Flora diverged in more than age. I already told you how she, before her father's commission, defended Pedro and Paulo, whenever they spoke badly of each other. She naturally continued to do this, but the change of regime brought the occasion to defend both monarchists and republicans, depending on whose opinion she listened to, Paulo's or Pedro's. A spirit of conciliation or justice, she placated the anger or disdain of the interlocutor: "Don't say that . . . They are patriots, too . . . It is important to excuse excess . . ." They were just statements, without passion or principle behind them, and the interlocutor always concluded: "You are too good, my lady."

Well, Aires's way was the opposite of this benign contradiction. You will remember that he always used to agree with his interlocutors, not for disdain of the person, but in order not to dissent or fight. He had observed that convictions, when thwarted, disfigure a person's face, and he did not want to see others' faces that way, or give to his own an abominable appearance. If he gained something, so be it. But not profiting anything, he still preferred to remain in peace with God and men. Thus the arrangement of affirmative gestures and phrases that left all parties quiet, and himself calmer still.

One day, since he was with Flora, he spoke of that habit of hers, saying it appeared studied. Flora denied it was; it was her natural inclination to defend whoever was absent, who could not respond. What is more, it placated the twin she was with and then the other.

"I also agree."

"And why do you always have to agree?" she asked, smiling.

"I can agree with you, because it is delightful to go along with your ideas, and it would be bad taste to refute them. But truthfully there is no calculation in this. With others, if I agree, it is because they say what I think."

"Then I have already caught you in a contradiction."

"It could be. Life and the world are nothing else. You haven't learned that yet, because you are young and inexperienced, but believe me that the advantage is all yours. Innocence is the best book, and youth the best school. Please excuse my pedantry, sometimes it is a necessary evil."

"Don't accuse yourself, counselor. You know that I believe nothing against your word or your person. I find your very contradictions agreeable."

"I also agree."

"You agree with everything."

"Look here, Flora; excuse me, counselor."

I forgot to say that this conversation took place at the door of a fabric and fashions shop on the Rua do Ouvidor. Aires was going in the direction of the Largo São Francisco de Paula, and he saw the mother and daughter seated inside, choosing some fabric. He entered, greeted them, and walked to the door with the daughter. Dona Cláudia's call interrupted the conversation for a few moments. Aires looked out at the street where women of all classes walked back and forth, men of all work, without counting the people standing on both sides and in the center. There was neither a great hubbub nor pure quiet, but something in between.

Perhaps a few people were known by Aires and greeted him. But his soul was so immersed in itself that, if he spoke to one or two, that was the most. Every now and then, he looked back into the store, where Flora and her mother consulted with the shopkeeper. He heard the words exchanged even now. He was curious to know if the girl had finally chosen one of the twins, and which one. Anything would have been satisfactory. He was already disappointed that it had been neither, even though he didn't care whether it was Pedro or Paulo. He wanted to see her happy, if happiness was marriage, and happy the husband, regardless of the exclusion. The excluded one would be consoled. Now, whether it was for love of them or love of her, one cannot say for sure. At most, to raise the tip of the veil, it would be necessary to look into his soul even deeper than he himself could. There one might find, among the ruins of his half-bachelorhood, a faded and late-blooming flower of paternity, or more properly, the longing for it.

Flora brought back the fresh red rose of the first moment. They spoke no longer of contradictions, but of the street, the people, and the day. No more words about Pedro and Paulo.

LXXXVIII

No, No, No

They, wherever they were at that moment, could speak or not. The truth is that, if neither one was willing to let go of the young woman, neither felt sure to win her, as much as he thought she might be inclined to accept him. They had already reached an agreement that the rejected one would accept his fate and would leave the field to the victor. If victory were not achieved, they did not know how to resolve the battle. It would be easiest to wait, if passion did not grow stronger, but passion did.

Perhaps it was not exactly passion, if we give to this word its sense of violence. But if we recognize in it a strong inclination to love, an adolescent love or a little more, that was the case. Pedro and Paulo would have yielded the hand of the young girl, if they were to consult only their reason, and more than once they were on the verge of doing it. That was a rare impulse, which quickly disappeared. Her absence was insufferable, her presence necessary. If it were not for what happened and what I will narrate in the pages ahead, there would be enough material for this book to go on forever. All I would have to tell is the yes and the no, and what they thought and felt, and what she felt and thought, until the editor said: enough! This would be a book of morality and truth, but the story would go on endlessly. No, no, no . . . We must continue it and finish it. Let us begin by telling what the twins negotiated with each other, a few days after that dream or delirium of the young Flora, that night in her room.

L X X X I X

The Dragon

Let us see what they negotiated. They had been to the theater with Aires one evening, killing time. You know this dragon. Everyone has given him the hardest blows they can; he kicks, expires, and revives. So it went, that night. I don't know which theater it was, nor which play, nor which genre. Whatever it was, the purpose was to kill time, and the three left him stretched out on the floor.

They went from there to a restaurant. Aires told them that a long time ago, when he was a young man, he would end the evening with friends his own age. It was the time of Offenbach and the operetta. He told anecdotes, summarized the plots, described the ladies and the roles, almost recited passages by heart, snatches of the arias, and the words to the songs. Pedro and Paulo listened attentively, but they felt nothing of what awakened echoes in the soul of the diplomat. On the contrary, they felt like

laughing. What did they care about an old cafe on Rua Urugua-
iana, which had become a theater, was now nothing, people who
had lived there and starred, passed through and exited before they
came into the world? The world began twenty years before that
night and would never end, like the breeding pen for eternal
youths that it was.

Aires smiled, because he felt that way at 22, and he still remembered his father's smile, already an old man, when he said
something like this. Later, having acquired of time the idealistic
notions he now possessed, he understood that the dragon was
both alive and dead, and it was just as important to kill it as to
feed it. Nevertheless, the memories were sweet, and many of
them were still as fresh as if they were from the evening before.

The difference in age was great, he could not go into details
with them. It remained as a memory, and he changed the subject.
Pedro and Paulo, however, fearful that he would notice the disdain that his longing for remote and strange times provoked in
them, asked him for information, and he gave what he could
without intimacy.

In the end, the conversation was worth more than this sum-
mary of it, and their leave-taking was slow. Paulo continued to
ask about Offenbach, Pedro requested a description of the pa-
rades on September 7 and December 2. But the diplomat found a
way to jump to the present, and particularly to Flora, whom he
praised as a lovely creature. The eyes of both agreed she was
lovely. He also praised her moral qualities, her delicacy of spirit,
gifts that Pedro and Paulo also appreciated, and thus the conversation and finally the negotiations, which I referred to at the beginning of this chapter and which demand another.

The Agreement

"As far as I can tell, one of you likes her, if not both," said Aires.

Pedro bit his lips, Paulo consulted his watch. They were already on the street. Aires concluded with what he knew, that yes, both loved her, and he did not hesitate to say it, adding that the young woman was not like the republic, which one could defend and the other attack. It was imperative to win her or lose her for once and for all. What would they do, once the choice was made? Or was the choice already made and the rejected one stubbornly insisting on trying to win her back to himself?

Neither one spoke right away, since both felt the need to explain. They felt the choice was not clear or decisive. And moreover, that they had the right to wait for her to declare her preference, and they would try like the devil to win it. These and other ideas floated around silently inside them, without getting into the open. The reason, and there must be more than one, is easy to understand. First, the subject of the conversation, then, the gravity of their interlocutor. As much as Aires opened the door to frankness with the two young men, the fact remained that they were young men and he was old. But the topic itself was so seductive, the heart, despite all, so indiscreet, that there was no remedy but to talk, albeit to pronounce denials.

"Don't deny it," interrupted Aires. "Grown-up people know the wiles of young folks and guess right away what they are up to. It is not necessary to guess, it's enough to see and listen. You both like her."

They smiled, but now with such bitterness and dissimulation that they revealed the displeasure of their well-known rivalry. That rivalry was recognized by others, and so it must be sensed by Flora, and the situation seemed to them to be more complicated and inextricable than before.

They had arrived at the Largo da Carioca; it was one o'clock in the morning. One of Santos's carriages was waiting there for the boys, at the advice and order of their mother, who sought every occasion and means to encourage them to do things together. She insisted in trying to correct nature. She took them on many excursions, to the theater, on social calls. That night, since she knew they were going to the theater, she had her husband lend them the carriage, which took them to the city and waited for them.

"Please get in, counselor," said Pedro. "The carriage is big enough for three. I'll ride on the front bench."

They got in and took off.

"Well," continued Aires, "it is certain that you like her, and equally certain that she has not chosen between the two. She probably does not know what she is doing. A third person would resolve the crisis, because you would soon console yourselves. I also found consolation as a young man. Not having a third, and not wanting to prolong the situation, why don't you two come to some agreement?"

"Agree to what?" asked Pedro, smiling.

"Anything. Find a way to cut this Gordian knot. Each one of you should follow his calling. You, Pedro, will try first to untie it. If he cannot, Paulo, you pick up Alexander's sword and strike the blow. Then everything will be done and finished. Then destiny, which awaits you with two lovely creatures, will bring them to each one of you by the hand, and everything will fall into place, on earth as in heaven."

Aires said a few more things before getting out at the door of his house. Once alighted, he asked again: "Are we in agreement?"

The two nodded their heads in assent, and once they were alone they said nothing. They were thinking, of course, and perhaps the time seemed short between Catete and Botafogo. They arrived home, climbed the garden stairs, spoke of the temperature, which Pedro thought delightful and Paulo abominable, but they did not say anything, so as not to irritate each other. The hope of an agreement brought them along to relative and fleeting moderation. Long live the anticipated fruits of the next day!

There was their room awaiting them, a haven of order and grace, comfort and repose. Their mother gave the final touches to their room each day; she took care of the flowers in the porcelain vases, she herself put them outside the window at night so they would not breathe in the fragrance while they were sleeping. There were the candles at the feet of the two beds, placed in their silver candleholders, one engraved with Pedro's name, the other with Paulo's. The little rugs were made by her own hand, the curtains also by her, and finally the picture of her and her husband on the wall between the two beds, in that same place where the portraits of Louis XVI and Robespierre, bought on the Rua da Carioca, had hung before.

At the foot of each candleholder they found a note from Natividade. This is what she said: "Does either one of you want to go to Mass with me tomorrow? It is the anniversary of Grandfather's death, and Perpétua is feeling poorly." Natividade had forgotten to tell them before, and in fact could do fine without them, particularly by carriage, but she liked to have them with her.

Pedro and Paulo laughed at the invitation, and one of them proposed that to please their mother, they both go to Mass with her. The acceptance of the proposal came promptly. It was not harmony, but a kind of dialogue in the same person. Heaven seemed to write the peace treaty that both would have to sign. Or if you prefer, nature corrected their inclinations and the two combatants were beginning to reconcile their inner selves with their external appearance. I would not swear to this, I just report what one could be led to believe based on the look of things.

"Let's go to Mass," they repeated.

A long silence ensued. Each one ruminated over the agreement and the manner of proposing it. Finally, from bed to bed, they discussed what seemed best, they proposed, argued, amended, and concluded without a notarization, just a verbal agreement. There were few clauses. Admitting they could not guarantee Flora's choice, they agreed to wait for it during a short period of time, three months. Once she chose, the rejected one pledged himself to try nothing more. Since they were certain of what the choice would be, the agreement was easy. Each one expected to do nothing more than eliminate the other. Nevertheless, at the end of the period, if no choice had been made, it was necessary to adopt a final clause. They decided to resort to chance, and the one chosen by luck would leave the field to his rival. Thus passed an hour of conversation, after which they gave themselves to slumber.

XCI

Not Just the Truth Should Be
Told to a Mother

At nine o'clock the next morning, Natividade was ready to go
to the Mass that she had requested at the church in Glória.
Neither of her sons appeared.

"They must be asleep."

And two, three, four, five times she went to the door of their
room to check if there were any sounds, in answer to the note she
had left. Nothing. She concluded that they had come in late. She
didn't guess that they were sleeping on an agreement, nor what
the agreement was about. As long as they were sleeping on soft
beds, all was well. Anyway, she put on her gloves, went down-
stairs, got into her carriage, and went to church.

The Mass was for the anniversary of her father's death, as the
note had explained. An old custom. Her father had his Mass, her
mother another, her brothers and relatives others still. She did not
forget dates of death, just as she did not forget birthdays, whoever
it might be, friends or relatives. She remembered them all by
heart. Sweet memory! There are people you do not help, and they
fight with themselves and with others because you have neglected
them. Happy are those you protect. These are the ones who know
the special sadness and happiness of a 24th of March, a 10th of
August, a 2nd of April, a 7th and 31st of October, a 10th of November, the whole year, its private joys and sorrows.

Returning home, Natividade saw her two sons in the garden,
waiting for her. They ran to open the door of the carriage for her,
and after helping her out and kissing her hand, they explained
their failure to appear. They had both resolved to go but slept.

"Sleepy and unwilling," concluded their mother, laughing.

"It was just sleepiness," said Pedro.

"We just got up," added Paulo.

They both tried to take her arm. Natividade satisfied them by
giving one arm to each. In the house, while changing clothes,

Natividade reflected that if Flora had made a request, they would have awoken early, however late they had gone to bed. Memory would serve them as an alarm clock. That passed like a quick shadow, but she soon reconciled herself to the difference. Thus, it was not out of jealousy but to give them other seductions, and to separate them from the war over the lovely Flora, that the mother insisted on taking her sons to Petrópolis. They would go up to the mountains the first week of January. The season promised to be excellent. There were invitations to parties, she told them the names of the hosts and noted that Petrópolis was the city of peace. The government can change down here and in the provinces . . .

"What 'provinces,' Mother?" asked Paulo.

Natividade smiled and corrected herself: "In the states. Forgive the carelessness of your mother. I know they are states now. They are not like the old provinces, they don't wait for their governor to come from the Court . . ."

"What 'court,' baroness?"

Now both laughed, mother and son. Once their laughter had subsided, Natividade continued: "Petrópolis is the city of peace. It is, as Counselor Aires said the other day, a neutral city, it is a city of all nations. If the capital of the republic were there, the government would never be deposed. Petrópolis, you should notice that the name, despite its origin, remained and will remain, is for everyone. They say the season will be charming."

"I don't know if I can go just yet," said Paulo.

"Nor I," said Pedro.

One more time they were in agreement, but their agreement probably meant divorce, reflected the mother, and the pleasure those two words gave her died quickly. She asked them what reason they had to stay and for how long. If they had been established with their medical practice and lawyer's office, fine. But if neither one had yet begun their career, what would they do down here when she and her husband . . .

"That's exactly it, I have to do some clinical work at the Santa Casa Hospital," responded Pedro.

Paulo explained himself. He would not practice law, but he did need to consult certain documents of the eighteenth century in the National Library. He was going to write a history of land claims.

None of this was true, but not just the truth should be told to mothers. Natividade reasoned that they could do everything between the two launches to Petrópolis. They could travel down to Rio, have lunch, work, and then at four go back up, like everyone else. In the mountains they would have visits, music, balls, a thousand lovely things, not counting the mornings, the temperature, and Sundays. They defended their studies, which needed many consecutive hours of attention.

Natividade did not insist. It would be quicker for her to wait for her sons to finish the library documents and the residency at the Santa Casa. That idea made her heed the importance of seeing the young doctor and the young lawyer established. They would work with other reputable professionals and would get ahead and succeed. Perhaps the scientific career would give them the greatness announced by the cabocla at the Castelo, and not politics at all. One can shine and climb in any career. Here she criticized herself for having imagined that Batista would open the way for the political career of one of them, not realizing that Flora's father would barely be able to continue his own obscure career. But the idea of command returned to occupy her head, and, filled with that, her eyes turned first to Pedro, then Paulo.

They reached an agreement. They would come up on Saturdays and would go down on Sundays. The same for religious holidays and gala occasions. Natividade counted on force of habit and the attractions.

On the boat and in Petrópolis the subject of conversation was the difference between the two sons, who only went there once a week, and the father, who carried the burden of so much business on his shoulders, but still traveled up every afternoon. What could they be doing down there, when there were so many lovely eyes to attract them and hold them here? Natividade defended the twins, saying that one went to the hospital and the other to the National Library and they studied a lot, at night. The explanation was acceptable, but aside from stealing a topic from the wagging tongues that summer, it could be an invention of the boys. Naturally, they were womanizing.

The truth is that they charmed Petrópolis during the few hours they spent there. Besides everything, they had their similarity and their wit. The mothers said nice things to their mother, and asked the true reason that kept them in the capital, not as I said, plain and simply, but with a fine and insidious art, a wasted art, because their mother insisted on the hospital and the library. That way, the lie, once served up firsthand, was served secondhand, and not for this better believed.

X C I I

A Secret Awakens

Well, what secret is there that is not discovered? Wit, good will, curiosity, call it what you will, there is a force that drags out here everything that people try to hide. Secrets themselves get tired of remaining silent—silent or sleeping. Let us keep that other verb, which serves the image better. They get tired, and they help in their own fashion what we attribute to the indiscretion of others.

When they open their eyes, the darkness makes them uneasy. One ray of sunshine is enough. Then they ask the gods (because secrets are pagan) for just a little twilight, dawn or evening, since the dawn promises day, while the evening falls again into night, but however late it may be, to breathe clarity is everything. Secrets, my friend, are also people. They are born, they live and die.

Now what happens, when a ray of sun penetrates their solitude, is that it hardly ever leaves, irreversibly and gradually the light grows, tears through, pools up, and ends up dragging the secret by the ear into full day. Vexed by the strong light, at first they travel by whispers from ear to ear, sometimes written in notes, even though namelessly so that one can hardly guess whose they are. That is the period of infancy, which passes quickly. Youth leaps ahead before adolescence, and then the secrets seem strong and ubiquitous, knowledgeable as newspapers. Finally, if old age arrives, and they do not mind their gray hair, they take over the world and perhaps manage, I don't say to be forgotten but at least tiresome. They enter into the family of the sun itself, which is born for all, according to a copybook motto from my childhood.

Copybooks of my childhood, oh copybooks! I wanted to end this chapter with them, but the topic would have neither nobility nor interest, and once again would interrupt our story. Let us remain with the divulged secret, that is enough. An elegant summer resident did not disguise her shock when she found out the two brothers were so close on a subject that could break up the best of friends. A first secretary in the diplomatic corps suggested that it could be a joke the two were playing.

"Or the three of them," added another summer visitor.

They were on an excursion by horse to Quitandinha. Aires accompanied them and said nothing. When they asked him if Flora was pretty, he answered yes and spoke of the weather. The first summer guest asked him if he could tolerate such a situation. Aires sighed, like someone who has traveled a long distance, and declared that at the feet of a priest he would be obliged to lie, so black were his sins. But there, on the road, in the fresh air, among ladies, he confessed that he had killed more than one rival. That if he remembered correctly, he must be carrying seven corpses on his back, done in with various weapons. The ladies laughed. He continued in an ominous voice. Just once had he escaped dying first, and he made up a Neapolitan anecdote. He praised his dagger. One he had owned many years ago, with the best steel in the world, he had been obliged to give it as a present to a bandit, his friend, when the man proved that he had just committed his twenty-ninth murder the day before.

"Here's for your thirtieth," he said, giving him the weapon.

A few days later, he learned that the bandit, with that dagger, had killed the husband of a lady, and later the lady, whom he loved hopelessly.

"I left him with thirty-one first degree murders."

The ladies continued to laugh. Thus he was able to divert the conversation from Flora and her lovers.

XCIII

Neither Weaves nor Unravels

While they inquired about her in Petrópolis, Flora's moral situation was the same, the same conflict of affinities, the same balance between preferences. Once the conflict ceased, the equilibrium collapsed, the solution would come rapidly, and as much as it might hurt one of the lovers, the other would triumph unless that dagger of Aires's story intervened.

Thus passed the weeks from the time Natividade traveled to the mountain resort. When Aires went down to Rio de Janeiro, he did not neglect to visit her in São Clemente, where he found her just the same as always, except for the silence in which he saw her immersed one time. The next day he received a card from Flora, asking his pardon for her lack of attention, if that is what it was, and sending him her fondest regards. "Mother asks that she also be remembered to you and to the family of the baroness." That remembrance expressed the consent obtained from her mother to write the letter. When he returned to Rio, he hastened to São Clemente, and Flora repaid with happiness the silence of that other morning. Still, her mood was not spontaneous or constant; she had her moments of melancholy. Aires returned a few times again that week. Flora appeared at first to be in her customary gay mood and then lapsed into her altered state of the last few days.

Perhaps the cause of those lapses in conversation was the journey that the young girl's spirit was making to the home of the Santos people. One time her spirit returned back to say these words to her heart: "Who are you that you neither weave nor unravel? It would be better to leave them for once and for all. That would not be difficult because the memory of one would destroy that of the other, and both would be lost with the wind, which sweeps the old leaves and new, as well as dust particles so light and small they escape the human eye. Go on, forget them. If you can't forget them, try not to see them anymore. Time and distance will do the rest."

Everything was finished. All that was left was to write the words of her spirit into her heart so that they would serve as a reminder. Flora wrote them, with a trembling hand and blurred vision. As soon as she finished, she saw that the words would not go together, the letters became confused, then they vanished, not all at once, but piecemeal until the muscle ejected them. In valor and impetuosity one could compare her heart to the twin Paulo; her spirit, in its artfulness and subtlety, would be the twin Pedro. That was what she thought after some time, and with this, she explained the inexplicable.

In spite of everything, she did not understand the situation and resolved to do away with it or with herself. That entire day was restless and complicated. Flora thought of going to the theater, so the twins would not find her home at night. She would go early, before visiting hours. Her mother ordered the box, her father approved the diversion when he came home for dinner, but the daughter ended up with a headache and the box seats went unused.

"I'll send them to the Santos boys," said Batista.

Dona Cláudia was opposed and kept the box. The reason was a mother's. Since the choice had not been made, and the marriage still not arranged, she wanted to see them there with her daughter, talking, laughing, debating whatever it was, with their eyes glued on her. Batista did not understand right away or later, but so as not to displease his wife he did not send the tickets to the boys. Such a good occasion! It was not a lot to them, who had money to burn, but the gift was in the thought and also in the little note he would write to them, in sending the tickets. He even composed it in his head, even though it was now useless. His wife, seeing him quiet and serious, thought he was angry and wanted to make peace. He waved his hand softly. He composed the little note, put in a measured witticism, folded the paper, and addressed it to "the young apostles Pedro and Paulo." The intellectual work made Dona Cláudia's opposition harder to bear. It was such a nice note!

X C I V

Opposing Gestures

How can one roof cover such diverse thoughts? And that other vast roof, our sky, either clear or stormy, covers them with the same zeal that a hen shelters her chicks. And don't forget man's very cranium, which covers them as well, not just diverse thoughts but opposite ones.

Flora, in her room, was not concerned with notes or boxes at the theater. Nor did she pay attention to the headache, which she did not have. The headache was a handy and acceptable excuse, which could be brief or long, depending on the need of the occasion. Do not suppose that she is praying, although she does have a crucifix and an oratory in her room. She would not ask Jesus to free her soul from that clashing inclination. Sitting at the edge of her bed, her eyes gazing at the floor, certainly she thought of something serious, unless it was nothing at all, which also transfixes one's eyes and concentration. She bit her lips without anger, and put her head between her hands as if she wanted to arrange her hair, but her hair remained as before.

When she got up, it was completely dark, and she lit a candle. She did not want the gas light. She wanted a soft glow that would give as little life as possible to the room and to her furniture, and that would leave some corners of the room in half darkness. The mirror, if she went to it, would not reflect her everyday beauty, with the candle placed on top of an old desk, in the distance. It would show her the note of pallor and melancholy, it's true, but our little friend did not think herself pale nor did she feel melancholy. There was in her deranged sadness on that occasion a small touch of weariness.

How all of this combined in her, I don't know, nor did she. On the contrary, Flora seemed at times to be taken by fright, other times by a vague restlessness and, if she searched for the repose of a rocking chair, it was to leave it right away. She heard the clock strike eight. In a little while, Pedro and Paulo would probably arrive. She thought of telling her mother not to call her down. She was in bed. That idea did not last the time it takes to write it. And in fact it's already gone, now that I am on the next line. She held back in time.

"That's pointless," she said to herself. "It's enough not to appear. Mother will say that I am sick, and because of that we did not go to the theater, and if she comes up, I'll tell her I can't come down . . ."

The last words came out in a loud voice, so as to firm her resolve. She tried to lie down, and thought she better do it when she heard her mother's footsteps in the hall. All these alternatives could present themselves spontaneously. Nevertheless, it is not impossible that it was also a way of shaking any unpleasant memories. The young lady feared chasing after them.

The Third

Fearing those thoughts, what was Flora to do? She opened one of the windows to her room, which faced the street, leaned over the balcony, and looked up and down. She saw the starless night, the few people walking by, silently or talking, a few rooms lit and open, one with a piano. She did not see a certain figure of a man on the opposite sidewalk, looking at the Batista house. She did not see the figure, nor would it matter to her who it was. As soon as the figure saw her, it trembled and did not unfasten its eyes from her, nor its feet from the ground.

Do you remember that summer visitor to Petrópolis who attributed a third lover to our little friend? "One of the three," she said. Well, here is the third, and it could be that still another appears. This world belongs to lovers. Everything else is dispensable; the day will come when even governments can be done away with, and anarchy will organize itself as in the first days of paradise. As far as food is concerned, from Boston or New York will come a process by which people nourish themselves from simply breathing the air. It is lovers who will be perpetual.

This one was an official in an administrative bureau. Generally such officials marry early. Gouveia was single, he was courting the young ladies. One Sunday at church, he had noticed the daughter of the ex-governor, and he left the church so much in love that he did not want another promotion. He had fancied many girls, accompanied a few, but this was the first one to really wound him. He thought of her night and day. The Rua de São Clemente was the path that took him and brought him from his place of work. If he saw her, he looked at her intently, stopped at a distance, in the doorway of a house, or then appeared to look at a passing carriage and then diverted his gaze from the carriage to the young woman.

When he had been a clerk, he had written verses; once he had been appointed an official, he lost the habit, but one of the effects of passion was to restore it. Alone, at his mother's house, he spent paper and ink to put his hopes into meter, and the verses followed one after the other, lined up like companies of a battalion. The title would be the colonel, the epigraph the brass band, once he ordered the march of his thoughts. Would that be reinforcement enough for the conquest? Gouveia printed some in newspapers with this dedication: "to someone." But not even this made the city surrender.

Once he got it into his head to send her a declaration of love. Passion comes up with outlandish ideas. He wrote two letters, not in the same style, in fact they were contrary to each other. The first was of a poet. He used the *tu*, as in the verses, lots of adjectives, he called her a goddess in allusion to the name Flora, and quoted Musset and Casimiro de Abreu. The second letter was the official's satisfaction upon the clerk. It came out in the style of reports and memoranda, grave, respectful, with Excellencies. Comparing the two letters, he ended up choosing neither. It was not just the diverse and contrary texts, it was principally the lack of acknowledgment that led him to tear up the letters. Flora did not know him and at best fled from knowing him. Her eyes, if they met his, immediately turned away, indifferent. Just once he thought they might be pardoning him. That this brief ray of light opened the tiny buds of his hope (I am beginning to sound like the first letter) was possible and even true; so true that he arrived late to work. Fortunately, he was an excellent employee. The director gave him a quarter of an hour grace period, and he accepted the headache, the cause of a sad insomnia.

"I fell asleep only at dawn," the official explained.

"Sign."

Then Gouveia's godfather died and left him three contos of réis in his will. Anyone would consider this a boon. Gouveia found two, the legacy and the opportunity to enter into relations with Flora's father. He ran to ask him to accept the job of counsel for administering the will, taking care of the fees and expenses immediately. In a little while, he went to seek him out at home, and so that the lawyer would tell his family about the new client, he used many subtle and clever expressions, told anecdotes about his godfather, proclaimed philosophical concepts and a plan to become a husband. He also described his administrative situation, the imminent promotion, praise received, commissions and bonuses, all that distinguished him from other colleagues. In addition, nobody in his department had a bad word to say about him. Even those who thought they had been overlooked because of him ended up confessing that the preference given to Gouveia was deserved. Not all of that was true; he believed it so, at least, and if he did not believe all of it, he did not deny any of it. He wasted time and work. Flora never heard about the conversation.

She neither heard about it nor noticed the shadowy figure now, as I said before. I also said that the night was dark. I add that it began to drizzle, and a cool breeze picked up. Gouveia had an umbrella, and he was going to open it, but then he hesitated. What went on in his soul was a struggle similar to the one between the two drafts of the letter. The official wanted to shelter himself from the rain, the clerk wanted to get wet, that is, the poet was being reborn against all the elements, without fear of harm, ready to die for his lady as in the times of chivalry. An umbrella was ridiculous; to save himself from a cold was to deny his adoration. Such was the struggle and the outcome. The clerk won, while the rain came down heavily, and others hurried by with their umbrellas. Flora went inside and closed the window. The clerk waited a while longer, until the official opened his umbrella as did the others. At home he found the sad consolation of his mother.

XCVI

Withdrawal

That night passed without incident. The twins came, Flora did not appear, and the next day two notes asked Dona Cláudia how her daughter was doing. The mother responded that she was well. But Flora did not receive them with the usual happiness. There was something wrong that made her quiet. They asked her for music, she played. That was good because it was a way of withdrawing into herself. She did not respond to their handclasps as they supposed she had until a short while ago. Thus it was that night, and so it went on the following. First one then the other arrived early, thinking it was the presence of the rival that confused the girl. But precedence was worth nothing.

XCVII

A Private Christ

All of this took such a toll on her that she ended up asking her Christ for an appointment for her father—a post as governor or any other commission far away from Rio. Jesus Christ does not distribute government posts in this world. People here hand them over to those who deserve them, by a system of secret ballots, put inside a wooden urn, counted, opened, read, added, and multiplied. True, the commission could come: the question is whether Jesus Christ would aid all those who ask him for the same thing. Commissioners must be infinitely more numerous than commissions. That objection was soon expelled from Flora's spirit, because she asked her Christ, one of old ivory, left her by her grandmother, a Christ that had never denied her anything, and to whom other people did not come to bother him with supplications. Her mother had her own Christ as well, the confidant of her ambitions, the consolation of her disappointments. She did not resort to her daughter's. Such was the naive faith of the girl.

Certainly she had already asked him to free her from those complicated feelings which would not yield to one another, that tiresome hesitation, that pushing and pulling on both sides. She was not heard. The reason would perhaps be that she did not give a clear explanation of what she wanted, as I have done, perhaps scandalizing the reader. In fact, it was not easy to ask in words, spoken or even just thought. Flora did not compose her supplication. She put her eyes on the image and forgot herself, so that the image could read the desire that resided inside her. It was too much to ask a favor of heaven and expect heaven to guess what it was. That is what Flora concluded, and she decided to change her approach. She did not make it. She did not dare to tell Jesus what she could not tell herself. She thought of both of them, without confessing it to either one. She felt the contradiction, without daring to face it for very long.

The Doctor Aires

O ne day it seemed to the mother that her daughter was
nervous. She questioned her and discovered that Flora
was having dizzy spells and lapses of memory. That was just the
day that Aires appeared for a visit, with messages from Natividade. The mother spoke to him first and confided her fears to
him. She asked that he question her as well. Aires put on the
airs of a doctor, and when the young woman appeared and the
mother left them in the parlor together, he took care to question
her cautiously.

A futile intent, because she herself initiated the conversation,
complaining of a headache. Aires observed that headaches are the
malady of lovely young women, and then, admitting that the saying was banal, he uncovered the cause. He did not want to lose
the chance to tell her what everyone knew and was talking about,
not only here, but also in Petrópolis.

"Why don't you go to Petrópolis?" he concluded.

"I hope to take another longer trip, a much longer one . . ."

"To the other world, I'll wager?"

"You're right."

"Do you already have a ticket?"

"I'll buy it the day I leave."

"You might not find one. There is a lot of traffic for those des-
tinations. It's better to buy one ahead of time, and if you like, I
will take care of it. I'll buy another for myself, and we will go together. The crossing, without acquaintances, must be tedious.
Sometimes, even people you know can be tiresome, as happens in
this world. The nostalgia for life is agreeable. The people on
board are common, but the captain inspires confidence. He does-
n't open his mouth, he gives his orders with gestures, and there is
no record of his ever having shipwrecked."

"You are making fun of me. I think I have a fever."

"Let me see."

Flora gave him her wrist. He said gravely: "Yes; a fever of forty seven degrees Celsius. Your hand is burning, but that proves that there is nothing, because those trips are made with cold hands. It must be a cold, talk to your mother about it."

"Mother cannot cure anything."

"She can, there are home remedies. In any case, ask her, and she can call you a doctor."

"Doctors give tonics, and I don't like tonics."

"I don't either, but I put up with them. Why don't you try some homeopathic remedies, which are tasteless, unlike allopathic ones?"

"Which do you think is best?"

"The best? Only God is great."

Flora smiled, a pale smile, and the counselor noticed something that was not the fleeting sadness or the mood of a child. Again he spoke of Petrópolis, but he did not insist. Petrópolis was the aggravation of the present situation.

"Petrópolis has the problem of rains," he continued. "If I were you, I would leave this house and this street. Go to another neighborhood, the house of a friend, with your mother or without her."

"Where?" asked Flora anxiously.

She looked at him, waiting. There was no house of a friend, or she could not think of one, and she wanted him to choose one, wherever it was, and the farther away the better. That was what he read in her listless eyes. That is reading a lot, but good diplomats have the talent of knowing everything people tell them with the expression on their faces, and even the contrary, what they don't tell them. Aires had been an excellent diplomat, despite the Caracas adventure, if that itself didn't sharpen his skill at uncovering and covering up. All diplomacy resides in these two related verbs.

In the Name of Fresh Air

"I'll arrange a good house for you," he said to her as he left. Since he had been in Petrópolis, Aires had not dined with his sister in Andaraí on Thursdays, as he had arranged with her in chapter XXXII. Now he went there, and five days later Flora moved to her house, to get some fresh air. Dona Rita would not allow Dona Cláudia to bring her daughter, she herself went to fetch her in São Clemente, and Aires accompanied the three of them.

Flora's youth in Dona Rita's house was like a rose blooming at the foot of an old wall. The wall became younger. The simple flower, although pale, brightened the scarred mortar and the bare stones. Dona Rita was delighted. Flora repaid the hospitality of the lady of the house with such innocence and grace that the lady said she would steal her from her mother and father, and that made them both laugh.

"You gave me a wonderful present with this young lady," wrote Dona Rita to her brother. "She is a fresh soul and she came at a good time because mine is getting decrepit. She is very docile, she talks, plays, and draws delightfully well, she has made sketches of several local scenes, and I go out with her to show her the worthwhile views. Sometimes she looks sad, her eyes go blank, and she sighs. But I ask her if she misses São Clemente, she smiles, making some gesture of indifference. I don't speak to her about her nerves, so as not to upset her, but I believe she is getting better . . ."

Flora also wrote to Counselor Aires, and the two letters arrived the same day in Petrópolis. Flora's was a long and cordial thanks, interlaced with expressions that she missed him. That confirmed the other letter, although he had not read it yet. Aires compared them, reading the young girl's letter twice to see if she was hiding more than appeared on paper. In sum, he trusted the remedy.

"As long as she does not see them, she will forget them," he thought. "And if in the neighborhood anybody takes a fancy to her, she might end up married."

He answered both that same evening, telling them that on Thursday he would lunch with them. He wrote to Dona Cláudia, enclosing his sister's letter, and went to spend the night at Natividade's house, to whom he showed the five letters. Natividade approved of everything. She only noted that her sons did not write to her, and they must be desperate.

"The Santa Casa Hospital cures, and so does the National Library," replied Aires.

On Thursday, he went down to lunch at Andaraí. He found them just as he had read about them in the letters. He questioned them separately, to hear from their mouths the confessions sent on paper. They were the same. Dona Rita seemed even more delighted. Perhaps the most recent cause was what the young lady had confided to her the evening before. Since they had been talking about hair, Dona Rita referred to what has been mentioned in chapter XXXII, that is, that she had cut hers off to put it in her husband's coffin, when they buried him. Flora did not let her finish. She took her hands and squeezed them hard.

"No other widow would do that," she said.

Now Dona Rita took her by the hands, put them on her shoulders, and finished the gesture with an embrace. Everyone had praised her for the sacrifice of the act. This was the first person who found it unique. And then another long embrace, longer still . . .

C

Two Heads

The embrace was so long that it took up the rest of the chapter. This one begins without it or another. The very handclasp of Aires and Flora, while prolonged, also ended. The luncheon took longer than usual because Aires, besides being a conversationalist extraordinaire, could not get enough of hearing the two, principally the young woman. He found in her a touch of languor, weariness, or something akin, which I cannot find in my vocabulary.

Flora showed him the drawings she had done, landscapes, figures, a sketch of the Tijuca road, an old fountain, ruins of a "Half-Built House." It was one of those houses that somebody had started to build many years ago and nobody finished, leaving only two or three walls, a ruin without a history. There were other drawings, a flock of birds, a vase at a window. Aires leafed through them, full of curiosity and patience. The intentions of the work made up for its imperfection, and its fidelity was approximate. Finally, the young girl tied up the strings of the folder. Aires, suspecting there had been a last and hidden drawing, asked her to show it to him.

"It's a sketch, it's not worth it."

"Everything is worth something. I want to follow your artistic trials, let me see it."

"It's not worth anything."

Aires insisted. She could not refuse again, so she opened the folder and took out a piece of thick paper on which two identical heads were drawn. They did not have the perfection she desired. Nevertheless, the names were unnecessary. Aires pondered the work for a few moments and two or three times lifted his eyes to look at the artist. Flora waited for him, expectantly. She wanted to hear praise or criticism, but she heard nothing. Aires finished looking at the two heads and put the drawing back with the other papers.

"Didn't I tell you it was just a sketch?" asked Flora, trying to pull a few words out of him.

But the ex-minister preferred to say nothing. Instead of finding the influence of the twins almost extinguished, he found it to be consolation in their absence, so vivid that memory was enough without the presence of the models. The two heads were joined by a hidden link. Flora, as Aires's silence continued, perhaps understood part of what passed through his spirit. She took the drawing and gave it to him. She did not say anything or write anything on it. No matter what it was, it would be indiscreet. Besides, it was the only drawing she had not signed. She gave it to him as if it were a token of repentance. Then she tied up the folder again, while Aires silently tore up the drawing and put the pieces in his pocket. Flora stood speechless for a moment, her mouth open, but then she took his hand, thankful. She could not hold back two little tears, like two ribbons that tied up forever the portfolio of the past.

The image is not good, nor is it true; it was what occurred to Aires on the way back from Andaraí. He wrote it in his *Memoirs*, then crossed it out, and wrote a less definitive reflection. "Perhaps it is a tear for each twin."

"This may end with time," he thought, heading for the boat to Petrópolis. "It doesn't matter, it's a knotty case."

The Knotty Case

T he twins also thought the case complicated. When they went to São Clemente, they got news of the girl without any confirmation of her return. Time went on. It wouldn't be long before they consulted a fortune-teller, as two people did long ago.

Technically, they did not count the weeks of separation, since the choice had not been made, and the consultation might yield the opposite of the young lady's true inclination. A fair reflection, although a self-interested one. Neither one of them wanted anything but to prolong the battle, hoping to win it. Nevertheless, they did not trust each other with this twin thought. Each now felt exclusive, and affection now had its modesty and need to remain silent. They no longer spoke of Flora.

Not just of Flora. With their opposition growing, they resorted to silence. They avoided each other. If they could avoid it, they did not eat together. If they did dine together, they spoke little or not at all. Sometimes they talked, to avoid creating suspicion in the servants, but they did not notice that they spoke clumsily and in a forced manner, and that the servants would gossip about their words and expressions in the pantry. The satisfaction with which they communicated their discoveries and conclusions is one of the few things that sweeten domestic service, which is generally harsh. They did not, however, get to the point of figuring out everything that was making the twins more and more adversarial, the touch of hate which was growing in the absence of their mother. It was more than Flora, as you know; it was their very irreconcilable personalities. One day there was big news in the pantry and the kitchen. Pedro, on the pretext of feeling the heat more than Paulo, changed rooms and went to sleep poorly in another, that was no less hot than the first.

Visions Require Half-Light

Meanwhile, the lovely girl did not banish them from her own bedroom, much as she tried to get away from them. Memory brought them back by the hand, they entered and stayed. Later they would leave, either on their own or pushed out by her. When they returned, it was by surprise. One day, Flora took advantage of their presence to make a drawing identical to the one she had given to the counselor, more perfect now, much more finished.

She would also get tired. Then she would leave her room and go to the piano. They would go with her, sit on either side of her, or stand in front of the piano, and listen with religious attention, now to a nocturne, now to a tarantella. Flora played to the taste of each, without deliberation. Her fingers obeyed the mechanism of her soul. So as not to see them, she bent her head over the keyboard. But her field of vision kept them in her sight, if it was not the breathing she felt next to her or in front of her. Such was the subtlety of her senses.

If she closed the piano and went to the garden, she often would find them walking there, and they greeted her with such good spirits that she forgot her annoyance for a few minutes. Later, without her asking them to go, they left. At first, Flora was afraid they had abandoned her completely, and inside herself she called to them. Both returned immediately, so docile that she convinced herself that their flight was not a flight, nor did they feel despair, and she did not evoke them anymore. In the garden, the disappearance was more rapid, perhaps because of the extreme brightness of the light. Visions require half-light.

CIII

The Room

I know, I know, thrice I know, that there are many visions on those pages there. Ulysses confesses to Alcinöos that it is troublesome to tell such things. It is for me, too. I am, however, obliged to do so, because without them our Flora would be less Flora; she would be some other person I never knew about. I knew this one, with her obsessions or whatever you want to call them.

Notwithstanding, and despite having picked up some depression and nerves, Flora did not neglect to present herself well, make herself more beautiful, and have more than one unknown lover, who sighed for her. She did not lack those who admired her from afar and then went to watch her, at least on the green bench, at the garden gate, next to Aires's sister. It could be she met some of them, such as Gouveia, for example. Truthfully, it was as if she did not see them.

One of them was worth more than all because of his carriage, drawn by a beautiful pair of horses, the neighborhood capitalist. His house was a mansion, the furniture made in Europe, empire style, Sèvres china, Smyrna carpets, and a vast bedchamber with two beds: one a single bed, the other a double. The second bed was awaiting his future wife.

"She must be the wife," he thought one day, upon seeing Flora.

He was middle-aged. His face was battered by the winds of life, despite many splashes of eau de cologne. His body lacked agility, and his manners had no grace or naturalness. It was Nóbrega, that one of the banknote of 2,000 réis, the fertile note, which left many others after it, more than 2,000 contos. As far as the recent notes were concerned, their grandmother was lost in the mists of time. Now times were bright, the morning sweet and pure.

When he saw the young woman and had the thought recorded above, he was surprised at himself. He had seen other ladies, and more than one had sent him messages with her eyes, signaling the emptiness of her heart. This was the first one who truly captured his fancy and made him stop to think. He returned to see her.

The neighbors noticed the frequency of the capitalist's visits. Finally, Nóbrega had himself invited into Dona Rita's home, to the displeasure of his own circle, who felt themselves neglected by their habitual host. Nóbrega, however, had given orders for all to be served and received as if he himself were present.

His absence did not cause him to lose his friends. On the contrary, the servants could testify to what they all thought of the "great man." Such was the name that had been given to him by his private secretary and that stuck. Nóbrega could barely spell and had no command of syntax, useful studies, for sure, but which did not add up to moral worth; and moral worth, said all who followed the secretary, was his principal and greatest merit. The faithful scribe added that, if it were necessary to take off his own shirt and give to a beggar, Nóbrega would do so, even if the shirt were embroidered.

Right now, this love was, in fact, an act of charity. In a little while, his sudden liking turned into a grand passion, so great he could not contain it and resolved to confess it. He hesitated about whether he should declare it to the girl herself or to the lady of the house. He did not have courage for either. One letter would take care of it all, but the letter required style, warmth, and respect. If only Flora's gestures had told anything, even if little, fine. The letter would then be a reply. But the girl's gestures told him nothing. She was simply courteous and gracious. Nothing she did went beyond that.

Dona Rita noticed Nóbrega's leanings and thought he was the best solution for her guest. All the uncertainties, anguish, and melancholy would end in the arms of a rich man, esteemed, respected, in a mansion with a carriage at her command. She herself compared it to the grand prize of the Spanish lottery.

Finally, Nóbrega's secretary drafted, in the best language he could, a letter in which the capitalist asked Dona Rita the favor of an interview with his beloved.

"Don't write sweet little words," he advised his secretary. "I like this girl most of all because I feel protective of her. It is not a lover's letter. The style should be serious . . ."

"A dry letter," concluded the secretary.

"Not totally dry," corrected Nóbrega. "A flattering letter, but not forgetting that I am not a child."

Thus it was done, in fact, overdone. Nóbrega thought that the style could be a little softer. It wouldn't do any harm to put in two or three words appropriate to the goal, such as beauty, heart, feeling ... So it was finally done, and the letter was carried to its destination. Dona Rita was very pleased. That was just what she wanted. She had a plan to close out, by her own act, a melancholy story, to which she would give, on its last page, a dazzling conclusion. She did not think to tell her brother about it, because she wanted him to receive the news as a fait accompli. She reread the letter. She was disposed to go immediately, but there are people for whom the adage that says, "the best part of the party is in the anticipation," sums up all life's pleasure. Dona Rita was of that opinion. Still, she understood that those are the kind of letters one doesn't keep for too long, nor are they the kind that one answers casually. She waited for twenty-four hours. The next morning, after they had breakfasted, she read the letter to the girl. It was natural that Flora should be startled. She was, but it did not take her long to laugh, a frank and loud laugh, as she had not yet laughed in Andaraí. Dona Rita was very alarmed. She had supposed that, not the person, but the advantages and position argued in favor of the candidate. She forgot the hair offered to her husband's tomb. She advised the girl, stressed the social standing of the suitor, the present and the future, the splendid situation that this marriage would give her, and finally, Nóbrega's moral qualities. The girl listened quietly and laughed again.

"Are you sure I will be happy?" she asked.

"I think so. Now, the future will tell whether you will be or not."

"Let's wait for the future to arrive, which appears to be taking a long time. I do not doubt the qualities of that man, he seems good, and he treats me well, but I don't wish to marry, Dona Rita."

"Really, you are of the age ... But don't you at least want to think about it for a few days?"

"I've already thought about it."

Dona Rita still waited another day. The negative reply, if Flora should change her mind, would be a disaster. To use her own terms, a great disaster, splendid position, profound sentiments. Dona Rita went to extremes for that rich man of the final years of the century.

The Answer

Not wanting to give the answer point-blank, Dona Rita consulted the girl, who replied simply: "Tell him I don't intend to marry."

When Nóbrega received the few lines that Dona Rita had sent, he was shocked. He had not counted on a refusal. On the contrary, he was so certain of acceptance that he had the whole engagement planned out. He imagined the young woman, her timid eyes, her closed mouth, the veil covering her pretty little face, his delicacy, the words he would speak to her as they entered the house. He had already composed an invocation to the Holy Mother for their happiness. "I will give you a carriage," he said aloud to himself, "and jewels, many jewels, the best jewels in the world . . ." Nóbrega did not have a precise idea of what the world was; it was just an expression. "I will give you everything, little silk shoes, silk stockings that I myself will put on you . . ." He trembled and flushed as he put on her stockings. He kissed her feet and her knees.

He had imagined that she, upon reading the letter, would be so amazed and grateful that at first she could not answer Dona Rita, but then the words would gush out of her heart. "Yes, ma'am, I want to, I accept. I have thought of nothing else." She would write immediately to her father and mother to ask their permission. They would come at a run, astonished. But seeing the letter, hearing their daughter and Dona Rita, they would not doubt the truth and would give their consent. Perhaps the father would deliver it to him in person. And nothing, nothing, absolutely nothing, a plain refusal, an impertinent refusal, because, after all, who was she, besides a beautiful girl? A creature without a penny to her name, modestly dressed, no earrings, he had never seen earrings in her ears, not even two little pearls. And why had they pierced her ears, if they had no earrings to give her? He thought that the poorest girls in the world pierce their ears so that earrings can shower on them from the sky. And this one comes along, and refuses the richest earrings that the sky could rain on her . . .

At dinner, the friends of the house noticed that he was preoccupied. That evening, he and his secretary went out on foot. Nóbrega searched within himself for the coldest and most indifferent gesture that he could, almost frivolous, and announced to his secretary that Flora did not wish to marry. One cannot describe the amazement of the secretary, and then his consternation, finally his indignation. Nóbrega answered magnanimously: "It wasn't malicious. Perhaps she thought herself beneath, far beneath, the fortune. Trust me that she is a good girl. It may also be, who knows, that it would be bad for her heart? That girl is sick."

"Sick?"

"I don't say it for a fact, I just say it could be so."

The secretary nodded his assent.

"Only illness could explain the ingratitude, because the act is pure ingratitude."

Here his tone became indignant, a sincere tone, like the others. Nóbrega enjoyed hearing it, it was a kind of sympathy. This brought him to an idea he had before they left the house: he raised his man's salary. That could be considered wages of sympathy. The beneficiary went even further, concluded it was the price of silence, and nobody ever was the wiser.

Reality

The illness that was given as an explanation for refusal of the offer of marriage became a reality in a few days. Flora took lightly ill. Dona Rita, so as not to alarm her parents, tried to treat her with home remedies. Then she called for a doctor, her own doctor, and the face that he made was not a good one; in fact, it was bad. Dona Rita, who was accustomed to reading the gravity of her illnesses on his face, and always thought them to be very grave indeed, took care to advise the girl's parents. The parents came right away. Natividade also came down from Petrópolis, not immediately. In the mountains, there was fear of some disturbances below. She came to see the girl and, at her request, stayed for a few days.

"Only you can cure me," said Flora. "I don't believe in the remedies they are giving me. Your words are good and your affection . . . Mother, too, and Dona Rita, but I don't know, there is a difference, something . . . See, I'm almost laughing . . ."

"Yes, yes, laugh some more . . ."

Flora smiled, still that pale smile that appears on the mouth of a sick person when the illness allows it, or she defeats the seriousness that comes with pain. Natividade spoke encouraging words to her. She made her promise that she would come to convalesce in Petrópolis. The illness began to recede. Dona Cláudia accepted Dona Rita's offer and stayed there. Natividade went that night to Botafogo and returned in the morning. Aires would come down from Petrópolis every other day.

The twins also came to ask for the invalid. Now more than ever, they felt the strength of the bond that tied them to the girl. Pedro, already a doctor although without a practice, put more authority into his questions, made better diagnoses, but the hopes and the fears were shared by both. Sometimes, they spoke louder than was usual or polite. The reason, as egotistical as it might seem, was pardonable. Suppose that visiting cards could speak: some, more impatient, would proclaim their names so the courtesy of their presence would immediately be known, as well as their anxiety. Such care on the part of the two was unnecessary, because she knew they had come, and she received the regards that they left her.

Thus Flora passed her days. She wanted Natividade always with her, for the reasons she already gave and for another, that she did not tell, and might not even have known, but we can suspect it and print it. There was the blessed womb that had engendered the twins. Instinctively, she found in it something special. As far as the influence it exercised on Flora, for this or any other reason, Natividade did not know. She was just content that now, and in such a crisis, Flora did not lose the friendship she felt for her. They spent the hours together talking, if it did no harm to talk; or else one held the other's hands in hers. When Flora dozed, Natividade stayed to contemplate her, her face pale, her eyes sunken, her hands hot, but preserving the grace of her healthy days. The others entered the room on tiptoe, craned their necks to watch her sleep, spoke in gestures or in whispers so soft that only the heart could guess them.

When she seemed better, Flora asked for a little more light and sky. One of the two windows was opened, and the sick girl filled with life and laughter. Not that the Fever had gone entirely. That livid witch was in the corner of the room, its eyes fastened on her. But either because it was tired, or out of some imposed obligation, it nodded off occasionally. Then the sick girl felt only the heat of the ill that the doctor measured at thirty-nine, or thirty-nine-and-a-half degrees Celsius, after consulting the thermometer. Fever, seeing this gesture, laughed without scandal, laughed to itself.

C V I

Both Who?

We were at the point where one of the windows of the room increased the amount of light and sky that Flora asked for, despite the fever, which was in fact low. What happened next should take a book. It was not right away, it took long hours and some days. There was enough time so Flora and life could have a reconciliation or a farewell. Both one and the other could be extensive; they could also be short. I knew a man who became ill when he was old, if not from old age itself, and he spent an almost infinite time in his final farewell. He was already asking for death, but when he saw the fleshless face of his final friend spying through the half-open door, he turned his head away and hummed a nursery song, to deceive her and live.

Flora did not resort to such songs that were in fact still so close. When she saw the sky and a patch of sun on the wall, she enjoyed herself naturally, and once she wanted to draw, but they did not let her. If death peeked at her through the door, she had a shiver, it is true, and she closed her eyes. When she opened them, she looked at the sad figure, without either running away or calling to her.

"Tomorrow you'll be ready, and in a week or sooner we will go to Petrópolis," said Natividade, hiding her tears, but her voice did the work of her tears.

"Petrópolis?" sighed the invalid.

"There you will have a lot to draw."

It was seven o'clock in the morning. The evening before, when the twins had left, the fears of death had grown. But fears are not enough; it is necessary that reality follow behind. Thus hope. Hopes are also not enough, for reality is always urgent. The dawn brought some relief. At seven o'clock, after Natividade's words, Flora was able to sleep.

When Pedro and Paulo returned to Andaraí, the patient was awake, and the doctor, without giving much hope, ordered measures which he declared were energetic. All had marks of tears on their faces. That evening Aires appeared, bringing news of agitation in the city.

"What is it?"

"I don't know. There was talk of demonstrations supporting Marshal Deodoro, other rumors of a conspiracy against Marshal Floriano. Something is going on."

Natividade asked her sons not to become involved in the confusion. Both promised and kept their word. When they saw the look of some streets, groups, patrols, weapons, two machine guns, the Itamarati building illuminated, they were curious to know what was going on. It was a vague idea which did not last two minutes. They ran home and slept badly that night. The next morning, the servants brought them the newspapers with the news of the evening before.

"Has there been any message from Andaraí?" asked one.

"No, sir."

Still, they wanted to glance over the papers quickly. They could not. They were anxious to get out of the house and to find out the news of the night before. Although they took the newspapers with them, they did not read with concentration. They saw names of people imprisoned, a decree, movements of people and troops, all so confused that they found themselves at Dona Rita's house before they understood what was happening. Flora was still alive.

"Mother, you are sadder today than you have been."

"Don't talk so much, daughter," said Dona Cláudia. "I am always sad when you're sick. Get better and you'll see."

"Get better now," intervened Natividade. "When I was a girl I had a similar illness that laid me out for two weeks, until I got up, when nobody expected it."

"So you don't expect me to get up anymore?"

Natividade wanted to laugh at the abrupt conclusion, hoping to cheer the girl up. The invalid closed her eyes, opened them in a little while, and asked them to check if she had a fever. They came, she did, it was very high.

"Open the window wide for me."

"I don't know if that would be good for you," pondered Dona Rita.

"It can't do any harm," said Natividade.

And she opened it, not all the way, but halfway. Flora, although very weak, made an effort and turned toward the light. She stayed in that position without moving. Her eyes, opaque at first, stopped, until they became fixed. People entered the room slowly, and muffling their steps, delivered and took messages. Outside, they waited for the doctor.

"He's taking a long time; he should be here by now," said Batista.

Pedro was a doctor. He proposed to see the patient. Paulo, unable to enter, too, opined that it would be disagreeable to the attending physician. Besides this, Pedro lacked practice. Both of them wanted to attend Flora's passing, if it had to come. Their mother, who heard them, came out of the room, and learning what it was about, said no. They could not come in. It would be better if they went to call the doctor.

"Who is it?" asked Flora, seeing her come into the room.

"It is my sons, who both want to come in."

"Both who?"

That word made them believe that delirium had commenced, if it wasn't already ending, because in fact, Flora said nothing more. Natividade stuck to the delirium theory. Aires, when they repeated the dialogue to him, denied it was.

Death did not delay. It came more quickly than they had feared. All the women and her father surrounded the bed, where the signs of agony were approaching. Flora ended like one of those sudden afternoons, not so sudden that the longing for the day gone is not poignant. She ended so serenely that the expression on her face, when they closed her eyes, was less that of a corpse than of a sculpture. The windows, open, let in the sun and the sky.

CVII

State of Siege

A ll funerals are alike. That one had the feature of passing through the streets during a state of siege. Well considered, death is nothing more than a cancellation of the freedom to live, a perpetual cancellation, while the decree of that day lasted only seventy-two hours. At the end of seventy-two hours, all freedoms would be restored, except that of coming back to life. Whoever had died, was dead. That was Flora's case, but what crime could she have committed, except that of living, and perhaps of loving, one does not know whom, but loving? Pardon these obscure questions, which are not consequent, in fact are contradictory. The reason is that I cannot recall this demise without pain, and I can still see that funeral . . .

CVIII

Old Ceremonies

T he coffin is being brought out. All take off their hats, as soon as it comes through the door. People passing by stop. The neighbors lean out of their windows, some climb up on railings of the balconies, because the families are bigger than the space; at the doorways stand the servants. All eyes examine the people who carry the coffin: Batista, Santos, Aires, Pedro, Paulo, Nóbrega.

This one, even though he no longer visited the house, had asked for news of the invalid and was invited to carry her graceful body. In the carriage, in which he brought his secretary and which was pulled by the most handsome pair in the cortege, Nóbrega reminded his secretary: "Didn't I tell you she was sick? She was very sick."

"Very."

I won't go to the extreme of affirming that he was pleased at Flora's death, simply because it had made him right in declaring her ill when she was perfectly healthy. But that nobody would be her husband was a kind of consolation. There was more; suppose she had accepted the proposal, and they had married. He thought now of the splendid burial he would have arranged for her. He designed in his imagination the carriage, the richest of all, the horses and their black plumes, the coffin, an infinity of things that as he imagined them, seemed done. Then the tomb: marble, gold lettering . . . The secretary, to pull him out of his sadness, talked about objects in the street.

"Does Your Excellency remember the fountain that was here years ago?"

"No," grumbled Nóbrega.

Once again, all funerals are alike. Thus the likely tedium of the gravediggers, opening and closing graves all day long. They don't sing, as in *Hamlet,* tempering the sadness of their calling with verses of that calling. They lift the coffin down into the lime and give a spade to the guests, for themselves a shovel with which they fill the grave. The father and a few friends stood at the foot of Flora's grave to watch the earth fall in, at first with that grim, hollow thud, then with tiring rhythm, as much as the poor men hurry. Finally, all the earth was in and they placed the wreaths on top, from parents and friends: "To our beloved daughter." "To our saintly friend Flora from your friend Natividade, who misses you." "To Flora, from an old friend.", etc. All done, they began to leave. The father, walking unsteadily between Aires and Santos, who gave him their arms. At the gate, they took their carriages and left. They did not notice the absence of Pedro and Paulo, who stayed behind at the foot of the grave.

C I X

At the Foot of the Grave

Neither one of them counted the time they spent in that place. Suffice it to say that it was filled with silence, contemplation, and longing. I don't confirm it, so as not to trouble you now, but it is possible they also cried. They had handkerchiefs in their hands; they wiped their eyes. Later, with fallen arms, their hands holding their hats, they appeared to look at the flowers covering the grave, but in reality they were gazing at the being within it.

Finally, they made an effort to tear themselves away and to say good-bye to the deceased, we know not with what words, nor whether both used the same words. The meaning would be the same. Since they were facing each other, they were struck with the idea of shaking hands over the grave. It was a promise, a sworn oath. They came together and walked down to the gate, silently. Before reaching the gate, they reduced to words the gesture made over the grave. They swore perpetual reconciliation.

"She separated us," said Pedro. "Now that she is gone, let her unite us."

Paulo confirmed this statement with a nod.

"Perhaps she died for that very reason," he added.

Then they embraced. Neither gesture nor word showed emphasis or affectation; they were simple and sincere. The shade of Flora certainly saw, heard, and inscribed that promise of reconciliation on the tablets of eternity. Both, with a common impulse, gazed back one more time at Flora's grave, but the grave was now distant and hidden by large tombs, crosses, columns, a whole world of departed people, almost forgotten. The cemetery had an air that was almost gay, with all those wreaths of flowers, sculpted facades, busts, and the white of marble and limestone. Compared to the recent grave, it seemed like a rebirth of life, neglected in a corner of the city.

It was hard for them to leave the cemetery. They had not thought themselves so bound to the dead woman. Each of them heard the same voice, with the same sweetness and special words.

They had arrived at the gate, and their carriage came to fetch them. The face of the coachman was radiant.

One cannot explain that expression of the coachman, except that, concerned about the delay, and not expecting the two customers to stay so long at the gravesite, he had begun to suspect they had accepted the invitation of some friend and returned home. He had decided to wait a few more minutes and then to go, but the tip? The tip was doubled, just as the pain and the love had been; let us say it was a twin.

C X

Let It Fly

J ust as the carriage flew from the cemetery, so also this chapter will fly, destined to say first that the mother of the twins managed to take them to Petrópolis. Now they alleged neither the hospital of the Santa Casa nor the documents of the National Library. The hospital and documents repose now in plot number . . . I don't set down the number, so that some curious person, finding this book in the National Library, can take the trouble to investigate and complete the text. It is enough to supply the name of the deceased, which has already been told and told again.

Let this chapter fly, like the Mauá train, up the mountain, up to the city of repose, luxury, and gallantry. There goes Natividade with her sons, and Aires with the three of them. Up there, at night, as Aires returned to the house of the baron, he could see the effects of the sworn peace, the final reconciliation. He knew nothing of the pact between the two young men. Neither did the father or mother. It was a secret kept in silence and in the sincere desire to remember a being who had united them by dying.

Natividade now lived for the love of her sons. She took them everywhere or kept them for herself, so she could enjoy them more deliciously and to test them in action, helping the corrective work of time. News and rumors from Rio de Janeiro were the subject of conversation in the houses that they visited, but these did not tempt them to forego their voluntary abstinence. Entertainment called them little by little, an excursion by carriage, or on horseback, and other diversions brought them together.

This was how they spent their time until the Santos family went back down to the capital, even against Natividade's wishes. She was afraid that, if they were closer to the government, political discord would destroy the recent harmony of her sons, but they could not stay here. Others were leaving. Santos wanted to get back to his old routine, and he gave a few good reasons that Natividade later also heard from Aires. It could be a planned coincidence of ideas, but if they were good, they should be accepted.

Natividade entrusted the perfection of her work to time. She believed in time. I, as a boy, always saw him drawn as a white-bearded old man with a scythe in his hand, which made me feel afraid. As for you, my gentleman friend or lady friend, depending on the sex of the person who reads me, if not two and of both sexes, an engaged couple, for example, curious to know how Pedro and Paulo could be following the same creed . . . Let us not speak of that mystery. Content yourself with knowing that they intended to keep the oath of that place and time. Time brought the end of the season, as in other years, and all Petrópolis left Petrópolis.

A Summary of Hopes

"When one does not wish it, two cannot fight": such is the old proverb that I heard as a lad, the best age to hear proverbs. In maturity they should already be part of the baggage of life, fruits of ancient and common experience. I believed this one, but that was not what gave me the resolve never to fight. It was because I found it in myself, that I gave it credence. Even if it had not existed, it would have been the same. As for how I came not to want to, I cannot answer, I don't know. Nobody opposed me. I got along with all temperaments. I had few disagreements, and I only lost one or two friendships, so peacefully, in fact, that the lost friends did not stop greeting me in the street. One of them asked me forgiveness in his will.

In the case of the twins, both wanted not to fight. It seemed they heard a voice from beyond or on high that constantly asked them to keep peace. A greater force, therefore, and a change in the formula: "If no one wants it, then no one will fight."

Naturally, the acts of government were approved and disapproved, but the certainty that it could again inflame their hatred made Pedro and Paulo keep their opinions to their personal friends. They thought nothing in each other's presence. Disagreements about the theater or the street were immediately snuffed out, much as the silence pained them. It must not have pained Pedro as much as Paulo, but there was always some suffering. Changing the subject, they forgot everything, and their mother's laughter was their reward.

Their careers would separate them soon, while their common residence brought them together. Everything could be arranged. The interests of their professions served this purpose, as did their personal relations, and finally habit, which is a lot of it. I summarize here, as best I can, Natividade's hopes. There were others, which I will call conjugal. The young men, however, did not seem inclined to them, and whoever tested the heart of their mother would already detect a premature jealousy of her future daughters-in-law.

C X I I

The First Month

O n the eve of the day of the first month after Flora's death, Pedro had an idea, which he did not share with his brother. He would have lost nothing by doing so, because Paulo had the same idea and also kept it to himself. From it is born the present chapter.

Under the pretext of visiting a sick person, Pedro left home before seven o'clock. Paulo left a little later, with no excuse. Faithful reader, you will guess that both went to the cemetery. You will not have guessed, nor should it be an obvious conclusion, that each carried a wreath of flowers. I do not say they were the same flowers, not only to respect the truth, but also to discourage any idea that there was intentional symmetry in the act and in the coincidence. One was forget-me-nots and the other, I believe, was of immortelles. Which was which is not known, nor does it have any bearing on the tale. Neither one had a card attached.

When Paulo arrived at the cemetery and saw his brother from a distance, he felt like a person who has just been robbed. He wanted to be the only one, and he was the last. The presumption, however, that Pedro had brought nothing, not even a leaf, consoled him for the priority of the visit. He waited for a few moments; and then, realizing he might be seen, he took a detour and walked between the tombs, until he was behind Flora's grave. There he waited for about a quarter of an hour. Pedro did not want to tear himself away. He seemed to talk and listen. Finally, he said good-bye and left.

Paulo slowly walked over to the grave. As he was about to lay down his wreath, he saw the other one freshly placed there, and realizing it was from his brother, had an impulse to go after him and make him confess the visit and the remembrance. Don't take this impulse the wrong way. It passed immediately. What he did was to place the crown of flowers which he had brought on the end corresponding to the feet of the dead girl, so as not to pair it with the other, which was at the head.

He did not see, nor even guess, that Pedro naturally had stopped for an instant, to look back and to gaze once more at the buried girl. So it was, but when Pedro saw his brother, in the same place where he had been, with his eyes on the ground, he also had his impulse to confront him and take him away from that sacred place. He preferred to hide and wait. The gestures of piety, whatever they were, he had given them first to their shared beloved. He had been the first to evoke Flora's shade, to speak to her, hear her, sigh with her over their eternal separation. He had gone before the other; he had remembered her sooner.

Thus consoled, he could have gone on his way. If Paulo left immediately afterward and saw him, he would understand that he had made his visit in second place and would be stricken. He took a few steps in the direction of the gate, stopped in his tracks, turned around, and hid once again. He wanted to see his gestures, see whether he prayed, whether he crossed himself, to be able to unmask him when he made fun of ecclesiastical ceremonies. He then felt that this was a mistake. He would not admit to anyone that he had seen him praying at Flora's grave. On the contrary, he was capable of denying it, or at least, of making a gesture of denial.

While these imaginings passed through his head, each one undoing the next, arguing without words, accepting, rejecting, waiting, his eyes did not leave his brother, nor did his brother leave the grave. Paulo made not a single gesture, he did not move his lips, he had his arms crossed and his hat in his hand. Nevertheless, he could be praying. He could also be speaking silently to the shade or to the memory of the dead young lady. The truth is that he did not leave the place. Then Pedro saw that the conversation, evocation, adoration, or whatever it was that kept Paulo at the grave was taking a lot longer than his own prayers. He had not kept time, but evidently Paulo had already been there longer. Discounting impatience, which always makes the minutes longer, it still seemed certain that Paulo was spending more minutes of longing than he had. In this way, he gained in the length of the visit what he had lost in time of arrival at the cemetery. Pedro, in his turn, was now the one who felt himself robbed.

He wanted to leave, but a force which he could not explain would not let him lift his feet or take his eyes off his twin. With much effort, he was finally able to move them and make himself walk around the other gravesites, where he read a few epitaphs. One from 1865 was barely legible, and one could not tell if it was a tribute of filial or conjugal love, maternal love or paternal, because the adjective had been worn away. It was a tribute, it used the formulas adopted by stonecarvers to save their customers the effort of composing one. Noticing that the adjective was eaten away by time, Pedro said to himself that his love was a perpetual noun, needing nothing more to define it.

He thought of other things to distract himself from his humiliation. He had done everything in a hurry. If he had taken longer, the other one would be enduring the wait. Time went on, the sun beat on the face of his brother, and he did not budge. Finally he gave signs that he was about to leave the grave, but he circled it, and stopped at each of its four corners, as if he were trying to find the best place to see or evoke the person kept inside.

All this done, Paulo retreated, walked down the hill, and left, taking with him Pedro's curses. This one had an idea, which he immediately rejected, and you would have done the same, my friend. That was to return to the grave and add to the time he had previously spent. That idea rejected, he wandered around for a few minutes, until he left, without finding a trace of Paulo.

C X I I I

One Beatrice for Two

I f Flora saw the gestures of the two brothers, it is likely that she would descend from heaven and find a way to hear them in perpetuity, a Beatrice for two. But she did not see them, or it seemed to her that it would not be fitting to leave heaven. Perhaps she saw no need to return here, to serve as patroness of a duel she had left in the middle.

As for the duel, if it were to continue, it was not over the same insults. Don't forget that it was at the foot of that same field that the two made their eternal peace, and while the field did not undo their pact, it certainly rekindled a little of the old rivalry. You will tell me, and with apparent reason, that if the girl still separated them, dead and buried, she would have separated them still more had she descended in spirit. Completely wrong, my friend. In the beginning, at least, they would swear to do what she commanded.

C X I V

Practice and Bench

A few months later, Pedro opened his medical office, where people went when they were sick, and Paulo his law office, where those needing justice procured his services. One promised health, the other winning a case, and often they were able to deliver, because they lacked neither talent nor luck. Besides, they did not work alone, but each with an experienced and well-known colleague.

In the midst of the events of the time, among which loomed the rebellion of the navy and the fighting in the south, the bombardment of Rio's harbor, the inflamed speeches, imprisonments, brass bands, and other noises, they were not lacking for issues on which to disagree. Nor was politics even necessary. Now the number of occasions and subjects was growing. Even when they agreed, by coincidence and in appearance, it was to disagree right away and permanently, not deliberately but because it could not be any other way.

They had lost the accord, achieved by reason and sworn by love in honor of the dead girl and their living mother. They could hardly endure the sight of each other, nor stand to listen to each other. They began to avoid everything where the occasion and the place might conspire to separate them even more. In this way, their professions divided their paths and their relationship. Natividade hardly noticed the bad feelings between her sons, since the two seemed resolute in their love for her, but she finally noticed it, and she continued to be determined to bind them closely and in everything. Santos enjoyed the idea of furthering his own health and interests through the medicine and maneuvering of his sons. He only feared that Paulo, given his political tastes, would look for a Jacobin bride. Not daring to say anything about this, he took refuge in religion, and he did not attend a Mass at which he did not place a private and secret prayer for protection from heaven.

Exchange of Opinions

That was when Natividade noticed the first signs of an exchange of inclinations which seemed more purposeful than a natural effect. Nevertheless, it was very natural. Paulo started to oppose the government, while Pedro moderated his tone and meaning and ended up accepting the republican regime, object of so much dissension between them.

His acceptance of the government was not rapid or total. It was, however, enough to feel that there was not an abyss between him and the new government. Naturally, time and thought accomplished this effect on Pedro's spirit, if we don't admit that he, too, harbored the ambition of a great destiny, his mother's hope. Indeed, Natividade was delighted. She, too, had changed, if there could be a change in a simple mother's soul, for whom all regimes were measured by the glory of her sons. Pedro, in fact, did not give himself over entirely; he held some reservations about the people and the system, but he accepted the principle, and that was enough. The rest would come with age, she said.

Paulo's opposition was not to the principle, but to its execution. "This is not the republic of my dreams," he said, and he set about trying to reform it in three stages, with the finest flower of human institutions, not present or past, but future. When he spoke of them, one saw the conviction in his lips and in his elongated eyes, like the soul of a prophet. That was another opportunity for the two to disagree. Dona Cláudia was convinced that it was some calculated plan of both never to agree, an opinion that Natividade would have finally accepted, were it not for Aires.

He, too, had noticed the change and was ready to accept that explanation, because of the comfort that he found in agreeing with the opinion of others, a position which did not tire or annoy him. Even better if he could agree with a simple gesture. This time, however, he spoke his mind.

"No, baroness," he said, "don't believe it is intentional."

"But what could it be, then?"

Aires took some time to choose his words, so they would sound neither pedantic nor trivial. He wanted to say what he thought. Sometimes speaking is no less difficult than thinking. After three minutes, he said confidentially to Natividade: "The reason seems to me to be a restless spirit in Paulo and a conservative nature in Pedro. One is content with what exists, the other thinks it is little or much too little and wants to go beyond where men have gone. In sum, they don't care about forms of government, as long as society stays put or leaps ahead. If you don't agree with me, then agree with Dona Cláudia."

Aires did not have that sad sin of opinionated people: he did not care about being accepted. This is not the first time that I say it, but probably it will be the last. In truth, the mother of the twins did not want another explanation. Not for this would discord die between them, they who simply changed weapons to continue the same duel. Hearing this conclusion, Aires made an affirmative gesture, and called Natividade's attention to the color of the sky, which was the same before and after the rain. Supposing there was something symbolic in this, she tried to find it, and you would do the same, reader, had you been there. But there was nothing.

"Have faith, baroness," he continued a little later. "Count on circumstances, which are also fairies. Count on the unexpected. The unexpected is a kind of extra god, to whom it is necessary to pay some homage. He can have a decisive vote in the congress of events. Imagine a despot, a court, a message. The court discusses the message, the message canonizes the despot. Each courtier takes it upon himself to define one of the virtues of the despot, his gentleness, pity, justice, modesty . . . Finally, they arrive at his greatness of soul, and news arrives that the despot has died of apoplexy, a citizen has assumed power, and liberty has been proclaimed from the throne. The message is approved and copied. Then one clerk is enough to change the course of History. It means everything that the name of the new chief be recognized, and the contrary is impossible. Nobody dons the mantle of power without this; not even you, my lady, know what a clerk's memorandum can do. Just as in funeral Masses, you simply switch the name of the intended—Petrus, Paulus . . ."

"Oh, don't curse my sons!" exclaimed Natividade.

C X V I

The Return Home

" So they were elected deputies?"

"They were. They take office on Thursday. If they were not my sons, I would say that you will find them even more handsome than you left them, a year ago."

"Say it, feel free, baroness. Pretend they are my sons."

Aires had just returned from Europe, where he had gone with the promise of staying just six months. He broke his promise. He spent eleven. Natividade was the one who rounded out his absence to a year, which she had truly felt, as had Dona Rita. Blood, in one of them, habit in the other, made it difficult for them to withstand the separation. He had gone on the pretext of taking the waters, and as much as those in Brazil were recommended to him, he did not want to try them. He was not used to the local denominations. He had the impression that the waters of Carlsbad or Vichy, without those names, would not cure as well. Dona Rita insinuated that he was going to check on the young ladies he had left there, and concluded: "They have got to be as old as you are."

"Who knows if they are not older? Their job is to get older," retorted the counselor.

He wanted to laugh but could not go beyond threatening to do so. It was not the reminder of his own age, or the dotage of others, but rather the injustice of fate that filled his inner vision. He knew very well that the young ladies had succumbed to time, just as cities and institutions do, and even more quickly than the latter. Not all of them would have gone early, to fulfill the saying that attributes premature death to the love of the gods. But he envisioned some of them like that, and now he remembered sweet Flora with her fine graces . . . his laughter did not go beyond a threat.

Both wanted to detain him, Santos too, who lost in him a reliable companion for his evenings. But our man resisted, embarked, and left. Since he wrote regularly to his sister and his friends, he gave the true reason for his delay, and it was not love affairs, unless he was lying, but he was past the age of lying. He affirmed that yes, he had regained some strength, and so it seemed when he disembarked, eleven months later, on the Pharoux docks. He had the same air of an elegant old gentleman, fresh and well groomed.

"But then, elected?"

"Elected. They take office on Thursday."

C X V I I

Two Inaugurations

Thursday, when the twins took their seats in the Chamber, Natividade and Perpétua went to see the ceremony. Pedro or Paulo arranged seats of honor for them. The mother wanted Aires to go, too. When he arrived, he already found the two ladies seated, Natividade looking through her eyeglass at the president of the Chamber and the deputies. One of these was reading the official register, and nobody was paying attention to him. Aires sat a little farther back and, after a few minutes, said to Natividade: "You had written me that they were candidates from opposing parties."

Natividade confirmed the news. They were elected in opposition to one another. Both supported the republic, but Paulo wanted more republic in it, and Pedro thought there was enough and to spare. They showed themselves to be sincere, ardent, ambitious. They were well accepted by their friends, studious, well-informed . . .

"Do they finally love each other?"

"They love each other in me," she responded, after composing the sentence in her head.

"Well, that friendly terrain should be enough."

"It is friendly, but aged. I may be missing tomorrow."

"You won't. You have many more years of life. Take a trip to Europe with them, and you will see that you will return even more robust. I myself feel doubled, as much as that tasks my modesty, but modesty forgives all. And later, when you see them as great men in their careers . . ."

"Why should politics separate them?"

"Yes, they could be great in learning, a great doctor, a great jurist . . ."

Natividade did not want to admit that learning was not enough. Scientific glory seemed comparatively obscure to her. It was quiet, cloistered in an office, and understood by few. Politics, not so. She wanted only politics, but that they should not fight, that they should love each other, and rise together. So she thought to herself, while Aires, letting go of the notion of science, ended up declaring that, without love, nothing could be accomplished.

"Passion," he said, "is half the battle."

"Politics is their passion: their passion and their ambition. Perhaps they are already thinking of the presidency of the republic."

"Already?"

"No, that is, yes. Keep it a secret. I questioned them separately, and they confessed that that was their ruling dream. It remains to be seen what one will do if the other rises first."

"Overthrow him, naturally."

"Don't joke, counselor."

"I am not joking. You are concerned that politics will tear them apart. Frankly, I'm not. Politics is an incidental, just as young Flora was another . . ."

"They still remember her."

"Still?"

"They went to her anniversary Mass, and I suspect they were also at the cemetery, not together and not at the same time. If they went it is because they truly loved her. Thus, she was not incidental."

Although Natividade deserved his frankness, Aires did not insist on his own opinion. Instead he focused on hers, confirmed by the very fact of the visit to the cemetery.

"I don't know whether they went," Natividade corrected herself. "I suspect they did."

"They must have gone. They really cared for the girl, and she loved them. The difference is that, since she could not make them one, as she saw them in herself, she preferred to close her eyes. The mystery is not important. There are other, darker ones."

"It seems that the ceremony is starting," said Perpétua, who was looking at the Chamber floor.

"Come up front, counselor."

The ceremony was the customary one. Natividade wanted to see them come in together and together confirm their oath of office. They would enter just as she had carried them in her womb and brought them into life. She was satisfied with admiring them separately. Paulo first, then Pedro, both serious, and she heard them from up above repeating the oath with a clear, firm voice. The ceremony was curious for the galleries, thanks to the resemblance between them. For the mother, it was moving.

"They are now legislators," said Aires, when it was over.

Natividade's eyes were filled with pride. She rose and asked her old friend to accompany her to the carriage. In the hall they found the two new deputies, who came to greet their mother. It is not recorded which one kissed her first. Since there was no internal protocol in this other chamber, it could be that it was both at once, as she placed her face between their mouths, one cheek for each. The truth is that they did it with equal tenderness. Then they returned to the Chamber.

CXVIII

Things of the Past,
Things of the Future

As she entered her carriage, Natividade noticed the Church of São José next door and a bit of the Morro do Castelo in the distance. She halted.

"What is it?" asked Aires.

"Nothing," she responded, entering and extending her hand to him. "I'll see you soon?"

"Soon."

The sight of the church and the hill awakened in her all those scenes and words that were recorded in the first two or three chapters. You will not forget that it was at the foot of the church, between it and the Chamber, that the coupé had waited for her and her sister.

"Do you remember, Perpétua?" said Natividade, when the carriage began to move.

"Remember what?"

"Don't you remember it was there that our carriage was waiting when we went to the famous cabocla of the Castelo?"

Perpétua remembered. Natividade noticed that right near there must be the hill where they had climbed with difficulty and curiosity, to the house of the cabocla, among all the other people who rose or descended as well. The house was to the right, it had a stone stairway . . .

Rest assured, my friend, I won't repeat those earlier pages. She could not resist evoking them, nor stop them from coming by themselves. Everything reappeared to her with its old freshness. She had not forgotten the little figure of the cabocla, when her father called her into the room: "Come in, Barbara." The idea that she was now grown, and far away, returned to her state, which was then a "province," living rich where she had been born poor, did not occur to our friend. No, all of her returned to that morning in 1871. The little cabocla was that same light and small creature, her hair tied up on her head, looking, talking, dancing . . . Things of the past.

When the carriage was about to turn along the Praia de Santa Luzia, skirting the Santa Casa Hospital, Natividade had the idea, but just the idea, of turning back and going to the Morro do Castelo, climbing the hill again, to see whether she would find the fortune-teller in the same place. She would tell her that the two nursing babes, whom she had predicted would be great, were now deputies and had just taken their seats in the Chamber. When would they fulfill their destiny? Would she live to see them great men, even if she were very old?

The presidency of the republic could not be for two, but one could have the vice presidency, and if he thought it too little, they could later switch offices. Great things were not lacking. She still remembered the words she heard from the cabocla, when she asked what kind of greatness lay in store for her sons. "Things of the future!" responded the Pythoness of the North, in a voice she would never forget. Even now it seemed to her that she could hear it, but that is an illusion. At most it is just the wheels of the carriage rolling and the hooves of the horses sounding the words: things of the future! things of the future!

CXIX

Which Announces the Following

All stories, if one cuts them into slices, end with a last chapter and a next-to the-last chapter, but no author admits that. All prefer to give them their own titles. I adopt the opposite method. On top of each one of the next chapters, I write their precise names, their concluding role, and, without announcing their particular subject matter, I indicate the milepost at which we find ourselves. This assumes that the story is like a railroad train. Mine is not exactly that. It could be a canoe, if I had put in water and wind, but you saw that we only traveled by land, on foot, or by carriage, and we paid more attention to the people than to the ground we covered. This book is not a train or a boat. It is a simple story, which happened and is about to happen, which you may see in the two remaining chapters, short ones.

CXX

Penultimate

This one is yet another obituary. Young Flora died a few back, and here old Natividade goes to her death. I call her old, because I read her certificate of baptism. But truthfully, neither her

248

deputy sons, nor her white hair, gave this lady the appearance that corresponded to her age. Her elegance, which was her sixth sense, eluded time in such a way that she kept, I won't say the freshness, but certainly the grace, of her younger days.

She did not die without a private conference with her two sons, so private that not even her husband attended it. Nor did she insist on that. It is true, it is true, Santos was weeping everywhere. He could hardly hold back his tears, if he heard his wife making her final requests to her sons. Meanwhile, the doctors had already told her that she was dying. If I did not see those health officials as the discerners of life and death, I could give a twist to my pen, and, against scientific prediction, have Natividade escape. But then I would be committing a facile and cheap trick, besides a false one. No sir, she died without delay, a few weeks after that session in the Chamber. She died of typhus.

So secret was the conference between her and her sons, that they did not want to tell anyone about it, except for Counselor Aires, who had guessed it in part. Paulo and Pedro confessed the other part, asking him for silence.

"Didn't you swear to secrecy?"

"Positively not," said one.

"We only swore to do what she asked us," explained the other.

"Well then, you can tell me. I will be as discreet as the tomb."

Aires knew that tombs are not discreet. If they say nothing, it is because they would always tell the same story. Thus the reputation for discretion. It is not a virtue, it is lack of novelty.

Well, what their mother did, when they came in and closed the door to the room, was to ask each one to come to one side of the bed and hold out their right hand to her. She joined them, without strength, and closed them in her burning hands. Then, with her expiring voice and her eyes bright only from fever, she asked them a great and single favor. They were weeping and silent; however, they guessed what it was.

"A last wish," she insisted.

"Tell us what it is, Mother."

"You will be friends. Your mother will suffer in the next world, if she cannot see you as friends in this one. I ask for little. Your life cost me a great deal, and raising you did as well, and my hope was to see you become great men. God does not will it, so be it. I want to know I have not left behind two ungrateful sons. Go on Pedro, go on Paulo, swear you will be friends."

The young men were crying. If they did not speak, it is because their voices would not come out of their throats. When they could finally speak, their voices trembled, but they were clear and strong.

"I swear, Mother!"

"I swear, Mother!"

"Friends forever?"

"Yes."

"I want no other farewell. Just this, true friendship, which will never be broken."

Natividade still held their hands tight, felt them tremble with emotion, and remained silent for a while.

"Now I can die in peace."

"No, Mother, you aren't dying," both interrupted.

It seems that their mother wanted to smile at this expression of confidence, but her mouth could not carry through her intention, in fact, it made a grimace that frightened the two boys. Paulo ran to get help. Santos entered into the room disoriented, in time to hear a few last whispered words from his wife. The agony began right away and lasted a few hours. Adding up all the hours of death throes that have transpired in this world, how many centuries would they make? Of these, some would be terrible, others melancholy, many desperate, few tedious. In sum, death comes, however long it delays, and plucks its victim away, either from the weeping or the silence.

Last

C astor and Pollux were the nicknames that a deputy gave to the twins, when they returned to the Chamber, after the seventh-day Mass. So close was their union that it seemed like a deal. They entered together, walked together, left together. Two or three times they voted together, to the great scandal of their respective political friends. They had been elected to oppose each other, and they ended up betraying their electorate. They heard hard words, sharp criticism. They wanted to resign from office. Then Pedro found a way to compromise.

"Our political duty is to vote with our friends," he said to his brother. "Let us vote with them. Mother only asked us for personal concord. On the floor, nobody will make us attack each other. In debate, and in our votes, we can and must dissent."

"Seconded. But if one day you think you should come over to my camp, do so. Neither you nor I mortgaged our judgment."

"Seconded."

Even personally, this agreement did not always last. Contrasts were not rare, nor were impulses, but the memory of their mother was so fresh, her death so close, that they suppressed whatever movement they were inclined to make, much as it cost them, and they lived in harmony. In the Chamber, their political dissent and personal fusion made them more and more remarkable.

The Chamber finished its work in December. When it reconvened in May, only Pedro appeared. Paulo had gone to Minas, some said to see a girlfriend, others that he was hunting for diamonds, but it seems he just took a vacation. Shortly thereafter he returned, entering the Chamber alone, unlike the year before, when the two brothers had climbed the stairs together, almost glued to each other's side. The eyes of their friends quickly noticed that they did not get along, and soon that they detested each other. There never lacked someone indiscreet who would ask one or the other, what had happened between the two sessions. Neither one would answer. The president of the Chamber, on the advice of the leader, nominated them to the same committee. Pedro and Paulo, in turn, asked to be excused.

"They are different," said the president, in the coffee room.

"Completely different," confirmed the other deputies present.

Aires heard about that conclusion the next day, through a deputy who was a friend of his, who lived in one of the boarding houses in Catete. He had gone to lunch with him, and in conversation, as the deputy knew of Aires's relationship with his two colleagues, he told him about the radical and inexplicable change from the previous year to this one. He also told him the opinion of the Chamber.

None of this was new to the counselor, who had witnessed the bonding and unbonding of the twins. While the other spoke, he reviewed their life and times, reconstructing the battles, the contrasts, the mutual aversion, barely disguised, occasionally interrupted by some stronger motive, but persistent in their blood, like a virtual necessity. He had not forgotten the pleas of their mother, nor her ambition to see them become great men.

"Since you, sir, are close to them, tell me what made them change," concluded the friend.

"Change? They haven't changed at all; they are the same."

"The same?"

"Yes, they are the same."

"That's not possible."

They had finished lunch. The deputy went back up to his room to freshen himself. Aires went to wait for him at the door to the street. When the deputy came down, he had a look of discovery in his eyes.

"Now, wait, can it be . . . Who knows whether their mother's inheritance didn't change them. It could have been the inheritance, questions about the estate . . ."

Aires knew it was not the inheritance, but he did not wish to repeat that they had been the same, since the womb. He preferred to accept the hypothesis, to avoid argument, and he left, patting his buttonhole, which held the same, eternal flower.

Counselor Aires and His Moviola

An Afterword

Carlos Felipe Moisés

Translated from the Portuguese by Elizabeth Lowe

*E*sau and Jacob (1904) is the next-to-last novel of Machado de Assis and shares with the last, *Aires's Memoirs* (1908), a common "authorship" attributed to a retired diplomat, Counselor Aires, a fictional character. In his free time while in service, he dedicated himself to filling various notebooks which comprise a "diary of remembrances," as one reads in the "Note to the Reader" of *Esau and Jacob*. In retirement after his return to Rio de Janeiro, he proceeds with the task, but his writings are only published after his death. In this same note, the "editor" Machado informs us that Aires left seven notebooks in all. The first six constitute the diary per se, in which the counselor is at the same time narrator and main character. These will be published under the title *Aires's Memoirs*. The seventh, unnumbered notebook is identified by a title, "*Last*," and contains the story of the Carioca twins, Pedro and Paulo Santos.

In this seventh, more voluminous notebook, Aires is not the main character. He has merely a supporting role, and he dedicates himself to collecting memories not of himself, but of others. It is the "last" of his notebooks, but that counts for little. It is above all the last novel of Machado's in which the story has minimal independence and autonomy beyond the narrator's intrusions. Not so in *Aires's Memoirs*, where action and reflection are all of one piece, and the interventions of the narrator are combined with the episodic mass, of which he himself is a protagonist.

I.

In referring to the title, Machado informs us that he has preferred *Esau and Jacob*. In the counselor's diary, the analogy between Pedro and Paulo and the twins of Canaan is just insinuated (chapter XIV) and would pass unnoticed by most readers. The decision to imprint it on the title, taken by Machado de Assis, is what forces us to compare the Carioca twins with the Biblical twins. In this subtle game are hidden successive and stratified layers of fiction upon fiction.

The action occurs between 1870 and the last decade of the nineteenth century, a period of great transformations that were decisive for the history of Brazil (see the Foreword). The important events of the period are registered in the novel, but the protagonists hardly notice; it is as if the events had nothing to do with them. Whether there is a monarchy or a republic, for example, is of little importance to them, as long as their personal prerogatives are not at risk. All fear, at most, that the new regime will break their windows, like those of the poor teashop proprietor, Custódio (chapter LXIII). Natividade worries that the change will aggravate the rivalry between her sons, since one declares himself a republican and the other a monarchist, less out of conviction than from pride. Santos, father of the twins, a banker and a capitalist, shows himself worried about political change, but soon allows himself to be comforted by the counselor, moved not by any good argument, which the counselor does not offer if he has any, but by his friend's indifference. Right away, Santos puts aside his conservative scruples and, as a businessman, takes excellent profit from the newly established order, an example followed by the lawyer Batista and others.

As for the twins, the essential has already been suggested. Paulo is a republican and Pedro is a monarchist, since that day when, as adolescents, walking into a frame shop on the Rua da Carioca, Pedro acquired an engraving of Louis XVI and Paulo would not be outdone: he bought one of Robespierre (chapter XXIV). At home, each one hung his portrait at the head of his bed, like a spiteful trophy, which his rival was forced to live with, since they shared the same room.

There is something behind this political divergence. From the beginning of the novel we learn that "Paulo was more aggressive, Pedro more wily" (chapter XVIII), and at the end Aires confirms that "a restless spirit resides in Paulo and a conservative nature in Pedro" (chapter CXV), so that, years later, the twins switch positions. The impulse that motivates them, in sum, is the need to antagonize each other. The rest is incidental.

For this reason Flora, daughter of Batista and Cláudia, has a salient role in the plot. Pedro and Paulo let themselves be enchanted by the graces of the young woman, they court her simultaneously, but wait passively as the impasse is perpetuated. They do not fight for her, they do not set off to conquer her (the reader will remember the Biblical tale of the various wives and concubines of Esau and Jacob), and they end up forming a secret pact, according to which they will wait until *she* decides on one of them, the rejected one being obliged to leave the scene. Now Flora's dilemma is precisely hesitation between the two of them. Both are attracted to her and she, divided, is incapable of choosing: "In valor and impetuosity one could compare her heart to the twin Paulo; her spirit, in its artfulness and subtlety, would be the twin Pedro" (chapter XCIII).

At a certain moment, Flora is the object of the passion of another fellow, Gouveia, and she also attracts the attentions of a wealthy old bachelor, Nóbrega. Instead of amusing herself with this tangle of suitors, instead of feeling, who knows, flattered by the persistent pursuit of three gallant young men or by the advantageous proposal of a wealthy entrepreneur, Flora becomes upset and anguishes over her situation. The twins don't leave her mind, the indecision persists, and she daydreams about the two, fusing them into just one person. Her hallucinations yield a few moving pages, such as those of the chapter titled "The Long Night" (chapter LXXXIII). She is advised to change surroundings, and she spends a season in Andaraí, in the care of Rita, the counselor's sister (chapter CIX). But it's useless. The illness advances and she dies.

The twins sincerely feel their loss. They shake hands over her tomb and swear eternal friendship. "She separated us," says Pedro. "Now that she is gone, let her unite us" (chapter CIX). But everything soon is transformed into a pretext to stir up the old rivalry. Paulo's pain, in front of the same tomb, a month later, is overshadowed by the annoyance he feels at knowing that Pedro has paid his visit to the grave before him. Pedro, for his part, prides himself on having arrived first, but cannot accept the fact that his brother stayed longer than he did. Less than a year later, the reconciliation is practically forgotten.

Pedro graduates in medicine and Paulo in law, and they begin to exercise their professions. Soon they run for seats in Congress and are elected. Natividade attends their inauguration and exults over the confirmation of the cabocla's oracle. She has a notion to return to the Morro do Castelo to relay this good news, but she abandons it (chapter CXVIII). Then she dreams of the presidency of the republic for each of them.

Later, gravely ill, she implores: "Go on, Pedro, go on Paulo, swear you will be friends." Both give her their word, and she insists: "Friends forever?" The brothers reaffirm their promise and then she concludes: "I can die in peace" (chapter CXX). But the promise is soon broken; the twins return to their habitual antagonism. In the last chapter, Aires diagnoses them with a "mutual aversion, barely disguised, occasionally interrupted by some stronger motive, but persistent in their blood." And he concludes that "they had always been the same since the womb" (chapter CXXI).

2.

Once the novel ends, a reader who might have been attracted by the title could ask, Why "Esau and Jacob"? How to associate such pale lives, such weak wills and banal destinies, to the heroism of the twins of Canaan? In this peaceful end-of-century province of Rio de Janeiro, which goes to bed a monarchy and wakes up a republic, what is equivalent to the enormous effort to unify the Jewish people around monotheism? Or to the endless struggle of Jacob, who mocked his brother, deceived his father, and relied on the cleverness of his mother to win primogeniture and to change the destiny of an entire people? What are the greater motives of the twins of Botafogo, beyond personal rivalry?

The confrontation suggested by the title will disappoint the reader who accepts it unequivocally. In choosing it, Machado perhaps intended that the Biblical passage remain present in our minds, not just to remind us of an anecdotal coincidence in their origins, but also to stress the contrast between the two stories. In a world of petty values and interests, this is the sort of Esau and Jacob that we get. Instead of offering us an epic novel, patterned after the Biblical tale, Machado puts into action, one more time, his irony and skepticism, with the subtlety he is famous for. To be honest, the title does not promise that Paulo and Pedro will have lives and ambitions analogous to those of Esau and Jacob. The analogy is derived from the expectations of the reader, who is compelled to accept at last that the title could be just a red flag: see how Pedro and Paulo *do not* resemble Rebecca's sons. See what our civilization was at its beginnings, and what it has been reduced to.

3.

Perhaps this is all just a question of point of view. If it were told by Pedro, it would be one story, by Paulo another. Flora would have her own version, which would not be the same as Natividade's. How many stories could be added to the tale? But this is just speculation. The one who really tells us the story is the retired diplomat who, in his diary of well-crafted phrases, lays out the lives of the people with whom he associated or associates, in addition to his own.

Esau and Jacob is a novel with a love story, centered on the triangle composed of Flora, Paulo, and Pedro. It is also the story of the ambitions of two vain and persuasive women, Natividade and Cláudia, and the novel of a few equally ambitious, pusillanimous men, devotees of power. And it is the novel of the insuperable dualism that separates the twin brothers. Finally, it is a novel of manners, with priceless observations about end-of-century Rio de Janeiro, as well as a political novel, given the persistence with which its pages register the grave events of the period. But one can also affirm that *Esau and Jacob* might be simply the novel of Counselor Aires, he who is its real protagonist, the point of convergence of all the other characters. Accustomed to fine Machadian irony, the reader will not be surprised by this small maneuver and will be prepared to rethink the whole story, according to the perspective imposed by the skeptical and insinuating eyes of the counselor.

Machado had already used the technique of the character-narrator in other novels, but what is unique in *Esau and Jacob* in this respect is that the writer entrusts the task of narrating the story to a secondary character. In the case of *Dom Casmurro*, for example, the narrator is Bento Santiago, the protagonist, permanently at the center of the action. Aires, however, is just an extra, at the margin of events. Except for one or another episode, none decisive, the story narrated by him only comes to his attention after the events. Aires is not a participant or even a direct observer of the main action. This invites us to reflect on the question of narrative focus, or the point of view adopted by the narrator.

Aires begins by revealing that, on a certain morning in 1871, two sisters, Natividade and Perpétua, traveled from the suburb of Botafogo to Morro do Castelo hill, with the mission of consulting a famous half-breed Indian fortune-teller, whose name is Barbara. The chapter is short, but it describes in detail the climb uphill, the dwelling where they are received, the physical and psychological characteristics of the cabocla, the state of mind of the sisters, which manifests itself through "nervous and confused gestures" (chapter I), a good part of the dialogue between the fortune-teller and her client about the future of the twins, and so on. Aires only learned this from the confidences of Natividade. Would those confidences have been laced with so many details? Let's say that she gave him the essentials. In the transit to paper, imagination must have embroidered the rest.

Similar situations are repeated throughout the book. Aires relates events which he could not have witnessed, and does it with a wealth of factual and psychological detail. There is always someone to reveal secrets and intimacies, and he is always attentive to everything, invariably disposed to listen. Thus, one understands that he is well informed about all that goes on. With some good will, the scenario is almost plausible, and could justify the point of view adopted in *Esau and Jacob.*

It happens that, if we venture there, we will be following a false lead, that is, of the plausibility of the point of view. The previous argument would only apply to the specific case of the character who narrates, that is, the character who relates what he himself experienced or witnessed, sometimes falling back on indirect testimony. That is the case of the narrator of *Dom Casmurro.* There we may properly ask, how does Bento Santiago manage to describe what occurs outside his range of vision? But that is not the case of the counselor, a narrator-character sui generis.

By entrusting the telling to him, Machado leaves it up to Aires to assume the perspective of the omniscient and omnipresent narrator, the narrator who does not need to be eyewitness or privileged confidant to be informed about everything. By a kind of literary license, such a narrator functions as if he were always present, with access to the most secret intimacy of the other characters. The omniscient narrative focus, although not at all plausible in terms of our reality outside fiction, is easily accepted by a reader. What pleases us, as we begin reading a novel, is the idea or illusion that we too will become privileged spectators. We will learn everything, even the most secret intentions of the characters, nothing will escape us. Such is the promise guaranteed by the intervention of the omniscient narrator. At the end, we will not have had access to the facts through the unilateral testimony of this or that participant, but through the irrefutable testimony of someone who sees all and knows all. That cannot be the case with our Aires, but from the first page we accept it as if it were.

To reinforce this, Machado displays another technique, starting with chapter XI, "A Unique Case!", when Counselor Aires makes his first appearance as a character. Until then, various figures had entered the scene but Aires had not made any reference to himself. Santos, upon visiting his friend Dr. Plácido, meets a common acquaintance. Plácido is a spiritist; Santos would consult him about the twins, to confirm or refute the prognosis that Natividade had obtained from the cabocla. Entering, he is immediately hailed by Plácido: "'Come, come,' he said, 'come help me convert our friend Aires. For the last half hour I have tried to inculcate in him the eternal truths, but he resists'" (chapter XI). It is the first reference that the counselor makes to his own person.

Before the father of the twins can declare the purpose of his visit, Aires reacts with good humor: "'No, no, no, I'm not resisting . . .'" and the narrator adds, on the same line: "chimed in a man of about 40, extending his hand to the new arrival" (chapter XI). Wouldn't the reader expect to find, "I chimed in," instead of, "a man chimed in," since the narrator and character are the same person? It happens that, forty pages into the novel, we are already used to the absent presence of Aires, we are used to associating with a narrator who lives outside the action. As the events unfold, the counselor leads us through the circuitous routes of the story, highlighting his/our condition of privileged observer. The omniscient focus allows us to fulfill a secret desire to see without being seen, to observe without being observed, to listen without having to respond. We penetrate the intimacy of others without revealing our own. For the reader this is how it will always be. For the narrator, it must be a matter of adopting the point of view of the counselor.

After being announced in the scene just mentioned, the counselor addresses not us, his habitual listeners, but the other actors, and in this sequence we are introduced to a person different from the narrator, as if he were a stranger. In the next chapter, the description continues in the same tone: "That man Aires who just appeared still retains some of the virtues of the times, and almost none of the vices" (chapter XII). The counselor continues to talk about himself as if it were about another person, as if he were introducing a new character. After a fashion, that is what is happening. The Aires that the reader knows by this point in the story is the omniscient narrator, a persuasive but neutral voice, a kind of accomplice who will lead him along to the end of the narrative. The Aires who reveals himself now is the character, a stranger. Who is he? What does he do? What does he look like? Where does he live? With whom does he live? Such is our natural curiosity, which must be satisfied by the narrator. Starting with chapter XI, every time the character Aires appears on scene, the narrator Aires will say "he is," and not "I am."

There is not just one Aires, there are two. Here, close to us, guiding our steps, he is the gentlemanly, good-humored, and spirited figure of the narrator, with whom we become acquainted from the first lines. We count on his constant presence, unhurriedly to filter, with bonhomie and grace, what most interests us: the story of the twins Pedro and Paulo. A little later on, we meet Aires the character, a sporadic presence who interacts and dialogues with the other characters, but not with us. The narrator of *Esau and Jacob* thus accomplishes what the Portuguese poet Fernando Pessoa (1888–1935) describes with the neologism *outrar-se* (to turn oneself into the other). Certainly to do this, but not in the classical manner, through the doubling of personality, but rather in the Kierkegaardian manner. When Aires appears in the notebooks of the counselor, the latter becomes concomitantly an other, referring to himself as a character in the third person. "*J'est un autre*," Rimbaud would say.

Here again, plausibility means little. We accept the artifice with good grace, it does not bother us that the same actor plays two different and apparently incompatible roles: there, the occasional figure, whose vision is limited to the few episodes in which he participates; here, an Aires who knows and sees all, and shares with the reader the privilege of essential vision, essential because it is distant and free, the vision of someone who does not allow himself to be ruffled by pressing demands, able to rise above personal involvement. Thus is Aires the narrator. Aires the character would not have the same impartiality, immersed as he is in circumstances, at the mercy of unilateral interests like everyone else. In chapter XII, we find out that a long time ago he was attracted to Natividade, "but as soon as he saw the interest was not reciprocated, he changed the subject." He had been married, a loveless marriage, and was widowed. And later, Santos thought of getting him married again, to Natividade's sister Perpétua, also a widow, but the attempt was unsuccessful. The widower rejected by Natividade would possibly tell another story, distorted by his previous involvement with the protagonists. Thus the artifice through which the counselor splits in two: one occasionally participates in the action, the other narrates. The goal is to gain perspective, not just in relation to the people involved in the central plot, but also in relation to oneself, now turned into an Other.

Once the artifice is understood we remain with the impression — false, one should immediately add — that there are really two counselors. That is not so. The same essential aspect characterizes both facets of his personality: absence, the refusal to become emotionally involved. Just as the narrator removes himself from the scene, adopting the omniscient posture capable of apprehending the essential truth which underlies individual differences, the character Aires behaves the same way in relation to the people in his circle. Attentive to everything, sought out by everyone, he never exposes himself, he never commits to anything. Even when urged to do so, he refuses to reveal his opinions, he always finds a way to change the subject, with a volley of humor, a spirited jibe, a sibylline quotation.

A retired diplomat, a citizen of the world, a refined and cultured man without commitments or ambitions, solitary but cultivated by many friends, a neutral and curious observer of the behavior of others and himself—the counselor approximates the ideal of skepticism, the ideal of someone who systematically throws doubt on all the statements which are cast before him as truths, notwithstanding always appearing to be in search of the utopia of absolute truth. The deeds of the character hint at the posture fully assumed by the narrator. In the same way, the knowledge we acquire of the latter, on each page, leads us to understand the character better. One throws light on the other.

The counselor calmly observes the agitation of the people around him and detects—what? Anxieties, misunderstandings, various fears, desires and ambitions, many doubts, precarious certainties. A mother preoccupied with the destiny of her sons who, the more they are loved, become all the more insecure. Uncertainty in face of the future, energy spent on earning and fear of losing, projects of conquest at any price, the cleverness of some, the naiveté of others, the fragility of almost everyone. Humanity appears engaged in a battle, against whom and to what end, nobody can say. "War is the mother of all things," Aires philosophizes, quoting Empedocles (chapter XIV).

The counselor, in conclusion, is in fact a narrator sui generis, less interested in telling a singular story than in practicing his vocation as an amateur philosopher. The people around him, and he himself, are interesting above all as examples of the human condition in general. It is toward this abstract goal that he directs his well-tuned instruments of analysis and reflection.

4.

One of the preeminent marks of the counselor's style on the story is its slow narrative pace. The facts are transmitted to the reader in a measured, unhurried manner. Whatever the original rhythm of events, as they are put on paper, they are funneled, so to speak, into a Moviola, that instrument of film editors that allows them to control the speed of the film they are viewing. In it Aires unspools his memories. After a few pages, the reader understands: the humor, the temperament, and the spirit of the counselor maintain enviable uniformity. Nothing seems to perturb him. Yet the contrast with the narrated story is glaring.

Right at the beginning, we are told of the hurried and nervous manner with which Natividade and Perpétua venture to a strange place which they suppose to be dangerous. We are made to notice that their hearts beat faster, their pulse accelerates, but the narrative preserves its own rhythm, it does not allow itself to be infected by the action. Throughout the book there are many passages in which the facts precipitate and the characters move quickly and with agility, but the narrator never alters his pace. The pressures of daily life oblige the characters to vary enormously their rhythms of action, from unbridled rushing to a slow walk. The counselor's rhythm is always the same. It comes from within, from a certain spiritual disposition. It is the rhythm of one who places himself at a distance from events, does not nourish ambitions, has no great dreams to realize and for this reason is a stranger to anxiety.

Machado knows that this rhythm is not one that will endear him to the majority of readers, who are used to moving through novels with their attention fixed on the thread of the plot, curious to find out how conflicts will be resolved. Their preference is for abundant and uninterrupted action. Machado foresees that the counselor's style will perhaps be disappointing. But he makes no concessions. Rather, he invests it with an occasional savage irony, such as to ask the reader's pardon for not dwelling on explanations which "eat up time and paper, hold up the action and end up in boredom. It's best to read with attention" (chapter V).

One has only to think of the example of the protagonists. If they were not in such a hurry to live, in such a hurry to conquer and shine,

Natividade, Santos, and the others would perhaps enjoy life more. In case the reader has not understood the lesson, Aires gives another: if the hurry to live life is an incurable disease, at least one should overcome the hurry to read. With fine irony, the narrator protracts the action and addresses the impatient reader, criticizing him: "Frankly, I don't like it when people go about guessing and composing a book which is being written methodically" (chapter XXVII). A book written methodically— that is an appropriate definition. In daily life, events collide, appeals multiply, and sometimes a trivial incident can change the direction of an entire life. There is no method empowered to withstand that, and Aires knows it. But in books things are different. In his book, in his diary, in his memories, in the story which only he knows, the mass of life is shaped by his own sovereign free will, imposing on the external chaos the order, or the dream of order, that his serene spirit dictates.

The narrative slowness, one can see, relies on the precious device of digressions, to which the narrator resorts without hesitation. The thread of the story is successively broken, and Aires seems to find pleasure in pretending that he will get lost in its detours. But he does not get lost. A scene left in suspense, lines and paragraphs before, is picked up again and the picture filled in. Better said, it is completed little by little at a punctuated pace, dependent on stimuli and associations that, by the side of the main road, happen to attract the counselor's attention. The picture is never completely finished. Method, yes, but one which does not sterilize and turn artificial, because it knows how to live with disorder and the unforeseen.

The episode mentioned above, the encounter between Aires and Santos at the home of Dr. Plácido, is an excellent example of this procedure. Interrupted at the end of chapter XI and apparently forgotten, the conversation between Santos, Plácido, and Aires is taken up again at the opening of chapter XIV with no cuts: "'Stay, please stay, counselor,' said Santos, gripping the diplomat's hand. 'Learn the eternal truths.' 'Eternal truths demand eternal hours,' mused the latter, checking his watch" (chapter XIV).

We can almost hear the grinding of the Moviola, unfreezing the action, making the film roll again. The image is not gratuitous. It is meant to suggest the cinematographic or theatrical atmosphere with which action is imbued, in the hands of the counselor. Instead of deluding us with the suggestion that Natividade, Santos and the twins, Flora and the rest, are people of flesh and blood, occupying a space similar to ours, the narrator insists on making it clear that this is about two distinct spaces: us here, engaged with reality, with the truth of life; over there the stage or the screen where certain actors play their roles, pure fiction. The inverse could also be true; Aires is not restrictive.

The counselor invites us to reflect on the story, with perspective and distance. He does not ask but rather warns us not to identify with the characters, suggesting that none of these lives can compensate for our possible lack of dreams and accomplishments. Whatever the destiny of Pedro, Paulo, or Flora, it will not alter our own destiny. The reality in which we are involved proceeds on its course, and out here we cannot rely on the Moviola of the counselor to freeze the action and stop time, which flows on inexorably. Aires is an illusionist intent on undoing illusions.

To stop time . . . "Time is an invisible fabric on which one can embroider everything: a flower, a bird, a lady, a castle, a tomb. One can also embroider nothing. Nothing, on top of the invisible; that is the most subtle work of this world, and for that matter, of the other" (chapter XXII). There perhaps resides the grand ambition of the counselor: to stall the march, to "embroider" time, to impede its progress, not so that he becomes paralyzed, placing himself at the margin of life, but on the contrary, so that it will be possible to enjoy the plenitude of each moment, holding off death. Distancing is an illusionist effect. Aires's style reduces the action to a few scenes, interwoven with digressions that have no apparent purpose but at the same time register a limitless number of features and details, rich in materiality and concreteness, even regarding the geographical space occupied by the characters.

With brief but sure notations, the narrator spreads before us an ample and colorful map of the city of Rio de Janeiro, a palpable territory where the protagonists move about. With this, distancing does not imply absence. The tendency to digressions and reflections of a general nature does not signify taking refuge in fantasy but paradoxically to come closer to reality. Not just superficial reality, which is quickly shown and forgotten, but a more substantial reality that hides behind appearances and is not revealed immediately.

It is aiming at that reality that the counselor tries to adjust the focus of his lens, in search of the real meaning of life, the ultimate meaning of all things. Flora, defined by him as "inexplicable," is his favorite model of the human being who is a little lost in herself, divided between conflicting interests and in search of a direction. But the picture is repeated in the others. Santos and Natividade, Batista and Cláudia, and above all the twins, who together symbolize the inherent duality of the human condition—all seem absorbed in a tumult of tiring and innocuous errands. What do they want, after all? Toward what just and defined direction do their efforts point?

Without drama or overemphasis, not even in the face of death, the counselor passes on to us an understanding and good-humored image of people who live their lives in reaction to circumstance, lives whose meaning needs to be redone with each change (the monarchy is ended, long live the republic!), empty as they are of a deeper meaning. For this reason they fight, they struggle, they go in circles and seem to advance, but they do not progress, since they are always returning to their point of departure.

5.

"The concept of history" which one sees there, according to Alfredo Bosi, "is that of cyclical time: a history woven of recurrent acts, if not symmetrical ones, and propelled by the 'nature of the species.' A concept alien (at least in outline) to the evolutionist metaphor of the arrow of time, the time of linear progress which supported the political values of the generation of 1870 and of the young Machado, but which could no longer dominate the scenario of ideas at the end of the century."* We can confirm it in comparison with the Biblical twins, our point of departure and now of arrival.

In the context of the Scriptures, the differences between Esau and Jacob are broad and deep, and accompany them for their entire lives. The dispute for primogeniture in which they are engaged transcends by far

---

* Alfredo Bosi, *Céu, Inferno* (São Paulo: Ática, 1988), p. 71.

the individual destiny of either one. Esau is an idolater; Jacob stays faithful to the beliefs of his ancestors. Esau, the hunter, represents a dissipated lifestyle, nomadic and potentially polytheistic. Jacob opts for the sedentary life, a premonition of the desired settlement in the Promised Land. The rivalry between them, therefore, represents the dispute between these two ways of life, the foreshadowing of a profound upheaval. Having wrested the rights to primogeniture, having engendered twelve sons, Jacob would change his name to Israel. From then on, his people could take on the condition of a chosen people.

In Pedro and Paulo, what do we have? A surface rivalry of futile motives, mere "reciprocal aversions," says the counselor, "persistent in the blood." Esau and Jacob engage in combat with a firm purpose. What is the purpose of the animosity between Paulo and Pedro? The counselor seems to insinuate that the passage from the monarchy to the republic could have represented, in the career of the Carioca twins, something equivalent to what the passage from a nomadic to a sedentary life, from polytheism to monotheism, represented for the sons of Rebecca and Isaac. But Pedro and Paulo's rivalry does not go beyond the personal limits of vanity and envy.

Along these lines, Aires suggests yet another common element to the two histories: the intervention of the supernatural. Yahweh listens to Isaac and determines that his wife will conceive; He also attends to the appeal of Rebecca, revealing to her the prophecy about the twins which she carries in her womb. He appears later before Jacob, at the top of a ladder, through a messenger angel. In the case of the Botafogo twins, the supernatural also plays its part through the cabocla Barbara, the fortuneteller, and through Dr. Plácido, the scholar of "eternal truths." And that's all. The difference is too blatant for us to dwell on it. Let us remain with what is essential. In the Biblical passage, the supernatural represents the grand design, the overarching purpose, able to lend a firm meaning to the trajectory of generations. In the story of Pedro and Paulo, the supernatural is reduced to credulity and speculation, meant to pique the fantasies of the most impressionable.

As for the rivalry between Pedro and Paulo, will this not have been fed by the obsession with which their mother, after visiting the cabocla, insists on demanding that they be friends? How much of the lack of direction and purpose in these muted lives, incapable of directing their own destinies, could be due to their difficulty in *outrar-se*, "turning themselves into the other," that is, seeing in the Other not their enemy but their complement? How much of all this is due to the loss of faith in a higher Providence?

Machado de Assis is too skeptical and discreet to challenge us explicitly with such questions. Nevertheless, there they are, among many questions that his *Esau and Jacob* invites us to consider at our own risk.

Notes

Note to the Reader

1. Ab ovo = "from the egg," from the origins.

Chapter I

3. "Dico, che quando l'anima mal nata" = "I say that when the ill-born soul"; Dante, *The Divine Comedy*, *Inferno*, Canto V.

3. Morro do Castelo = "Hill of the Castle," Rio de Janeiro hill leveled in the early twentieth century.

5. *Eumenides* = Aeschylus, *The Furies*; the line, "if there are Hellenes . . ." is spoken in the Prologue by Pythia, priestess of the temple of Apollo at Delphi.

Chapter II

8. "Better Going Down Than Going Up" = Luis Vaz de Camões (1524–80), *The Lusiads* (1572), Canto V, in reference to a crewman's retreat downhill from Africans onshore, just before the crew's encounter with the prophetic giant Adamastor.

8. 50,000 réis = about U.S. $25; 1,000 réis (one *mil-réis*) exchanged for 50 U.S. cents in 1870. Large sums were quoted in contos (1,000,000 réis, or one million réis), approximately U.S. $500.

8. Croesus = king of Lydia, fabled as the inventor of coinage. His lavish gifts to Pythia, the priestess of Apollo's oracle at Delphi, are recorded in Herodotus, *The Histories*, Book 1.

Chapter III

10. Tostão, vintém = a tostão was 100 réis, about a nickel; a vintém was 20 réis, about a penny.

10. "Ni cet excès d'honneur, ni cette indignité" = "neither such an excess of honor, nor such an indignity." Jean Racine, *Britannicus*, act II.

12. The Gospel = on giving alms, *Matthew* VI:3–4.

Chapter IV

12. Praia de Santa Luzia = beach in Rio de Janeiro popular for swimming,

later filled in to create the Praça de Paris.

13. Igreja São Domingos = church formerly located in the present-day Praça da República.

13. Maricá = town in the province of Rio de Janeiro.

14. Stock market fever = first stock boom in Rio de Janeiro, 1851–55, following a reform of the Commercial Code.

Chapter VI

18. Teatro Lírico = theater founded 1871, demolished 1933.

18. Fluminense Casino = social club of Rio's high society in the mid-nineteenth century.

18. João Fernandes = a failed Portuguese fifteenth-century adventurer who was captured by the Moors.

Chapter VIII

23. Paraguayan War = War of the Triple Alliance (of Brazil, Uruguay, and Argentina) against Paraguay, 1865–70.

24. *"On ne prête qu'aux riches"* = "only lend money to the rich . . .," first half of a French proverb, which ends: " . . . because they have good credit, while the poor only have needs."

24. Spiritist = Brazilian occultism had many branches, but "Spiritists" were usually disciples of the French writer León-Denizárth-Hippolyte Rivail (1804–69), pseud. Allan Kardec, whose doctrines reached Brazil in the 1860s.

Chapter IX

26. Rio Branco law = also known as "the Law of the Free Womb," or "Law of Free Birth," passed September 28, 1871, when José Maria da Silva Paranhos (1819–80), viscount of Rio Branco, was prime minister (1871–75). The law declared all children born henceforth of slave mothers free— after serving their mother's master to the age of 21. It was Brazil's second emancipation measure, after the closing of the African slave trade in 1850.

26. Nova Friburgo palace = in 1870, it was a private residence that had been built by Antonio Clemente Pinto, baron of Nova Friburgo. Acquired by the government in 1896, it became the Catete Palace, official residence of the president.

Chapter XIV

36. Esau and Jacob = *Genesis* XXVII: 22–23.

37. "War is the mother of all things" = saying attributed to Greek philosopher Empedocles or Heraclitus.

Chapter XV

37. "Teste David cum Sybilla" = *Dies Irae*, the thirteenth-century hymn for requiem Masses: "Both King David and [the pagan oracle] Sybil say our lives end in ashes."

Chapter XIX

48. Cape of Storms, Adamastor = named by Bartolomeu Dias upon its first passage in 1488, renamed Cape of

Good Hope by Vasco da Gama in 1497, when he had an easy passage. In Camões, *Lusiads*, Canto V, Vasco da Gama hears glorious and dire predictions from the giant Adamastor, who long ago, pursuing the nymph Thetis, had been turned into the Cape of Storms, tormented by the waters surrounding him.

Chapter XX

49. "Baroness" = Brazil's monarchical Constitution of 1824 and later laws provided for the creation of non-hereditary titles of nobility. While initially granted sparingly, by the 1870s titles were virtually sold to worthy candidates who made large donations (10 to 20 contos, approximately U.S.$5,000 to $10,000) to the emperor's charities.

Chapter XXIII

53. "Day that Pedro I fell" = on April 7, 1831, Brazil's first emperor, Dom Pedro I (1798–1834), was forced to abdicate in favor of his young son, Dom Pedro II (1825–91).

53. Dom Pedro II School = officially chartered secondary school in Rio de Janeiro, attended by sons of the elite.

55. "Israel wept for the onions of Egypt" = *Numbers* XI:4–5.

55. Habeas corpus = a Brazilian law similar to the English writ of habeas corpus requiring the release of prisoners held without due process. Some famous habeas corpus briefs were filed during the 1890s to free political prisoners.

Chapter XXIV

56. Madame de Staël, Corinne = Anne Louise Germaine de Staël (1766–1817) kept a progressive Paris salon before the Revolution, and was exiled by Napoleon. She was often identified with the heroine of her novel *Corinne* (1807).

57. Dom Miguel de Bragança (1802–66) = pretender to the Portuguese throne after João VI's death in 1826. Miguel's elder brother Dom Pedro declared Brazilian independence in 1822 and became Brazil's Emperor Pedro I, abdicating the Portuguese throne to his daughter Maria. From 1828 on, Miguel reigned as regent, betrothed to his niece Queen Maria II. He persecuted Portugal's liberals. When Brazilians forced Pedro I to abdicate in 1831, Pedro returned to Portugal in 1832 as king (Pedro IV of Portugal) and leader of the liberals. He defeated Miguel in 1834, and died soon after. Maria II took the throne. In exile, Miguel I remained the hope of reactionary absolutists, including many of the poor of Lisbon.

Chapter XXVI

62. Law and medicine = to balance regional interests, the government chartered two law academies, in Pernambuco and São Paulo, and two medical academies, in Bahia and Rio de Janeiro. The São Paulo law academy was known for radical literary and political fads.

Chapter XXIX

65. Camões, "from a certain father" = *Lusiads*, Canto III, referring to the

son of King Henrique, Prince Alfonso (1109–85), who fought a civil war against his ambitious mother Teresa for possession of Portugal. As Alfonso I, he established Portugal's independence from Moorish and Spanish kings.

Chapter XXX

66. Ribeirão das Moças = a fictional town in the unnamed province Batista administered.

68. São Cristóvão = site of the emperor's palace in Rio de Janeiro, also the Quinta da Boa Vista.

Chapter XXXI

69. Sinimbu administration = João Lins Vieira Cansanção de Sinimbu (1810–1906), viscount of Sinimbu, was called by Dom Pedro II to organize a new Liberal party cabinet in 1878, after ten years of Conservative party dominance. Liberal Ministries then governed until 1885, but failed to reform electoral laws or slavery.

Chapter XXXII

72. Catete, Largo do Machado, Praia de Botafogo, Praia do Flamengo = fashionable districts just south of the center of Rio de Janeiro; Andaraí was semi-rural.

Chapters XXXII, XXXIII

73. "I would flee to a far-off place" = a twist on *Psalm* LV:7, "Lo, then, I would wander far off, and remain in the wilderness."

Chapter XXXV

77. Orpheus = Greek semi-divine musician, devoted to Apollo, who attempted to rescue his wife Eurydice from the underworld. Later, dismembered by devotees of Dionysus, his head became an oracle more famous than Delphi, until Apollo silenced it.

Chapter XXXVI

78. Homer = Homer, *The Iliad*, Book I, opens with the discord among gods and men.

Chapter XXXVII

80. Abolition of slavery = decreed May 13, 1888, a week before Paulo's speech.

Chapter XXXVIII

81. Rua do Ouvidor = the central street of Rio de Janeiro's commerce.

Chapter XLIII

92. 1848 liberal = following the forced abdication of Dom Pedro I in 1831, a regency governed in the name of the underage Pedro II. There were many separatist revolts, urban uprisings, and slave rebellions. In 1841, a centralizing faction declared the majority of Pedro II and brought him to the throne at age 15. Revolts continued, including revolts of federalist liberals in Pernambuco in 1848. Conservative "Conciliation" Ministries of the 1850s included moderate members of liberal parties. This political compromise lasted almost through the beginning of the Paraguayan War in 1864.

93. Princess regent = Princess Isabel (1846–1921), daughter of Pedro II, substituted for him as regent while he sought medical care in Europe. She signed the decree abolishing slavery.

Chapter XLVII

99. *Matthew* IV:1–10 = the temptation of Christ by Satan.

99. Rise of the liberals = after the abolition of slavery under the Conservative Ministry in May 1888, the Conservative coalition collapsed. The emperor called Afonso Celso de Assis Figueiredo (1837–1914), viscount of Ouro Preto, to form a Liberal party cabinet on June 7, 1889. Ouro Preto antagonized military officers, bringing on the republican coup.

101. Rubicon = Roman general Julius Caesar defied an order by crossing the Rubicon River in 49 B.C., thus symbolizing his irrevocable decision to usurp power and take Rome.

101. Saquaremas, Luzias = factions that became the Liberal and Conservative parties in the 1840s. The viscount of Albuquerque, Antonio Francisco de Paula e Holanda Cavalcanti de Albuquerque (1821–68), is supposed to have said, "there is nothing more like a conservative than a liberal in power." Among the leading conservatives who formed the Progressive party faction of the Liberal party during the Conciliation were: Pedro de Araujo Lima, the marquis of Olinda; José Tomás Nabuco de Araújo; and Zacarias de Gois e Vasconcelos (who helped Machado de Assis enter the civil service).

Chapter XLVIII

103. Ball on the Ilha Fiscal = November 9, 1889, a ball for Chilean naval officers visiting Rio on the *Almirante Cochrane*.

105. Baron of Mauá = Irineu Evangelista de Sousa (1813–89), Brazilian entrepreneur of the mid-nineteenth century.

106. "Hail Macbeth" = William Shake-speare, *Macbeth*, Act 1, scene 3.

108. Plutarch = Plutarch (46–120), a Greek writer of the Roman Empire, is known primarily for his *Parallel Lives* of Greek and Roman political and military leaders, such as Julius Caesar. He was a priest of the Pythian Apollo at Delphi.

108. Third reign = the pro-clerical Princess Isabel, and her unpopular French consort the Count d'Eu, would have inherited Pedro II's throne, commencing the Third Kingdom of the Brazilian Empire.

Chapter XLIX

110. St. Sebastian = patron saint of Rio de Janeiro, which was founded on his feast day, January 20.

Chapter L

110. Evaristo = Evaristo da Veiga (1799–1837), pamphleteering journalist whose *Aurora Fluminense* first attacked Pedro I, then later moderated.

Chapter LI

114. "Blessed are those who are present" = parody of the Sermon on the Mount, *Matthew* V:1–12.

Chapter LII

115. Praia Grande = a beach on the Ilha do Governador near Rio de Janeiro.

Chapter LIII

119. Cont of Oeiras = Sebastião José de Carvalho e Melo (1699–1782), best known as the marquis of Pombal, dictatorial prime minister of Portugal from 1750 to 1777.

Chapter LV

124. Proudhon = Pierre Joseph Proudhon (1809–65), *La Pornocratie ou les femmes dans les temps moderns.*

Chapter LIX

133. Buridan's Ass = philosophical parable speciously attributed to the French scholastic philosopher Jean Buridan (c. 1300–58): if a hungry ass is placed exactly between two equal amounts of food, will he turn to either, or will he starve to death, unable to choose?

Chapter LX

134. Passeio Público = park and promenade in Rio de Janeiro, built 1799–1803.

135. Deodoro = Field Marshal Manuel Deodoro da Fonseca (1827–92), general who led the Republican coup on November 15, 1889, overthrowing Emperor Pedro II to become the first president.

Chapter LXI

137. Xenophon = Xenophon, *Ciropaedia*, Book 1, the life of Persian King Cyrus

the Great (599–530 B.C.), who defeated King Croesus (see chapter II). Xenophon also wrote *Anabasis* about the fratricidal war between Cyrus the Younger (424–401 B.C.) and his brother Artaxerxes II (c. 404–359 B.C.).

Chapter LXIII

142. *Laemmert's Almanac* = city directory of Rio de Janeiro.

Chapter LXIV

145. Beaurepaire Rohan = Brazilian field marshal, from a French noble family.

Chapter LXIX

155. Bosom of Abraham = parable of *Luke* XVI:22.

Chapter LXXI

159. "The style is not the man" = inversion of a phrase of the French naturalist Georges Louis Leclerc Buffon (1707–88): "The style is the man."

Chapter LXXII

160. Dissolution of Congress = the early republican regime was wracked by tensions among President Deodoro da Fonseca, his vice president Marshal Floriano Vieira Peixoto (1839–95), Congress, and the state governors. On November 3, 1891, President Deodoro dissolved Congress; civil wars in the states began. Floriano overthrew Deodoro on November 23. But rather than share power with Congress, Floriano made himself dictator. He intervened in the states, replacing many

governors. In Rio de Janeiro, Admiral Custódio bombarded the Candelária church. Floriano held the presidency from 1891 to 1894, when he was forced to turn it over to Prudente de Morais, a civilian from São Paulo.

161. Roland = Madame Roland (1754–93), who kept a salon of the Girondins during the French Revolution, and was guillotined.

Chapter LXXIII

163. Encilhamento = literally, "saddling up" before a horse race, nickname given to the inflationary financial bubble of 1890–92, caused by new financial policies facilitating limited-liability stock companies and by monetary policies creating several banks of emission.

164. Candide and Cacambo = José Basílio da Gama (c. 1741–95), author of the epic poem, *O Uruguai*, which tells of the love of Cacambo for Lindóia during wars against Jesuit missions in Paraguay. The narrator must be mistaken when he says that Voltaire's *Candide* (1759) took the character Cacambo from Da Gama's *O Uruguai* (1769); both probably took the name from chronicles.

Chapter LXXVI

170. Carceler = a popular café in Rio de Janeiro in the 1870s.

Chapter LXXXI

178. "Two souls live in my breast" = Johann Wolfgang von Goethe, *Faust* (1808–32), Part I.

Chapter LXXXV

187. Constitution of February 24, 1891 = the republican Constitution.

Chapter LXXXIX

192. Offenbach = Jacques Offenbach (1819–80), German-born composer of French comic operettas including *Orpheus in Hell* (1858).

193. 7th of September, 2nd of December = Brazilian holidays commemorating, respectively, the declaration of Independence by Pedro I and the birthday of Dom Pedro II.

Chapter XC

195. Gordian knot = in legend, King Gordius of Phrygia (the adoptive father of King Midas) had tied an intricate knot on his oxcart; an oracle predicted that whoever could undo it would rule all Asia; much later the future king Alexander the Great undid it at one stroke, by cutting it with his sword.

Chapter XCV

207. Flora = Roman goddess of flowers and gardens.

207. Musset = Alfred de Musset (1810–57), French romantic poet.

207. Casimiro de Abreu = Casimiro José Marques de Abreu (c. 1839–60), Brazilian romantic poet.

Chapter CIII

219. Ulysses and Alcinöos = Homer, *Odyssey*, Book 8.

Chapter CVI

227. Itamarati = the Itamarati Palace, built in 1854, housed the provisional government in 1889, and later, the Foreign Ministry.

Chapter CVII

229. Seventy-two-hour state of siege = state of emergency decreed by Floriano Peixoto on April 10, 1892, to stifle demonstrations in favor of restoring ex-President Deodoro. It was followed by severe political repression.

Chapter CVIII

230. *Hamlet*'s gravediggers = William Shakespeare, *Hamlet*, Act 5, scene 2.

Chapter CX

232. Mauá train = the Mauá Railroad, opened in 1854, went from the port of Mauá to Petrópolis.

Chapter CXIII

238. Beatrice = in Dante, *The Divine Comedy*, the spirit of Beatrice leads the poet to Paradise.

Chapter CXIV

239. Rebellion of the navy, etc. = events of Floriano Peixoto's presidency, including the rebellion of the naval squadron in Rio's harbor (1893–94), which was partly in support of the civil war in Rio Grande do Sul and other states of the south (1892–95), partly monarchist.

239. Jacobins = nativist and militarist followers of President Floriano Peixoto; their newspaper took the name of the French Revolution's radical Jacobin faction.

Chapter CXXI

251. Castor and Pollux = in the Greek myths, Castor and Polydeuces, sons of the coupling of Zeus and Leda. As Castor and Pollux, they were the patrons of Roman knights.